Dinner
and a
Murder

#2

Ballad Publishing
Lincoln, Nebraska

Dinner and a Murder

LAINE BOYD

Ballad
Publishing

Book design copyright 2015 by Ballad Publishing. All rights reserved.
Cover design and interior design by Ballad Publishing
Cover illustration by Theresa Ann

Published by Ballad Publishing Company
PO Box 6193
Lincoln, NE 68506, USA

Ballad Publishing Company and the "MANDOLIN" logo are trademarks of
Ballad Publishing Company or an affiliated company

Library of Congress Control Number: 2015948914

Published in the United States of America
ISBN-13: 978-0-9899689-6-6
ISBN-10: 0989968960
1. Fiction/Suspense/Thriller/Crime Fighting/Family
2. Fiction/Mystery/Suspense/Police Family

Other Books by Laine Boyd

Unharmonious

Coming soon from Laine Boyd

He'll Find You

In loving memory of my parents, Vic and Joretta,
who modeled sacrificial love, commitment
and cheerful service to each other for over 51 years,
and encouraged me always to follow my dreams.

Acknowledgements

I am indebted to a number of people, whose specialized knowledge and insight provided invaluable assistance in a variety of fields: Sandi Hafner, R.N., Leland Boyd, retired police detective, Kevin Burgdorf, retired police detective, Mary K. w.d.-Turner, John and Mary Kelly, and Bryan Boyd, all provided input on specific topics. I deeply appreciate their willingness to share their expertise and experience in their respective fields, and their patience as I peppered them endlessly with questions. It is my hope that I have not taken too much liberty with the information my sources provided to me. If I have not been as accurate as I should have been, or taken too much liberty with certain scenes in this story, the fault lies with me and not with those who were so generous with their time and willingness to provide me with their perspectives.

Gloria Harrison, Kris Hillen, Sandi Hafner, Rick Rodriguez and Lisa Mozingo provided support as my fantastic test readers. Their input was priceless and I am beyond grateful for their help and the time they invested.

A special thank you is extended to Peggy McAlister, whose cheerful and generous sacrifice provided for the widespread sale of my books locally. Her efforts and support are deeply appreciated.

St. Louis attorney John Goffstein provided tremendous encouragement by giving everyone on his very long holiday gift list a copy of my last book, Unharmonious. His generosity has touched my heart.

Thanks to my editor, Madeline Bien, for her help and input. I also want to thank Theresa Ann for her compelling artwork for the cover.

Finally, I would like to thank Ballad Publishing for taking a chance on me, first with Unharmonious, and now, with Dinner and a Murder. CaSondra Poulsen has been a joy to work with. I appreciate her wisdom, her insight, her suggestions, and her patience more than even I have words to say.

I cannot thank all of these wonderful people enough for the confidence they have shown in me, and their unfailing support. Their cheerful encouragement, helpful advice and contagious excitement provided food for the soul. May I never forget to count my many blessings!

Part One:
The Original Crime

September 15, 1865

A silver crescent moon hung over St. Louis, its shimmery light largely obscured by gathering storm clouds, pregnant with the threat of rain. Captain Josiah Mansford quietly slipped off of his ship, the *Mississippi Jewel,* and into the shadows along the mighty river. He looked around to see if he had been observed. Confident his movements had gone unnoticed by anyone on the docks, he crept into the forest and hid among the trees, watching, listening. Turning his head and squinting to see, he checked his pocket watch in the scattered beams of moonlight that filtered through the clouds. The *Jewel* would not cast off until dawn— another two hours or so. Enough time, if he was careful. He had made certain that he was seen in several places on the ship before he left. If asked, a number of crewmen and staff could honestly swear they had seen him. But Captain Mansford also had a back-up plan. Just in case. He hurried deeper into the woods to the place he had left Sultana, his fastest Arabian mare, tied to a tree. He mounted the jet-black steed, kicked her into a gallop, and sped furiously toward home.

The rain began as a light drizzle, but steadily increased. Thunder clapped and lightning sparked across the sky, frightening the horse, but Josiah, an expert rider, urged her on before stopping a quarter mile from his home. He dismounted, and tied her to an enormous oak tree with abundant foliage and long low branches that would shelter her from the coming storm. He crept toward his home and snuck in through the kitchen door at the back of the house. He paused for several moments to steady his breathing. Josiah was a large man to begin with, but now forty-eight years old, he was feeling his age, and his expanding girth hampered his efforts to move as he had when he was younger. He smoothed his gray beard. It was damp, as was his uniform. There would be no time to dry himself by the comfort of a warm fire. He would have to return to the *Mississippi Jewel* as soon as he was finished with the business at hand.

Josiah crept up the servant's narrow staircase at the back of the house, avoiding the steps with creaky boards. He stopped and listened. The servants' quarters were on the third floor of his spacious home. The servants, at least those he had not fired recently, were sleeping. The house was quiet. He slipped into the bedroom of Mrs. Lena Anderson, the housekeeper. She lay on her back, snoring, and did not stir as he walked to her bed. Her gray curls fell haplessly from beneath her nightcap. Taking a pillow, Josiah Mansford muffled his pistol and pressing it to her ample chest, shot her through her treacherous heart with no more than a faint popping sound from his weapon. Lena Anderson's bright blue eyes opened in surprise and her head rose slightly from the pillow. Then, her eyes closed as her head fell back, her tight gray curls bouncing against her pillow.

It serves her right, the lousy mick. She knew about the deception and hid it from me. Because of her omission, Josiah Mansford branded Mrs. Anderson a most disloyal employee. *I should have known better than to trust an Irishwoman.* He had taken pity on her as she told her sad tale of losing her husband, and hired her to supervise the house staff—a position for which she was unworthy, having chosen to keep his wife's dirty little secret from him. Josiah narrowed his steel blue eyes and set his jaw in grim satisfaction. One traitor in his household had been eliminated. He would not tolerate disloyalty. They would pay. They would *all* pay.

Down the hall from Lena Anderson's room was the small bedroom of Hettie Jefferson, the maid and part-time cook. *Ungrateful darkie.* As a kindness, he had taken Hettie and her little mulatto daughter in. He had given her room and board and a salary, more than she deserved. He even allowed her to sleep under his roof, safe within the confines of his beautiful home. He could have made her sleep in the barn with that idiot half-wit, Donnie, but Josiah gave her a room on the third floor with the other servants—a generous gesture indeed, considering all the trouble these black-faced intruders to his country caused. Every time he saw the child, it sickened him to think of her cavorting with a white man.

Josiah had hired Hettie because he had been unable to procure a maid, having dismissed the last several as incompetent, and she was the only woman willing to work for him. She, too, had betrayed his trust by keeping his wife's affair from him. He imagined her laughing at him behind his back as scandal loomed over his fine house. She would pay for her sins. Nobody could treat him with that kind of disrespect, especially the likes of an inferior life form such as Hettie Jefferson.

Without making a sound, he opened the door to her room. She was sleeping peacefully, unaffected by the thunder and lightning roaring outside, oblivious to the man with a loaded pistol approaching her bed. Josiah watched Hettie through narrowed eyes, her small body motionless except for the faint rise and fall of her chest, unlike the fat Irishwoman, snoring away in her beer-soaked dreams down the hall had been. Again using a pillow to muffle the sound, he shot Hettie, first in the throat, and then through her heart. Where was the child? He did not see her. Probably running through the streets begging while her mother slept.

Josiah left Hettie's room, closing the door behind him, satisfied that his disloyal staff had gotten what they deserved. When Gordon, his butler returned, he would enlist his assistance in replacing them.

Gordon Saunders, the faithful butler, had been granted several days off to visit his ailing mother in Alton, across the river. Saunders had alerted Josiah to the shameful activities taking place when Josiah was away from home. In hushed tones, Saunders informed him that Josiah's wife and her lover met in the barn, and after the servants' lights went out, they moved into the house. While Saunders' news was most unwelcome, Josiah had suspected as much. His butler merely confirmed his suspicions, and by so doing, spared his own life. Saunders would be rewarded upon his return.

Annalise, Josiah's young and beautiful wife, had defiled herself in an adulterous affair. With a scoundrel, no less. He snorted at the thought. Had she really believed that her scandalous behavior could escape his attention? Josiah seethed with anger as his steely blue eyes narrowed even further. Her behavior had made him a laughingstock throughout St. Louis society. *Nobody* made Josiah Mansford a laughing stock and got away with it. He knew that Annalise believed that Josiah was now on the *Mississippi Jewel*. He had told her the departure time had been changed before he left earlier that evening. She never questioned it, so anxious was she to be with her paramour. Annalise had even put her arms around Josiah's neck, kissed him, and told him she would miss him. *Lies!* Tonight, he would end her deception, once and for all.

Josiah reloaded the pistol. He stood at the top of the grand staircase, admiring his weapon. He stroked the fine grip and fingered the barrel. It was a beauty of a gun. He smirked as he remembered taking it from a dying Confederate soldier. The hand-carved silver grip was inlaid with pearl and ivory, and the gun shot true.

He moved to the middle landing of the grand staircase, which afforded a full view of the front door and graceful entryway, glistening with Italian marble flooring. The wide, polished mahogany staircase shone like glass. A massive banister crowned exquisite, intricately carved balusters. The staircase emptied out into the entryway in a widening finish, like the train of a bridal gown, elegant and flowing. On the landing, where Josiah stood, the staircase branched upward, both to the left and to the right, leading down different hallways lined with bedroom doors. His eyes swept over the far hall and lingered on the last door on the right—the bedroom he shared with his bride, Annalise. His knees weakened.

"Annalise, Annalise." His heart felt faint as he whispered her name. She was one of the most beautiful women in all of St. Louis. Josiah's chest ached when he thought of her betrayal. She was half his age, but the moment he saw her, he had wanted her, needed to have her as his own. She was expensive to keep, but he had plenty of money, the ill-gotten fruit of war profiteering. He was willing to pay an exorbitant price to have her. Annalise Mansford wore the latest fashions, red lip color from Paris, and owned more jewelry than any other woman in the city, which she loved to flaunt. She wore diamonds or pearls, even while horseback riding. Josiah had given her a two carat emerald necklace, a perfect jewel, with a solitary emerald cut, surrounded by diamonds set in platinum. It matched her eyes which flashed flirtatiously beneath thick black eyelashes against her pale skin, set off by her long, black hair. Annalise Mansford was dazzling to look at. She mesmerized men with a single, sultry glance. But as Josiah waited in simmering anger, the stench of adultery rendered her ugly. Thinking of her caused him to taste bile. He swallowed hard as the bitterness burned a path down his throat.

It would not be long now. The storm had grown fierce and would soon force the whore and her current lover out of the barn. Josiah sneered at the thought. *They belong in the barn with the rest of the animals.*

At last, he heard the door opening and watched in disgust as Annalise and Stefan tumbled in, giggling as they fell over each other, dripping wet from the rain. Her beautiful white dress was soaked through and clung immodestly to her supple body, leaving little to the imagination. Her long, slender neck was adorned with the emerald and diamond pendant Josiah had given her. Tonight would be the last time Annalise would wear the stunning piece. Her long black hair spread haphazardly, plastered against her face and neck. Her ruby red mouth gaped open in raucous laughter, mocking her wedding vows, as Stefan ogled her in unconcealed lust. Stefan LeBlanc was young and slender with dark hair parted down the middle. He sported a pencil thin mustache that Josiah thought looked ridiculous. *He isn't even man enough to grow a full beard. A fop.* They embraced and kissed passionately, mercifully ending the obnoxious laughter.

Josiah used the moment of silence to cock his pistol. The click echoed through the foyer and Annalise and Stefan broke apart and stared in open-mouthed horror at Josiah on the landing as he aimed the pistol at them.

Annalise's deep green eyes grew wide with fear and surprise as she struggled to speak. Her voice was hoarse and weak. "Josiah!"

He suppressed a smile to see her caught, like a rat cornered by a hungry cat. *That's what she is—a trapped rat!*

"Now—now see here, man," Stefan began, putting his hands up. But Josiah cut him off.

"How long did you think you would get away with this? In *my* house? Under *my* roof?"

"Please, Josiah, put the gun down," Annalise pleaded. "The servants will hear you."

Josiah laughed. "Oh, I don't think there's anyone around to hear anything, you wretched trollop. Did you really think I would let your servants see another day after they betrayed me?"

"Josiah!" she gasped. "You killed them? Why? They knew nothing! They knew nothing at all!" It pleased Josiah to hear Annalise on the edge of hysteria.

"Liar!" His face contorted with rage. His booming voice reverberated through the house. "After all I've done for you. After all I've given you, you carry on with a dandy boy? You will die for your betrayal. But first, it's time to rid the earth of that vile scum!" He pointed the pistol at Stefan.

"You'll—you'll never get away with this," Stefan threatened, but his hollow stammering only amused Josiah.

"Won't I?" Josiah answered. "If the police come, who's to say I didn't catch an intruder violating my wife and shoot him trying to save her? Who's to say I didn't miss? Perhaps my aim isn't all that perfect. Let's just see."

He fired. Annalise screamed as Stefan crumpled to the floor. Josiah's smile chilled the air as he stared at a trembling Annalise. He raised the gun again, aimed at her and pulled the trigger. She collapsed next to Stefan, her long white dress staining crimson with blood.

Josiah checked his pocket watch. All had gone as planned. He had ample time to retrieve Sultana and put her in the barn. Donnie the half-wit would take good care of her in the morning. The boy slept so soundly nothing ever woke him. But Donnie was good with the horses. It was all he was good for. Josiah would be back on the *Mississippi Jewel* in plenty of time for her launch at dawn.

It was then that Josiah heard the crying of a child pierce the now quiet house. Surprised, he looked up and saw four-year old Ginnie Jefferson, staring wide-eyed at him from between the balusters of the third floor, wailing for her mother. Josiah realized Ginnie must have been hiding under the bed, afraid of the storm, when he killed Hettie. Had she witnessed everything? Surely, no one would believe such a young child, and a mulatto at that.

But he could not take that chance. He fired at the child and she flew backward, hitting the floor with a thud. Josiah breathed a sigh of relief. Nothing could stop him now. There was no one left to thwart his plan. Justice had been served.

Yet, one more sound shattered the silence, as Stefan, before his final breath, fired his own revolver—the last deed he would ever commit—and Josiah Mansford tumbled down the grand staircase, shot through his own wicked heart. The last thing Josiah's hate-filled eyes saw before eternity was the crystal chandelier over the foyer, its candles flickering, swaying gently from the ceiling.

Donnie Smith woke with a start and sat upright in the small bunk he shared in the barn with a big orange tomcat he named Pumpkin. Something wasn't right. It was dark outside, so he knew it wasn't time to get up. So why had he woken all of a sudden? What was wrong? Donnie rubbed his sleepy eyes, got out of bed and put on his clothes. He stepped around to the stables and began to check on his beloved horses. Well, not his, exactly. Donnie was only fourteen years old. He knew the horses belonged to the Captain, of course, but they were his charges and he took very good care of them. The Captain let him sleep on a bunk in the barn, and every morning, Hettie brought him delicious biscuits with cream gravy and scrambled eggs. Donnie could get hungry just thinking about Hettie's biscuits and gravy and eggs. Hettie was kind to him. She never made fun of him like the boys in town did. He knew it wasn't time for breakfast, so he couldn't think about that right now. Something was wrong.

Donnie got out of bed and began to check the stalls. The Belgian draft horses, Bud and Minnie, were sleeping, their flaxen manes flowing over their rich, chestnut necks, almost to their shoulders, their forelocks reaching to their eyes. He checked on Myrtle the mule, who was also sleeping. The spirited Palomino that Mrs. Mansford rode woke and walked to the bars of her stall, ready for a treat. "Hi, Mirage," Donnie cooed to her, petting her nose. He checked on Trixie, the little brown Welsh pony the Captain had bought for his young niece, before the cholera killed her. The Morgans, Princess, Duchess and Star, were safe in their stalls. Millie, the brown and white Arabian, was sleeping, and Midnight, another Arabian, was just beginning to stir. He rounded the corner to the large stall, and stopped, horrified to find Sultana's stall empty. *The Captain's black Arabian is missing!* Donnie knew she had been safely locked in her stall when he had gone to bed. *Where can she be?*

Panic-stricken, Donnie ran outside. The first rays of sun were beginning to lighten the eastern sky. He strained to scan the pasture, but saw nothing. Donnie ran toward the entrance of the property, calling her. No answer. He ran further, toward the edge of the city, and ran right into Bobby Malley, one of the constables.

"Whoa, there, Donnie, boy!" Malley exclaimed, taking the lad by his shoulders. "Where ye be goin' in such a hurry? It ain't even time for ye to be outta bed!"

"Su-Su-Sultana is gone, sir, I gotta f-f-f-find her," Donnie tried to explain, breathless.

"Now who's Sultana, boy?"

"Cap'n Mansford's prize Arabian. I woke up and know'd somethin' were wrong and when I checked the horses, Sultana was missing. I gots to find her. The Cap'n, he'll be mad cuz it's my job to take care of the horses."

Constable Malley put his arm around Donnie and said, "Let's go have a look, Donnie, eh? I'll go and check things out with ye and we'll see what's what, eh?"

Donnie, somewhat placated, agreed and ran ahead, with Bobby Malley right behind him. They reached the stables and Malley's own check of Sultana's stall confirmed what Donnie had told him.

"Let's go and ask up at the house, boy. Maybe the Cap'n or someone took Sultana for a ride."

Donnie looked up at him with doubtful pale blue eyes. Constable Malley did not understand the horse's routine, but he was a policeman, so Donnie figured he must be smart.

They walked up the stone steps to the large wooden front doors and knocked. No answer.

"Mr. Saunders is in Alton. His mum's sick. Mrs. Anderson or Hettie should be awake." He hoped Hettie was making biscuits now. The sun was almost up.

Constable Malley knocked harder this time, and the door opened a bit under the pressure. That was odd. The staff should be up. He pushed it open a little more and called in.

"Hello?"

No answer. That was odder still. He opened the door further and saw the bodies. First Annalise, then Stefan, whom he did not recognize, crumpled by the door, and the body of Captain Josiah Mansford, a few feet away, sprawled at the bottom of the staircase.

"Donnie, Donnie boy!" he exclaimed, backing out of the house and placing his hands on Donnie's shoulders. "Did ye hear anythin' last night? Ye said ye woke up and knew somethin' was wrong. Did ye hear a noise? Did ye see anythin' wrong?"

"No, sir," Donnie answered solemnly, shaking his head. "Just Sultana's stall were empty. I need ta find Sultana. She won't be in the house, sir. Ain't no horses goes in people's houses."

"Donnie, somethin' very bad has happened here. I need ye ta go wait in the barn till I get back, ye hear?"

"But the horse!"

"I'll be back fast. I need to get help. We'll find Sultana. Now go and wait like a good boy till I return."

Donnie obeyed. He knew if you were bad to a policeman and disobeyed, you could go to jail. Donnie did not want to go to jail. He fidgeted in the barn for a few minutes before deciding he better give the horses their hay and their morning brushing. If Constable Malley had still not come back, he would lead them out to the pasture and clean their stalls.

Bobby Malley ran toward the city, blowing his alert whistle as hard and as long as he could. It did not take long before his superior, Johnny Leary, joined him with three others on foot patrol and they hurried back to the Mansford Mansion, while Malley filled them in.

They entered the home and surveyed the bodies on the floor. "Looks like Captain Mansford interrupted a burglar," Malley said, as they tried to piece together what had happened. St. Louis had its share of crime, even murder, but not in such posh areas as this, and certainly not involving such prominent and respectable citizens as the Mansfords. The homes in this spacious area, situated at the northernmost end of the city, were large with some acreage. The wealthy and the privileged dwelled in safety and comfort, yet were still a short distance from the city, where most of them worked.

Then they heard it. It started low, and grew in intensity, volume and pitch. An eerie wailing, high pitched and frantic, like a wounded animal, coming from somewhere in the house—echoing, it seemed, through the walls.

"Mary and Joseph," Malley said, making the sign of the cross.

"It's comin' from upstairs." Leary cautiously began climbing the steps.

The wailing grew louder the higher Leary climbed.

The officers below heard him gasp.

"Come up here! Now!" Leary urged, running full tilt up to the third floor. The others hurried upstairs to join him.

Little Ginnie Jefferson lay in her own blood, her eyes wide with fear and pain, struggling for air, half crying, half moaning, as she stared at Johnny Leary.

Leary rushed to the child, but as he neared her, he could see that little Ginnie was beyond help. Sitting beside her, Leary cradled her head with his left arm and held her flailing hand in his right hand. "It's all right, child, don't worry. There, there." He tried his best to comfort her, in spite of her hopeless condition. No child should die alone, afraid and suffering.

The others arrived and stared in disbelief at the dying child in her blood-soaked nightdress.

"Boss man, he hurt mama. Den he hurt me, Ginnie." She gasped for air and with one final wail, went limp in Leary's arms. Leary held her lifeless body for several more minutes, then tenderly laid her down and stroked her head, damp from perspiration. He had seen children die of the cholera, but never from violence. "What kind of a monster would kill a child?" he asked out loud, looking in desperation at his men.

"What in heaven happened here?" one of the others asked, surveying the carnage.

Leary stood, shaken, and answered, "We're going ta find out." He walked toward the third floor servants' rooms, beginning with the small room at the end of the hall. They found Hettie's body, then Lena Anderson's. They entered the butler's room and found it empty and neat, with the bed made.

Malley suddenly spoke. "Oh no! I left Donnie in the barn. He said Mr. Saunders, the butler, was in Alton with a sick relative. Donnie is tryin' ta find one of Josiah Mansford's Arabians." He started for the stairs. "I told 'im I'd be right back."

"Go on. Horses is all that poor boy knows." Leary said, as Malley bounded down the stairs.

Malley found Donnie in the stall, brushing Minnie, one of the large Belgian draft horses.

"Donnie, let's go look for Sultana together."

Donnie already knew she wasn't in the pasture or on the way toward the city. The only place left to search was the woods behind the house, and the woods would eventually lead to the riverfront. Donnie was afraid to go into the woods, but Bobby Malley said he would be right there with him.

As they walked, Donnie called Sultana's name over and over. After a quarter mile, he stopped and listened.

Malley didn't hear anything, but Donnie turned off toward the left and soon found the frightened horse entangled in the low-lying limbs of the large old oak tree. He watched as Donnie spoke to the animal in soothing tones. The frightened Arabian stopped struggling, and Donnie came closer, talking to her every step of the way. With patience, the boy began to untangle the horse from the tree, while she stood placidly, as if to tell Donnie she trusted him.

"The storm sceered her," Donnie said as he hugged Sultana around her graceful curved neck. "Most horses, they don't like storms. She'll be okay. She's hungry." He gently removed the bit from her mouth and led her home.

He put Sultana into her stall, removed her tack, and gave her hay and water. After brushing her, he led her out to pasture with the other horses and Myrtle, the mule. Locking the gate, Donnie started back toward the barn to muck the stalls. His stomach was beginning to growl.

Johnny Leary and the other officers walked out of the house. Leary sent the others back to their posts and joined Malley, who was watching Donnie work, happily shoveling manure from the stalls. Word of the murders was already spreading. The bodies were dispatched to the morgue to wait for someone to claim and bury them. Donnie finished mucking the stalls and tapped Bobby Malley on the arm. "When is Hettie going to come with my biscuits and gravy and eggs?"

Leary heard the question and sighed. What would become of the boy, he wondered. All anyone knew about Donnie Smith was that his mother was a prostitute who had sent him to Annalise Mansford to help with the horses. The mother was never seen again. There was no way of knowing who his father was, much less where he might be found. No one could have imagined that Donnie had such an extraordinary gift with the animals, but when Josiah had seen it, he realized that Donnie could be had for cheap labor. Donnie was a sweet and trusting boy, but would always need someone to look after him.

Leary and Malley exchanged glances. How much would Donnie understand? How much *could* Donnie understand? "Donnie, why don't you stay right here, while I go and see about some breakfast for you?" He left Malley with the boy and started for the house.

"Thank you for goin' to the woods with me, sir," Donnie said, remembering his manners. "I don't like goin' in them woods. Sultana, she don't like it neither. She's happy to be back at pasture. I hope Hettie puts some bacon on my plate. I'm real hungry."

Bobby Malley shifted uncomfortably and tried one more time to see if Donnie could shed any light on what had happened. "Donnie, somethin' very bad happened at the big house last night. Ye said ye woke up just before sunrise. When do ye usually wake up?"

"The sun comes full in through the barn windows and I get up then. I care for the horses all day and after I put them to their stalls at night, I go to sleep. Hettie brings me meals and sits and talks with me. Sometimes Ginnie comes too."

"Do ye have any idea why ye woke up last night? Did ye hear a noise, or feel somethin'?"

"I just know'd somethin' was wrong, that's all."

Donnie was not going to be any more help than that, so Malley let it go. He wasn't too certain what went on in the simple mind of Donnie Smith. Beyond his extraordinary gift of working with horses, he figured Donnie didn't think about much else.

Leary appeared with some bread and jam. Donnie's face fell with disappointment, but he was hungry, so he ate it with gusto while the policemen talked to each other.

Malley positioned himself so his back was to Donnie. "Saunders will be here soon. I hate to take him from his sick mum, but we need a few answers." He looked over his shoulder at Donnie, who was licking the last of the elderberry jam off of his fingers. "We could take Donnie to the workhouse, I s'pose, but I don't think that's really a very good idea."

A woman's voice broke in before Leary could answer, causing the men to jump. "It's quite a terrible idea, in fact!"

Neither of the policemen had seen Adeline Merriweather approaching. Wearing an ivory muslin dress trimmed in ivory lace with a matching jacket, and an ivory hat with peach and pale blue flowers circling it, she walked with an air of style and confidence. Her brown hair was pulled back into a bun somewhere under her hat. She was clearly disapproving of what she had just heard.

"Why, Mrs. Merriweather, how nice to see you this mornin'." Johnny Leary tipped his cap with a short bow.

Adeline Merriweather ignored the small talk and planted the pointed tip of her ivory parasol firmly beside her feet. "Now see here. Donnie won't last ten minutes in a place like the workhouse. He owes no debt to society. He's committed no crime. He certainly does not belong in a filthy place filled with filthy people and no one to care for him." She pointed a finger at each of the policemen and shook it as if she were scolding a naughty child. "You of all people should know that. Shame on you. All that poor boy knows is horses. Until the Mansford estate can be settled, those horses will need care. I see no reason why he cannot stay exactly where he is, doing exactly what he knows and loves." She paused for a rare moment of silence. "At least for the time being, until other arrangements can be worked out." Having finished her diatribe, Mrs. Merriweather inhaled and stood tall.

Adeline Merriweather may have been a busybody, but underneath her nosy exterior, beat a kind, compassionate heart. She was a temperate and pious woman of action, leading the Ladies Mission Society at the Baptist church, the Children's Summer Bible School, as well as teaching Sunday school. She organized numerous charity events in St. Louis and was used to getting her way. Adeline Merriweather had brought Donnie to church when he was a young boy. She knew he did not understand all that was taught, but he liked the cookies and could play with children who would not treat him with the cruelty he endured before being left at the Mansford place by his now-absent mother.

Adeline Merriweather was the subject of some controversy in St. Louis society for her outspoken views on the evils of slavery and it was suspected, although never proven, that the prim and proper lady of the Merriweather home may have participated in the Underground Railroad, relocating slaves from the South to freedom in the North. Her husband was prominent in politics and in the church, so she was careful not to do anything that might place him in an untenable position. The Merriweathers made their position on slavery clear, but any action they may have taken beyond that was unknown. Adeline Merriweather was a force to be reckoned with, but if she had any ideas to help Donnie, Leary was open to hear them.

"He has to eat, Mrs. Merriweather," Leary said.

She shot a withering look at him that indicated she thought him an idiot.

"I live no more than ten minutes from here. I am certain we can see to it that Donnie is fed." She glanced into the barn, taking note of the supplies. "It looks as if the horses have plenty to eat for now. I assume they will be auctioned?"

"Likely," Malley chimed in. "Who's gonna tell 'im?" He motioned toward Donnie.

"Run along, now," she ordered them. "I'll take care of the boy."

Having nothing more to do for now at the Mansford property, the policemen left.

Having finished every last crumb on his plate, Donnie looked up and saw Adeline Merriweather standing in front of him. He grinned at her, showing crooked teeth, remembering how nice she always treated him. She smelled good all the time. Not as good as the horses, but like a lady who wore flowers. He remembered how she would bring him to Sunday school when he was little and would let him pick his cookies first. She never allowed anyone to be mean to him. Donnie liked Mrs. Merriweather.

She smiled at him. "How are you Donnie?" she asked sweetly. "I hear there was quite a bit of excitement today. Are you all right?"

"Yes ma'am. Sultana is home. Hettie didn't bring me my biscuits and gravy and eggs. I wanna see Hettie and Ginnie. Trixie misses Ginnie. She likes children."

Mrs. Merriweather sat down on the bench next to Donnie. She still smelled like flowers. "Let's see, now. Trixie is the little Welsh pony, isn't she? It's good that she likes children, because ponies are nice and small for children."

"Yes, ma'am. All my horses like children. Myrtle's sometimes stubborn, but Trixie is just the right size. I'm gonna show Ginnie how to ride, but she needs to be six and she's only four now."

Mrs. Merriweather took Donnie's hand. She spoke to him as if he were a child. "Donnie, I'm afraid I have some very bad news to tell you and that it's going to make you sad. But I want you to try and be very brave. Do you think you can do that?"

Donnie looked at her with a bewildered expression, but nodded his head.

"Good boy. Do you remember when the policemen went into the big house? I'm sorry to tell you this, Donnie, but something terrible happened last night. Do you remember when you used to come to Sunday school and we would talk about heaven?"

Donnie nodded. Mrs. Merriweather ran her fingers over the top of his head and patted his shoulder. She resumed holding his hand.

"Well, Donnie, Hettie and Ginnie aren't going to be here anymore." Her voice cracked and her eyes misted. She continued to hold Donnie's hand, patting it, sandwiching his hand between her hands. She sniffed and tried without success to sound cheerful. "They are in heaven with Jesus now. They died last night. I know you'll miss them very much, but we will not see them again here. Do you understand?"

Donnie looked up at her, his eyes brimming with tears. "Yes, ma'am. Are they happy in heaven?"

"Oh yes, dear. They're both very, very happy. Donnie, the other people that lived in the big house, Miss Lena, Miss Annalise and Captain Mansford—they too have died. Today is just a very, very sad day."

"Are they happy in heaven too?"

Adeline Merriweather wasn't certain how to answer Donnie's question. Annalise's scandalous affairs were quite the talk of the town, and Captain Mansford's reputation was one of a greedy, short tempered devil. She was not well acquainted with the Mansford staff, but knew that on Sunday mornings, Hettie and Ginnie always dressed up and attended the service at the colored church. Adeline and others from her church would take baskets of food and supplies to that church after their own services ended and she had recommended Hettie for the position with the Mansfords. Adeline was aware of Hettie's kindness toward Donnie and assumed that she would see them in heaven when it was her time to go. There would be no color divide in heaven as there was here. Rather than answer Donnie's question, she changed the subject. It was wrong to judge.

"Donnie, dear, there will be some changes coming. I know Hettie used to bring you food. I'll be sure you have food every day. I may bring it, or my maid or my cook may bring it, but you won't have to worry about your meals. For the time being, you may stay right here and care for the horses. How does that sound?"

Donnie brightened as he sat up straight. His light blue eyes widened and his freckles ran together as he smiled. "Will you bring me cookies? With the raisins?"

She stroked his choppily cut hair. "Of course. And you just let me know if you need anything else."

Lena Anderson's family, the McBrides, lived in Ireland. Her late husband had one surviving sister, Ida, who, with her husband William, buried Lena's body after a small funeral mass at the parish cemetery. Ida could not bear to tell the McBrides of the terrible manner in which Lena died, so she wrote to them and told them Lena had taken ill and not recovered. She felt it would be much easier, and being an ocean away, they would never hear news that could only cause deeper despair. After talking it over with her husband, they agreed it was a kindness to spare them the truth.

Stefan LeBlanc, the slimy paramour of Annalise, was buried in a pauper's grave. Nobody knew who he was or where he came from and nobody claimed his body.

Captain Josiah Mansford and his wife, Annalise were buried at the Bellefontaine Cemetery not far from the Mississippi River. The attendees for the double funeral were Gordon Saunders, who made the arrangements, the staff and crew of the *Mississippi Jewel* and a handful of the couple's neighbors and acquaintances.

Gordon Saunders, the faithful butler of the Mansford Mansion, oversaw the arrangements for disbursement of the estate, with the help of the Mansford's solicitor. After helping himself to choice pieces of Annalise's jewelry, Saunders arranged for an auction to dispatch of the horses and property. Having secured a position as a butler in Chicago, Saunders departed St. Louis before the final disposition of the estate, happy to leave the entire sordid mess behind him and move on to greener pastures.

After the news of the murders faded and the funerals were over, a boy of fifteen years stood in the rain beside the double graves of Hettie and Ginnie Jefferson. The sun began its slow descent, but the boy stood motionless, unaware of the rain or the coming nightfall. The rain mingled with his tears, running down his face in flowing rivulets. He was tall and gangly, with a typical teenage body, not unlike a spindly legged colt. The kindly minister from the colored church conducted the service and presided over the burial. The money raised by his poverty-entrenched congregation purchased the plain wooden crates that held their bodies. When the rain began to fall, the congregation that had gathered to mourn a senseless loss dissipated and hurried to their homes. But the lanky teenager remained.

Ezra Jefferson stared at the fresh mounds of dirt beneath which the bodies of his mother and little sister lay. So much promise. So much work. So many tears, yet, all their hopes and plans had come to this. Few people knew of Ezra's existence. Hettie had confided in the minister and his wife, but no one else knew much about Hettie, other than she was a sweet, quiet soul with a half-white child. It was assumed she had been raped by a past owner and left to raise the little girl alone. Questions were never asked and explanations never offered.

Brother Samuels tried to comfort the young man, but his words sounded hollow, even to him. Grief was a way of life that the elderly gray-haired minister knew Ezra would eventually learn to embrace. Sensing that the young man wanted to be left alone, Brother Samuels placed a comforting hand on Ezra's shoulder, squeezed and left the boy to make his peace. If the lanky teenager noticed Brother Samuel's attempt to comfort him, he did not show it. Ezra continued staring.

He remembered his mother telling him how she had met Caleb Jefferson, a white man who secretly worked in the Underground Railroad system. He had helped in the St. Louis drop-off, transporting escaped slaves from Mississippi, Alabama and Georgia, to safe houses over the river and into Illinois, where others would then take over to transport them further north. Caleb owned a dry goods store in town, a respectable business, but never discussed his true feelings about any issues in public, hiding instead behind a well-executed façade of meekness and shy solitude.

On a chilly April night, he met Hettie and three other escaped slaves at the safe house, as planned. That night, the weather turned severe with thunderstorms, hail and heavy rain, so the plan to move the slaves to the next location had to be postponed. Caleb remained with his charges in case there was trouble. Staying too long in one place could attract unwanted attention. He had vowed to God and to himself to do his part to keep this group of frightened fleeing slaves safe and help them reach freedom, regardless of the risk to his own life. The safe house was cold and drafty. Hettie, a quiet young slave from Mississippi, made coffee for him as a gesture of gratitude. When he thanked her, he noticed for the first time how lovely she was. Scars etched on her face and neck did not detract from her beauty. She exuded a sweet spirit, in spite of all she had endured in her young life.

The dangerous weather continued unabated, stranding the group for three more days, during which time, Caleb found himself increasingly drawn to Hettie. When the storms passed and it was safe to move the escaping slaves, Caleb took Hettie aside and confessed his feelings to her. He told her that he loved her and asked if she would stay on as his wife. Of course, they could not be legally married anywhere in the state of Missouri— it could mean a death sentence for both of them—so they were secretly married before God and God alone. They told no one. Hettie posed as Caleb's cook and housekeeper and they kept a small bedroom for her off the porch of his modest home to perpetuate their ruse, should anyone become suspicious.

One year later, Ezra was born. He was much lighter skinned than Hettie and Caleb wondered if he might be able to pass his son off as white, but as the child grew older, he retained enough of Hettie's features that to make such a claim would have aroused more interest than they cared to attract. Since Caleb continued to keep to himself and Ezra was quiet and well behaved, the family garnered no attention and the couple continued to live publicly as a businessman with his cook and maid, but privately as husband

and wife. Caleb continued his work with the Underground Railroad, confident that all of his secrets were safe.

When Ezra was ten years old, Hettie discovered she was once again pregnant. The couple considered moving north and decided that after the next group of slaves arrived, the family would continue north with them and find some place to settle. Caleb had been saving money for such a time as this and they began to make their plans.

Caleb, Hettie and Ezra met at the safe house to wait for the expected slaves, as Caleb had done so many times over the past several years. But that night, their plans were tragically altered. They had been discovered and betrayed. Instead of receiving a group of escaped slaves, when Caleb looked outside the window, he saw an angry mob in the distance approaching, carrying torches and weapons. He rushed Hettie and Ezra out through the back of the house and told them to run as fast as they could toward the river and wait at a second secret place used by the Underground Railroad. He would run in a different direction as a decoy and meet with them once he had escaped the encroaching mob. Hettie was frightened, but did as her husband told her, grabbing biscuits to put into her pockets before leaving. Once away from the safe house, she looked back to see where Caleb was, only to watch in horror as the mob bore down on him. She sobbed, holding little Ezra close to her and watched, her hope fading, as the harsh truth erupted that the child growing within her would never meet her father.

Determined not to let Caleb die in vain, Hettie did not risk going to the docks, fearing more hiding places had been discovered, but ventured into the wooded area just beyond. Pregnant, grief-stricken and alone with a ten-year old son and only a small amount of money, Hettie and Ezra slept in the forest for a few nights, sheltered by the dense woods. She found nuts and wild berries to eat to supplement the biscuits she had brought with her, but knew she could not live long in such a manner.

As mother and son journeyed through the woods, they came upon a small church at the edge of a clearing. Hettie could tell by the building that it was not a white church. The building was not much bigger than a shed and in need of paint. None of the windows had pretty shutters like the white churches and one of the windows was broken. But a cross hung over the doorway, and for Hettie, it was a sign of welcome. She looked inside and saw a man kneeling in prayer at the altar. He turned when he heard the door open and looked upon the small, thin woman with her child, obviously fathered by a white man. The man stood and walked toward her.

"Hello? I'm Brother Samuel. I'm the pastor of this church. Can I help you?"

Hettie began to cry and told Brother Samuel all that had happened. He arranged for her to stay with him and his wife until after the baby was born. He told her he thought he could find work for her, but Ezra would need to go away to work and Hettie would only be able to see him on Sundays at church.

"I believe it will be too dangerous for you to be seen with two half-white children. It'll raise too many questions."

It was a terrible proposition, but Hettie saw no other way.

Two years after Ginnie was born, Mrs. Adeline Merriweather arrived at the church, as she had on many Sunday afternoons with food baskets, clothing and blankets for Brother Samuel to distribute to the neediest in his flock. Brother Samuel spoke with her about Hettie's situation. Adeline's household had a full staff, but her neighbor, Josiah Mansford, a hard and angry man, could not keep hired help because he was so odious. He was desperate for help, and his wife, Annalise, had announced it would be fashionable to have a colored maid on the payroll, seeing as she thought that slavery might be going out of style with the new Republican President.

Ezra, who had recently turned eleven, was sent to a nearby family farm to work and continued to see his mother and sister only on Sundays, and Hettie moved into the Mansford home, where she and Ginnie had a bedroom, meals and meager pay.

When Ezra turned fourteen, he found work that paid a little more, and every Sunday, gave his mother half his earnings. He determined to work hard and save enough money to move them all north, as his father had intended. Ezra remembered Caleb well and wanted to honor his father's memory by becoming a man of integrity as Caleb was, keeping his mother and his sister safe.

Now, staring at their graves, their dreams were shattered, their hopes and plans, dust. The rain had slowed to fine droplets and moonlight had replaced the sun. Ezra stooped and pulled up a handful of wet grass. He sprinkled it over the mounds of dirt and turned. Walking through the misty rain, Ezra Jefferson disappeared into the night.

Adeline Merriweather brought Donnie his dinner of fried chicken, mashed potatoes, green beans, biscuits and gravy, and of course, cookies with raisins for dessert. Donnie was happy to see her. For several days, she had brought him food and checked on him. Tonight, she sat by him and told him they needed to talk. Changes were coming and she wanted Donnie to be prepared.

"Donnie, do you remember when the people in the big house died and I told you that things were going to change?" she asked. She sat beside him as he finished the last of his dinner.

"Yes, ma'am."

"Donnie, there's going to be an auction tomorrow and the following day. I want you to be prepared. Do you think you can be a brave boy?"

"Yes, ma'am."

"I'll see you in the morning." Adeline Merriweather patted Donnie's hand in hers, and left.

When Donnie got up to care for the horses, a crowd was gathering outside the big house. He watched as furniture, paintings, draperies, lamps, clothing and all kinds of items, large and small, were removed throughout the day. He did not feel sad at all. He told Mrs. Merriweather when she brought his lunch that he was very brave. When he led the horses and the mule out to pasture, he noticed that several people were at the fence, looking at the animals. He imagined they were saying what a good job he did taking care of them.

In the morning, the crowd had returned, and this time, they began to lead the horses out in front of the barn.

The auctioneer brought out Bud and Minnie, the chestnut Belgian draft horses with the long, flowing flaxen manes, and Myrtle, the mule. He talked about them and then sang out numbers while people in the crowd raised their hands. Then the auctioneer stopped and a farmer tied Bud, Minnie and Myrtle to the back of his wagon and left.

"Wait! Stop!" Donnie shouted in alarm. "Where are you going with my horses? You can't take them!" Donnie started to run after them, but the farmer kept going, and Donnie could not keep up with him. He turned around and saw the Arabians being led out to the man standing behind the podium.

The man started singing out numbers again while people raised their hands, and soon beautiful Sultana was taken away. Donnie watched in alarm, not understanding, and began to wail. Some of the people in the crowd laughed at him, mocking his pain. He had grown accustomed to the cruelty of others, but to watch helplessly as strangers led away his beloved horses was unbearable.

Midnight and Millie were bought as a pair, and then Mirage, the majestic Palomino that belonged to Annalise. Donnie's agony increased to hysteria. Didn't these people know you couldn't break up the herd? He didn't understand, and he knew the horses didn't either.

Adeline Merriweather watched the unfolding scene in anguish. She dabbed at her eyes with her husband's handkerchief and squeezed his arm for support. Her heart broke for Donnie. She had to do something, but the Merriweather barn was full and they had neither need nor room for additional horses. She had lain awake many of the past several nights praying that God would provide for Donnie. But Adeline Merriweather was more a woman of action than a woman of faith, in spite of the sermons she'd heard extolling virtues to the contrary. Finally, she could stand no more. She walked resolutely to a man in the crowd and spoke with him, as Princess, the young Morgan filly, was auctioned off. Donnie saw Mrs. Merriweather press something into the man's hand before returning to her husband's side. Some of the crowd began to leave.

Finally, the only horses left were Duchess and Star, the two older Morgans, and Trixie, the Welsh pony. The man to whom Adeline Merriweather had been speaking continued to raise his hand as the auctioneer called out the numbers, until no other bidders remained. Before he approached the podium to take the horses home, the man walked over to Donnie.

"Donnie, do you know who I am?"

"No, sir," Donnie sniffed, wiping his nose and his face with his sleeve. "Please don't take my horses." Donnie's face was red and tear streaked.

"My name is Chester Brown. I don't live very far from here. I've bought Duchess and Star for myself and my wife, and Trixie for our daughter. But there's one more thing I need, Donnie, and I'm hoping you might be willing to help me out."

Donnie looked up at Mr. Brown with puffy eyes and cocked his head sideways.

"You see, son, I need a stable boy to help me with my horses, and I hear you're just about the best man for the job. You won't have to live in the barn. You can live in your own bedroom. My wife will give you three meals every day and I'll pay you two dollars a month. How does that sound to you?"

"I like to sleep in the barn. I like to be near my horses."

Try as he might, Chester Brown could not make Donnie understand that a room in a house was better than a bunk in a barn, but Donnie agreed to the rest of the deal.

The Mansford property stood emptied of every fine possession. Donnie ran into the barn one last time to retrieve his pillow and blanket and to bid farewell to the empty stalls of his beloved horses.

The Merriweathers remained arm in arm where they had been standing until they saw Donnie and Mr. Brown leading the horses away, with Pumpkin, the big orange tomcat, trotting after them.

Part Two:
The History of Mansford Mansion

1865-2015

Over the ensuing years and decades, the deserted Mansford property fell into disrepair. The families who could afford that type of real estate shunned it, for the gruesome murders within its walls cast a sickly pall over the place. Its former glory tainted by scandal and rumor, the abandoned property became forlorn. Its once beautiful gardens overtaken by weeds, the lifeless home took on a formidable appearance, haunted by the tragedies of the past and threatened with a sense of ominous foreboding. The porch sagged and the chimneys crumbled. If prospective buyers did, perchance, venture inside, they left in a hurry, saying something "just didn't feel right."

On occasion, hobos hopping off the trains took shelter in the house, but left within minutes, sometimes reporting sounds of a crying child coming from upstairs. The crystal chandelier swayed, absent a breeze. The house remained unlived in and unattended to for many years, earning a reputation of being haunted. Teenagers ventured inside at night, seeking a thrill or going on a dare, only to run out, shaken and terrified.

On September 15, 1915, the state of Missouri took over the property with the intention of turning it into a children's home. Construction workers swore they heard a child crying as they set up their tools. They would look for the child and, not finding her, return to discover their tools moved. Some claimed to hear a woman scream, and others told of noises that sounded as if a heavy object was falling down the grand staircase. In any event, little work was accomplished, and after a carpenter was found dead for no apparent cause, the state shifted the property to a low priority on the never-ending list of taxpayer-funded projects. Eventually, the paperwork was lost in a sea of red tape and once again, the house sat empty and neglected.

On September 15, 1965, the barn caught fire and burned to the ground. Because it was reported that a child could be heard crying, the charred mess remained untouched. No one, including the state employees, was willing to work cleanup duty.

In the spring of 1970, the city announced that the Mansford property would be torn down and replaced with a neighborhood playground. Although the area had not been posh and fashionable for decades and languished in swift decline, efforts were undertaken to rehabilitate the failing neighborhood and others like it in hopes of attracting families back to the city. Businesses and residents had left in droves for the suburbs, citing crime and deteriorating neighborhoods and schools as the primary reasons.

Thomas and Barbara Arbogast, a wealthy couple from the affluent suburb of Clayton, decided the place could be turned into a profitable upscale bed and breakfast. Thomas Arbogast was known for imbuing the Midas touch on every business venture he undertook, and he smelled money in this one. Thomas and Barbara petitioned the city of St. Louis for permits and presented a convincing case to city officials that their plans would do more for the revival of a questionable neighborhood than tearing down an historic, although notorious, landmark and replacing it with a playground. The city council agreed, especially after calculating that the cost of the tear down, clean up and building of the park far exceeded the tax abatement the Arbogasts proposed in exchange for their assuming full financial responsibility. It was a win-win proposition, if they succeeded.

Thomas and Barbara, cynics to their core, scoffed at the idea of ghosts, believing the old rumors to be poppycock, the product of overactive imaginations and willful ignorance. It was 1970, for heaven's sake.

The rehabbing process began in August, first with the outside clean-up, and by September, moving inside to rehab the mansion. Thomas and Barbara personally oversaw the project and hired like-minded people who were not prone to superstition and suggestion.

By Thanksgiving, the home had new wiring, indoor plumbing, central heating and air conditioning, and the foundation had been shored up. The entire exterior had been tuckpointed and the bricks cleaned. The only complaint was that the third floor was always cold—a phenomenon the construction workers could neither explain nor remedy. Undaunted, Barbara suggested that the third floor be used for laundry and storage of all supplies. The original plans were altered to accommodate her ideas. Problem solved.

Over the Christmas holiday, the Arbogasts vacationed in Hawaii, leaving orders for new windows to be installed, along with general structural repairs. When they returned, most of the crew had quit, citing strange noises and creepy feelings of being watched. Thomas and Barbara were furious. One of them had been at the site every day throughout the project. It was nothing more than an old house in serious disrepair. Nothing more unsettling than a stray cat walking in and eating one of the workmen's lunches had happened in the previous months. They made a public show of moving a bed into the house and spending the night there. Having slept without incident, they emerged unscathed the next morning, and announced they were accepting bids to finish the work and would pay double time for anyone willing to work weekends.

The project was completed in July of 1971, almost an entire year after it began, and four months ahead of the predicted completion date of November. Most of the original wood and fixtures had been restored to their original beauty, with only the most seriously damaged requiring replacement. It had gone over budget, but the Arbogasts were certain that any shortfalls would be recouped when the Mansford Mansion Bed, Breakfast and Tea Room opened two weeks before Thanksgiving. Within three days of opening the reservation lines, the Arbogasts' gamble paid off. They were booked full, well into April and soon were taking requests for small wedding receptions. Interest and enthusiasm were high and climbing. Thomas and Barbara calculated they would be in the black by the first week of March. They hosted a lavish celebration dinner at Tony's, the priciest five star restaurant in St. Louis, with champagne, steak, lobster and all the trimmings, inviting their closest friends and select members of the local media. Toasts were made and glasses raised many times, hailing the couple's success and future prosperity.

However, the celebratory mood soon faded, as guests staying at the mansion reported having nightmares and hearing eerie sounds in the foyer, including the echo of a child crying. While some reported their stay was quite comfortable, with delicious food and luxurious accommodations, others said the place gave them the creeps and nothing could persuade them to darken the doors of Mansford Mansion again. They claimed no amount of paint or polish could rid the house of its maleficent aura. It soon became difficult to keep staff for the same reasons it was difficult to retain clientele.

The Arbogasts broadcast on numerous occasions that they would yet again spend the night in the house. Eventually, they slept in every room, each morning appearing before the press, relaxed, refreshed and unharmed. But the negative publicity generated by vocal clientele demanding refunds far outweighed the Arbogasts' claims of rubbish, and business fell off dramatically. By Valentine's Day, the Arbogasts announced that Mansford Mansion would close its doors. All existing reservations had called to cancel. Nobody considered the place suitable for a romantic Valentine dinner. Once again, the house, though refurbished to its original magnificence, stood vacant and abandoned.

Over the next forty years, various business entrepreneurs attempted to make a run of the place. Restaurants opened and closed, business centers renting rooms to small firms and sole practitioners came and went, and the building, like the surrounding neighborhoods, fell into decline.

By 2015, Mansford Mansion suffered major deterioration. The house was sold at a tremendous loss to Alan Cunningham, a local businessman with plans to turn it into a mystery dinner theater. Cunningham reasoned that if all the rumors were true— the crying, screams and thumping sounds—it would only add to the ambiance he desired to create anyway. Why not turn the negatives into positives?

While his idea was plausible, Alan Cunningham needed financial backers. He was not a wealthy man by any means and had never succeeded at anything, other than playing Count Dracula in his high school play, having been chosen for his looks, rather than any acting ability. He was tall and thin, in his late thirties, with a receding hairline. His large, bulging brown eyes matched his small amount of remaining hair. His sizeable aquiline nose dwarfed his receding chin and his pale complexion gave the appearance of a vampire who avoided the sun. His shirt sleeves were too short, which accentuated his long, bony fingers. Alan paced incessantly, a trait that drove others to distraction. His character was shady on a good day and he saw the Mansford Mansion Dinner Theatre as an easy way to make fast money. Cutting corners wherever possible, he served cheap, tasteless food and adorned the place with chintzy decorations. Payroll was usually late. Much needed repairs and updates to the building were ignored. If the place looked like it was falling down, what better way to add to the atmosphere?

But in spite of his penny pinching, the business was failing. All he needed was one good break. Alan visited the History Museum in Forest Park and the downtown library to review the colorful past of the mansion in search of some clue that might bring him success. As he studied whatever materials he could find on the house's history, a pattern emerged. Alan noticed that every fifty years, a major event occurred. Fifty years to the day after the murders, a workman was found dead in the house. Fifty years to the day after that, the barn burned to the ground. Fifty years after that, was . . . *this year*!

Part Three:
The Present Day Crime

August 7, 2015

Chapter 1

"Please, Daddy, please? It's my birthday and this is what I really wanna do! Oh, please, pleasepleaseplease, *please*? I get to be queen for the day on my birthday. That's the rules. Please say yes! Okay, Daddy?"

Adam Trent had just gotten home from a long day at work and no sooner walked in the door, before Amy, with the persistence of an alarm clock, attacked him with her birthday request, almost an entire month before the major event. He looked imploringly at his wife, Jenna, for help.

"Those are the rules, Adam," Jenna reminded him sweetly, as she finished slicing the last of the potatoes. "Birthdays are special and we all get to pick what we want."

"Jenna, hon, do you really think that's the healthiest option for our little girl?"

"I'm almost a teenager. I'm almost *eleven*! That's practically old enough to drive. I'm not a little girl anymore, Daddy! I love haunted houses! And this is *the* fifty year mark, and that makes 150 years, and look," Amy exclaimed, bringing him the entertainment section of the Post-Dispatch and pointing. "Something big always happens every fifty years. I don't wanna miss it!"

The quarter page ad warned that the 150-year anniversary of the Mansford Mansion murders was the event of the century and implied that missing it would constitute a tragedy of epic proportions.

Adam removed his gun, badge and holster and set them on the kitchen counter, breathing in the enticing aroma of whatever Jenna had baking in the oven. The kitchen always smelled good when he came home from work and he was looking forward to dinner. He sat down on a kitchen chair and glanced at the mail. Immediately, Amy was standing in front of him, smiling ear-to-ear while she wrapped her arms around his neck. Her brown eyes stared into his with the unblinking determination of a cat. Her long golden brown braids, freckles and lavender glasses told him she was still his little girl, regardless of her arguments to the contrary.

Powerless to resist her charms, Adam put his arms around his daughter and hugged her. He leaned his forehead into hers until their noses were almost touching. "Amy, you know there's no such thing as haunted houses. There are no ghosts, and everything that has ever happened at that property can be easily explained. What you're asking me and your mother to do for your birthday is to take you into a bad neighborhood, eat a meal of questionable digestibility, sit through a drama that is nowhere near as good as your fourth grade play, and pay way too much money for the privilege. We always have so much fun on your birthday. I really think you'll be disappointed if we agree to this."

"No I won't. I promise." Amy pulled away and pointed again at the ad in the Post. "The paper says the seats will fill up fast, so we have to get our reservations in now. I get to pick what I want for my birthday and this is what I want! *Pleeeease* say yes!"

Adam looked at his wife, but Jenna appeared preoccupied with dinner preparations.

Undaunted, Amy continued. "If the meal isn't very good, we can go to the Fountain on Locust for ice cream later. We all love the Fountain, Daddy! How 'bout we go there, too? I won't be too full. Promise! Cross my heart and hope to die, stick a needle in my eye. Okay?"

"Okay to stick a needle in your eye? Are you sure?"

"Daddy! You're aggravating me!" Amy stood in front of Adam with her hands on her hips.

Adam pressed his lips together to keep from laughing.

Jenna listened with amusement to the banter between her husband and their daughter. She placed the Potatoes Dauphinois into the oven. "We'll eat in about 45 minutes. Amy, why don't you give Daddy a few minutes to change clothes and get comfortable? When daddies get home from a hard day at work, they need a few minutes to themselves, even if there *is* a very special occasion coming up in a month."

"A month and a week," Amy corrected her.

"All right, a month and a week. Besides, it's time to set the table and help me with the salad."

"Thank you," Adam whispered as he rose and kissed his wife on her forehead. He picked up the newspaper, along with his things on the counter and left for the bedroom to change clothes and enjoy a few minutes of peace and quiet before dinner.

Amy pouted, but put the plates and silverware on the table.

Jenna talked to her as she tore the lettuce and chopped the celery, carrots, peppers and scallions. "Sweetheart, there's one thing you need to learn about men, whether it's your Daddy, or, when you're all grown up, your husband. They're always more agreeable when they have a full stomach. Now, when Daddy comes to dinner, I don't want to hear another word about your birthday or the haunted house."

"But Mom…"

"No buts, Amy. Give it a rest and we'll talk about it after dinner. Blue looks hungry. Have you fed her and given her fresh water?"

"Blue always looks hungry. Come on, Blue."

The big blue and white pit bull padded behind Amy, wagging her tail at the sound of the food bag being opened. Amy sat down next to the dog, petting her and talking to her as Blue ate the kibble her human put in her bowl. Blue had always been a great listener.

Jenna finished working in the kitchen, washed her hands and hung her apron on the pantry door hook. She rested on a stool and watched as Blue sat and listened while Amy pontificated on the important details of her birthday. The two had been inseparable for almost eight years. Blue acted as Amy's guardian angel and friend since they met on the most terrifying day of Jenna's life.

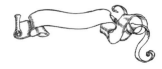

Amy was a late-in-life baby welcomed by Adam and Jenna after Jenna had suffered four heartbreaking miscarriages. The Trents had given up on having a baby—a decision Jenna's doctors supported after years of testing without satisfactory results. When Jenna, at the age of thirty-seven, discovered she was pregnant, neither she nor Adam allowed themselves to feel the joy and excitement of anticipating a child's arrival. Instead, they tried to prepare for yet another inevitable loss in the ensuing weeks. But this time, Jenna did not miscarry, and six months into her pregnancy, they dared to choose names and prepare the nursery. Five weeks later, Amy was born prematurely, but viable. Her lungs were small and she spent two weeks in an incubator, but when she reached five pounds and three ounces, she was allowed to come home, where she thrived with few problems. Adam and Jenna brought the tiny infant to their small two-bedroom bungalow in the Carondelet Park neighborhood.

When Amy was three years old, Jenna joined a neighborhood play group where around a dozen pre-school aged children met one day a week in St. Louis Hills' lovely Willmore Park, not far from the Trent's home. Although Amy was small for her age, she enjoyed the outings. She was a friendly child with no fear of strangers, or of anything, as far as Jenna and Adam could tell.

Toward the end of the afternoon, the Jasons, as Jenna referred to them, started a fight. Another fight. Jason Watson and Jason Olinger were three-year-old terrorists, as far as Jenna was concerned. They bullied the other children and started fights as soon as their mothers turned their backs. Jenna had considered removing Amy from the play group because the Jasons could not be trusted and Jenna was afraid that Amy might get hurt. Worse, their mothers thought their sons' behavior was cute, which aggravated Jenna to no end. Once again, the Jasons started a playground brouhaha and soon, loud wailing could be heard from their latest victim. Jenna, along with several other mothers, intervened to break it up, offering comfort to yet another wounded toddler. It was over within minutes, but when Jenna stood to collect Amy and start for home, Amy was nowhere in sight.

Panic gripped Jenna like a vice—it was a parent's worst nightmare. Jenna called her daughter's name, as she searched the area with her eyes, her feet frozen to the ground in fear. Each time she called, the only response was the faint echo of her own voice. Terrified, Jenna realized that Amy was in fact, missing. She grew more and more frantic. Where could a toddler have gone in only a few minutes? She searched her memory. Had there been strangers watching the children as they played? No. She was certain she would have noticed. Adam had taught her to always be aware of her surroundings.

The other mothers joined the search to no avail, and Jenna, hysterical, called Adam. Would they bring the search dogs? She continued looking, venturing into the heavily treed area by the hiking trails beyond the playground. The sun would be setting soon. The temperature was dropping and Amy was wearing only a little sun dress. What if Amy had fallen into the lake or into River Des Peres? Surely, she could not have gotten as far as the cemetery! She continued calling, running deeper into the park and off the trails. She prayed, "God, please send an angel to watch over Amy. Please keep her safe."

Jenna heard the wail of a police siren approaching and knew Adam would soon be at the park. She did not want to return to the playground area. Backtracking would waste valuable time. She knew she must continue to search before the sun set. Trekking still further into the trees, Jenna stopped cold when she saw Amy's little legs lying motionless in the distance by a tree, her pink glitter sandals reflecting the fading sunlight. A lump formed in Jenna's throat and her knees buckled. She stood trembling, unable to move, staring at Amy's inert legs, fearing the worst. Summoning her courage, Jenna drew nearer to the still child. She suddenly stopped. A huge pit bull was lying on top of the toddler. Had her daughter been harmed? Amy had no fear of dogs. Had this pit bull attacked her and was now guarding its prey? Jenna shuddered to think such a thought as the knots in her stomach tightened. She took one cautious step closer, then another, watching the dog with each careful step. The dog did not growl or move, but cocked her head, with her ears forward as she watched Jenna approach. Then Jenna saw Amy's tiny arm, wrapped around the dog's neck. She then realized the two had snuggled together and this strange dog was keeping Amy warm as she slept beneath her. The dog, a blue-gray pit bull with a white stripe down the middle of her face and a white chest and socks, looked up at Jenna with large curious amber eyes. She had no collar, but seemed gentle. Amy appeared to be unharmed as she slept peacefully under the animal. Jenna called to her in a soft voice, so as not to startle the dog.

"Amy."

The child woke up, and seeing her mother, smiled. She hugged the big dog that had kept her warm and comfortable and then wiggled out from beneath it.

"Amy, step away from the dog and come to mommy."

"My gog," Amy announced and hugged the animal again.

Jenna's cell phone rang.

"I found her, Adam. She's okay, but we have a small problem."

Adam ran to their location and stopped when he saw the dog standing calmly beside his daughter.

"Amy," he coaxed her, kneeling in the grass. "Come to daddy. Tell the doggie goodbye and let's go home."

"My gog," Amy insisted, hugging the dog around the neck so tightly Jenna feared a vicious reaction. But the dog stood placidly beside Amy.

Jenna took a step toward the pair and the dog wagged her tail. She was calm, allowing Jenna and then Adam, to pet her. But just as Amy refused to leave her new companion, neither would the dog leave Amy.

They took both the dog and Amy home. Adam tried in vain to find the owner. There was no clue as to where the dog came from, but she was gentle and well-behaved.

"She has to be somebody's pet," Adam insisted three days later. "She's good with children, obedient and sweet."

"Adam, we've placed ads in the paper and left our names with the Humane Society, the APA, and Pet Finders. No collar, no chip and nobody has claimed her."

"Besides Amy."

"What should we do?"

Adam shrugged. "Find a good vet and get her spayed. Looks like we have a dog." He reached down and scratched the new family member behind her ears. The dog leaned into Adam's leg and wagged her tail.

Amy named her Blue and the Trents officially adopted her. Jenna referred to the newest family member as her Blue Angel because she had prayed that God would send an angel to keep Amy safe, and He had. It wasn't quite what she had expected, but then, she knew God always had a better plan.

Adam squeezed Jenna's hand after dinner. "Delicious, Babe. Thanks for a great meal. Lemon rosemary chicken, buttered carrots, and those creamy potatoes. Hit the spot."

"I helped with the salad," Amy chimed in. Before she could continue hammering on about her birthday, Adam cut her off.

"Especially the salad. You're gonna be a great cook just like your mother, peanut." He tweaked her nose, putting his thumb between his index and middle fingers.

Amy rolled her eyes. "Daddy, I'm too old for that. My nose is still on my face."

"Well, 'scuuuze me," he teased, returning her nose to its rightful place.

Jenna grinned at her husband and brushed his hand with hers. He was still as handsome as the day she met him. She had fallen hard for the young patrolman and had watched with pride as he rose through the ranks to detective sergeant. Adam would always be her hero.

"Hard day at work?"

"Yeah. We finally closed the Cranston murders and gave the D.A. enough hard evidence to convict. Cranston was a squirrely devil, but we all knew he was guilty. Proving it was another matter. But like all criminals, he screwed up and that sealed the deal. I'm glad that one is behind us, at least until trial."

"Glad you got him. What an evil man! Just thinking about what he did gives me the creeps. Everyone is safer because of all you did to get that twisted monster off the streets."

"Aw, shucks, ma'am. Just doin' my job." Adam tipped his imaginary cap to his wife. It was his favorite line and always made her laugh. "It was a team effort," he reminded her, referring to his partners, Bo and Connor, in the Homicide Division. "And it cost us our vacation this summer. More to sock away for next year, I guess," he sighed. "Maybe we can still get away for a few days before school starts. Maybe a long weekend in Branson or down at Table Rock Lake."

"Or we could plan for my birthday at Mansford Mansion," Amy reminded him.

"It *is* the birthday rule, Adam," Jenna added, as if he needed another reminder.

"Et tu, Jenna?" Adam looked up at his wife and put his head in his hands, defeated.

"Aw. You're so cute when you pout. And quote Shakespeare. Sort of." Jenna patted Adam's head.

He took her hands in his. "Stop picking on me. It's not nice to bully your husband."

"You're even cuter when you pout and give me puppy dog eyes. It's just dinner and a murder, and like you said, we can hit the Fountain for ice cream later. I doubt Amy will be scarred for life by the experience."

"Like there's not enough crime in my life as it is," he moaned in resignation.

Amy pounced on the moment of concession and hugged Adam. "Oh, thank you, Daddy! Thank you! This is gonna be my best birthday ever! Can Amanda come? Please? She's my best friend and I know she wants to come, so can she? Huh? Can she?"

"Of course," Adam said. "It's the birthday rule."

Jenna said, "I'll call Amanda's mother in the morning before making the reservations."

Amy jumped and cheered. "Yay! Can I get a cell phone?"

"Don't push it, kid," he answered, pinching her nose.

Amy screwed up her face, making her freckles blend together and looked at her parents through squinty brown eyes. Blue padded over to her side carrying her leash in her mouth, creating a perfect diversion.

"I'm taking Blue for a walk." Amy clipped the leash on the ecstatic Blue and the two friends left.

Jenna put her arms around Adam's strong shoulders and kissed the back of his neck. "You're such a good daddy," she whispered. "It's just one night. Everything will be fine. You'll see."

Adam looked at his wife. They had been married over twenty years. She had aged well, in spite of the years not being kind to her. Jenna had wanted a large family, but with each miscarriage, a little bit of Jenna died as well. When they realized they would never have a child, they applied to over a dozen agencies to adopt, but the adoption agencies told the Trents they were too old to be considered for a baby. Heartbroken, they looked into foreign adoption, but the salaries of a policeman and a librarian were woefully inadequate to pursue that option.

Jenna spiraled into depression. Adam knew she was in a dark place and sinking deeper, beyond his reach. He realized he needed strength much greater than his own to be the man she needed. Although Adam was a man of strong faith, he found himself shaken as he feared losing the woman he loved with all his heart. He had always prided himself on being able to solve his own problems, but understood that Jenna's sorrow and desire for a child were beyond his reach. He sought and received wise counsel from their pastor that led him to a deeper understanding of his wife, and in the end, Adam determined that this trial would bring him closer to God and closer to Jenna, no matter what the outcome. He chose to trust that God had a plan, even though Adam had no idea what that plan might be.

Amy had been an answer to prayers the Trents had stopped praying. When they brought their tiny daughter home, Adam saw the sparkle of life return to Jenna's eyes. He thought Jenna was even more beautiful than when he first saw her driving her shiny red, vintage Mustang GT convertible down Jamieson Avenue more than twenty-five years ago.

He was a young, first-year patrolman and she was the prettiest creature he had ever laid eyes on. She was waiting at the red light at Jamieson and Chippewa and he was in the parking lot of Ted Drewes Frozen Custard, watching the morning traffic. The car caught his eye first—a gorgeous piece of automotive history, flawlessly restored. He glanced at the driver to see who the lucky guy was to call that classic beauty his, but to his surprise, the driver of the dream car was unquestionably a she—a she so pretty, he forgot all about the car. When the light turned green, the 'stang turned onto Chippewa and drove right in front of Adam's squad car, a temptation Adam could not resist. He pulled his cruiser into the traffic, maneuvering it behind her Mustang, making a note of the license plate. He turned into the parking lot of Donut Drive-in, home of the best donuts in St. Louis, and ran the number. Adam learned her name was Jenna Willows and she lived in an apartment on Jamieson on his patrol route, so he surmised she must have just left home. He was relieved to see she had no record and no red flags.

Adam watched for her car every day, hoping she would go over the speed limit, have a tail light out, something. He needed some excuse to meet her, but could find none. For all of his Marine swagger, Adam had always been tongue-tied around women, and when he did manage to say something, he usually sounded as though he suffered from bone jarring stupidity. He just wanted a chance to meet her and not sound like an idiot. All he knew was that the lovely Jenna Willows took the same route from Jamieson to Chippewa every morning. Although she didn't live very far from his apartment in Holly Hills, he had never seen her in any of the neighborhood haunts. He wondered where she worked, but didn't dare follow her. The last thing he, or the Department, for that matter needed was a harassment complaint. Adam told himself that if he could just talk to Jenna Willows one time, he would not say something stupid.

One afternoon, after his shift ended, Adam was on his way home when up ahead on Jamieson, he saw a red Mustang GT convertible parked on the side of the road with its flashers on. It had to be her! At last. He hoped she would be as beautiful on the inside as she was on the outside. Nothing could be worse than if this mystery woman he had been dreaming of meeting turned out to be a nasty witch.

Popping a breath mint in his mouth, he pulled his car in back of hers and got out to see if she needed help. He was still wearing his uniform and hoped that would help garner her trust. Otherwise, he thought, she might be alarmed at a strange man approaching her. He walked over to her car.

"Trouble, ma'am?" He tried to sound confident.

The mysterious Jenna Willows looked up and her soft brown eyes met his. His legs turned to jelly.

"I'm afraid so. I was on my way home from work and my car started making a terrible noise and shaking. I didn't feel safe to drive it, so I pulled over. I've called a tow truck and it should be here soon."

She didn't sound nasty, he thought, relieved. Just a little concerned, which he could understand. Her voice had a clear, bell-like quality. He wanted to hear more of it.

"It's a beauty of a car. What year is it?"

She smiled and the world grew brighter.

"Thanks. 1966. My dad spent years restoring it before he died. He passed it on to me. It's in great shape and I keep it meticulously maintained. Never had any trouble until now. I don't know what's wrong with it." She got out of the car, stepping to the sidewalk, and Adam followed, happy he didn't have to stand in the street.

"Hmm. Could be the rear end or the U-joints. Do you have a good mechanic? How about a ride home? Need a lift?"

"I only let the Johnson brothers over in the Central West End touch my car. I trust them. I was just going through my phone directory when you pulled up. I work at Machacek Library over on Scanlan. I get off work earlier than my friends, so I don't have anyone to call for a ride for another hour or two."

Now he knew where she worked. He wondered why she took such a long roundabout route when she worked such a short distance from home.

"How far are you from home?" he asked, even though he already knew where she lived.

"I'm a little more than a mile down Jamieson, close to the park. Once they pick up the car, I can walk home."

"I could take you home," Adam volunteered. "I live over in Holly Hills. We're practically neighbors. I'm Adam. My shift is over and I was just on my way home. It's my first year on the force, so I don't have my own squad car yet to take home."

"That's very kind, but I couldn't trouble you. I'm Jenna, by the way." She offered her hand and he shook it, taking care not to squeeze too hard.

"It's no trouble—no trouble at all," he said, hoping he didn't sound too eager. Or, too desperate. "I was going to stop at Imo's for a pizza and go home to watch the Cardinal game. You're not five minutes away. And if I'm not being out of line, those don't exactly look like walking shoes." He pointed to her feet, which appeared to him to be covered with devices of torture.

Adam's curiosity finally got the better of him. He had to know why she took such an unusual route from home to work. "Haven't I seen this car going east on Chippewa in the morning? That's an awfully long route to work."

She laughed. "Yes, you have. I stop at World's Fair Donuts on Vandeventer to pick up breakfast for the library crew," she answered.

Adam raised his eyebrows. "Donut Drive-in is right up here. Why not go there? It's much closer, and they have the best donuts in town."

She looked at him doubtfully. "Well, Officer Adam, I know it's bad form to argue with a cop, especially about a subject as serious as donuts, but it's World's Fair Donuts, hands down."

"Donut Drive-in," he announced with great authority.

"World's Fair," she insisted, unmoved.

He crossed his arms. "I'm a cop and when it comes to donuts, I'm telling you, it's Donut Drive-in."

"Oh yeah? Give it your best." She stood with her hands on her slender hips. Adam accepted the dare.

"One. Word. Apple fritters."

"That's two words. Cream horns."

"Buttermilk old fashioned."

"Milk chocolate cake. Beat that, cop."

"No problem. Old school style. Deep fried sugar and fat."

"Seriously? Deep fried sugar and fat? That's your best?"

"Okay, blueberry cake donuts. Blueberries are good for you. It's health food."

Jenna giggled, rendering her unable to answer.

"Point goes to Adam. I declare myself the winner." He pumped his fist into the air in victory.

Jenna shook her head and kept laughing.

The tow truck arrived and the goddess of the vintage Mustang convertible supervised as her car was secured for transport. Once the car was on its way to the Central West End, she turned her attention back to Adam.

"All right. I'll take you up on your offer of a ride home on one condition. Let me at least buy the pizza. Deal?"

It was the best deal Adam had ever made. He didn't make it home in time for the baseball game that night. They stayed at the pizza parlor talking until the manager began to put the chairs on top of the tables before closing. Adam studied Jenna as she talked. Her long brown hair had been pulled back in a ponytail, he presumed, so it wouldn't get tangled when she drove with the top down. Her skin was clear and creamy. Not too much make-up. He felt he could talk to her for the rest of his life. Adam Trent was undeniably smitten.

More than twenty years later, nothing had changed. They had suffered together through the heart-wrenching loss from four miscarriages and other trials. They had persevered through difficult times, when Adam's job put Jenna and newborn Amy in danger. They had endured financial hardship, the loss of Jenna's mother, and the guilt Adam suffered as the sole survivor when his unit of Marines was ambushed and killed, resulting in flashbacks and violent nightmares. But their marriage remained strong. Adam's love for Jenna had only grown deeper.

Adam stood and helped his wife clear the table. "Adam, she's growing up. Amy's not going to be a little girl forever, you know."

"She's always going to be my little girl."

"You know what I'm talking about."

"And this haunted house nonsense. Jenna, what if this gets around at church? I don't think this is a healthy choice—falling for a gimmick that centers around a tragedy?" He had the plates and salad bowls neatly stacked and started for the kitchen.

"The more you forbid it, the more tempting it's going to become to her. Let her have her fun and we can be the voice of reason. She'll look back on this and laugh. We need to choose our battles wisely, especially as she gets older. This isn't a battlefield to die on. Wait until the day some teenage boy comes to the door for her." Jenna gathered the remaining dishes and followed Adam, who was loading the dishwasher.

"Thanks, babe. Like I need to think about *that* now! Any boy that wants to take *my* daughter out is going to have to have a little chat with me first. It'll be a good time for me to be cleaning my gun."

Jenna laughed and kissed him on his forehead. "Shall I make the reservations in the morning, Herr Commandant?"

"Sure," he answered, walking to the living room window and peeking out the curtain to check on Amy and Blue as they made their way toward home. "You know, Blue is getting up in age. How do you think Amy will take it when she no longer has her best friend?"

"Blue's got a little arthritis, but she's still got plenty of life in her. Let's not pay the toll before we get to the bridge."

"We've had her almost eight years, now, Jen. How old do you think she really is?"

"The vet said she thought Blue was right around a year when she came to us. Amy was three. Blue is around nine. She's in good health and should have several years left of devoted friendship to Amy. She's a great dog. I feel safe with her when you're working the night shift and we're home alone."

"Jenna, she's never even barked. She's as gentle as a lamb."

"Blue's never been tested. I think she'd rise to the occasion if she felt her pack, her family, was threatened."

"I hope we never have to find out." Adam watched as Amy and Blue circled around to the back yard for a game of fetch before coming in. He shuddered at the thought of the damage Blue's teeth could do if she ever did feel the need to protect her family.

"She was a good girl. As usual," Amy announced upon their return. She hung Blue's leash on the door handle and gave her a treat. Then she trotted over to her father and held her arms out in front of her. Adam picked Amy up by her wrists and swung her around in circles, while she squealed in delight. It was their nightly ritual, and Adam realized with a sinking heart, that this too, would eventually come to an end, as Amy would soon grow too old to play airplane.

"Okay, peanut." Adam set her down on her feet. "Start getting ready for bed. Mom will make your birthday reservations in the morning."

"It's still light outside. Why can't I stay up longer?"

"The school year is just around the corner, so we need to start moving bedtime back earlier. You got to stay up late all summer."

"I'm almost in junior high," she whined, stifling a yawn.

"Don't remind us," Jenna mumbled under her breath.

Chapter 2

September 15, 2015

At Amy's insistence, the Trents arrived early at Mansford Mansion for the advertised event of the century. She also insisted they drive Jenna's car. It would be so embarrassing to arrive at such a momentous occasion in a police cruiser.

Amy's friend, Amanda, woke up sick that morning, and was unable to join the festivities. Although disappointed, the absence of her friend did not abate the birthday girl's excitement for long. Amy had practically memorized the flyer. It rehashed with dramatic flair, the original murders and the different theories as to who did it and why, although, there was never any real question.

Adam resented that a true historic tragedy had been turned into a circus event for profit and was concerned that by bringing Amy, they might be encouraging the development of a taste for the morbid in their precious little girl. The flyer further made a big deal of the house's history of being haunted, playing up every story that was even vaguely out of the ordinary—a gimmick which Adam found tiring. But, as he had been reminded now on numerous occasions, it was Amy's birthday and so they were going to have a great time, like it or not.

As the Trent family walked up the steps to the porch, Adam noted numerous code violations—broken and sagging steps, protruding nails, a dim light bulb flickering overhead that buzzed at intermittent intervals as if it would short out at any minute.

The house was situated in one of the worst crime districts in the city, far from Adam's clean, safe District Two neighborhood, where the officers were so bored that a dog bite could elicit a response from every squad car in the district. He knew who he could mention the hazards to, if he wanted to make trouble. But with the area as crime-ridden as it had now become, he doubted whether anyone would care about the code violations. He hoped the kitchen was sanitary enough to survive eating the food. It was probably teeming with bacteria. Adam shuddered at the thought and checked his wallet to be sure his health insurance cards were in place, should his family end up in the emergency room with ptomaine poisoning or salmonella, or whatever else might be lurking in their food to make them sick.

They entered the house through the front door, which made a loud creaking noise when they opened it. On the foyer wall hung large portraits of Josiah and Annalise Mansford. They were good copies, Adam assumed, probably taken from old news clippings. Captain Mansford's portrait displayed a stern countenance with a disapproving glare that even now, a hundred and fifty years later, sent a chill through whomever glanced at it, but the portrait of Annalise reflected a hauntingly beautiful woman.

Alan Cunningham appeared, stepping out of the shadows of the dimly lit foyer. He was dressed in black from head to toe. The color made him appear a ghastly white. Adam thought he looked creepy, but Amy seemed enthralled with the experience. "Is that *the* chandelier?" she asked wide-eyed, pointing to the light fixture overhead.

"It is," Cunningham answered, trying to sound mysterious as he raised his eyebrows into a high arch. "You are the first victims, er, I mean, *guests*, to arrive. Welcome. You may sit at any table you wish, except for the long one in the middle, which is reserved for a large party of brave souls. The bar is straight ahead. Mike, our very capable bartender, will take good care of you. The gift shop is over here, to the right. Many lovely things in there." He gestured flamboyantly. Adam noted his long, pale fingers with manicured nails. *Still creepy.*

Adam surveyed the dining area and chose a table toward the rear against the far wall, where he could watch the room. It was a common habit of cops. Never leave your back exposed, and sit where you can observe everything. Jenna was used to her husband's idiosyncrasies and took her seat, but Amy balked.

"I want to sit in the front, right in the middle."

But Adam leaned toward Amy and said in a low voice, just above a whisper, "You might miss a clue if you can't see the whole room. This is the best table in the house. You can see everything."

Her eyes widened. She nodded her head in agreement and winked at her father. "You're so smart, Daddy. That's why you're a detective, right?"

He put his finger to his lips and whispered again to her, "Shhh! That's our little secret, peanut. Don't tell anybody who we really are." He winked at her with a twinkle in his eye.

She giggled with delight and whispered back. "Roger that. Nobody will know. Can we go see the gift shop?"

Jenna put the menu down and rose. She knew Adam needed to look over the room, in keeping with his habitual dining-out security idiosyncrasies. Taking Amy to the gift shop would be a good excuse to let her husband be the cop he would always be, even when he was off duty.

Adam's dark eyes met his wife's. "Don't be too long. And don't buy anything. They'll start taking dinner orders once everyone has arrived, which should be soon." He had no sooner spoken, when the sound of car doors closing outside was heard, announcing the arrival of other guests. Adam glanced at what he considered a sorry excuse for a menu and thought ahead to dessert at the Fountain on Locust. It was the best place in town, famous for delectable ice cream concoctions. Their lunch and dinner food was also good, made with locally farmed ingredients and no harmful additives, which appealed to Jenna. But their ice cream desserts were the stuff dreams were made of. They would head there right after dinner.

Adam surveyed the room. It was smaller than he had imagined. The stage ran the length of the front end of the room. A large gracefully curved marble fireplace adorned the far wall, flanked by two tables. The Trent's table sat behind the fireplace and the other table was in front of it. The remaining area would not have seated more than twenty-five or thirty guests, but was only set up for four tables of four and one table of six. *Small crowd for such a momentous occasion, not to be missed.* Tonight was the kickoff for the 150-year anniversary of the original murders. The same play would be re-enacted every weekend for the month of September. *Who in their right mind celebrates the anniversary of a tragedy as such that occurred here?* He knew Alan Cunningham by reputation only, and decided after assessing the room, that the rumors of Cunningham being in deep financial trouble were true. This was his swan song, Adam supposed—a last-ditch effort to make ends meet.

The cheerful chattering of voices drew his attention toward the entryway of the room as four women emerged. They were all nuns. The eldest was wearing a shoulder length veil and walked with a cane, which she rested against the table after she took her seat. Adam guessed their ages ranged from the mid-twenties to the late seventies. Dressed in gray or navy skirts with matching blazers and white or pink blouses, they chose the table closest to the entry. Adam could tell by their light-hearted banter that the nuns, in spite of the difference in their ages, were friends.

"Isn't this fun?" one of the older nuns said.

"Yes. Please tell the Porters thank you from all of us, Sister Cecilia Marie. It was so thoughtful of them to give such a nice gift."

The eldest spoke. "You have done much for their little boy. He has many special needs. It was a nice way for them to show appreciation for your dedication and hard work."

Sister Cecilia Marie appeared to be the youngest. She flushed at the compliment. "It was very kind of them. Christopher just needs a little extra help, that's all. I'm happy to give it to him. And it's so rewarding to see his progress! But I'll admit I was surprised when they gave me four tickets to tonight's dinner theater. That was *quite* generous. I could think of no other friends with whom I would've liked to share this gift than the three of you." She leaned forward and lowered her voice. "I've always wanted to go to one of these things!"

"Me, too," chimed in the others.

Jenna and Amy returned. Amy was excited and talking non-stop. "Dad! Dad! Guess what they have in the gift shop? They have the emerald and diamond necklace Annalise Mansford was wearing when she was murdered and it's only thirty dollars and they have pieces of the house for sale and books about the ghosts and more of her jewelry and..."

Adam looked at his wife and pursed his lips. "Sounds awfully macabre, Jenna."

Jenna took her seat and changed the subject. "More guests are arriving. I see there's a group of nuns over there. Looks like they're enjoying themselves."

Adam mumbled, "Maybe they're here to perform an exorcism."

Jenna kicked Adam under the table and gave him a dirty look.

"Ow! That's gonna bruise," he said.

"Amy, did you choose your dinner?" Jenna asked her daughter, ignoring Adam.

The menu was meager. Entrees offered were steak of no particular cut, baked chicken breast or vegetarian pasta with equally uninteresting sides. A children's menu was available, offering grilled cheese and tater tots or a hot dog and chips. Some sort of dessert would be offered with the final act of the play.

A man and woman arrived and took their seats at the table on the other side of the fireplace, in front of the Trents. They were in their mid-thirties. The woman was an attractive blonde who needed to lose a few pounds, but was dressed in style. The man was average in height and weight with light brown hair and blue eyes. Adam observed their body language, noting obvious tension between them. They did not seem angry, but rather, on edge. The man ordered a beer and the woman asked for a mixed drink. She reached for his hand and Adam, seeing her rings, concluded they were married, but perhaps not happy about it. Her husband did not withdraw his hand, nor did he respond to her touch. Adam thought they seemed out of place and wondered what they were doing here. The man downed his beer and when he ordered another, his wife looked away.

Soon after the couple had been served their drinks, two men entered and took the last available table other than the large table in the center of the room. They were dressed in business suits, and if Adam thought the last couple looked out of place, he couldn't figure these two out at all. One was much older, tall, slender and tanned, with a ring of grayish hair framing a mostly bald head. He carried himself with the air of a man who was successful, both on and off the golf course. The other man was younger, pudgy and in his mid-forties, with a receding hair line and brown eyes framed by gold-rimmed glasses. Adam studied them and thought perhaps they were considering buying this place and had come to look it over.

Two waitresses were working the floor. One was stunningly beautiful, with long, dark hair, full black eyebrows and eyelashes and full lips with a light café au lait complexion. Adam could not tell whether she was Hispanic, Indian, Middle Eastern or even light-skinned black. She glided gracefully to the Trent's table and greeted them. "Good evening and welcome to Mansford Mansion. My name is Jasmine and I'll be taking care of you this evening. Have you decided what you'd like, or do you need more time?"

As if three choices presented a challenge. Adam decided the biggest mystery of the evening was what kind of beef was on the menu, so he ordered chicken. Jenna ordered pasta and Amy asked for grilled cheese. Jasmine thanked them and moved over to the nuns and then the businessmen.

"What an extraordinarily beautiful girl," Jenna said to Adam.

"What? Oh, I hadn't noticed," he answered.

"Nice try. You'd have to be dead or blind not to notice. I wonder what she's doing working in a place like this?"

Adam wondered the same thing. He looked at his watch. The program was supposed to start at 6:00. It was now 6:15.

A loud commotion was heard at the front door, followed by five raucous adults causing a scene as they entered the dining room. They took their seats at the large table. The patriarch of the clan, a corpulent man in his late sixties with a small amount of gray tufted hair, wire rimmed glasses and a beard took his place at the head of the table. His adult children, two men and two women, fell in line and sat in seats which Adam surmised had been permanently assigned since childhood. While the new guests in their noisy attention-grabbing entrance had piqued Adam's interest, what he found even more noteworthy was the effect the latecomers had on the other guests in the room.

The businessmen stared in open contempt at the large table before turning their backs and huddling together. They were too far away for Adam to hear what they were saying, but the younger man kept looking back at the family and began wiping his forehead with his handkerchief. When the two men broke apart, the older companion sat up and looked straight ahead.

The married couple became visibly nervous as their unspoken tension mounted. The husband ordered a third beer and the wife ordered another mixed drink. Adam noticed the husband's left eyelid was twitching and he kept balling up his fist. The wife looked back once at the newcomers' table, flushed, and rubbed her temples. They downed their drinks in a hurry and ordered more. Adam made a mental note to keep an eye on the couple when it was time to leave, in case they were in no condition to drive.

The nuns fell silent as all four stiffened their backs and sat up straight. Their pleasant smiles faded and they all looked as if they had eaten something rotten, which Adam would not have had any trouble believing, except the food had not yet been served. They leaned their heads toward the middle of the table and whispered, but Adam could not make out what they were saying. The youngest nun, Sister Cecilia Marie, looked over her shoulder and glared at the patriarch of the family. The eldest

nun placed her hand upon Cecilia Marie's forearm and leaning
forward, whispered in her ear. Sister Cecilia Marie turned back
to her companions and the sisters fell silent.

Jenna and Amy were reading through their programs, oblivious
to the commotion around them.

Adam heard the father of the group address his grown children
in a loud, disparaging voice. "I suppose *this* was the best you
could do for my birthday? This was Cedric's idea, I suppose.
He's the dumbest of the bunch. What a sorry lot you all turned
out to be."

One of his daughters spoke. She was underweight to the point
of emaciation, with dark circles under her eyes and a sallow
complexion. Her sparse brown hair hung in limp strands and she
pulled on it nervously, twisting the ends. She reminded Adam
of a timid mouse. "Father, please. We just thought you might
enjoy a little something different—dinner and a play. You know,
it might be fun."

The other daughter snorted in derision. She appeared to be the
youngest of the four. She had badly dyed coal black hair, dark
eyes and an overabundance of garish black make-up. "Esme,
you're pathetic," she sneered as she lit a cigarette and inhaled
deeply. "Why do you even bother to order dinner? We all know
as soon as you eat anything, you'll be in the bathroom puking it
all up. When are you going to stop trying to please the old fart
and tell him he's lucky he's even having a birthday?"

Alan Cunningham hurried over to the table. "Ah, miss, I'm
sorry, but this is a no-smoking establishment."

"Oh really?" the young woman answered with an air of
indifference. She blew smoke in Alan's face. "I didn't realize
this was an *establishment*," she said with scorn, drawing out her
words. She took another puff and blew the smoke in his face
once again. She shrugged her shoulders with exaggeration and
ground her lit cigarette out on the table top. "Sorry." She curled
her upper lip.

"Oh Lucinda, really? Stop. Just stop." It was one of the sons.
Turning to Alan Cunningham, the man offered an apology. "I

am so sorry for my sister's poor behavior. Apparently, she still hasn't mastered the art of good manners. We'll cover the cost of a new table for you. My sincerest apologies."

The elder brother spoke up. "That's Roland for you. All prim and proper, making excuses for Lucinda and *apologizing*, of all things." Cedric sneered. "Harringtons don't apologize. Just ask dear old Dad."

The Harringtons! That's who they are. Adam had been enjoying the entertainment at the larger table before the curtain on stage went up for the program, which by now was running quite late. He had never met any of them, as they stayed just out of legal trouble. The Harringtons' reputation was well known. Wealthy, snobby and believing they were entitled to whatever they wanted, the family was famous for being obnoxious, rude and dysfunctional—especially the father, Edward Rupert Harrington, III. The idle rich and proud of it, Adam thought. He tried to remember the various stories that swirled around the Harrington family.

Roland Andrew Harrington, the son who had apologized to Alan Cunningham, was the only Harrington sibling who worked for a living. Outwardly successful, having forged a career as a financial analyst, he remained unmarried, it was speculated, for fear of turning anyone unfortunate enough to be his wife into a Harrington.

"If Mother were alive to hear you, she would be ashamed," Roland retorted.

"That's enough!" boomed Edward. "You'll not bring my Catherine's name into your snickering and bickering! How could I have ever fathered such a lot of losers?"

Esme shrunk further into her chair, twisting her hair even tighter around her bony finger. Roland looked uncomfortable. Cedric and Lucinda exchanged glances and smirked.

Mariah, the second waitress on the floor, had the bad luck to be assigned to their table. She was young, petite and attractive. After the commotion the family had caused, Jasmine Jones whispered to Mariah that she would handle the rest of the tables and the girls agreed to split the tips between them. Mariah whispered back to Jasmine, "Thank you. This table will probably be all I can handle. What do you wanna bet Nimrod over there won't even tip?"

Jasmine answered back in a whisper, "What do you wanna bet that I won't even make enough to bet?"

They returned to their customers, as Jasmine had now picked up the married couple.

"Can I get you something to drink?" Mariah asked returning to Edward.

"Whiskey," Edward replied, looking down his nose at her in disapproval. "Hope you have a green card. And be sure you wash your hands before you touch my food."

Mariah set her jaw and refused to look at him. She moved on to Esme, who meekly asked, "Water, please?"

Lucinda ordered four cocktails that no one had ever heard of, and rolling her eyes, asked if a Cabernet was too much to ask for.

"One Cabernet," Mariah repeated through clenched teeth before addressing Roland, who politely ordered iced tea.

She came to Cedric last. "Cosmopolitan, darlin'. And your phone number," he leered at her. Mariah took the order and turned to leave. Cedric reached out to grab her from behind, but she moved away before he could touch her and he came up empty handed.

"Just your type, Cedric," his father snorted in disgust. "A waitress, and a spic at that. Let's see, now. The last four women were strippers, over on the East Side, right? And before that a couple of cashiers at Wal-Mart. And before that, a barmaid. You really know how to pick a woman with class."

Cedric sneered in derision, narrowing his eyes and curling his upper lip. He and Lucinda could have been twins, Adam thought, if it weren't for the age difference. Cedric was tall and thin, but strong. Adam could see definition in his lower arms. His black hair was slicked back with a middle part and he had a thin dark mustache. Cedric pulled out a cigarette, but after looking at it, returned it to his pocket.

"Dear Cedric," Lucinda spoke. "Nice to see you got over your mommy complex. I hope you don't father any bastards with your harem of classy women. I'm not sharing any of *my* inheritance when the old guy kicks it."

"Can't happen soon enough for me," Cedric answered.

"We'll see who gets what," Edward threatened. "I'm meeting with my attorney in the morning. It's time for a new will."

Esme's hands began to tremble and she shifted in her seat. Lucinda seemed unconcerned as she studied her bright red fingernails.

Roland spoke. "It's your money, Father. You can leave it to charity for all I care, if you can even think of any. *That* would be a first."

Alan Cunningham interrupted the Harrington drama by stepping onto the stage. So far this night was not going as planned. They were running late because they waited for the Harrington party to arrive and now, he would have to pay overtime. At least his damaged table would be paid for. He would charge that wretched family the maximum amount. And then some.

He blew into the microphone, creating a popping noise, and began. "Ladies and gentlemen, welcome to Mansford Mansion. It was brave of you to come. Let me explain how the evening will unfold. As I speak, your servers, Mariah and Jasmine, will be bringing your drinks. The drama will begin as your salads are served. Between each course, there will be a short intermission at which time you may order refills on your drinks. Or, if you prefer, please feel free to cozy up to the bar. Mike, our bartender, will be happy to serve you. The final act will coincide with dessert. Enjoy your evening." Alan exited the stage and the program began.

Adam found the drama at the Harrington table far more entertaining than the drama for which he had paid. Edward Rupert Harrington, III complained about everything. The drinks tasted off, the food was stale and the play was lame. He never missed an opportunity to insult or criticize his children. While Adam agreed about the food and the play, he cringed at every hurtful barb this man hurled at his children. No wonder they were a dysfunctional mess.

At each break, Cedric left the table to go to the bar, as did the nervous man who had come with his wife. Esme left for the restroom. Roland and Lucinda remained at the table.

"Adam," Jenna whispered after the entrees were served. "Stop staring at those people. It's rude. Besides, you've barely touched your dinner. We came together, as a family. We are here, at *this* table, celebrating Amy's birthday. Would you please join us?"

"Sorry," he said, chagrined.

Amy turned and faced her parents, putting a finger to her lips. "Shhh! I'm trying to figure this out! Annalise just said the servants didn't know anything, but the Captain said they did and he already killed them!"

Adam and Jenna pressed their lips together in a joint attempt not to laugh, and Adam poked his wife in fun. Jenna was right, he knew. Adam needed to ignore the Harrington family and pay attention to his own.

Dessert was served as the last act of the play commenced. "Mmm. Hank's cheesecake. At least we're ending dinner on a tasty note," Jenna whispered to Adam.

As they started to eat their cheesecake, Cedric Harrington sneezed with such force, Adam jumped.

"That was appetizing," Adam mumbled to Jenna. "Hope he covered his mouth or we'll all get sick."

"Quit being such a germophobe. Would you please make the tiniest effort to enjoy this evening?"

Amy turned around to shush her parents again. From somewhere off stage came the loud screams of a woman. Adam started to jump up in response, but then realized it was part of the drama. Overdone by a long shot, the screaming continued. Adam gritted his teeth. *Whoever that actress is, she needs acting lessons. And we need earplugs.*

Mike Davey, the bartender, came around the corner and looked around the room. He glanced up at the stage, then back to the dinner guests, and hurried back to the bar.

Cedric sneezed loudly again and Adam shuddered. Jenna suppressed a laugh. She scooted her chair toward her husband and whispered in his ear. "You're the bravest man I know, and here you are, afraid of germs."

"You can't shoot germs." He whispered back and nibbled on her ear. "More people die from dirty conditions than violence."

Amy turned around and glared at her parents. "You're both exasperating," she whispered.

"Big word for a little girl," Adam whispered back.

"I'm almost a teenager," she hissed.

The play was finally over and the lights came up. The cast took their bows on stage to mediocre applause. As the guests gathered their belongings and prepare to leave, Adam stole one last look at the Harrington clan. Apparently, Edward Rupert Harrington, III had gotten bored enough or drunk enough to fall asleep. He was sitting upright in his chair with his head drooped onto his chest.

Esme spoke to him. "Father? Come on, Father, that wasn't so bad. Wake up, Father." She jostled him and he fell over, landing on the floor with a thud. Esme screamed. The rest of the room fell silent as everyone looked toward the floor where Edward Rupert Harrington, III lay motionless.

Adam leapt from his seat, identifying himself as a police officer and knelt by the figure on the floor. He felt for a pulse but found none. "He's dead," he announced, and called for an ambulance.

Judging from the man's size and the redness of his face, Adam surmised that Mr. Harrington had suffered a heart attack. While his instincts screamed within him to suspect this was not a natural death, there was no immediate evidence to support otherwise. He administered CPR, but held little hope of revival. The other guests looked on in silence.

The ambulance arrived within minutes, along with a fire truck. The paramedics took over for Adam and, catching his eye, shook their heads, but continued to work to bring life back to the lifeless body. Adam whispered into the ambulance driver's ear. The driver responded with a single nod. The EMS crew continued their efforts a few more minutes, and then gave up. Edward Rupert Harrington III would be officially pronounced dead when they reached the hospital. The paramedics prepared to remove his body.

"Was your father a cardiac patient?" Adam asked the family.

Lucinda responded sarcastically, "How can you be a heart patient when you never had a heart?"

"Lucinda! Please! Father is dead. Can't you show a little respect, even once?" Esme, the mouse, had spoken up.

"Oh, Esme, you can stop trying to please him now. He's gone and you're free. Why don't you finish his cheesecake? It'll taste just as good coming up as it did going down," Cedric sneered, unaffected by his father's sudden passing.

"Yes, Officer. Our father had a heart condition," Roland said.

Adam looked around at the rest of the guests and again noted their odd reactions to what had occurred. The nuns made the sign of the cross. That much could be expected. Jenna was the only person in the room whose body language reflected an appropriate reaction. Adam could see his wife was upset. Her eyes were wide and her lips parted. Amy stared with wide-eyed fascination, certain that the event could be attributed to a ghost or some such baloney. He wasn't even certain his daughter understood what had happened. The others seemed surprised, but relieved—even smug. He made a mental note to write down all he observed once he got home. Adam had found over the years that first impressions were telling and usually accurate.

"I don't know about the rest of you, but I'm going home. Need my beauty sleep," Lucinda announced, yawning. She glanced once more at her bright red fingernails and picked up her handbag to leave.

"Can we go home?" Esme asked Adam.

"Of course. It looks like your father died of a heart attack. I have no reason to keep you. It's your choice if you want to accompany the ambulance. But you're certainly free to go." *For now.*

Adam turned to Jenna and whispered in her ear that he would return in a few minutes. He left in a hurry. The other guests followed, as if they needed to distance themselves from the dead man. The eldest nun, Sister Agnes Pauline, approached the Harrington clan to offer her condolences.

"I'm sorry for your loss."

Lucinda snapped at her, "Why? It's no loss for me! If anyone else is honest, it's no loss for them either."

Roland intervened and placed his hand on Agnes Pauline's shoulder. "Thank you, Sister."

Sister Agnes Pauline joined her friends and they exited the building.

When Adam returned to retrieve Jenna and Amy, Jenna shot him a questioning look. "Just taking down license plate numbers in case this turns out to be a little more than what it looks like," he whispered to her.

"Are your Spidey senses tingling?" she teased.

"Let's just say something isn't kosher in the deli."

"I'll follow the ambulance," Roland volunteered. He was somber. Whether that was heartfelt, or nothing more than a show of propriety, Adam could not tell. "Would you like to ride with me, Esme?"

"Eeewww. I mean, like, he's dead and all. Gross," she replied, having recovered from the shock of her father's passing.

The paramedics hefted the behemoth's body onto a stretcher and the family followed them out.

"This was a great birthday," Amy exclaimed. "I thought that fat guy was just another guest. He sure surprised me! Can we go get ice cream now?"

Jenna and Adam exchanged glances. "Amy, honey," Adam began. "That man really died. That was not an act."

Amy sobered. She looked at the floor, then up at her father. "I'm sorry, Daddy," she said, blinking up at him. "I thought that was the big finish." Jenna put her arm around Amy and pulled her close.

Adam watched the couple who had been drinking get up and leave. They both appeared to be in full possession of their faculties, but time had passed and they had consumed a meal. He thought perhaps the shock of a death at dinner might have contributed to their apparent sobriety as well.

The Trents were the last of the guests to leave Mansford Mansion. Adam saw Alan Cunningham in the foyer, fluttering his pale hands. He heard Alan tell the staff to gather in the upstairs dressing room for a meeting. Adam imagined Cunningham would use Harrington's death as yet another marketing gimmick to recoup his losses.

"Mr. Cunningham," Adam began. "Do you have the names and contact information for this evening's guests?"

"Of course, Officer. Why?"

"Just hang on to it for a while, will you?"

Adam ushered his family out the door before Mr. Cunningham could say anything else.

Chapter 3

"City Morgue. You kill 'em, we'll chill 'em." Dr. Vincent Sutter answered his phone as he bustled down the hall of the morgue. He saw Adam walking toward him and covered the cell phone. "Hey, Adam, good to see you. Hold on a sec." He returned to his call. "Lemme call you back, huh? I should have those results this afternoon." Hanging up, he turned his attention to his guest, and greeted him with a firm handshake. "So what brings you by the hallowed halls of my cheery dungeon on this beautiful fall morning? It is fall, isn't it?" The head coroner for the St. Louis City Morgue always seemed upbeat to Adam, in spite of spending his working hours with dead bodies—a number of which entered eternity sooner than natural causes would dictate.

"Mornin' Doc," Adam answered. "I'm down here unofficially, at least for now."

Dr. Sutter raised his bushy eyebrows and looked at Adam over his glasses. "Social call? I'd have baked a cake!"

"Thanks, but no thanks. You all got a body down here last night. White male, late sixties. Edward Harrington."

"You mean Edward Rupert Harrington, III." Doc Sutter grinned.

"That'd be him. My family and I had the distinct pleasure of being seated at the table next to him when he died last night. Amy's birthday dinner."

Doc Sutter winced. "Ouch. Sorry. Poor kid."

"Yeah. Anyway, it looked like a heart attack, but I wanted to see if anything looked suspicious to you."

"Avril Markham has his autopsy on her schedule. She's our new assistant coroner. Should get to it later this week. Do you want to talk to her?"

"Sure, if she's got a minute."

Doc walked Adam down the gray tiled hall to a doorway on the left and peered through the glass panel in the door. The newly hired assistant coroner was shutting the cooler door and pulling off her gloves. She was young and attractive with blunt cut blond hair, fair skin and green eyes. She moved with long, confident strides and straight posture. Walking to the sink, she scrubbed her hands and forearms vigorously, then stepped to her right and sat down at her computer. Adam watched her fingers fly over the keyboard with lightning speed. Her right hand clicked the mouse and she stood, turning off her screen. Despite her youth, Dr. Avril Markham gave Adam the impression that she was serious and efficient.

"It's okay to go in, now," Doc said to Adam. They entered her autopsy room and Adam recoiled from the chemical smell. He supposed he would never get used to it.

"Avril," Doc Sutter began. "This is Detective Sergeant Adam Trent. He'd like to talk to you about the Harrington autopsy for a few minutes. You got some time?" Doc Sutter always treated his staff with the utmost courtesy, but it was understood that his requests were, in fact, orders, politely issued. His staff respected him and complied without complaint.

"Of course, Doc. I just finished with our fourth gang-banger this week. Like you always say, 'you stab 'em, we'll slab 'em.' Have a seat. I'll be right with you." She motioned to a metal chair against the wall and opened a file cabinet to pull out a manila folder.

Avril Markham's serious demeanor melted in the presence of the living. She seemed to have caught Doc Sutter's infectious cheerful attitude. As he turned to thank Doc, he asked in a low voice, "Does she have enough experience if Harrington turns out to be homicide, rather than heart failure?"

Doc Sutter assured him. "No worries, my man, no worries. She's young, but she's thorough. Only the best for the homicide capitol of the Midwest." He turned to leave. "Gotta get going. Nice seeing you, Adam. People are dyin' left and right to get in here. Hey, don't be a stranger."

Adam could think of thousands of places he would rather be than in the morgue, alive *or* dead. He supposed you needed some type of offbeat humor to be able to work in a place like this for an entire career. He could hear Doc whistling as he walked back down the hall to his office.

"Now, Detective Trent," Avril Markham began, opening the folder and scanning the contents.

"Adam."

"Okay. Adam. Oh! I see you were the one who told the ambulance driver that you thought this might be a suspicious death. Good thing. At first glance, Harrington looks like a heart attack. But you were correct to suspect otherwise."

"What can you tell me?"

"His autopsy isn't scheduled for a few more days, but I could get started on him first thing tomorrow if you want him expedited. I promise to be thorough. Just so you know, because of your request, we started the tox screen as soon as he arrived last night. Some poisons weaken and dissipate if too much time elapses between death and autopsy. That raises the risk of losing important evidence. The rest of him can be started tomorrow morning if you request it. Feel free to stop by in the afternoon, if you like. Gowns, gloves and masks are right outside the door. If I'm working on a body, please put them on and come on in."

"Thanks, Dr. Markham."

"Avril."

News of Edward Harrington's death at Mansford Mansion spread like an epidemic. Even before the autopsy had been performed, reporters were announcing the tyrant's heart condition did him in. Headlines on the rumor rags screamed,

Mansford Ghost Strikes Again! 50-Year Curse Alive and Well, Claims Another Life! Adam made no attempt to conceal his disgust, but did try to learn as much about the deceased man as he could before the autopsy report was released.

Edward Harrington's reputation as a ruthless businessman was bolstered by numerous stories. He had a Midas touch, amassing great amounts of wealth by stepping on others or cheating them, but never quite breaking any laws. At least, he was never caught breaking the law. While he was adept at making money, he hurt or damaged everything and everyone he touched, including his own children. That he would be mourned by many, or even any, was doubtful.

To no one's surprise, Alan Cunningham used Harrington's death to his financial advantage, claiming that once again, the 50-year curse had befallen Mansford Mansion. To his utter delight, ticket sales soared for the remainder of the month. Mansford Mansion was booked to capacity, with a waiting list.

"Jen, hon, did you see or hear anything that night?" Adam asked when he returned home.

Jenna was curled up on the sofa reading the latest release from the library. Adam could smell the rich aroma of beef stew drifting in from the kitchen. Jenna set her book down and stretched. "Nothing you wouldn't have already noticed. I wasn't paying that much attention. I left for the restroom at one of the breaks and the skinny, mousy daughter was in there throwing up. I didn't think the food was *that* bad."

"From what I hear, I think that was her own doing." Adam sat beside his wife.

"I see. Well, with a father like *that*, I'd be surprised if an eating disorder was *all* she had. The one brother, the snide one, was up at the bar at every intermission. Wouldn't leave that poor little waitress alone."

"Yeah, everything about that night was off, but there was nothing obvious or in your face."

Amy entered the room and Adam and Jenna stopped talking.

"Why are you talking so quietly?" Amy asked. "What is it I'm not supposed to hear?"

"Well, Nosy Rosy, if we wanted you to hear, we would have included you in the conversation," Adam said.

"Tell me!"

"Amy, we're discussing something for Daddy's work. I think Blue needs to go for a walk."

"Is it about the haunted house? Did the ghost kill that man? It did, didn't it! I knew it!"

Adam's patience was running thin. "Amy, there are no such things as ghosts. Now, go walk the dog."

As if on cue, Blue trotted over to Amy with her leash in her mouth. Amy stomped off with the dog in tow. "You're just mad 'cuz you don't wanna admit I'm right!" Pre-teen and dog made their dramatic exit, opening the door wide and letting it slam behind them.

"Yeah, that must be it," Adam mumbled.

Jenna laid her head on his shoulder. "Sorry I can't be more helpful, sweetheart. I wasn't paying attention to anyone else's table. If I remember something unusual, I'll let you know. You're upset because it happened right under your nose and you didn't catch it and you think you should have. Don't take it out on Amy."

Dr. Avril Markham looked up to see Adam peeking into the window of her autopsy room door and motioned for him to enter.

"Your suspicions were correct, Adam. This was no heart attack. I'll put all the gory details in my report, but Edward Harrington was murdered. Cyanide poisoning. No doubt about it. There was enough cyanide in his body to kill him several times over. My complete report should be ready sometime next week. There are still a number of tests left to run."

"Can you tell me how the poison was administered?"

"It looks to me like the man ingested everything in sight. Did you notice if he was experiencing discomfort or shortness of breath?"

No. My wife made me participate in our daughter's birthday dinner. She has a thing about manners and all. Had I been able to watch the Harrington drama unfold instead of participating in a dinner I didn't approve of in the first place, I could have either stopped the crime from happening, or at least seen who did it. "Not that I could tell. He griped about everything. Said his drinks tasted off, the food was terrible. In spite of all his complaining, though, he ate and drank anything that wasn't nailed down. I didn't have any alcohol, but I can attest that the food was terrible. But everyone else at the restaurant seemed to survive the meal without keeling over."

"He could've been given small doses early on and then a large dose right before dessert. It could've done the trick, but you would've heard him struggling for breath. Was it noisy in the restaurant?"

Adam remembered the over-emoting screamer from off stage. Her shrieking could have covered up a thundering herd of elephants.

"There was one part, toward the end, where there was screaming coming from off stage. It was loud and went on for quite some time. I suppose that could've been enough of a distraction that no one would have noticed."

"If the victim had been given a very large dose toward the end of the meal, then time of death would have been within a few to several minutes. I'm afraid I can't get more specific. Different people may react to the same toxin in different ways."

"I was right there and honestly thought he'd had a heart attack. His face was all red, plus, the guy looked like the poster child for heart failure." Adam's shoulders sagged as he shook his head.

"Don't be so hard on yourself. Cyanide can easily mimic a heart attack. It was an easy mistake to make. The paramedics didn't see anything to raise concerns, but the level in his tox screen was excessively high. No way was this an accident."

"Thanks, Avril."

"You bet."

Adam left the morgue and headed back to the police station. He reported his conversation with Dr. Markham to his captain, Gavin Peterson. "When the official autopsy report is released, I'd like to be assigned this case, Cap. I knew something wasn't right that night, but it was an apparent heart attack and I had no reason to hold anyone. The entire evening was off and now a man is dead—not that anyone will miss him. But murder is murder. It's still a crime, and we need to find the truth."

"You mean it wasn't the ghost of Mansford Mansion?" Captain Peterson asked, in mock surprise.

"No sir. Imagine that. Something a little closer to this world and the nasty here and now, I'm afraid. But if you can convince the coroner's office to delay releasing the autopsy results for a few more days, that might give me an edge in my investigation."

"Consider it done. You've got the lead on this. We'll let the assumption of heart failure ride for a while. I suppose you'll start with the grieving children?"

"You got that right. They're about as loony as it gets, but I didn't peg them as dangerous. It gripes me to no end that a murder took place right under my nose and I never even saw it. I'll tell you this much, though. Something was wrong that entire evening. A very unusual assembly of guests. And they all had a strange reaction both to Harrington's arrival and his departure. More to this than meets the eye."

"Keep me up to date on your progress, Adam."

Chapter 4

The Harrington home was situated on an exclusive barricaded street in the city's fashionable Central West End. Built in the early 1900s, it was a three-story castle that boasted old-world architecture, complete with intricate and ornate finish work, leaded glass windows and a carriage house in the back that was bigger than anything Adam could ever dream of owning. Some of the carriage houses in the neighborhood had been converted into mother-in-law residences, guest homes, hobby shops or used for storage. But the Harrington's had been turned into a luxury garage.

The doorbell was answered by a woman whom Adam assumed was the housekeeper. She had an air about her that told him jobs were hard to come by and she would like to work anywhere on the planet that wasn't here. Her shoulders slumped and she looked at Adam as if life could not be more distasteful. Adam inquired as to the whereabouts of his suspects.

"Cedric is here. You can tell by the smoke. Esme seldom leaves, so she's here, of course. Heaven only knows where Lucinda is or when she'll be back. Roland doesn't live here. He works downtown at one of the brokerage firms and lives in a loft on Washington Avenue. Who do you want to talk to first?" She opened the door to admit Adam and he followed her into the foyer.

"Would you please ask Cedric to come downstairs?"

She gave him a tired nod and trudged up the wide staircase, leaving Adam alone in the cavernous foyer. He looked around. With fourteen-foot ceilings, large rooms, dark wood paneling and crystal chandeliers, the place screamed old money. On the wall of the foyer were portraits of Edward and Catherine Victoria, his deceased wife. Edward looked much the same as when Adam had seen him at the dinner theater, only somewhat younger—rotund, with thinning light gray hair, round glasses, a bulbous nose and a disapproving countenance. But the artist that painted Catherine's portrait had been sensitive to capture her spirit, not merely her image. Adam saw a sad woman with soft features who appeared as if she was trying to look as stern as her husband, but couldn't quite pull it off. As he studied the portrait of Catherine Victoria, he was moved with compassion. He saw a woman with a broken spirit. Her pleading eyes bore silent testimony of her entrapment in an unhappy marriage. While Adam could not excuse the Harrington siblings' terrible behavior, he could only imagine how miserable it must have been to grow up in this loveless tomb of a house with a monster for a father.

Cedric followed the housekeeper down the stairs. He seemed none too happy to see Adam waiting for him.

"And to what do I owe the pleasure of this visit, occifer?" he asked, jutting his chin out and garbling his speech on purpose. Adam had not seen Cedric close up at Mansford Mansion. He noted Cedric's mustache was crooked and his skin was almost as oily as his black hair. *I thought Brylcreem went out of business. Looks like he got more than a little dab.*

"Mr. Harrington, I need to ask you a few questions about your father's death," Adam began, ignoring the blatant disrespect.

"The old coot kicked the bucket from overeating, over drinking and choking on his own venom. You were there. You saw it, same as the rest of us."

"You left out the part where he was poisoned, Mr. Harrington. But you're right about one thing. I was there and I did see and hear much of what went on at your family's table."

Adam maintained a straight face, but was gratified to see that something he said made an impact on Cedric. He watched with satisfaction as the sneer on Cedric's face faded.

Adam continued. "I overheard your father threaten that he was going to change his will. He didn't get the chance to do that. Now you do know, don't you, that if you had anything to do with his death, not only will you go to prison, you'll also lose any right to your inheritance?"

Cedric shifted his feet, but rebounded at once. "I don't know anything about poison, occifer. If I remember correctly, I flunked out of chemistry. Too bad. But we *all* hated dear old dad. We all might have had motive, but means and opportunity? Good luck, Charlie. The world is better off without him. To know him was to hate him. I'm not sorry he's dead in the least. But that doesn't make me his killer." He snorted. "You got your work cut out for you, cop."

"What is your full name?" Adam maintained a wooden, professional demeanor. Disrespect was no stranger to law enforcement personnel, and Cedric Harrington's attitude was a dime a dozen.

"Cedric Rupert Harrington. Do I need a lawyer?"

"You're welcome to call your lawyer if you so desire." Adam paused, but Cedric made no move for a phone.

"Do you know what's in your father's will?"

"A whole ton of money, the most important thing in the world to him. The old fart should have gotten a trust, but he was too cheap to pay a lawyer to draw one up. Far as I know, we all four split even Steven, except that Esme, Lucinda and I have to give Roland money for his share of the house whether we stay here or sell the place and move. Dear old Roland. Had to sully the family name by getting a job and being self-supporting and all that respectable crap. What's the world coming to?" He lit a cigarette and blew smoke at Adam.

Adam set his jaw and tried not to inhale. He determined to remain in control of the conversation, and continued his questioning, ignoring Cedric's behavior. He would not allow Cedric to get the upper hand.

"Where were you during the break between the main course and dessert?"

"Probably at the bar."

"Did you get your father a drink or bring him any food?"

"That's why they have waitresses, or don't you eat out much on a cop's salary? Look, all I want is what's mine. How soon before we get the money?"

"As soon as his killer is caught."

Cedric rolled his eyes.

"Do you know why your father threatened to change his will?"

"Just another one of his ridiculous control tactics. He never would've done it. Who else would he leave his fortune to? Charity? No way."

"How often did your father threaten to change his will?"

Cedric shifted from one foot to the other and swallowed. "All the time. Nobody ever believed him."

He's lying. "Why do you think your father threatened to cut you out?"

Cedric stared at Adam and said nothing.

"Didn't approve of your lifestyle, you think?"

Cedric narrowed his eyes at Adam, took a long drag on his cigarette and exhaled toward Adam. He refused to answer. Adam blew the smoke back into Cedric's face.

"Here's my card. Let me know if you remember anything."

Cedric took the card, flicked it with his fingers, and watched without interest as it landed on the table in the foyer,

"I'd like to see your sister, now."

"Lucinda's out. Dunno where, dunno who she's with, dunno when she's coming back, and don't care."

"Your other sister."

"Edie!" Cedric yelled for the housekeeper. She arrived within moments of being summoned. "Edie, go get Esme. The cop wants to talk to her." Cedric stalked out of the room.

Esme came down the stairs so lightly that Adam would not have noticed her had he not been standing at the foot of the stairs where he could see her. She was little more than a skeleton and was balding in some places. Her sallow complexion was exacerbated by the dark circles under her eyes.

"Would you like to sit down, officer?" she asked, showing him into the living room. "I'm sure Cedric didn't bother to ask. Would you like a glass of water or a cup of coffee?"

"Thank you, Ms. Harrington. I'll just take a seat, if you don't mind."

"I suppose this is about poor Father," she squeaked, as she sat across from Adam. She studied the floor and twisted her thinning hair around one finger, never making eye contact.

"It is, ma'am. I need to ask you a few questions," he said, afraid she might break or melt at the slightest provocation.

"May I have your complete name, please?"

"Esme Frances Harrington," she answered meekly. "I'm twenty-five years old."

Looks more like fifty-five. Adam began to write in his notebook. He knew he needed to deal with her gently, but that didn't make her any less a suspect.

"I understand you and your siblings took your father to the Mansford Dinner Theater to celebrate his birthday, is that correct?"

"Yes."

"What made you decide to go there?"

"We got an ad in the mail. Fifty percent off for a table of four or more."

"I see. Whose idea was it to go?" Adam pulled out his notepad and began writing.

"Cedric's, I think. Or maybe Lucinda's. I can't really remember." She pulled at the threads of her chair and returned to twisting her hair.

"How did you feel when your father threatened to write a new will?"

She was silent for a few moments, then responded in a quiet voice. "Afraid."

"Had your father often talked about a new will?" Adam leaned toward her.

"Oh, no. Never." She started to lift her head, but returned to studying the floor. "After mother died, he rewrote his will, but he didn't like to pay lawyers."

"Can you tell me where you were during the break between the main course and dessert?"

"I needed to use the restroom." She stopped twisting her hair and began to pick at her fingernails.

"Did you stop at the bar?" Adam pressed his fingertips into his eyebrow.

"No. Father didn't approve of women drinking alcohol." Esme traced her foot around an imaginary pattern on the carpet.

"Do you keep any poisons in the house, Ms. Harrington?"

"I don't think so. Maybe some bug spray. I could ask Edie."

"Who's Edie?" Adam continued to write in his notebook.

"Our housekeeper."

"Oh, right. Yeah. Can you think of any reason your father would cut you or your siblings out of his will?"

"He didn't approve of us." She switched from picking at her fingernails to picking at the upholstery on her chair.

Adam had no difficulty understanding why Edward did not approve of Cedric and Lucinda, but Esme and Roland?

"Why was that?"

"Because mother tried to love us and he wanted all her attention. He made our mother very sad."

"Did you see anyone put anything in your father's food or drink the night he died?"

For the first time, Esme looked at something other than her shoes. She gave Adam a puzzled look, cocking her head toward her shoulder and frowning. "No. He had a heart attack."

"Did he take heart medicine?"

"Yes," she answered, returning to study the floor.

"What did he take?" *Sheesh! This is worse than pulling teeth.* Adam sighed and looked around the room.

"I don't know. It's in his bathroom, I guess."

"How did you feel after he died?"

"My stomach didn't hurt so bad."

"Ms. Harrington, your father was poisoned. He didn't die from a heart condition."

Esme raised her eyebrows, but continued to avoid eye contact. Adam took the slight shift in body language to mean the information surprised her.

"Can you remember anyone tampering with his food or drink?"

"No."

"Ms. Harrington, here's my card. Would you please give me a call if you remember anything out of the ordinary that night?"

"Yes."

"Thank you. I can see myself out."

Adam walked to his car, shaking his head. He could not remember interviewing anyone so cooperative, yet gleaning so little information. He didn't think it was an act, but wasn't certain that Esme's unresponsive answers weren't designed to deflect suspicion from her.

Adam pulled onto Kingshighway and headed toward the exit to take 64/40 east into downtown. He had plenty of time to speak with Roland Harrington before the 5:00 mass exodus from downtown began. He called Captain Peterson and requested an unmarked car be dispatched to watch the Harrington house for Lucinda's return. If she returned while he was with Roland, it would be a short trip back to the Central West End.

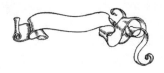

Bill Meyers sat in Sid Friedman's office, fumbling through papers. Perspiration dotted his forehead and his deodorant was failing him. His hands shook as he blotted his forehead with his handkerchief. The two had not spoken to each other all day. Sid broke the silence. "At some point, Bill, we're going to have to talk about the elephant in the room." Sid closed the manila file folder on his mahogany desk and tried to make eye contact with the younger partner of Friedman and Meyers.

Bill put his stack of papers down and looked away. "Awfully convenient, wasn't it? Harrington buying the farm last night?"

Sid cast a sly glance at the younger partner. "Yes. Like a gift from heaven. Don't look the proverbial gift horse in the mouth. He's gone and with him, our troubles. Good riddance." Sid leaned back in his leather chair and put his Gucci loafers on his desk, crossing his feet at the ankles.

"Sid, how can you—I mean, he's dead and all."

"It was a heart attack. That's why you should take care of yourself," he said, looking Bill up and down, increasing Bill's discomfort. Bill needed to lose weight, but then, being the junior partner in the acquisitions business, he didn't have time for golf or exercise, like the fanatical Sid. All work and no play had turned Bill into a dull boy, indeed. Sid did not miss the opportunity to salt the wound.

"Take me, for example." He patted his trim stomach. "I eat right, get plenty of exercise and I'm in bed by 10:30 every night. Sleep like a baby. Harrington's only exercise consisted of stepping all over people to get what he wanted. And now? Crushed like a bug. And we are back in business."

"Sid! There was a cop there! I thought I was gonna keel over right alongside Harrington!"

"The cop was out of uniform and he was there with his family. Will you relax? Sheesh! We were just guests, out for a little fun. Just like everyone else. I couldn't believe the luck! Perfect timing for the old rat to kick the bucket."

"Don't you think that looks just a little suspicious?"

"Why? Did you kill him? Did you force him to eat and drink everything in sight?"

"No! No, no, no! But his death is very fortuitous for us, don't you think?" Bill's forehead was wrinkled and damp. He wiped it again with his handkerchief.

"Gift horse, Bill, gift horse! Yes, fortuitous. The perfect word, I'd say. Now, go run the new figures and rewrite our projections. Life is good and business is better. Friedman and Meyers didn't become one of the most successful acquisition brokerage firms in town without taking a risk now and then."

The younger partner heaved his tired body out of the chair, and wiping perspiration from his face, sat down at his own desk across the expansive open hall and began working on a new set of figures. He would start exercising. Maybe this weekend.

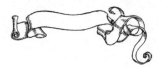

Adam entered the small branch office on the 18th floor of a high rise on Olive Street, where a pleasant receptionist greeted him. She picked up her telephone and announced Adam's presence to Roland Harrington, then offered Adam coffee.

Roland Harrington did not keep him waiting. A gentleman with impeccable manners, Roland was relaxed and cordial as he greeted Adam. He invited Adam into his office which boasted a breathtaking view of downtown. The Arch was at eye level overseeing the Mississippi River, which gave the deceptive appearance of flowing peacefully beneath its span. Busch Stadium was beginning to fill with faithful Cardinal fans, clad in red, pouring in for the late afternoon game. Adam took note of Roland's office. No family photos, no personal mementos, no artwork. The sole décor other than a desk, computer and a few chairs consisted of a desk calendar and a framed photo of a dog with questionable parentage.

"That's Fergus," Roland volunteered, following Adam's gaze to the photo. "He was due to be euthanized at the shelter. They had to make room for other unwanted dogs, and Fergus had overstayed his welcome. I had stopped by to drop off papers for a client who volunteered at the shelter and she insisted on taking me to see the dogs before I left. There was Fergus. My, was he a mess! Dirty, tangled fur, skin and bones. He looked frightened and man, did he smell! But when he saw me, he wagged his tail. The rest is history. Whoever said money can't buy love, never visited an animal shelter. Turned out to be the best friend I ever had."

Adam smiled and thought of Blue. "I understand. I got somebody else's throwaway also. She'd come to our bedroom and wake us if our little girl spiked a fever in the middle of the night or had a bad dream." Adam paused, and taking out his notebook and pen, returned to the purpose of his visit. "Mr. Harrington, I won't keep you long. I imagine you need to get home to feed and walk your friend."

"Don't worry, Detective Trent. I hire a dog walker to come in twice a day. Fergus is well cared for when I can't be there for him. I assume this visit is about my father?"

"Yes, sir. I've spoken with your brother and your sister Esme. They may have called you?"

"No, not at all. We are not exactly close. I could apologize for my siblings' behavior that night, but it wouldn't do any good. We only see each other on the mandatory dates. Christmas, Thanksgiving and Father's birthday. Now that he's gone, I doubt I'll see them again. Other than DNA, we have nothing in common. We're a far cry from a Norman Rockwell family portrait, as I'm sure you've noticed."

Adam nodded. "Do you mind if I ask you a few questions?"

"Not at all. Please have a seat." Roland pulled out a chair on the other side of his desk and walked around to his chair and sat.

"Thank you," Adam said. He sat and took out his notebook and pen. "What's your full name and age?"

"Roland Andrew Harrington. I'm thirty. Cedric is the oldest, at thirty-two. Esme is twenty-five and Lucinda is the youngest. She just turned twenty-one."

Adam wrote in his notebook. "Do you know which medications your father took?"

"No. He had chest pains a couple of years back and took something for his heart, but I don't know what it was. I guess it wasn't strong enough, huh?"

"Your father threatened to change his will. How would that have affected you?" Adam watched Roland for any signs of discomfort, but Roland seemed forthcoming and relaxed when he spoke.

"Minimally, if at all. I don't need him or his money. Feel free to run a credit check. I have no debts. I pay my bills on time. I pay the rent on this place, and payroll for my receptionist, an assistant and a secretary. And the dog walker, of course. Your questions seem a bit excessive for a heart attack, don't you think?" Roland got up and poured himself coffee.

"Your father didn't die of a heart attack, Mr. Harrington. He was poisoned."

Adam observed Roland's reaction. He raised his eyebrows, his mouth opened slightly and he took a step backward. But, as Adam reminded himself, a true psychopath might also behave surprised, as Roland did.

"Well, Detective, I must admit, I was *not* expecting to hear that. It looked to me like it was his heart."

"It was supposed to look like it was his heart," Adam said. He flipped a page in his notebook. "How was it that you and your siblings decided to celebrate your father's birthday at Mansford Mansion?"

"It certainly wasn't Father's idea. I believe it was Cedric or Lucinda, but I can't remember which." Roland returned to his chair and sipped his coffee.

"How did you feel about the suggestion?"

"I didn't care one way or another." Roland shrugged. "Like I said, it was an obligation. To honor our mother's memory, and for no other reason, I treated Father with respect—at least, as much as I could muster. But don't think for one minute that I've shed any tears over his departure. For that matter, I can't think of anyone who would. But it's always best to do the right thing, whether you feel like it or not."

"Do you have access to cyanide, Mr. Harrington?"

"Cyanide, was it? No. I don't keep any poisons at all in the house. I wouldn't put Fergus at that kind of risk. I don't even allow my cleaning service to use chemicals."

Adam nodded. He watched Roland to observe his reaction to his next question. "Had your father ever threatened to change his will before?"

"Not that I know of. He was too cheap to pay a lawyer. And besides, who else would he leave his money to? He hated everyone. And that feeling was mutual."

"Can you think of anyone who hated your father so much they would kill him?"

Roland Harrington sputtered and laughed. "I'm so sorry, Detective Trent," he said, wiping his eyes. "Everyone who ever knew Father hated him enough to kill him. Whoever did this should be given a public service medal. If you do catch the culprit, please let me know. I'd love to shake their hand and thank them profusely. For that matter, I'll even pay their legal fees."

"Can you give me any names? Did you recognize anyone at the restaurant? Was there anyone present at the Mansford Mansion that you can think of who might've wanted him dead so badly, they were willing to take a risk and actually kill him?"

"No. Sorry. Other than our own table, I didn't know anyone there that night. I don't mean to be rude. But you really do have your work cut out for you."

Adam decided to push Roland harder. Roland was smart, personable and, if he hadn't been a murder suspect, Adam would have found him likeable.

"You must realize, Mr. Harrington that the four of you stand to benefit from his death."

"In more ways than merely the financial benefits." Roland took another sip of coffee. "If you're asking me if I can point to one of my siblings as the most likely culprit, I'm afraid I can't. And trust me, that isn't coming from any sense of family loyalty." He set his coffee cup on his desk and leaned forward. Adam sat up straight. "Lucinda, as obnoxious as she is, is basically a frightened little girl underneath all that garish make-up. Esme is so damaged, I don't even know if there's any hope for her. She spent her entire life trying to earn Father's love and approval. Even now, after he's gone, she's lost and still craving his attention. And Cedric? He's a lout, all right. A poorer excuse for a human being you'll never meet, but I really can't see him having the brains or the intestinal fortitude to plan a crime, much less to carry it out."

"So that leaves you," Adam prodded, leaning forward.

Roland smiled and folded his hands together. "Well, Detective Trent. I *am* the only one with the brains and the drive to do it." He paused and leaned back in his chair. "The only problem is, I didn't. While I certainly hated my father, I saw him three days a year, no more. I have a successful career, my own money, my own place, my own life. Not to mention, I wouldn't put Fergus through that kind of separation. I inherit my portion of his estate for no other reason than an accident of birth. I don't need to kill my family to get away from them. I simply stay away from them. Three days a year of family togetherness hardly provides motive."

Adam paused from taking notes. "Did your father mention that anyone in the restaurant looked familiar?"

"No. Sorry."

Adam stood and thanked Roland Harrington for his time and help. He was not convinced it wasn't all an act, but he had been unable to catch the man in a lie.

Adam looked at his watch. It was getting late in the afternoon. Amy would be getting out of school soon. Adam needed to get back to the station to write his reports on his initial interviews. There had been no word on Lucinda's return. Adam thought about stopping by the courthouse to review the St. Louis City Court records to see if there were any legal proceedings against the Harringtons, but he had hoped to have Lucinda's interview finished before doing so. He knew he could check online, but sometimes the clerks were slow to enter and update cases. Adam preferred to have his hands on the physical files. He decided it would be more efficient to get Lucinda's interview finished before checking the records.

As Adam drove down Tucker, he changed his mind once more, chiding himself for being indecisive, a quality he eschewed. He pulled into the courthouse parking spots reserved for police cars to see if there was anything he could learn.

Adam walked a short distance when he saw a familiar figure descending the concrete steps. Harlan Royce, one of the most expensive criminal defense attorneys in St. Louis, was standing tall and confident as he approached Adam. Adam's stomach twisted in knots as the attorney drew near, clad in his fifteen hundred dollar suit which he accessorized with a smug look of arrogant satisfaction.

Normally, Adam didn't have a problem with defense attorneys. They had a job to do. Everyone was entitled to due process and a defense. But Harlan Royce was no run-of-the-mill defense attorney. He stopped at nothing to win, sacrificing truth and trampling victims and their families while collecting enough money to reduce the national debt. He took excessive pleasure in sticking it to the police and bamboozled juries with theatrics and drama. His appearance was dashing and his style elegant. He used all of these qualities to sway juries unfamiliar with the legal system, who, without ever realizing it, could be persuaded by his crafty manipulation. Harlan Royce had the means to hire investigators to research potential jurors that could be sympathetic to his clients, a luxury the understaffed district attorney's office lacked. Harlan Royce was representing Dr. Lionel Cranston.

"Detective Trent, nice to see you. Beautiful September afternoon." He offered a limp-wristed handshake, which Adam ignored, so Royce withdrew his hand.

"Mr. Royce," Adam replied curtly.

Before another word could be exchanged, Adam saw news vans descending on the courthouse like flies on rotten meat. His stomach tightened further as reporters rushed up the steps, microphones in hand, to the arrogant, smiling Harlan Royce. As an added bonus, the flamboyant attorney was on the courthouse steps with the detective who had been instrumental in the arrest of Dr. Cranston. It was a great day in St. Louis if you were a news reporter.

As the reporters shouted their questions, they shoved microphones into Royce's face as he posed for the snapping cameras, displaying perfect gleaming teeth. Microphones were pushed toward Adam's face. His jaw tightened as he clenched his teeth together. Unbeknownst to Adam, Harlan Royce, over the objections of the District Attorney, had obtained a new judge, the Honorable Lucas Dempsey. Dr. Lionel Cranston, dubbed the Doctor of Death, had been released on a million dollar bail when Judge Dempsey, in his questionable discretion, determined he was not a flight risk. Adam froze in sickened disbelief as the facts unfolded.

He tried to escape the mob of reporters, giving them nothing but a terse "No comment" in response to their shouted questions. He pushed his way up the steps and into the courthouse, where he rushed into the men's room to splash cold water on his flushed face. *How does any amount of bail justify letting that monster out?* Adam felt as if he had been kicked in the stomach. He turned the cold water on full blast and kept splashing his face. *When did this happen? Cranston threatened me, my team and our families! Why wasn't I told?* Grabbing a handful of paper towels, he dried his face. *What time is it? I have to reach Jenna before Amy gets out of school.* He slipped out of the courthouse through a side exit, and ran to his car. The reporters, still enamored with Harlan Royce, did not notice as Adam pulled out of the parking lot and sped to the police station.

Captain Peterson met him in the parking lot. His grim expression told Adam he had just heard the news as well. "Go home, Adam. Just go home. The D.A. fought the bail, but the judge ruled against him. Come back when you can work with a clear head. You know how this runs, Adam. Nobody expected Cranston could ever get out on bail, but you can never predict what a judge will do. Go and get your family to safety. When they're safe and you can concentrate on your work, come back. We'll talk then."

Adam opened his mouth to respond to Captain Peterson, but his Captain stood resolute. "Go home now. That's an order. The rest of your team has also been given leave for a day. Two if they need it. You'll be no different."

Adam turned on his heel and sped toward home, his teeth clenched and his hands digging into the steering wheel. Bail had been denied twice, but Royce's third attempt succeeded and he was granted a change of judge. All Adam held as just and right had been trampled.

He called Jenna on the way.

"Hi, babe. What's up?"

He could tell by her sweet answer that she had not watched television and had no idea what was going on. "Where are you?" Adam demanded, wiping perspiration from his forehead.

"On my way home. I work at the library on Fridays, now, remember? What's wrong, Adam?"

"Where's Amy?" he snapped, instantly regretting the tone he had taken with his wife.

"She'll be getting out of school soon. Adam, what's *wrong*?"

"Call the school and tell them to keep her inside until I get there. Meet me at the school. Now."

Jenna Trent was frightened. She heard fear in Adam's voice. She had always known her husband to be fearless and courageous. He had been her hero ever since the day he had come to her assistance when her Mustang had broken down. His cap had nearly swallowed his head and she could tell he was nervous in his attempt to make a gallant impression. She had fallen for him as much as he had fallen for her. He would never have given her such a curt order if something was not terribly wrong. Jenna called the school and relayed the message. Shaken, she sped toward Amy's school in St. Louis Hills.

There had been other times, she remembered, when Adam's work had placed her in danger. When Amy was two months old, Adam had worked a drug case and the gang involved learned where the Trents lived. Jenna was home alone and had placed Amy in her crib to sleep one night when she heard a car idling on the street outside their small Carondelet Park home. Standing to the side of the living room window, she peeked through the curtain and saw not one, but three cars lined up outside their home. She took her cell phone, hurried to the nursery and grabbed Amy, wrapping her in blankets. She called Adam, who was an hour away, working the case.

"Stay on the floor of the hallway, Jenna. Close the doors. I'll send someone for you."

"Adam, they're throwing rocks or something at the windows."

"Are the lights out?" he asked her.

"Yes, except for the one in our bedroom."

"Leave the baby on the floor and close all the doors leading into the hall. Stay low and quiet. Don't do anything to let on that you're home. I'm sending help and I'm on my way." She remembered his voice, strong and calm, but carrying an undercurrent of urgency.

"Adam, they've stopped. I hear the cars leaving. Is it okay to come out?"

"*No!* They'll be back. Jenna, do what I say. You have to trust me. Put your phone on vibrate so you don't miss a call. Do not make a sound, and keep the baby quiet."

Jenna sat on the floor of the hall with her back to the wall, cradling the sleeping baby in her arms, trying to slow her breathing and her heart rate. Several minutes passed. Her cell phone vibrated and she heard a soft knock at the back door. "Hello?" she whispered into the phone.

"Jenna, it's me. Kate Marlin," a voice whispered back. "I've got Robo with me at the back door. Let me in. Hurry."

Officer Kate Marlin and Robo, an enormous German Shepherd, were from the Canine Unit and lived a few blocks away from the Trent family. Jenna set the baby on the floor and dashed to the back door to let them in, locking it behind them with trembling hands. Robo could smell her fear and gave her one of his famous stares as if to assure her that he was ready to spring into action at Kate's command. Robo was a foreboding presence and Jenna derived some comfort from that. Dog notwithstanding, however, Kate arrived fully armed, a one-woman arsenal, prepared for war.

"Adam's on his way, but Robo and I were much closer." She kept her voice low.

Jenna whispered back, "I feel better with you here." Bent low, they made their way back to the hall.

"You need to stay in the hall with your baby with the doors closed. Robo and I will keep watch in the front room while we wait for reinforcements. Just stay low and quiet, got it?"

Jenna didn't need to be told twice. She remained in the hall, sitting on the floor with her back against the wall, holding Amy close to her chest, fighting the urge to cry and silently praying. It seemed like an eternity as they waited. Then, she heard the sounds of cars around her home. Was it the gang? Or was it the police? Jenna held her breath, remaining quiet, grateful her infant daughter was sound asleep, oblivious to the danger overshadowing her tiny life. Jenna had no idea how long she sat unmoving, listening for any type of movement or noise, but hearing nothing. Suddenly, gunfire shattered the silence. She could hear it coming from all directions. Jenna lay on the floor trying to cover little Amy with her body. She heard windows breaking, angry voices, sirens, screaming and banging, but she stayed down, holding her baby close and praying, her eyes squeezed shut. Eventually, all was quiet again and suddenly Adam was there, kneeling beside her, holding her and Amy together in his strong, reassuring arms. "It's over, baby, it's over," he said, helping her to her feet. To Jenna's surprise, Amy slept through the entire ordeal. They had only been home from the hospital a short time, and Amy, being a preemie, still slept much of the time, but now she stirred and started to cry.

Jenna ventured out from the hall to the rest of their small home. It looked like a war had been fought. Broken glass and debris covered the floor. Bullet holes dotted the walls, knocking off photographs which lay shattered. Surveying the damage, Jenna was sickened. She fought back tears and didn't know how she could ever get the mess cleaned and their home in good repair. The cost would be staggering.

Jenna walked to the bedroom and stood against the wall. She looked outside from behind the bedroom curtain. Ambulances had arrived to cart off the injured, and gang members were being loaded into police vehicles. One officer and four thugs had been wounded, three gang bangers killed and Robo had two more backed against a tree until they could be cuffed, daring them to move.

Adam brought up suitcases from the basement, and gently took the baby from Jenna. "Put some things together and take Amy and go stay with your mother for a few days. She'll be thrilled to see the baby and you'll be safe while I take care of things here."

"It's awfully late, Adam."

"It'll be fine, honey. Tell her what happened. I'm sure she'll understand."

"Are you coming too?"

"Later." He stroked her hair and kissed her forehead. "Call your mom and tell her you're on your way. If you don't feel strong enough to drive, I'll ask Kate to take you."

"No. That's okay. I'm fine." She turned to begin packing while Adam held Amy.

Jenna's mother lived in Ellisville, a quiet bedroom community about an hour west of the city, on a peaceful, tree-lined street in one of the older sections of the town. Jenna's father had passed away several years prior and her mother, whose health was failing, chose to remain alone in the home, turning a deaf ear to Jenna and Adam's concerns. When Jenna pulled into her mother's driveway, the porch light was on.

Three months later, the Trents purchased a small home near Lindenwood Park, in District Two, the safest neighborhood in the city. Abigail Willows, Jenna's mother, shaken by the earlier event, provided money for a down payment sufficient that Adam's income could meet the mortgage. Even though the St. Louis City Police Department no longer required its long-term employees to reside within the city limits, many of the officers, believing you defended best where you lived, chose to remain. Jenna's mother was not happy about their decision, voicing her opinion that they could just as easily live in the county, but she respected their choice in spite of her objections. Jenna and Adam enjoyed city living and wanted to remain. Adam had a short commute to work, and Jenna planned to return to the library once Amy was in school.

Now, as Jenna neared Word of Life Lutheran School where Amy was enrolled, she felt the same level of fear that had gripped her over ten years ago. She scanned the area before parking. Nothing at the school looked amiss—no barricades or ambulances greeted her. The school faced Francis Park, a beautiful park in the center of St. Louis Hills, with a circumference of one square mile, more or less, where walkers and joggers could be found completing laps any time of the day or night.

St. Louis Hills was one of the most sought-after neighborhoods in the city, with its manicured lawns, lovely flowering gardens, huge ancient trees and abundance of churches, many of which also sponsored schools. It was close to restaurants, two parks, and a short drive from Forest Park, St. Louis' urban jewel, home to free attractions such as the zoo, science center, art museum and more. The beautiful homes surrounding the park were expensive, and once on the market, often sold the same day. But, as Jenna observed, the neighborhood appeared peaceful.

Jenna breathed a sigh of relief that whatever Adam was upset about had not affected this quiet corner of the city. At least, not yet. As she walked toward the front door, Adam's car tore around the corner, screeching to a stop in the parking place beside her car. He jumped out of his car and ran toward her. He held her tight against his chest. She could hear his pounding heart.

"Where's Amy?"

"Adam, I just now got here. I was going inside to get her. Will you please tell me what in the world is going on?"

"Cranston is out on bail." He choked on his words.

Jenna felt her legs weaken. She held on to Adam as he steadied her and helped her sit on a bench outside the school. "Oh, no."

"I've already talked to my parents. I'm moving you and Amy out to their farm until Cranston is prosecuted. He *will* make good on his threats against my family and my team. I'm taking no chances. He's a lunatic."

"How could they let him out?" she asked, flailing her arms in frustration. Her eyes searched Adam's, pleading for an answer.

"Royce got a new judge who apparently, is also a lunatic."

"Or paid off!"

"Let's not go there. Honey, it's just too dangerous for you and Amy to be anywhere near me right now. My folks are expecting you."

"What about school?"

"Let's go talk to the principal."

School was letting out as Adam and Jenna entered the front doors of the building. They passed by Amy's home room and noted with satisfaction that her teacher was keeping her there while the other children left.

"Her teacher's smart. Looks like she gave Amy a special project to work on. That'll keep her busy for a while."

The principal met them in the hall and ushered them into her office, closing the door behind her. Adam explained the situation, stressing that if Amy was in danger, then the safety of the other children in her school would also be compromised. The Trents and the principal discussed the pros and cons of the various options available to best deal with the circumstances. Arrangements were made to have Amy's records transferred to a sister school in Union, Missouri. Adam's parents lived a short distance outside of Union on the same family farm that had been in the Trent family for generations. Adam and Jenna listened while Amy's principal explained the situation to the school principal in Union. As a precaution, the schools set up a dummy record changing Amy's name to Jessica Long. The paperwork would be changed back when it was deemed safe for Amy to return.

While the principal typed Amy's information into her computer, Jenna looked up at Adam. "Are we doing the right thing?" she asked.

Adam took her hand in his. "What do you mean?"

"Putting her in a strange new school with a new name. Do you think that's the best thing for her? If she stays at the farm, at least I can keep her close. And safe. I can teach her at home. This won't be for long, right?" Jenna's eyes searched Adam's.

"That's a good point, babe, but I think it'd be in Amy's best interest to try to keep things as normal as possible—not that any of this is normal, but she's used to going to school, having a schedule, a routine. Let's see how it works out. We can always change it later. How's that sound to you?"

Jenna leaned her head on Adam's shoulder and blinked back tears. He put his arm around her and pulled her close.

"I think Mr. Trent is right," the principal said. "Try to keep things as close as possible to what Amy's used to."

"Okay." Jenna sounded unconvinced.

Adam took her face in his hands and held it, brushing away a tear that escaped and started down her cheek. "It's not cast in stone, sweetheart."

She sniffed and nodded.

The principal stood. "All set. Amy's records have been copied, encrypted for security and transferred. We look forward to her return here when this is over for you. Best of luck. I'll keep you in my prayers. And let me reassure you. *All* of this is confidential."

"Thank you," they both said. They shook hands and walked out of her office.

Adam and Jenna breathed a collective sigh and walked to Amy's home room. Their daughter looked up at them with solemn eyes. Both parents coming to get her was not a good sign. "What's wrong?" she asked looking from one parent to the other.

"We'll tell you when we're on our way home, sweetie," Jenna answered.

Adam walked out of the school building first, and after surveying the surrounding area, motioned for Jenna to bring Amy. Jenna and Amy drove behind Adam's police car down Jamieson to the entrance to Highway 44.

"Amy," Jenna began. "Something bad has happened and Daddy doesn't believe it's safe for us to stay in our house right now. We're going to go and stay at Gomer and Oompa's house for a little while."

"What about Blue?" Amy asked.

Oh no! How could I forget about the dog? Jenna pressed the Bluetooth button on the steering wheel to call Adam.

"Don't worry, Jen. You and Amy meet me in the parking lot of Steak 'n Shake at 44 and 141. Give me twenty minutes and then order dinner for you and Amy. Get me a double cheeseburger, onion rings and an orange freeze—without the cholesterol commentary, if you don't mind. I'll turn around and get Blue and her things. Don't get out of the car. Just use the drive-through window."

"Mom, why do you always do what Daddy tells you? Why don't you think for yourself?"

This kid is hanging around Amanda too much. "Amy, just because Amanda's mother is going through a bitter divorce doesn't mean everything she says is correct. Her mom is angry toward all men, and if you listen to her, you'll start believing her poison. I know Amanda is your friend and she and her mother are going through a tough time, but that doesn't mean you have to believe everything she says. Your father is doing his best to protect us—to keep us safe from harm. Daddy has a very dangerous job and he knows what's best for us if his job affects us. Do you think this is easy for him? How is ordering a little dinner from a take-out window hurting anything? We're a family and if we don't work together as a family, and show each other love and compassion, then who will we have when we need each other?"

Amy was quiet a moment. "Blue chases the chickens."

Jenna sighed. The stress was taking its toll on her. "We'll have to keep Blue away from the chickens," she answered with a weariness in her voice that would not have been there had Cranston been kept locked up. *What kind of moron lets a psycho like Cranston out on bail? We should be home at our dinner table, laughing and talking, not fleeing for our safety.*

"Can I get an orange freeze too? Please?"

"Yes, Amy." Jenna felt a rush of exhaustion overtake her and fought back tears. They still had an hour to travel before reaching her in-laws.

They exited the highway and waited for Adam. He arrived sooner than the speed limit allowed. *Probably used the siren.*

Hope it didn't scare the dog! The family ate their dinner in the parking lot. Blue stared at the burgers until Amy finally shared with her.

"Was everything all right at home?" Jenna asked.

"So far, but we're not taking any chances. I picked up some clothes and things for you and Amy. Anything else you need, go and buy it, don't worry about the budget. You had two books on your nightstand, Jen. I put both of them in the car. I know how much you enjoy a little quiet reading time." Adam crammed the last of his cheeseburger into his mouth. "Dad has loaded all the guns in the house. Amy, you're not to touch them, understand?"

"Yes, Daddy." They'd had the loaded gun conversation on several occasions.

"And another thing. Do *not* call or e-mail any of your friends to tell them where you are, got it?"

"You don't have to be so bossy."

Adam hugged his daughter. "I'm not being bossy, peanut. I'm worried about your safety. I love you and your mother more than life and it's important that you listen to me so we can be together again soon."

They finished their dinner in record time and resumed their trip.

Daylight was fading when they reached the Trent farm, several miles outside of Union, Missouri. Blue jumped out of the car and ran to the chicken coop, but the chickens were already put up for the night.

"Hah, Blue! Fooled ya! The chickens are in for the night," scolded Emma Jo Trent to the big dog as she hastened off the porch to greet the family.

"Gomer!" Amy ran to her grandmother, who scooped her up and twirled her around in a big hug.

"Oh my, Amy! You just get bigger and bigger every time I see you. Let's see, now. Are you, what? About twenty-three years old now?"

"Oh Gomer! I'm eleven. I'm almost a teenager!"

Dwayne Trent came hurrying out to greet them.

"You cain't be no teenager, little girl! We don't 'llow no teenagers here!"

"Oompah, you're silly! You'll allow *me*!" She ran to her grandfather for a bear hug.

Emma Jo greeted Adam and Jenna with a warm hug, but her usual bright countenance was overshadowed by worry.

"You be careful out there Adam Joseph Trent. We'll keep our girls safe here. The principal of the Christian school goes to church with us and we've told him what's going on. He'll keep everything real quiet. He's good people, Adam, and he'll watch out for our Amy."

"Thanks, Mom." Adam put his arm around his mother's shoulders and squeezed.

"Come on in the house. Gomer's got hot cocoa and fresh baked cookies waiting for everyone." Dwayne held the door open and the family piled into the big comfortable farmhouse, where the rich aroma of homemade cookies could have melted everyone's cares away, if their cares had not been so dire.

"Amy, why don't you go get settled into that pretty pink bedroom we keep just for you?" her grandmother said. "Did you bring a bed for Blue?"

"She sleeps in bed with me."

"Not in this house. I don't cotton to no animals on my furniture."

"Gomer, I think just this once, it'll be okay." Dwayne winked at Amy and his wife. Emma Jo opened her mouth to object, but closed it and nodded to her husband.

"Thanks Oompah." Amy winked back at her grandfather and skipped to her bedroom to unpack. Blue trotted behind her.

"Mom, Dad, it's getting late. I think I'll spend the night here before heading back to the city."

"What has this man done that's so dangerous, Adam?" his mother asked.

"He's a doctor, Mom," Adam said, looking down the hallway to be sure Amy was out of earshot. "He's a self-appointed god of life and death. Anyone he deems unworthy of life, he injects with lethal medication. They might be old, handicapped in some way, or ill. He started with cardiac patients who were in the hospital. He injected them with high doses of potassium, causing cardiac arrest. Nobody even knows how many he killed before suspicion was aroused. Anyone he believes is a drain on society, he gets rid of them, like a bag of trash."

"Good heavens," Emma Jo exclaimed, placing her hand on her chest. "How could a doctor have such little regard for life?"

Adam sat on the sofa beside Jenna. "Then, he moved on to a drug called Curare. It acts by slowly paralyzing every part of your body until you stop breathing. Again, it took a while before anybody got wise. Dr. Cranston was on staff at a number of hospitals. He planned his murders meticulously. It took a long time to narrow the list of suspects to him, and even longer to build a case against him. But when we did, it was airtight. As the noose was beginning to tighten around the good doctor, so to say, he lashed out and made a huge mistake that sealed it for us. Arrogance was his downfall. That, and being just plain crazy, I suppose.

"Well," Emma said. "Pride goes before destruction. So what happened? What was his mistake?"

"He was caught inside Connor's home one night. Connor's one of my partners. The family was sound asleep. No idea how he got into their house. Tripped on the kid's skateboard and the crash woke up the whole family. Connor flew out of bed in his skivvies and got the handcuffs on Cranston. Caught him red-handed with a vial of the Curare in his pocket. He'd planned to use it on the children. Can you believe that? After we caught him, he vowed revenge on my homicide team and our families. There were three of us responsible for his capture: me, Connor and Bo. That was last month. Bail was denied twice before a new judge granted it today. We thought we were all safe, at least until trial."

"I suppose your fellow team members have evacuated their families as well?" his father asked him.

"Connor's the only one with kids. I can't imagine him leaving his loved ones open to certain danger. Bo's still single, but he's got a girlfriend, at least this week, so I'm sure he's got her someplace safe. I figured once everyone was safe, they'd rejoin the team and go after him again, but my captain said he wanted us all out of town. I just can't do that. Not with Cranston out there, free as a bird. Who knows where he might strike next? But I'll die before I put Jenna and Amy in danger."

Emma Jo spoke up. "How much does Amy know? She's so young to have to deal with this."

Jenna addressed Emma Jo's concern. "I told her on the way over here that a very bad man was out of jail and that her daddy and I felt we'd be safer if we stayed here. This is the second time Adam has had us leave home. The first time, Amy was home from the hospital just six weeks. We went to stay at my mom's for a few weeks." Jenna choked on her words.

Emma Jo rose to give Jenna a hug. "I'm sure you miss your mother, dear. At least Amy got to know her for a little while."

"What did you say about me?" Amy asked as she made her entrance with Blue at her side.

"We said we were wonderin' if you didn't like Gomer's hot cocoa and cookies anymore," Dwayne said.

"Maybe I better have some and I'll let you know!"

Adam's cell phone rang. It was the officer watching the Harrington house.

"Lucinda's home. What's next?" he asked Adam.

"I can't get there right now. Can you keep a detail on her? I'll try to get over there tomorrow." He hung up and turned back to his family. "I think I'll turn in now. I've got an early morning tomorrow. Mom, Dad, thanks for taking care of my girls." He gave Amy a hug and a kiss. Jenna stood to join him.

"Thanks for everything," she added.

"Our pleasure, you know that. We wish the circumstances were different. You'll be safe here."

Chapter 5

Adam rose before 5 a.m. He knew his parents would be up. Despite their advancing years, nothing ever changed with them. They ran the farm with little help. Coffee was brewing and the kitchen smelled like morning. Adam inhaled deeply, savoring the comforting aroma of breakfast. Jenna always had breakfast ready for him before he left every morning. She came downstairs, dressed in a robe. She had combed her hair, but wore no make-up. She looked tired and worried. Dark circles under her eyes emphasized deep crow's feet around her eyes. Her forehead was lined and her face puffy. They hugged each other and Adam kissed her forehead. "It'll be okay. God is in control. Just keep me in your prayers." He grabbed some bacon and a biscuit and, gulping down the coffee, thanked his parents again and left for the long drive back to St. Louis. Adam checked with the second shift watch on the Harrington house and was assured that Lucinda had not left. He accelerated to 95 miles per hour, stopping once for gas and coffee, and arrived at the Harrington castle a few minutes after 8 a.m.

Edie, the housekeeper, didn't arrive until 10, but Adam continued ringing the doorbell until a very sleepy Lucinda answered, in a foul mood.

"Ms. Harrington?"

"Yeah, yeah, what's so important that it couldn't wait?"

"I need to ask you a few questions about your father's death."

"Cedric told me all about it. I don't know anything. I haven't got any poisons and I haven't got any regrets. That about cover it?"

"Please state your full name."

Lucinda did not invite him in. Wearing a black nightgown and barefoot, she had slept with last night's make-up on and black lines and smudges were smeared on her face.

"Lucinda Madelaine Harrington. I already told you I don't know anything."

"How did you come to celebrate your father's birthday at the Mansford Mansion?"

"Cedric got a coupon or something. Said it would save us money and bug dear old Dad out of his wits. Which it did," she added, shrugging her shoulders. She looked down her nose at Adam and smirked. "It was a cheap way of aggravating the old man, so I was all for it."

"How would his threat to change his will have affected you?"

Lucinda rolled her eyes and stared upward, as if the ceiling had special wisdom to impart. "He wasn't going to change his will. It doesn't matter now anyway. The old fart is gone and we, his lucky children, inherit it all."

"Not if you played a part in his murder."

The smirk faded from her face. "Prove it, cop."

She shut the door in his face.

Adam retreated to his car and took out his notepad to jot down his impressions. He left for the station. He still had four viable suspects, but no helpful information.

He stopped at the first floor office at the end of the hallway to see Dr. Eli Gerwyn, the department shrink. Dr. Gerwyn provided counsel to the officers in a myriad of situations. Adam also considered the psychiatrist a good profiler, capable of analyzing suspects with a fair amount of accuracy. Adam tended to avoid Dr. Gerwyn because he didn't like feeling as if he, himself, were under the microscope, being analyzed, picked apart and labeled. Dr. Gerwyn was fine for those who could not deal with their issues by themselves, but Adam preferred to work out his own problems. He had made a single exception when Jenna had become severely depressed after the miscarriages and the rejections from the adoption agencies, but he had sought outside help that one time for her sake. Setting his nerves aside, he tapped on the doctor's door.

"Detective Trent. How nice to see you," Dr. Gerwyn offered his hand and Adam shook it. "What brings you to my office today?"

Said the spider to the fly. "I was wondering if I might pick your brain on my current case."

"Of course." Dr. Gerwyn gestured an invitation to enter. "How are you doing? I heard that Cranston was released on bail. That must have been tough for you. How's your family holding up?"

Already starting. "Oh, that. No worries. I'm fine." Adam waved his hand, dismissing Dr. Gerwyn's concern. "He'll screw up again and we'll get him again. I'm here about the Harrington murder, ah, hoping you could provide a little insight, if you've got time."

"It's my job to have time. Have a seat." He pulled a chair out for Adam. "How can I help?"

Adam filled Dr. Gerwyn in on the events that had transpired at Mansford Mansion and the ensuing interviews with the illustrious Harrington siblings. Dr. Gerwyn listened patiently, jotting down notes and nodding his head.

"So, Doc, what are your thoughts? Do you think you can help me narrow down a suspect, or rule anybody out? I'm running into dead ends here. Seems like the whole family is looney tunes in one way or another."

Dr. Gerwyn cleared his throat and straightened his posture. "Edward Harrington, the father, was without doubt, a narcissist. The world revolved around him and he manipulated others into submission, which has resulted in abnormal behavior in his unfortunate children. Cedric and Lucinda exhibit the same narcissistic tendencies as their father, only their behavior is also indicative of sociopathic tendencies. Narcissism and sociopathy are closely related. It's common to see an individual with both."

"So Cedric and Lucinda would never feel any guilt or shame for any wrongdoing?"

"Correct. A sociopath refuses to take responsibility for their behavior. They may lie with impunity, or steal. As children, they may fight, be cruel to animals, or start fires, all without any guilt or remorse. Anything dangerous, harmful or hurtful to others will always be someone else's fault. They're incapable of feeling remorse. You cannot rule out either one of them, Cedric or Lucinda, as suspects."

Adam wrote in his notebook as Dr. Gerwyn was talking. He looked up and asked, "What do you think about Esme?"

Dr. Gerwyn coughed and crossed his legs. "Esme engages in behavior to deflect, as a defense mechanism. Her eating disorder is a specific mechanism she uses to help her deal with a miserable childhood. Eating and vomiting are things she does not feel helpless to control. I believe Esme is too weak, not just physically, but also emotionally, to carry off such a crime as this. She would go to the bottom of my list. I don't believe Esme is a viable suspect."

Adam nodded in agreement. "That's what I thought. She's so mousy, and I don't think it's an act. She's like a shadow of a human being. But I'm not the expert you are in determining what lurks beneath a façade of weakness and frailty."

"Adam, all I have is your take on the Harrington siblings. So anything I say must, of course, come with the caveat of my not having the opportunity to examine these people in person. We must be clear on that."

"Of course, Dr. Gerwyn. This is all off the record. I'm just looking for your insight to help me figure these suspects out. I thought a little time talking with you might save me a lot of time chasing the wind if you can help me sort out the people who stood the most to gain by Harrington's death."

"If I could spend some time with each of them, I'm certain I could be more helpful."

Adam laughed. "I'm pretty sure that would be a tough sell, getting them in here to talk to you."

"Agreed."

"Which brings me to Roland Harrington, whom I find to be the most difficult to decipher." Adam leaned toward Dr. Gerwyn and cocked his head sideways. "There's a part of me that likes Roland a lot, Doc. He's pleasant, well mannered, kind, rescued this poor ugly dog. He's neat and clean—fastidious, even—and treats others with respect and dignity. He just seems so normal, but then, did you ever see that movie, *American Psycho*? I mean, wow, that guy was super normal on the outside. And I wonder if Roland could be like that?"

Dr. Gerwyn uncrossed his legs and leaned toward Adam. "I did see the movie, and I read the book as well. To be honest, I would have to meet and interview Roland in person. His behavior, his fastidiousness, minimalistic style, being polite and kind—those may also be a reaction to his upbringing. Roland has become the exact opposite of his father. Just as Esme uses her eating disorder as her specific mechanism to deal with a miserable childhood, so Roland uses his obsession with order and neatness as his defense mechanism to deal with his miserable childhood. As to your question whether Roland is genuinely as he seems, or covering up a dark and evil side, I can't say based on what you've told me. He could go either way. He could be at the bottom of the list, or at the top of the list. I'm sorry. I know that's not what you were looking for."

Adam stood to leave. "Thanks for your help. I was hoping to have more insight into Roland, but it's early in the investigation yet."

Dr. Gerwyn stood and offered his hand to Adam. "Sorry I couldn't have been more definitive on Roland, but I hope I've helped in some way with the others. How's your family dealing with the Cranston matter?"

Adam shook the psychiatrist's hand, and then took a step backward. "We're all fine, Dr. G. Everyone is safe and happy. Gotta go. Thanks again."

Chapter 6

Alan Cunningham sat at his desk reviewing the receipts and reservation book. Not that he would have *wished* anyone to die at his big event, but it certainly had been a tremendous boon for business. He might not have to sell the place after all. And even if he did, he would not take a loss. Which reminded him, in spite of the untimely death of their father, he needed to send the bill for a new table after that awful woman ground her cigarette out on his fine wood. Or wood veneer, whatever.

But what about that cop? He acted like he thought the death of Mr. Harrington had been suspicious. That would be icing on the cake, the whipped cream and cherry on the sundae. He had been told to keep the guest list. That had to mean the cop suspected something. Oh *this* was juicy, indeed!

He called his staff and announced that he was expanding the 150th anniversary event by a couple of extra nights per week. After assuring them they would be paid, and on time, of course, he notified the various media outlets that Mansford Mansion, due to high demand, would now be open Wednesday and Thursday evenings, in addition to the Friday through Sunday schedule. He would send a condolence card to the family. After all, he didn't want to seem too opportunistic.

Adam double checked the locks on the doors of the safe house he had been assigned. Captain Peterson insisted that Adam's homicide team stay in various hideaways until Cranston was off the streets. The safe house was an apartment in a large building with seven floors. Nice enough, but nothing like home. Adam went through the small rooms checking the security, and once confident he was alone, safe and unnoticed, took out his phone to call Jenna. He had gotten them both pre-paid throwaway phones for the duration of their separation so they could be certain their calls were private.

"Hi, sweetheart. How are you? Are you safe?" Jenna's voice was music to his ears.

"I'm fine, hon. It's so good to hear your voice. I miss you. Captain Peterson put us all in various safe houses around the city. I got one of the nicer ones. How are you and Miss Jessica Long handling things?"

"Jessica had a pretty good day at school. She's holding up well, all things considered. We're all praying for you. Your parents are angels. They've gone to great lengths to try to lessen the stress of this situation and their efforts are helpful. I'll still be glad when this is over and we can be together in our own home again."

"You can say that again."

They chatted a while longer and Jenna put Amy on the phone to tell her father goodnight.

Adam checked the apartment. All seemed safe and quiet. He sat on the sofa to read his Bible, and prayed that God would give him wisdom and courage. His head began to feel heavy. He checked the locks one last time, then retreated to the bedroom and laid his weary head down to sleep.

A taxi cab stopped in front of St. James the Greater Catholic Church in the Dogtown neighborhood of South St. Louis. A stooped figure wearing a shoulder-length nun's veil stepped out and hobbled into the church, leaning heavily on her cane. The taxi cab driver turned off the engine and remained parked for the return fare. The shadowy figure slipped into the confessional.

The priest hearing confession did not recognize the nun as being from his parish.

"Bless me Father, for I have sinned. It has been two weeks since my last confession, and my soul is troubled."

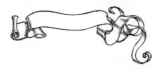

Ava Montel paced the floor of her tiny apartment in the Soulard area off of Broadway. She had walked the short distance to St. Louis Bread Company and treated herself to a bacon turkey bravo sandwich and a bear claw. It was more than she should spend, but her desire for immediate gratification won over her need for frugality, as it often did. Alan had finally paid the staff. Good thing. She was down to two ramen noodle packets and a half jar of peanut butter. She needed to find a better job, but for now, had to stay put, at least until the dust settled on what happened that night. A steady job with a regular paycheck would be nice, but now, thanks to Edward Harrington's well-timed death, Alan was opening the mansion two additional nights. Every little bit helped. Plus, she figured, it would look bad if she left now. What if someone found out?

Ava sat down to eat her sandwich, relishing the tasty blend of bacon, turkey and cheese on soft tomato bread. She wished she had ordered a brownie as well. Chocolate usually calmed her. But the bear claw would make a tasty dessert too. And the bear claw was bigger than the brownie.

She thought about her situation. No one could know. As if her luck couldn't have been any worse, there had been a cop there that night. *A cop*! And she had seen him out in the parking lot writing on a pad. Probably taking down license plates. Ava's hands began to shake and she set her sandwich down. If she took off now, it would look suspicious. She was an actress after all, wasn't she? Not much of one, she had to admit. But surely she could get herself through this mess if she was ever questioned. Ava had only been hired by Alan because she bore a striking resemblance to Annalise Mansford's portrait. Her looks had gotten her pretty far up until now. That was one of the few things in her favor. Ava had dropped out of junior college due to poor grades and poorer finances. She had no marketable skills, but when she had seen the job opportunity in the classifieds to portray Annalise Mansford, all she needed were green contact lenses. Once she got those, she applied for the job and was hired on the spot.

Ava set her half-eaten sandwich on her plate and paced some more. What if that cop came around and asked questions? What would she say? She peered out of her window. Everything looked normal. No cops. Chiding herself for worrying needlessly, she returned to her dinner and ate, finishing it off with the bear claw. Almonds were good for you. Good for your brain. Maybe dessert could help her think. With all those almonds, it was practically health food.

Ava poured a glass of wine from a bottle Mike Davey had given her when they were sure no one was looking. Mike was sweet on her, she knew. He was a nice guy, but not her type. No reason not to get what you could out of it, and if he snuck a bottle or two of good wine to her—well, she guessed, it wouldn't hurt to be nice to him. The sweet red liquid went down smooth as silk and calmed her.

After the second glass, Ava began to feel sleepy. She walked into the little bedroom at the back of the apartment, turned back the covers and climbed into bed, too sleepy to worry about answering any questions. For that matter, the police might not even ask her anything. Before turning off her lamp, she picked up the silver framed photograph she kept on her night stand. Ava stroked it with her finger, held it to her chest and lightly kissed it. *Goodnight, my sweet Roland.*

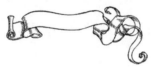

Charlie Dennison had just finished putting the last log in the fireplace in the family room of their home on Flora Place when his wife, Kimber, walked in.

"What do you think you're doing, Charlie?" she half asked, half demanded. She stood with one hand on a hip and the other waving an upturned palm. "Since when do we need a fire in September? We've barely turned off the air conditioner."

"You sure about that Kimber? I feel a little chill in the air. It's a perfect night for a fire." The hard edge in his voice cut her. His blue eyes narrowed beneath his thinning light brown hair as he looked at her, daring her to challenge him.

"Have you lost your mind?"

"Not at all," he replied, striking a match and fanning the logs. The flames jumped to life and began to build. Charlie opened his brief case and started to feed papers into the fire, watching with a sardonic smile on his face as the hungry flames consumed them.

"What are you—oh Charlie! I don't think that's such a great idea."

"Kimber, darling, why don't you go and get me a beer?" His loveless voice was flat and cold. His eyes never left the fire.

Kimber departed for the kitchen, returning with her husband's beer and a glass of wine for herself. "Don't you think the neighbors will wonder why we have a fire going when the temperature's only in the sixties?" she asked.

Charlie was halfway through the pile of papers. "I told you," he growled. "I felt a chill. Maybe I'm coming down with something."

"And you think that destroying every shred of evidence we have that Edward Harrington was going to ruin us is going to make a difference?" she asked, trying to control the rising pitch in her voice. "If they search Harrington's office, he'll surely have copies of everything."

"I was a silent partner, Kimber. Nobody knows my name. I wanted to keep it that way. Don't you realize what's at stake here? We could've lost our home, our retirement, everything. We're almost broke as it is."

Kimber wrung her hands. She walked back and forth beside her husband. "I wish we'd never gone to that dinner. It was a terrible idea."

Charlie scowled. "That's the first halfway intelligent thing you've said in a long time."

Kimber sat down heavily on the sofa with an audible sigh. She was close to tears. "Oh, Charlie. What's happened to us? Where did we go so wrong?" She looked around their spacious home, situated down the street from the Botanical Gardens in the historic Shaw neighborhood. Kimber had longed to live on Flora Place since she was a child. She had fantasized about living on the elegant private street graced by stately homes that stretched from Tower Grove to Grand Avenues. It was her favorite street in the city, full of history and old world charm. Their home had three working fireplaces as well as two that were decorative, wood beamed ceilings and ornate crown molding and finish trim. While not as expensive as the homes in the Central West End, the elegant homes on Flora Place were, nonetheless, out of the Dennison's reach. When they were able to obtain their home through a foreclosure sale, Kimber thought they were the luckiest couple in the world. She had hoped this would be a chance for her and Charlie to start over again.

"Where did we go wrong, did you say?" Charlie snorted. He turned and faced her for the first time. He stood, towering over her. "When the home we could afford wasn't big enough, grand enough, fancy enough. When the cars we could afford didn't make the right statement. When you were no longer happy with the diamond in your engagement ring that took me three years to pay off, but couldn't be seen a block away, so we had to replace it with a boulder. When the only clothes you would even consider buying had to have big name designer labels. When things became more important to you than I was."

And we're off! Kimber thought, dreading the escalation of an argument she had not intended to start. She closed her eyes and pressed her fingers to her forehead. *This is where I retort with accusations that Charlie spends more time with his alcohol than with me, that making deals under the table is easier money than conducting business that's legal and above-board—that he shuts me out and I feel so empty I fill my life with tangible things instead of that which really matters. And the list goes on and on until the fight comes full circle; nothing resolved, no steps forward, only each of us stepping back, closing off, shutting down. Another nail in the coffin of our lonely, empty marriage.*

This time, Kimber refused to take the bait. *A soft answer turneth away wrath.* A friend had quoted that Bible verse to her and urged her to try it if she wanted to start turning her marriage around. Nothing else she tried had worked. In spite of everything, Kimber still loved Charlie, still wanted things to be good between them, but she feared they had passed the point of no return. *A soft answer turneth away wrath*, she repeated to herself. There was something else her friend had talked to her about. *Forgiveness*. Yes, that was it! Forgiveness was another key to saving her marriage. Kimber opened her eyes and put her hands in her lap.

"I'm sorry, Charlie," she said in the softest voice she could manage. She reached toward him, but he pulled away. "I hope we can find some way to start over. Erase the past. If you want to sell the house… I'd rather have my husband back. You mean more to me than anything money can buy. I want us to be happy again."

Charlie, having failed in his attempt to escalate an argument, watched the last of his papers burn to ashes in cold silence, got up and stalked out of the room.

Kimber hung her head. *At least my soft answer didn't make anything worse.* She heard Charlie's footsteps going up the stairs. As soon as she heard her husband close the bedroom door, Kimber opened her purse and slipped the contents of a plastic bag into the fire. She stood and watched until nothing was left. Mesmerized by the quiet beauty of the fire, she watched in somber silence until the embers lost their glow and died, leaving a mound of ashes and a few clumps of charred wood.

As Kimber walked toward the staircase leading to the bedroom, she glimpsed her reflection in the hall mirror. She was beginning to show her age. She had gained weight since she and Charlie had married, but not a lot. She ran her hands over her mid-section and hips. Then she touched her face. Her face had gotten fuller, more rounded. If she gained five more pounds, she would need bigger clothes. That wouldn't do. She felt she could lose the extra weight if she was more careful about what she ate and exercised more. Her thick, blonde hair was pulled back into a low ponytail and clipped with a cloisonné butterfly barrette she had purchased at the gift shop at the Botanical Garden up the street. She touched the stress lines around her light green eyes.

Maybe some eye gel. I'll lose the weight and start using eye gel. Then, Charlie will want me again. I know he will. That decided, she went upstairs to bed. If the neighbors mentioned the smoke from their chimney, Kimber would tell them Charlie had gotten a chill and wasn't feeling well.

Chapter 7

The Honorable Lucas Dempsey paced the floor of his chambers, peeking through the slats of the window blinds, checking to see if by any chance the news vans had left to satisfy their bloodlust elsewhere. *If Ferguson was still having riots, then I wouldn't be dealing with those wretched reporters. The whole Ferguson mess drew the media vultures with lightning speed. I'm small potatoes in comparison.* He supposed timing was everything. And with nothing more newsworthy going on, the Lionel Cranston matter was lousy timing.

Judge Dempsey had taken an unplanned vacation the day after granting bail to Lionel Cranston. Doing so pushed his docket back a week, causing his already overloaded schedule to give his clerk a migraine, as she worked to accommodate the backlog of cases. He hoped the reporters would lock onto another story to sensationalize while he searched for ways to explain what in the world he was thinking when he granted bail for a heinous serial killer. The media vilified him for his decision. Certainly, this fiasco would cost him his position at the next election. Maybe not, though, he tried to console himself. Voters had notoriously short memories. That was part of the reason the country was in such a mess to begin with.

But he had no choice. When it came right down to it, the most important person Judge Lucas Dempsey had to protect was, well, Judge Lucas Dempsey. He did what he had to do.

He checked the blinds again, moving them apart imperceptibly. *Still a mob of reporters. Don't they ever go home?* It was almost seven o'clock. His first day back at work, he had managed to sneak through a side entrance early, before the main doors opened. He wondered if he could retreat the same way and walk several blocks to take the MetroLink, as he was sure there would be reporters waiting for him at his car. He couldn't elude them forever. He hoped he would not have to leave St. Louis. Or for that matter, leave the country.

Lucas Dempsey liked being a judge. Truth be told, he was proud of his position. He relished his entitlement to all the perks that came with the job. The money was good, but the power was better. The power was intoxicating. And there would be more money. He just had to be patient.

Carl Mendoza and Mark Vernon sat on the balcony of their two bedroom apartment sipping beer with a large plate of nachos on the table between them. Friends since high school, they had both chosen acting in college, but turned to bartending after failing to land any decent paying acting jobs. Rent and living expenses were cheaper if they split everything 50-50. Mark tended bar at the fashionable Cheshire Inn, while Carl worked at Helen Fitzgerald's, serving a noisier crowd. They made enough to meet their expenses and then some. Carl and Mark auditioned on the same day for the Mansford Mansion gig to pick up extra cash. Carl landed the part of the hapless Stefan LeBlanc, and Mark played Captain Josiah Mansford. Since Alan Cunningham announced the expansion of the 150th anniversary, they had to scramble to cover their bar-tending shifts. Both men were off work on Mondays and looked forward to their weekly ritual of relaxing and enjoying their traditional beer and nachos. The cool September evening provided the perfect ambiance for beer and nachos on the balcony.

"I think I've got everything covered," Carl said to Mark, picking up a cheese-laden chip.

Mark nodded. "I just need two more days for the month and I'll be good. It's a bummer, though, because we make so much more tending bar than we ever will working for Tightwad Alan."

Carl answered, "No joke, man. But we could also get discovered. The Mansion is sold out for the entire month-long event of the century. You never know who might be in the audience. This could be our big chance." Carl took a gulp of beer and leaned back in his chair, propping his feet on the balcony rail.

"The star of the show ought to be the guy that croaked. He's the only reason we have the sold out audiences to play to," Mark chuckled. "But you're right. The Muny Opera and the Fox Theater use local talent for fill-ins and small roles. And seriously, man, we're the only people down there who know how to act. Like, what planet did Ava come from?"

"She looks just like the portrait of Annalise. Scary, ain't it? She's pretty as they come, but she sure can't act, and I think she's a little nuts anyway. And Mariah? Overdid it just a bit on the off-stage screaming, I'd say." Carl straightened his chair and scooped up more nachos.

"Yeah. But at least *she* wasn't hired as an actress. Alan's too cheap to hire everyone he needs, so he makes the rest of the staff fill in. Brilliant, huh? Get a load of Jasmine. What a dish! So what's her story?"

"Yeah, and what is she doing working for Mansford Mansion? She ought to be a cover girl. Did you get her phone number?" Carl leaned back again, crossing his feet on the balcony railing.

"I don't stand a chance," Mark chuckled. He swallowed a mouthful of beer and assumed the same position as his friend. "She's way outta my league."

"Can you believe it was him—Harrington, who died? I about tossed my cookies."

"Do you think he recognized you?"

"With all the stage make-up and slicked down hair? Nah."

"Did you recognize him?"

Carl shifted in his seat and looked away.

"Carl?"

Mariah Flores kicked off her shoes and rubbed her tired, aching feet. She wished she could afford a pedicure. The extra nights at Mansford Mansion would mean extra money. Maybe she would treat herself to an afternoon at the spa. She didn't know how Ava and Jasmine survived without a second job, but then, she didn't know all that much about Jasmine. Jasmine didn't talk much about herself. She seemed to realize the effect she had on men, at least the guys at the restaurant, but she did not appear to be affected by it. Mariah couldn't figure Jasmine out. She thought Jasmine seemed pleasant enough, and was always willing to help Mariah, which Mariah appreciated. It was generous of her to split her tips with Mariah that night. *That night!*

Then, there was Ava. Everyone but Alan knew Ava stole from the restaurant—napkins, toilet paper, food, that sort of thing. Mariah knew Ava lived in a rat hole of an apartment close to the Soulard area. At times, she had been tempted to offer her the extra bedroom in her house. But Ava was a weird bird and Mariah thought it best not to get too close.

Mariah had been raised by her grandparents. They were hardworking people who taught her to be proud of any honest job. Her grandparents didn't have much money and lived in a small house in Affton, a working-class suburb south of St. Louis. Poppy had taken up photography after he was injured at the factory. He got quite good at it and was even able to make a small amount of money selling photos to local magazines, including a couple to the *Post-Dispatch*. Meemow worked in the housekeeping department, first at the Drury Inn, then later at Barnes Hospital. Before they died, they executed a beneficiary deed so Mariah would always have a roof over her head, even if it was modest. The furniture was old, but well made. While Mariah had the basic necessities, she longed for more—much more.

Mariah worked part-time as a nurse's assistant at a full-skilled nursing facility in St. Louis Hills. She was on her feet all day, caring for her charges, cleaning bedpans, mopping floors slick with all types of bodily fluids, helping the residents with the basic functions of life. It was difficult work, and at the end of her thankless shift, she had just enough time to drive home, shower, change, and get to Mansford Mansion to spend even more time on her feet waiting on people with different demands.

She ran a tub of hot water and poured in Epsom salts. She soaked in the tub, refreshing the hot water every few minutes, letting the Epsom salts soothe her aches and pains. Mariah remembered that night with deep satisfaction. Edward Rupert Harrington, III was dead. The very thought made her forget her tired, achy body. Her sleep would be filled with sweet dreams. Mariah relaxed as she soaked in the comforting, warm water, dreaming of a happier future.

Father Gerard heard the clock chiming. Confessions at St. Anthony's of Padua on Meramec had been slow, as usual, but Father Gerard doubted that it was because his parishioners were behaving well. He had been a priest too many years to believe in the inherent goodness of man. The chiming of the clock announced it was time to begin preparations to retire for the evening. He opened the door of the confessional and started to leave when he heard the heavy front door of the church open and the sound of light footsteps coming toward the confessionals. He resumed his seat and waited. Better late than never, if a troubled soul sought absolution. Father Gerard was surprised to see a Sister whom he did not recognize, and was curious as to why she didn't go to her own confessor. No matter, though. His calling was for all God's people, not just those in his own parish.

The woman's voice began. "Bless me, Father, for I have sinned. It has been three weeks since my last confession and my heart is heavy."

Chapter 8

Adam sat at his desk at the station scanning the interview notes he had taken on each of the Harrington siblings. All four of them had motive and opportunity and they all benefitted from their father's death. Discrepancies were minor, with the exception that Cedric said his father often threatened to change his will. *Why say that if it isn't true?* Minor discrepancies were to be expected in any case. Points of view differed and honest people could remember the same incident in different ways. These differences, rather than muddying a picture, often served to broaden it, providing a more complete story than if only one point of view were taken. They also made the teller more credible. If you asked ten siblings what it was like growing up in a large family, you could get answers ranging from, "there was always someone to play with," to "it was always noisy and there was no privacy," to "there was never enough milk." Each person told the truth as they saw it. Problems arose when the discrepancies were out-and-out contradictory.

Adam jotted notes in the margin, as he reviewed not only the factual statements, but his impressions of the Harrington siblings. Cedric and Lucinda were the most hostile, while Roland and Esme were the most forthcoming. Hostile or honest, though, none had been very helpful. All four children had an abominable upbringing and were damaged to one extent or another. Would their father's sudden death allow for healing or would their unresolved issues deepen their wounds? Was the hostility of Cedric and Lucinda merely evidence of unfathomable pain, or indicative of guilt? On the other hand, was the apparent honesty of Roland and Esme a cover-up for guilt, or was their pain manifested in other ways unrelated to the case? Each scenario presented its own set of questions.

Captain Peterson tapped on Adam's open office door. Adam looked up and motioned for him to come in.

"Just checking in on you and your team. Everybody safe and sound on your end?"

"Taken care of, Cap." He gave Captain Peterson a thumbs up sign.

"Good." Nobody wanted any details of where the families of the Cranston case detectives were. Peterson only wanted to know that they were safe.

"Your new digs okay?" he asked Adam.

"Not exactly home," Adam shrugged. "But they'll do. What's new on Cranston?"

Peterson folded his arms. "We're confident he'll screw up. We've got a twenty-four hour watch on him. And we got an order for an ankle bracelet. A thorough search was conducted at his home in Clayton. Syringes were found, which, of course, could be explained. He is a doctor, at least technically. But no curare, no potassium—nothing that could send him back inside until trial."

Adam was unconvinced. He rolled his tongue around the inside of his cheek. "Assuming the syringes were removed, right? Not that he couldn't get more." Adam regretted his remark. He looked down at his hands. "Sorry. I'm just not feeling all that warm and cozy about this." He set his paperwork aside.

"Look," Captain Peterson began. "His license has been revoked. He isn't allowed anywhere near any hospital, nursing home, any place. And remember—Cranston began to unravel while he was incarcerated. His confidence is shaken, regardless of whatever picture Harlan Royce portrays. We believe Cranston will make a mistake sooner than later, and when he does, we'll be there to make sure he stays put away until trial."

"Let's just hope nobody gets hurt in the interim." Adam tapped his pencil on his desk.

"Agreed. I gotta ask you, Adam. Do you feel up to the Harrington murder? Are you able to give it your full attention? If you say no, I can reassign it. The other two members of the Cranston team are on paid leave. The department wanted them away from here, for their own safety. I'm offering you the same deal."

"No." Adam was resolute. "No thanks, Cap. Jenna and Amy are safe. I'll do better if I'm busy working, as long as I don't have to keep looking over my shoulder for Cranston. I've done preliminary interviews on the four Harrington siblings," he said, picking up his notes and tapping them with his finger. "I believe it has to be one of them, but in all honesty, none of them stands out from the others as being more probable. I'm still waiting to see the full autopsy report. Dr. Markham doesn't have all her results in just yet. I'd like to see if cyanide poisoning is all they found. But based on the evidence I have so far, I can't tell you I suspect one sibling more than the other."

"Have you considered that all four of them might be in cahoots together?" Captain Peterson raised an eyebrow and shifted his weight.

"Oh, yeah. That'd be most logical. They all hated their father. They all were damaged to one extent or another by him and they all benefitted from his death. But they're not exactly close. I don't see the four of them getting along together long enough to pull *anything* off, much less a murder. Roland sees his family three days a year—Christmas, Thanksgiving and Harrington's birthday. Aside from that, he's distanced himself from them as far as he can. By his own admission, he has nothing in common with his family other than DNA." He resumed tapping his desk with the eraser end of his pencil.

"So, you think Roland is out as a suspect?"

"I'd like to. He's very pleasant and he was willing to answer all my questions. Never balked and tried to be helpful." Adam paused, setting his notebook aside on his desk.

"I hear a very big but coming." The captain leaned against the door jamb.

"Yep. Roland is the only one of the four who's smart enough to plan and carry out his father's demise. Roland himself pointed that out to me."

"Helpful," Captain Peterson replied drily.

"Right. He's congenial, perfect manners, nice guy and all. Plus, he doesn't need his father's money, as he also pointed out. He's successful on his own merits. Great work ethic. Hard not to like him, except that…" Adam touched his forefinger to his pursed lips.

"Lots of dangerous psychopaths can be described the same way."

Adam laughed out loud and leaned back in his chair. "Right! Except that lots of dangerous psychopaths can be described the same way!"

"So are you leaning toward Roland then?" Captain Peterson sat down in a chair across from Adam.

"Part of me is, but…" Adam frowned.

Captain Peterson leaned forward raising his eyebrows. "But?"

"But then there's Fergus." Adam resumed tapping his pencil on the desk.

"Fergus?"

Adam folded his hands in front of him. "He's got this dog he rescued from the shelter. Not a beautiful animal by a long stretch. No pedigree, nothing special. Fergus is actually quite ugly. But Roland took pity on him and snatched him from death. Cares for him like a child, provides the best of everything. That humanizes Roland quite a bit. I can't rule him out. He's the most capable, but he seems to have the least motive."

"What about the others?"

"Esme's a mess. Bulimic, weak, sickly, spent her life trying to gain her father's approval. She's got motive out the yin yang, but

I don't think she *could* pull this off. Not physically, not mentally and not emotionally. Dr. Gerwyn said as much."

"But people can surprise you."

"Yep."

"What about Cedric? He sounds quite hostile."

Adam recoiled. "He's vile—a womanizer who treats women with the utmost disrespect. But he's also lazy, and not all that bright. Out of the four, he's the only one that insisted his father was always threatening to change his will, yet the others said Harrington was too cheap to pay a lawyer."

"Maybe the father only threatened Cedric with a will change. Possible?" Peterson asked, turning his palm upward.

Adam shrugged. "Sure. Sounds good. I don't want to get too fixated on one thing, especially if it isn't relevant. That leaves the ever lovely Lucinda. Now there's a piece of work."

"What did their records checks and credit checks show?"

Adam consulted his notes, flipping through the pages until he found what he wanted. "Roland is clean. No surprise there. Not even a parking ticket, and he's more than solvent—earned his the old fashioned way. He worked for it. Esme is like a ghost in more ways than just her appearance. She's never worked—from what it looks like, she's never even lived. She's a sad case. No friends that I can discern, no hobbies or interests. Stays holed up in that castle waiting for her next meal so she can throw it up. Cedric has had minor incursions with the law—neighbor complaints and the like—but no serious trouble. Lucinda, however, has been picked up for soliciting prostitution, marijuana possession, curfew violations and shoplifting. However, with the exception of the shoplifting, never the same charge twice."

"Almost like she's trying everything once, but not sticking with anything," Captain Peterson said, rubbing his chin.

Adam nodded in agreement. "She was hostile and uncooperative. Except for Roland, the other three live in their father's home, don't work and don't contribute anything to anybody except grief. They all have their own daddy issues and those few skirmishes with the law, but it's a big jump to go from that to premeditated murder."

Captain Peterson frowned and leaned back in his chair, pressing his fingertips together. "What about the other guests? I hate to send you chasing down a rabbit hole, but is it possible someone else at the restaurant was responsible? In other words, could more than one person have had motive, means and opportunity? Did anyone else there that night benefit from Harrington's death?"

Adam grinned sideways—a telltale sign that a nerve had been hit.

The Captain laughed out loud. "Aha! You know, don't you, that you make that face every time someone mentions something you're chewing on? I hope you don't play poker, Adam. You don't have the face for it."

Adam smiled and nodded. He looked at Captain Peterson and pointed his forefinger upward. "That's the other thing that's been bugging me, Cap. The whole night was off. I couldn't quite put my finger on it that night, and, of course, we were there for Amy's birthday. I couldn't have been more off duty. It was an unusual gathering of people at the restaurant. It seemed to me that most of them didn't belong. And I couldn't figure out why they were there."

"Go on."

"All right. *We* were there for Amy's birthday dinner. The whole haunted house thing drew her like ants to candy. We got there first, so I got to choose our table. A group of four nuns was there. One of them had been given a gift of tickets for the evening and brought her friends. They were laughing and talking and having a good time."

"There's nothing unusual about that."

"Not yet, there isn't. Then this married couple walks in, but neither one of them seemed like they wanted to be there. Man drank a lot, but who knows? Maybe they're having marital problems, or maybe they just had a fight on the way over. Then, there's a couple of guys in suits. Looked like businessmen. I thought maybe they were thinking about purchasing the place and wanted to see firsthand what they might be getting into. So far, so good, right?"

Peterson rubbed his chin and leaned back in his chair, studying Adam.

"Then the Harrington clan arrives. Now, they were several minutes late, and made a grand and noisy entrance, so it wasn't surprising that the other guests were staring at them. That could be expected. But Cap—it was more than that. Everyone in that dining room seemed to be affected by the presence of the Harringtons. I know this isn't hard evidence, but the whole room was charged with something—a negativity, a tension, I don't know." He put his hands in front of him and spread his fingers apart, shaking his head.

"Just please tell me it wasn't the ghost of Mansford Mansion, Adam, or I *am* pulling you off this case and sending you on leave."

Adam laughed. "No. Nothing otherworldly, I'm afraid. Whatever was going on was strictly of this sphere. Which reminds me. How much longer can we have the coroner hold off on the release of Harrington's autopsy results?"

"I can't have them wait much longer. The media sharks need feeding. They've been having a heyday with the ghost line, but it's getting old. I can ask for another couple of days. Plus, the weekend will buy you two more days. After that, it'll look like we're holding something back. A final rendering of homicide will send them into another frenzy. Which reminds me, Adam– I'm keeping your name out of this." The Captain wagged a finger at Adam as though he were scolding a child. "You didn't smile pretty for the cameras on the courthouse steps the other day, so if I'm asked, I'll just say we're gathering a team to investigate."

"Fine by me." Adam shrugged. "Truth means nothing to the media. Facts that don't fit their agenda are tossed aside like yesterday's trash. They're all a bunch of vultures on the lookout for the next road kill. I'll be the first to admit—I don't handle reporters very well."

"Ya think?" Captain Peterson rolled his eyes and Adam shrugged again. "So what kinds of reactions did the other guests have when Harrington died?"

"Funny. What I observed was a combination of relief and discomfort. I had hoped by now to be building a case against one or more of the Harrington children, but after a preliminary investigation, I think we may need to cast a wider net."

"Cast away, Adam. Do you want a partner to help you? Sounds like a lot for one person to take on. Even if it is you."

Adam acknowledged the compliment. "Where's Connor? I haven't seen him lately."

"He's on Cranston leave. With the twins, the new baby and the four-year old, he and his wife now have four preschoolers in addition to a ten-year old son. The department thought it was safest for everyone with a family to get outta Dodge."

"I don't blame him. Talk about a target. I work well with him, but if he's not available, I'll work on my own and keep you updated, okay? You said Bo also took leave?" Adam raised his eyebrows.

"Your team didn't take leave, Adam. We sent them away. Like I said earlier, the department would like you to agree to leave as well, but you won't be forced. It's your choice."

"I won't, and you know I won't." he folded his arms across his chest. "I'll work this case whether the department wants me to or not. My family's safe, but I cannot rest until Cranston is back where he belongs."

Captain Peterson sighed and leaned back in his chair. "That's pretty much what I expected from you. Doesn't mean I like it or I agree with it. Be careful and watch your back."

"It'll take a little longer without the others to help. But I can still get it done."

"We'll have a new bunch of rookies coming in pretty soon. Graduation is just around the corner and there are some promising new kids who'll be joining us. It'd be a great opportunity to let them help with the grunt work."

"Hope to have this closed before graduation, Cap. But thanks."

"Daily reports, Adam." The Captain pointed a finger at him. "And if you don't come into the office, I want a phone check-in, got it? I don't want you incommunicado more than twenty-four hours at a time, tops."

"Yes, sir." Adam stood and gathered his notes.

Peterson retreated to his office and turning his back toward the glass partition, picked up his phone. He kept his voice low until he saw Adam leave in the reflection of his office window. "Just like we all figured. He's predictable as the sunrise. You got any questions? Good. Get to work and keep me posted."

Alan Cunningham was fluttering again with his hands, pacing nervously, excited that once again Mansford Mansion was the scene of a crime. Adam had had enough of the theatrics and decided to put a stop to the aggravation.

"Mr. Cunningham, since the death of Edward Harrington at your establishment, how has business been?"

"Oh! Never better!" he replied clasping his hands together. "Never better!" He resumed his fluttering.

"So you admit to benefitting financially from the untimely death of one of your customers?"

Cunningham stopped fluttering and his smile faded as Adam's implication was realized. Adam admired the effect his insinuation had on the ever-annoying Alan Cunningham.

"In the brochures advertising the big 150th anniversary of the original murders, you promised something big would happen.

Were you planning all along on one of the guests leaving in a body bag? That would've been quite the big finish."

"No, no, nothing like that. We didn't even get around to it, what with Harrington lying there, and all." Cunningham threw his hands into the air. "I assure you, detective, no murder was planned here—at least not by me."

"Before that evening, how was the restaurant doing financially?" Adam took his notebook and pen out and began writing.

Cunningham stared at the floor and fidgeted, balling his fists together, then straightening out his fingers and shifting from one foot to the other. Adam waited, enjoying Cunningham's obvious discomfort.

"Not—not very well, I'm afraid. If this event didn't pull us into the black, I was going to have to close."

"So Harrington's death and the swarm of media attention it drew was the best thing this place could have hoped for?"

Adam stared hard at Cunningham, making him squirm. He wiggled, as though his body was devoid of bones. Cunningham was unable to make eye contact with Adam. Adam didn't consider him high on the list of suspects, but he enjoyed having the power to stop that infuriating fluttering.

Jasmine Jones walked by carrying fresh folded tablecloths in her arms. She began to cover the dining room tables in preparation for the evening's guests. Adam wanted to talk to her as well. He thought she seemed out of place from the moment he saw her.

"Mr. Cunningham, I want a list of names and contact information for each guest that was present that night, as well as each one of the employees working that night. I'm going to speak with Jasmine while you get that information for me."

Alan stared at Adam, unmoving.

"I meant *now*, Mr. Cunningham."

"Oh yes, of course! Of course. Right away." He jumped as though he'd been stuck with a pin and retreated to the back of the house.

Adam moved into the dining room. "Jasmine, isn't it?"

The beautiful woman looked up and set down the tablecloths. "Yes. I remember you. You were the policeman here with the cute little girl for her birthday the night Mr. Harrington died. What an awful birthday memory for a child."

Actually, she thought it was pretty cool. "Right. Here's my card."

"Oh! You're a detective. How can I help you?"

"Mr. Harrington did not die a natural death."

Jasmine Jones raised her eyebrows in genuine surprise. "Oh my! How terrible. And you're investigating? I see." She read his card and then looked back at Adam. "I didn't wait on that table. As you may recall, the Harrington family, or at least most of the family, was quite difficult. Mariah had been given their table, as well as one other. But when I saw what kind of a night she was in for, I took her other smaller table and told her I would split my tips with her. It didn't take a rocket scientist to figure out she wasn't going to make any money that night." She motioned for Adam to sit, and took a seat facing him.

"That was very kind of you." He took out his notebook.

Jasmine smiled. "It was the decent thing to do under the circumstances."

She's beautiful, well-spoken and appears well educated. Is she for real? What's up with her? Why on earth would she be waiting tables here? "Can you tell me if you saw anything out of the ordinary, particularly with the serving of Harrington's drinks or food?"

She wrinkled her nose and shook her head. "I was pretty busy that night. We're not exactly overstaffed here. We pick up our food from the kitchen and bring it out to the tables, then go back for more. That's pretty cut and dried. And the timing has to coincide with where we are in the play, so we're always on the move. As to drinks, the servers can take orders and bring them, or, during the intermissions and before the show starts, our guests are welcome to go to the bar themselves. No one else got sick from the food, so am I to assume Mr. Harrington was poisoned?" She leaned toward Adam.

Adam ignored the question. "Are poisons kept on the premises?"

"Yes, but not in the kitchen. We keep rat poison and bug poison in Alan's office." She leaned closer to Adam and lowered her voice. "He's too cheap to hire an exterminator. And then there are the cleaning supplies. I doubt he uses organics, so I would assume there are poisonous substances in whatever he uses to clean."

"I see. And how long have you worked here, Jasmine?"

"I'm only here for the current season."

"That's curious," he started, but was interrupted by Alan Cunningham hurrying into the dining room.

"Here's the information you asked for." Alan shoved a piece of paper in front of Adam's face.

Adam took the paper and scanned it. Cunningham had complied with his request in a neat and orderly manner.

"Thank you, Mr. Cunningham. That will be all for now. I need a few more minutes of Jasmine's time, and then she may resume her duties. If you will excuse us?"

"Oh, of course. Certainly." He resumed his fluttering and left them alone in the dining room.

Adam flipped a page in his notebook. "Jasmine, what's your full name and address?"

"Jasmine Alyssa Jones, 212 North Kingshighway, #5-B."

The address sounded familiar to Adam, but he couldn't place it. "And why are you only working here for the 150th anniversary season? It's no more than a few short weeks, right?"

Another display of perfect white teeth. "I can assure you, Detective Trent, it has nothing to do with Mr. Harrington's death."

"Humor me." He studied Jasmine. She was self-assured, confident, but not cocky. And unlike Alan Cunningham, she did not seem at all intimidated by him. Adam suddenly remembered why her address was familiar to him. 212 North Kingshighway was the Chase Park Plaza. *Awfully ritzy digs for a waitress. Awfully ritzy digs for anyone.*

"You know the history of Mansford Mansion?" Jasmine asked.

"Everyone in St. Louis knows the history of this place." He sat back in his chair.

"I'm a direct descendant of Hettie Jefferson. Her great-great, five, greats, if you want to count them-granddaughter." She relaxed, sitting back in her chair and crossing her legs.

It was Adam's turn to be surprised. Captain Peterson was right about Adam. He had no poker face. His eyes bugged out and his jaw dropped as he sat up in his chair. Then he cocked his head sideways and looked at her with doubt. "Her daughter, Ginnie, was killed. She was a very young child. There were no descendants."

Jasmine crossed her hands in her lap. "There were. Hettie Jefferson had a son named Ezra. Hettie's husband was white and was killed trying to protect her and Ezra from an angry mob. Interracial marriages were quite taboo in the 1860s, as you know. Ezra lived elsewhere, working to provide for his mother and little sister. Few people knew about him. After Hettie and Ginnie were killed, Ezra, who was a teenager by then, was left orphaned and alone. Although young, he was smart and not afraid of hard work. He continued moving north and settled in New York, married a white woman and started his own family. They had several children, and many of them married white people. As America grew into a larger melting pot, Ezra's descendants intermarried. By the time the family tree reached my generation, there were several different races in the branches." She laughed. "The Jefferson family reunions look pretty unique."

That explained why Adam could not identify her heritage. "Are you from New York, then?" Adam found her story fascinating. Her easy manner put him at ease and he relaxed, sitting back in his chair.

"Connecticut," she replied.

"So, Miss Jones, what brought you to St. Louis? At this time?"

"Actually, it's Dr. Jones."

Again, Adam was surprised. "You're a doctor? And you're waiting tables?"

She flashed another broad smile. "I have a Ph.D. in psychology. I'm doing research on the effects of perception and expectation on reality." She leaned forward and lowered her voice. "Please don't tell Alan. He's clueless."

Adam nodded, intrigued. "Go on."

Jasmine became animated as she spoke. Her eyes sparkled as she wriggled in her seat. "I've known about the history of this house and the story of Ezra, the Underground Railroad and my own genealogy since I was a child. I knew about the fifty year curse, as some have called it, so I wanted to come to Mansford Mansion and observe firsthand the people who would be attending in expectation of something otherworldly, as part of my research. Acting as a waitress provided a great way to watch people unobtrusively. For example, your daughter's eyes couldn't have gotten any bigger, while you appeared bored. Totally unimpressed." She tucked her chin and raised an eyebrow at him.

Adam chuckled. "She was enthralled. I was here because it was her birthday, and my daughter and my wife ganged up on me."

"That was obvious," she answered drily, lowering her eyelids. "I'm collaborating with two other colleagues on this project. We're compiling our findings from so-called hauntings all over the country. People come to Mansford Mansion expecting something—they hope something spooky or otherworldly will occur. Or, on the other hand, they come expecting something gimmicky because they're not believers and wish to affirm their beliefs that such talk of ghosts is either fraudulent or for the simple minded. Every night, there's a mix of believers and scoffers. But most of the people who come to these types of events do believe there are ghosts, so they come with their own perceptions already in place. I observe everyone, and after each evening, I dictate what happened and people's reactions. I put a new tape in every night and when I return home to Connecticut, our department secretary will type and categorize all the dictation."

"I see. So what was the big finish supposed to be?" Adam resumed taking notes.

Jasmine rolled her eyes. "Because of my connection to Hettie and Ginnie, I was supposed to reveal my true identity at the end of the dinner. It was supposed to be dramatic and eerie. The lights were going to dim, and Alan had rigged the chandelier so he could make it swing as I spoke. As though the ghost was acknowledging my presence and giving me credibility, some such nonsense as that."

"But none of that happened because…"

"Because of our guest's demise, of course."

"So you spent that evening observing people. Did you see anything at all that struck you as odd or out of place?" Adam moved his chair closer to Jasmine.

Jasmine Jones nodded. "Detective Trent, I think just about everything and everyone that night seemed odd and out of place. That was my impression. But if you want to know if I saw anyone tampering with the food or drink, then no. I'm sorry I can't be of more help." She stood and began unfolding tablecloths and placing them over the tables.

Adam was not about to let a trained observer of human nature return to setting tables after admitting she thought everything was odd. He stepped around her. "Jasmine, er, Dr. Jones," he began.

"Jasmine is fine."

"Would you mind elaborating on that?"

"Not at all." Jasmine smoothed each tablecloth as she straightened them on the tables. "Except for your daughter and the nuns, who were enjoying an evening out, none of the guests seemed like they were here for the actual anniversary event. None of them really fit. At least it looked that way to me. Nobody seemed all that interested in the house or its history, and I remember wondering what even brought them here in the first place. And when the Harrington clan arrived—well, the air itself chilled. And *that* was no ghost."

My thoughts exactly. "Anything else?"

"No. That's about it."

Adam helped her straighten the tablecloth on the large table. "Jasmine, you have my card. Would you please call me if you remember anything that happened, or was said, that you might not have thought of now? I'd sure appreciate it. Thanks for your time."

She looked at the card again and slipped it into her pocket.

"Of course. I hope I've helped in some way."

Adam sat in his car outside Mansford Mansion studying the list Alan Cunningham provided. It was neatly typed and included more information than Adam had requested. He was satisfied to see his questions had rattled the irritating Cunningham, who couldn't have been more cooperative if he had tried. *It's almost as if Cunningham is going out of his way to show he had nothing to do with Harrington's murder.*

Adam checked his watch. Four o'clock. He thought he might have enough time to make it downtown to the office of Friedman and Meyers to question them, but if he was caught in traffic, he could end up making the trip for nothing. Unless there was a Cardinals game, the downtown crowd headed for home by no later than five o'clock sharp. Rush hour had already begun, so he decided downtown would not be the most productive choice. In due course, he would interview everyone, not that he had much hope of achieving any real results. Statistically, it had to be one of the Harrington siblings, but he could not shake off the reactions of the other patrons he had observed the night of the murder. He scanned the list again.

The Dennison family lived in South St. Louis. By the time Adam reached Flora Place, he figured they would be home from work. He ran their information on his computer to see if anything of interest appeared. A couple of traffic tickets popped up. Adam thought perhaps a DWI might show, given the amount of alcohol they consumed, but Mr. Dennison was either capable of holding a large quantity of alcohol, or he allowed his wife to drive if he was plastered. Or maybe he just plain got lucky and was never caught. On a whim, Adam ran their credit and was surprised to find their score was not as high as he would have expected from a couple that could afford a home on Flora Place.

He headed south, resigning himself to be stuck in rush hour traffic at its usual glacial speed. Good time to talk to Jenna. He missed her sweet, melodic voice.

"Hey baby, how's my beautiful girl?" he asked when she picked up the phone.

"Would it help if I tracked down Cranston and put the world out of its misery all by myself?" her strained voice asked through clenched jaws.

Uh oh, trouble. Now what? Please don't let it be Blue and the chickens again.

"What's going on, Jen?"

He heard her take a breath and sigh. "Amy's got a black eye, for starters."

"What? What happened?"

"She got in a fight!"

"Yeah? Did she win?"

"Adam! Not funny." Jenna was not amused. Adam pictured her lovely face wearing her famous exasperated look, brows knit and lips pressed together, and felt as if she was close enough to be sitting next to him. She was still beautiful when she was mad.

"Honey, Amy doesn't have a violent bone in her body. What was the fight about?"

"Some kid in class named Jason. It's always a Jason. Have you ever noticed that? What is it about boys named Jason?"

Adam suppressed a laugh. Jenna was getting worked into quite a state and he needed the comic relief. Since she couldn't see him, he knew his shins were safe from the painful kick of Jenna's trigger happy shoe. "Okay, so if we're ever blessed with another baby, we won't name him Jason. What happened?"

Another audible sigh. "This Jason kid made some disparaging remark about policemen. Amy took offense and he wouldn't take it back. Amy stood her ground and things escalated from there and it turned into quite a brawl."

"How big was this kid? Amy's just a squirt of a thing. Was she hurt?"

"He's twice her size, but she got a lot of good licks in. He went to the E.R., but Amy was treated by the school nurse. They're both suspended for three days."

"Put her on the phone." He did his best to sound stern. The traffic inched forward.

"Hi, Daddy!"

"Amy? I hear you got in a fight."

"Jason said bad things about the police."

"Peanut, you don't have to stick up for me. Sticks and stones, you know. My skin is a lot thicker than that, and yours should be, too."

"I'm sorry, Daddy. But I didn't like what he said, and I *don't* like this school and I wanna go *home* and I want my *own* school and my *own* friends, and my *own* teachers and I'm tired of pretending my name is Jessica!" With each objection, Amy's voice climbed higher in pitch and louder in volume. Having made her point, she lowered her tone. "And besides, I'm glad I hit him. My black eye looks pretty cool."

"I'm sure it does. Did you hit him with your thumb outside your fist like I taught you? Not inside your fist where your thumb could break?"

Amy's voice brightened. "Yes, Daddy!"

"That's my girl. So didja win?"

"You bet I did. All I got was a black eye. I did all the stuff you told me to do and I whomped him good!"

All right! That's my kid! "Okay, Amy. But I don't want to hear of you fighting any more, do you understand? I taught you what to do if you needed to defend yourself, not so you could go out and pick a fight. I want you to remember who you are and whose you are. You are a lady and I expect you to act like a lady. Can you imagine your mother getting into a fight?"

Amy giggled. "No, Daddy."

"Right, peanut. You couldn't have a better example to follow than your mom. Now I don't want to hear of anything like this happening again, do you understand?"

"Yes, Daddy. When are you coming back to Gomer and Oompah's house?"

"Next time I get a day off. Should be this weekend. Now put your mom on the phone. I love you."

"I love you, too."

Adam heard noise as the phone was being exchanged from daughter to mother.

Jenna's voice returned.

"Jenna, our little girl is sounding pretty stressed. I was afraid of the toll this situation would take on our family. You have your teaching certificate. Would you consider home-schooling until we're back in our own home?"

"Yeah," she replied. "She's unhappy at school, no question about that. I think having her help on the farm and doing her studies here might be better for her. Plus, I'd feel better knowing she's safe with us. We have all her books here. When we get her home, she can take the tests and do any catch-up work if she needs it. She misses you. So do I."

By the time they finished their conversation, Adam had arrived in the Shaw neighborhood.

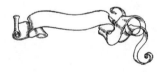

"What do you mean, there's been another delay? For heaven's sake, woman, it's a probate case with one heir! The forms have been sent in three times. The heir is the executor. There's only one person involved here. *One person!* This isn't rocket science. It's way past time to close that estate."

"I'm sorry, sir. Our computer system was hacked. We're working as fast as we can to repair the damage and update our records. The Cook County Court appreciates your patience."

Judge Lucas Dempsey slammed the phone down. He was shaking with anger and his face was red. He regretted yelling and losing his temper with the court clerk. A tirade like that could make him memorable. He should have held his tongue. *Lousy timing, the whole wretched mess.* He could not understand why his father had moved to Chicago, of all places, to live out his remaining years. He had pleaded with him to stay in the area, but the old man was stubborn as a mule. The entire estate closing would have been taken care of quickly and without fuss if Reginald Dempsey would have simply stayed in town where Lucas knew every judge for a hundred miles. The only judge Lucas Dempsey knew in Chicago had joined the growing list of Illinois governors languishing in prison.

Everything had gone according to plan until Lionel Cranston got caught being stupid. From that point forward, things began to unravel. And now there was an umpteenth delay in releasing the assets of his father's estate. He was so close, *so close* to having everything. And now, he feared, he was even closer to losing everything.

Chapter 9

Adam stood on the spacious front porch of the fine brick home of Charlie and Kimber Dennison. Like the other homes on Flora Place, the Dennison's home was well maintained, although, Adam knew, these old homes always needed some type of work done. Landscaping on the Flora Place homes was professionally sculpted, with beautiful manicured lawns and gardens planned to bloom three seasons a year. Flora Place remained a street of stately homes, reflecting the elegance and charm of a bygone era, in stark contrast to its immediate surroundings, which projected various stages of rehabbing. The Shaw neighborhood was a fascinating conglomeration of well-to-do professionals, working class folks, young families, retirees, artsy fartsies, drug dealers and other criminals, all living together as neighbors of a sort.

Adam pressed the doorbell and listened as melodious chimes echoed through the home. *Jenna would love to have a doorbell that chimed like that. That'll make a great welcome home gift.* He heard footsteps approaching and Kimber Dennison opened the door. She was well dressed in a green pantsuit that accentuated her green eyes and creamy peach-toned skin.

"Good evening, Mrs. Dennison? I'm Detective Trent from St. Louis Homicide. I'm investigating the murder of Edward Harrington and I'd like to speak with you and your husband, if he's home." He handed her his card. As she took it, Adam noted a faint shaking in her hands. Her color paled. She swallowed and opened the door wider, allowing him to enter.

"Murdered? Oh, my! I thought it was the food! The meal was enough to kill anyone! Please come in and have a seat. I'll go get my husband. Can I get you something to drink?"

Yeah, right. Someone on my little list is a murderer and poisoning drinks is his or her m.o. "No thank you, ma'am. I'm fine. I just need a few minutes of your time." *At least I hope it's just a few minutes. I'm getting hungry.* He missed Jenna's cooking and salivated at the thought of her homemade chicken pot pie. He could smell something tasty wafting through the house from the Dennison's kitchen. He would try not to keep them from dinner too long. He hoped the couple would remember seeing something that they may not have realized was important, but would be useful to Adam in his investigation.

"How did you come to be at the restaurant that evening?"

"We got a coupon in the mail," Kimber said. "It was a great deal. I thought it might be fun to go out with Charlie. He works very hard, you know. I'll go get him now." She left Adam alone in the living room.

She was gone several minutes. Adam looked around. The flooring was real hardwood with area rugs placed under tables and chairs. The furniture was a mix of contemporary and good quality antiques. The home seemed sparsely furnished, which made the rooms appear even larger. While they didn't seem to have much in the way of possessions, what the Dennisons did own looked tasteful and expensive. Adam noted ashes in the fireplace and thought it hadn't been chilly enough for a fire. *Who builds a fire in St. Louis in September?*

Kimber returned with an unhappy looking Charlie. Adam got the impression they had been arguing. While the house was a good size, Adam knew it wasn't so large that it would have taken such a long time to find another human in it. They both appeared nervous.

Charlie spoke first. Adam thought Mr. Dennison exerted too much effort to sound authoritative and wondered where this interview might lead him. *Hopefully, to an arrest, so I can concentrate on Cranston and getting my family home.* "My wife tells me that man at the restaurant was murdered? News to us."

Oh, really. "Did you know Edward Harrington?"

Charlie answered quickly—too quickly. "No! Of course not! How on earth would we know that man?"

Just a touch defensive, are we? Adam scribbled in his notebook. "Are you sure about that?" He stared hard at Charlie for several moments. Charlie stared back at him, determined to hold his ground.

Adam turned to Kimber. "Mrs. Dennison, did you know Edward Harrington?"

Kimber's eyes widened and her eyebrows arched. "Oh! Oh no! No, no, no."

Methinks thou dost protest too much. She's on the verge of tears. Interesting. Adam homed in on Kimber Dennison like a hawk swooping down to snatch a chipmunk dinner. "I think you did, Mrs. Dennison. Edward Harrington was murdered, and it has female killer written all over it. What I don't know is why he was murdered. Why don't you save us all a lot of time and tell me why you hated Edward Harrington so much you killed him?"

Kimber looked up at him with wide eyes, tears streaming down her face, her lips parted. She was trembling.

Deer in headlights. Amateurs. Like taking candy from a baby.

"What was your relationship with the victim, Mrs. Dennison?" he pressed her.

"That's enough," shouted Charlie Dennison. "You're harassing my wife. Leave her alone or I'll file a complaint against you. She doesn't know anything."

Adam turned his full attention to the raging bull in the living room. He remained calm, but firm. "This is a murder investigation, Mr. Dennison, and one or both of you are impeding it. We can continue this down at the station, if you prefer. Then you can explain to your neighbors why you both left your home with a policeman when you should've been sitting down to dinner. The choice is yours."

Adam silently prayed that the Dennisons would not lawyer up. He had no real evidence against them. But their defensive reactions told Adam there was gold to be found and he was not giving up. If they got a lawyer, he might as well go home. He had nothing other than their suspicious behavior, but he was banking on them not knowing that. There was treasure here and Adam was not going to stop digging until he unearthed something of value.

"My wife didn't kill that pig. Neither did I. But we're not sorry he's dead. The world's a better place without him."

"What was your relationship with him?"

"He was going to ruin Charlie's business," Kimber interrupted. "We would've lost everything. Edward Harrington was an evil man. We had no idea he'd be at the dinner theater that night. I wish we'd never gone!"

"All right. We're finally getting somewhere. What made you decide to go to Mansford Mansion that night? Neither of you strikes me as someone interested in haunted houses. Why were you there?"

"Like I told you, we got a coupon in the mail. It was such a good deal and I thought maybe if Charlie and I could just get out for a little fun, then maybe..." her voice trailed off.

Adam did not press her. He remembered seeing her reach for her husband's hand that night and how unresponsive Charlie had been, choosing his alcohol over her. She stole a quick glance toward the fireplace. Adam noticed.

"How was Harrington threatening to ruin your business, Mr. Dennison?"

"He was outbidding Charlie on a job—a big job that we were depending on," Kimber answered before Charlie could take a breath.

That's not it. Why fess up now and then lie? "Is that so, *Mister* Dennison? Can you elaborate on that for me?"

Charlie's shoulders slumped. He covered his face with his hands and sat down heavily on the sofa. Kimber rushed to his side and put her arm around him. Adam saw bewilderment written across her face as she knit her brows together and tilted her head sideways. Her lips parted, but no words formed. *They don't have their stories straight. This should be interesting.*

Adam walked purposefully to the fireplace, and bent down for a closer look. "A little early in the year for a fire, don't you think?" he asked, staring at the couple.

"Charlie wasn't feeling well. He took a chill and wanted to warm himself by the fire. These big old houses get drafty," Kimber explained.

"Don't insult my intelligence, Mrs. Dennison. I've been a detective far too long. What was Edward Harrington doing to ruin your business, Mr. Dennison?"

Defeated, Charlie Dennison sat slumped on the sofa, his elbows on his knees, his face in his hands. He removed his hands and Adam saw how red his face had become. His eyes were bloodshot and teary. Adam watched Mrs. Dennison, noting concern and confusion in her expression, as her brows furrowed even closer together over wide eyes. She reached toward him, but pulled back. *These two don't talk to each other. They're not even on the same page.*

"Look. We can do this the easy way or we can do this the hard way. It's your choice. But I'm going to get answers one way or another." Adam took his cell phone from his pocket and began to punch in numbers.

"What are you doing? Hey! Who are you calling?" Kimber sounded frantic.

"Looks to me like you were burning evidence here," Adam said, pointing to the fireplace. "I'm calling my Captain and we're going to get a warrant and have our crime scene techs go over every ash in this fireplace."

"No!" Kimber and Charlie both blurted out in unison. They looked at each other in surprise and Charlie sunk deeper into the sofa.

"I'm listening," Adam said. "I've got all night, for that matter." He closed his cell phone, sat down on a loveseat across from the couple, crossed his legs and leaned back, relaxed.

"Pictures," Charlie blurted out and began to sob.

Kimber shot him a quizzical look and jumped backward, her mouth flying open. "You knew about the pictures? How? I burned them."

"What are you *talking* about, Kimber?" he asked, horrified. He jerked his head up and looked at her with bulging eyes.

She wrung her hands and looked around the room, then looked at Adam. Tears began to roll down her cheeks and her lower lip quivered. "It was the first time. I'd never done anything so stupid in my life."

"What was that, Mrs. Dennison?" Adam was beginning to feel confused at the unexpected turn in the conversation. He felt his edge slipping.

"I was at the mall. West County Mall. There was a beautiful scarf from Roberto Cavalli. He's one of my favorite designers. I wanted it so bad. Charlie and I—we spent so much money on this house, there just wasn't anything left over after all the bills. I just wanted something nice. It was so stupid. I took it and slipped it into my purse."

"You shoplifted? A *scarf*?" Charlie asked her throwing his hands up. "Oh, what have I done?" he wailed, burying his face in his hands again.

Adam's confusion grew. He wasn't sure who was confessing to what at this point, but the conversation had taken a turn in a surprising direction. He decided to let it play out.

"I was caught. Of course. It was so humiliating. They took photos of me and I had to fill out paperwork. I was so embarrassed I wanted to die. But before the store security called the police, this man, I'd never seen him before, but it was Edward Harrington, walked in and paid for the scarf, and the extra charges the store wanted to let me go, everything, and took all the documentation. I didn't know who he was at the time, but he seemed to know me. I don't know how. He made me pay him money every month to keep what I did a secret. I was afraid of losing Charlie, and I didn't want a record. If Charlie found out, I thought he would leave me. That man mailed me photographs of the charges against me, and my photo —I looked terrible in it. He mailed those to me every month, a week before I had to pay him, just to remind me."

Charlie stared at his wife with his mouth hanging open.

"Then, when Charlie told me the same man was trying to ruin his business, I thought Harrington was toying with me. I just wanted to die."

"That's not a reason to kill him." Adam said.

"I didn't kill him. I didn't kill anybody!"

Adam took a deep breath and exhaled leaning his head back. He turned to Charlie Dennison. "Mr. Dennison, I don't think we've heard your side of this. What pictures were *you* referring to and how was Harrington threatening your business? The truth, please. Your dinner smells good and I wouldn't want it to burn."

"Oh, it's in the Crockpot, it can't burn," Kimber said.

Charlie Dennison looked away and was silent for several moments. He hung his head and mumbled, "Kimber, I'm sorry. I'm so, so sorry."

"No, Charlie! Please no! You didn't kill that man! You couldn't have! I know you could not have done that," she pleaded. She leaned into her husband and ran her hands down his arm.

"No," he sighed. "What I did was worse. Much worse." He sat, his eyes closed, his brow furrowed. A long silence followed. Charlie took a deep breath. When he exhaled, Adam could see him tremble. "Kimber, I had an affair. I wish it had never happened. I can't tell you how sorry I am."

Kimber's eyes spilled over with fresh tears. She withdrew from her husband and looked at him in disbelief, shaking her head. "Another woman? No! No, no, *no*! After everything we've been through together? You turned to someone else—when I was always here for you? How could you?" Her hands shook and she held them to keep them still. Her lips trembled as another river of tears streamed down her face, mingling with her make-up, and dripped off her cheeks, staining her blouse. Kimber stood and backed away from Charlie, pacing the room, wringing her hands. She sat down in a chair by the fireplace with her face buried in her hands. Her shoulders convulsed as she sobbed.

Charlie's simple confession explained everything—his angry outbursts, his refusal to accept her touch, his withdrawal from her no matter how she tried to show him love. Kimber heard her friend's voice in her head talking about forgiveness, urging her to forgive her husband. But her friend had counseled her about forgiving his surly behavior. Her friend could not have known what Charlie was guilty of. This was something terrible. Charlie had cheated on her, had broken his wedding vow. Betrayed her trust. She broke into more sobs, until she started coughing.

Adam noticed a box of tissues on an end table and handed them to her. She blew her nose and wiped her eyes. She sat with her eyes closed, thinking. She thought about leaving him, but Charlie had been the only man she ever loved. How could she forgive this? But, Kimber reasoned, if you sincerely forgive someone, surely, you forgive all. Wasn't that the way God forgave us?

Kimber stood from the chair with some effort to steady herself, walked to the sofa and sat next to her husband. "Charlie, you have hurt me—more than I could have ever imagined. But still—I love you. If our marriage is going to work, I must forgive you. There is no other way." She reached for him and he leaned against her, crying.

The couple held each other as they both cried. After several minutes, Charlie collected himself. "Harrington learned about the affair. I don't know how, but he sent photos to my office. He was blackmailing me. He threatened to mail the photos to you if I didn't pay up. There was no business deal. I made that up because I couldn't tell you the truth. I never wanted you to find out. I swear, Kimber, that affair was short-lived. I haven't seen that woman in months, but Harrington wouldn't give up. I've been so ashamed. I pushed you away, and wanted to make all of our problems your fault. I couldn't deal with my own guilt. I had to pay him every month and we were running out of money."

"Did you know Edward Harrington was going to be at the dinner theater, Mr. Dennison?"

"Heavens no! If I had known, I never would've gone. I was so upset when I saw him there. I thought he was going to tell Kimber everything."

"And I thought he was going to tell *you* everything," she sobbed.

Adam figured it was unlikely that either of the Dennisons walked around carrying cyanide in their possession on the off chance they might encounter someone they wanted to murder. What looked like a promising lead was fizzling out like flat soda. Adam asked if they had observed anything out of the ordinary or could provide any helpful information, but Charlie and Kimber had each been so wrapped up in their own fears, they had not been inclined to notice anything else. *Another dead end.* He left the Dennisons to patch up their marriage, thanking them for their time. He saw himself out, closing the door behind him.

It was past dinner time and Adam was hungry—too hungry to think clearly. He headed back to Highway 44, taking the Jamieson exit to his own neighborhood. He knew he couldn't go home—at least, not yet. Not with the Cranston threat hanging over him and his team. But he could still get dinner where he chose. He stopped by Mom's Deli on Jamieson for his favorite sandwich, a Beef and Philly on Rye. Despite the late hour, Mom's Deli had a line in front of the counter. Adam salivated as he watched the customers in front of him choose the meats and cheeses to be placed on fresh soft bread. His stomach growled in anticipation as he inhaled the smells of dinner. At last, it was his turn. The kid behind the counter beamed when he saw Adam and asked, "Your usual, sir?"

"You got it, Theo. How've you been?"

"All As and a B, sir."

"Very good. But it's only September. Keep that up for when I ask you again in May, right?"

The teenager flashed a toothy grin and gave Adam two thumbs up. He turned to prepare Adam's dinner.

A year ago, Adam had caught Theo running out of Donut Drive-in without paying. He caught the teen with no effort and drove him home to Theo's hard-working single mom, who hung her head in embarrassment that a cop had brought her son home. She marched Theo back to the donut shop and made him pay double for what he had taken. Adam believed Theo had potential and had taken an interest in him. Theo's mom was grateful for a positive male role model for her son and Theo responded well to the attention. Adam had talked to the owner at Mom's Deli, personally vouching for the kid, and Theo was hired for weekends and two school nights a week. He was an ace employee, and Adam checked in from time to time to be sure all was well. That, and Theo made the best Beef and Philly on Rye sandwich in town.

Adam ate his dinner at an outside table, savoring the fresh roast beef with the hot cream cheese, grilled onions, thin slices of pickles and thick gravy, soaking through the marbled rye bread. A small container of potato salad and a slice of Mom's Deli chocolate cheesecake topped off a dinner that was almost as good as something Jenna would put on the table. Almost. But not quite.

Jenna. His rock, his best friend and partner for life. Adam's heart ached from missing her and he wondered how much longer she, Amy and Blue could hold up under the strain. Amy's fight earlier was not a good sign. He hoped that keeping her home would have a calming effect. He hoped this would all be over soon and they could resume life as they knew it. Adam cursed Dr. Cranston, his attorney, Harlan Royce and Judge Dempsey. He also wondered how many chickens he would owe his parents when this was over.

Adam was tired. It had been a long day and he was no closer to cracking the Harrington murder than when the day started. He drove to the safe house to organize his notes. He would type his report tomorrow.

Darkness was settling over St. Louis. The morning would hail a hard-earned and long-anticipated Friday. Traffic going into the downtown area would be light. However, leaving downtown on a Friday afternoon brought exponentially more traffic. It was an every week phenomenon. The weather for the upcoming weekend promised to be stellar, which meant employers all over the area would have a large number of people calling in sick. It was common knowledge that nobody chose to live in St. Louis because of the weather. There was more lousy weather than good. Summers were hot and humid, winters were freezing and springs tended to be rainy. Autumn, the most beautiful season in St. Louis, was the shortest. So on the rare occasions that it was gorgeous outside, children and adults alike played hooky. It was a pleasant final thought that Adam entertained before allowing sleep to overtake his weary body and mind until morning.

A car turned slowly off the street, parked at the side of St. Ambrose Church on Wilson Avenue, and extinguished its headlights. Under a street lamp, the silhouette of a woman could be seen exiting the car, looking around her and hurrying into the church. The woman stood behind a pillar in the vestibule and surveyed the sanctuary. St. Ambrose was a very different cathedral from Our Lady of Sorrows, where she worked. But she did not dare go to her own church. Satisfied that St. Ambrose was empty, she entered. She noted the light in the confessional was on, and stepped inside. "Bless me Father, for I have sinned. It has been eleven days since my last confession, and my spirit is burdened."

Chapter 10

Mike Davey wiped down the counter of the bar at Mansford Mansion. Tonight had been the most lucrative yet. He had made enough in tips to make his final car payment and still have some spending money left over. He had almost decided to look for work elsewhere, being tired of short term jobs that offered nothing better than a miniscule paycheck. So many companies boasted that they hired veterans, but Mike found that the six years he served in the United States Navy had failed to give him any advantage in securing decent employment. He was the only employee to whom Alan paid a half-way decent wage. He was skilled at making good drinks and knew how to stretch the liquor without sacrificing taste. Mike was a big guy, muscular and in perfect shape with light brown hair, blue eyes and an amiable personality when tending bar. But his size and strength, coupled with full sleeve tattoos on his arms, gave him a formidable impression which allowed him to double as a bouncer—a job he was equally good at.

Ava Montel walked by on her way out. "Good night, Mike. See you tomorrow."

Mike waved and watched her leave. He thought Ava was beautiful. A little flighty and nervous. She couldn't act, and it was no secret she got the job because of her looks. He had tried to get close to her, but her response had been polite indifference. She was friendly enough with Mike, but unresponsive to anything more. Either that, or she was clueless, but he doubted it. Ava seemed grateful whenever he slipped her an occasional bottle of wine, but as much as he desired a closer relationship with her, it was clear she was not interested.

He thought she had acted strange the night that nasty old guy died. Edward Harrington was the only customer Mike had ever had who complained about one of his drinks. Mike shrugged it off. He had plenty of customers who were friendly and likeable, and lately, his customers had been extra generous in their tips. He had determined that one cranky grouch wasn't going to ruin his evening. And then the guy up and died. Mike had tried to move a little closer to Ava, thinking maybe she would draw close to him with the shock of a death right under their noses. Instead, she flitted about like a nervous Nellie with an odd look on her face. She avoided eye contact, he remembered, more so than usual. Her pace quickened and Mike thought she looked as though she were trying not to smile.

Mike remembered that night pretty well, and how that creepy Harrington guy, the son with the oily hair, had hung around the bar, leering at the women. Mike thought he saw the guy pinch Mariah on her bottom once, when the crowd got thick, but Mariah seemed to have not noticed, so Mike figured he must have been mistaken. For a smaller crowd, there seemed to be a lot of drinking. Now, with all the publicity the Harrington death brought, Mansford Mansion was packed to capacity. And the tips were rolling in.

Mike drove home, thinking how nice it would be to have Ava sitting next to him in his car that would be paid off Monday morning. He didn't know where Ava lived, only that she lived alone in an apartment in South City, around the Soulard neighborhood. He thought about her beautiful face. What was it he had read on her face that night? Shock? Sorrow? Relief? Yes! It was relief.

Carl Mendoza and Mark Vernon parked in front of their building and lumbered up the steps to the third floor apartment they shared. Carl went to the fridge and pulled out two beers while Mark kicked off his shoes, plopped down on the sofa and stuck his feet on the coffee table. He clicked on the remote and began routine channel surfing. Carl handed him a beer.

"Thanks, man," he said, guzzling half the bottle. "All these hours are starting to get to me." He yawned.

"Ditto, buddy," Carl said, plopping down on the far side of the adjoining cushion. "I'll be glad when the month is over and we can go back to tending bar. Never thought I'd say *that!*"

"Yeah. Working two jobs with long hours is getting old fast. I'm still hoping someone is out there looking for talent. I don't want to be in my fifties and still waiting to be discovered."

"I hear ya, bro."

Mark stretched before taking another swig of his beer. "I heard Alan talking to Jasmine this evening. Sounds like old Harrington had a little help getting into the hereafter."

Carl stopped his beer bottle midway to his lips, then set it down. He stared straight ahead. "Why would Alan say something like that?" he asked flatly.

Mark shrugged. "Seems there's a detective nosing around."

Carl did not move.

"Carl? Hey, are you okay?"

"Fine," Carl said. "It's been a long day. For that matter, it's been a long week. I got double duty tomorrow, so we won't be able to carpool to work. I'm tired. Goin' to bed." He rose, swallowed the rest of his beer, and leaving Mark alone on the sofa, retreated into his bedroom.

Mark channel surfed a few more minutes and then switched off the television. His own bed was calling, so he rose to answer the call. But as he tried to give in to the weariness creeping through his body, he found himself worrying about his friend in the bedroom down the hall. He hoped Carl hadn't done something stupid. Or illegal.

Ava Montel closed the door to her tiny apartment and locked it behind her. She was so tired she thought she might drop to the floor before she made it into bed. The extra hours were good only because there was more money and Alan had at least kept his word about paying on time. But she was exhausted. Ava closed her eyes and dreamed of what it would be like to have *him*, her dear Prince Charming, to take care of her. There would be food to eat, clothes she could shop for, even if she didn't need anything. A bright and wonderful future was waiting for her. Soon.

Ava looked out onto the street from behind the ivory lace curtains. All was quiet. That was good. No one had asked her any questions so far, so maybe this would blow over. She trudged into her bedroom, kicking off her shoes and letting her clothes drop on the floor, leaving them where they lay. Climbing into bed, Ava picked up the framed photograph perched on her nightstand. Smiling wistfully, she traced the photo with her finger and brushed it with her lips before returning it to its coveted position by her bed. *Soon, my love, soon. My sweet,*

sweet Roland. You'll take me away from all of this and we will be so happy.

Bill Meyers sat on the edge of his bed, drenched in perspiration. His hands shook and his breathing was heavy and labored. He rubbed his temples. *How can Sid act as though nothing is wrong?* He imagined Sid, sleeping soundly, as he claimed he did every night. Bill hadn't slept all week. His stomach was in knots and everything he ate made him feel like knives were stabbing him in the gut. He chewed a handful of antacids and chased them down with a couple of sleeping pills.

Bill didn't believe in coincidences. Especially when someone who was going to ruin your company suddenly dies at the same restaurant where you and your business partner are having dinner. Sid called it a gift horse. Gift horse indeed!

Sid is the risk taker. I'm the careful one. Friedman Meyers works because we have that yin and yang balance. Risk and caution. But maybe I should have been more careful before going in with him.

Sid killed Harrington. He must have. The reason he's sleeping so soundly is because he's gonna let me take the fall for it and then the whole business will be his. No wonder nothing bothers him. He's planning on coming out smelling like a rose while I pay the price for his crime.

Bill's hands continued to shake. He'd just showered twenty minutes ago and now, here he was, sweaty again. *I gotta get some rest. One thing's for sure. I am not going down for anything Sid has done.*

The sleeping pills made his head feel woozy. He lay back and pulled up the covers as the pills began to take effect. So he had taken a couple of extras. The prescribed dose was not strong enough. He needed more. He closed his eyes and at long last, sleep came.

Mariah Flores finished her bedtime routine and slipped into her nightgown. It had been another long day. She felt certain the stench from the nursing home was etched in her memory forever. Mariah feared growing old and losing control, feared needing strangers to attend to her most basic needs. She had been working on her feet all day and then again all night, waiting tables. At least business was up. She had even had a few nights where the tips were decent.

Mariah's cell phone rang as she was climbing into bed. It was him.

"No, baby, I'm never too tired to talk to you. We're in this together, right? We're in everything together. Just you and me." *And all that lovely money.* Mariah laughed, deep and throaty. "I'll see you soon. You worry too much. Everything's fine. Mmmhmm. Good night, love."

Chapter 11

Adam arrived at his office the next morning and sat at his desk to read over the report he had typed. *What am I missing about that night? I was there, just a few feet away! What is it?* The more the thought nagged at him, the more the answer eluded him. He wished he had his team together to brainstorm. Three brains were better than one.

Frustrated, Adam looked over the list of names Alan Cunningham had provided. There were several more interviews left to conduct. Bill Meyers and Sid Friedman had offices in a high rise downtown on Washington Avenue, a short drive from the police station on Clark Street. Their tickets had been purchased with a company credit card. That should mean they were there on business. After he talked with them, he would have the nuns and the remaining staff of Mansford Mansion to interview. Cunningham had listed the home addresses of the staff, but Adam felt certain they must have worked other jobs besides Mansford Mansion—he doubted Cunningham paid enough for anyone to be self-supporting, except perhaps the bartender. Dr. Jasmine Jones, of course, was being paid for her study, so whatever she earned as a waitress was of no consequence. It wouldn't have surprised Adam if she gave away all of her tips. She didn't need the money and Adam believed she was a kind-hearted person. But was she a suspect? He doubted it, but he could not rule her out. Her connection to the house was pretty eerie. Was there more? He studied the entire list, deep in thought, trying to make sense of the odd reactions he had observed at every table when the Harringtons arrived. And when Edward Harrington died. *Somebody somewhere knows something.*

Captain Peterson approached Adam's office. "Morning, Adam. You're in early. How's the investigation going?"

Adam handed the captain his report. "Still interviewing witnesses, Cap. Basically, I got nothin'."

"Need some help?"

"I thought my team was in hiding. Tell me you found Cranston dead in an alley somewhere, and I'll start assigning duties on the Harrington case!"

"No such luck. Sorry." Captain Peterson pulled a chair out and sat beside Adam. "Can I assign someone to help with the legwork? We still have several homicide detectives who weren't working the Cranston case with your team. I could pull someone if you need them."

Adam considered the offer. Some extra help would be nice, but to take another detective away from their own case load to help him didn't seem fair, especially with the department short-handed, and the murder rate in St. Louis climbing.

"Cap, I couldn't do that to someone else. It would hinder their own workload."

"What if I got you some help from outside of Homicide?"

Adam sat up straight. "That'd be great. I could use some help running down all the places you can purchase cyanide, and getting a list of who has made those purchases and when. Also, I need to know about the staff at Mansford Mansion—where the rest of them work during the day. Hard to believe their night job pays enough to live."

"How about Kate Marlin? She's smart and thorough."

"From K-9?" Adam shook his head. "I can't see Kate leaving her dog. Not for anything."

"Robo's retired now. He's too old and arthritic to work anymore. Kate's gonna keep him for the time he's got left. He'll be a hard one to replace. We've got a couple of new litters coming up soon, so Kate's in between pooches. Plus, she needs a little space to process. It's hard giving up Robo as her partner. I bet she'd welcome the distraction."

Adam sat up, encouraged. "Sure. I'd enjoy working with her." He began writing on a clean sheet of paper. "First up, let's see if we can trace all cyanide purchases in the bi-state area. If she finishes with that, there's more." He continued writing. "I'll be back later on. Out for more interviews. Thanks, Cap." He handed Gavin Peterson a list. "I realize there's a lot on here. I'd be grateful for whatever she can accomplish."

Adam left, walking with long, confident strides. He and Jenna had always liked Kate, and she would be a big help to him. A born tomboy, Kate was tall and muscular and as tough as any of the men with whom Adam worked. A fiery redhead with a non-nonsense attitude, she was a hard worker, bold and creative. Kate was not afraid to work outside the box. If she got half of the work on Adam's list finished, he would be thrilled.

Captain Peterson returned to his office, shut the door and picked up the telephone.

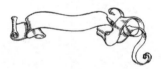

Adam arrived at the office of Friedman Meyers, LLC and waited in the reception area for several minutes. Looking through the glass doors, he saw the two men that were at the dinner theater talking. The younger retreated to his office looking unwell, his face pasty and puffy. The elder disappeared. After waiting several more minutes, he was shown to Sid Friedman's sprawling office, a lavish monument to Friedman's success.

The walls were decorated with numerous awards and plaques. Photographs of Sid with politicians and captains of industry dominated the shelves. Adorning the rest of the office were several ornate items which looked expensive. The back window, like Roland's office window, provided a spectacular view of downtown, but from a different angle than Roland's, and there was a large floor-to-ceiling window by the door where Sid could oversee the inside goings on of his firm as well. Adam noticed the younger partner across the open hall glancing frequently at them through the glass panel of his office while Adam met with the senior partner.

"How can I help one of St. Louis' finest today, Detective?" Mr. Friedman asked, showing him a chair opposite his massive mahogany desk. Sid Friedman's brusque manner made it clear he was a busy man and could spare little time. He spoke in a condescending manner which Adam resented. Adam positioned the chair so he could talk to Sid Friedman and still keep an eye on Bill Meyers. Taking in Friedman's perfect tan, perfect teeth and insincere manner, Adam managed to not cringe at the question.

Right. You keep me waiting because you can. What a phony, self-important snob. Adam leaned back in his chair, crossed his legs and took out his notepad and pen. *Maintain your professionalism, Adam. Guys like this are a dime a dozen.* "I'm investigating the murder of Edward Harrington. You were present the night he was killed and I would like to ask you a few questions."

"Murdered, was he? Hmm. I'm afraid I wouldn't know anything about that." Sid crossed his arms in front of his chest and tilted his head back so he looked down his nose at Adam.

Adam ignored the brush-off. "How well did you know Mr. Harrington?"

"Know him! I never met the man." The senior partner gestured with his arms out and palms upward.

"Are you sure about that?" Adam noted Bill Meyers across the way, mopping his forehead. "What type of business is Friedman Meyers?"

"For the most part, we're an acquisition brokerage firm. But we also dabble in a few local real estate matters."

An idea sparked in Adam's mind and he decided to go out on a limb with his next question. He could smell something fishy, and this guy stunk like week-old catfish. If his hunch was wrong, Friedman would shut him down in an instant. But if he was on the right track..."If Harrington had not died when he did, how much money would your company have lost after his maneuvering forced your big deal to fall through?" He stared at Friedman.

Friedman flinched. Adam's question struck home. *I knew it!* He saw the ever-confident Sid Friedman pale under his tan. Friedman swallowed.

"What big deal are you talking about? We have lots of big deals."

But Adam was adept at reading body language and Friedman had lost his huff and puff. Adam stood. "I asked you a question, Mr. Friedman. If you won't give me an honest answer, I'll see if Mr. Meyers can answer my questions with a little more accuracy."

Adam turned and walked with long, purposeful strides out of Sid Friedman's office across the open hall area into Bill Meyers' office, shutting the door behind him. Bill looked up at Adam like a frightened, trapped animal. He was all but drenched with perspiration.

Adam handed him his card. "I need to ask you about the Harrington murder, Mr. Meyers. Mr. Friedman was quite helpful, but I need to hear your side of the story before I can make an arrest."

Bill Meyers had worked himself into a state of near-collapse. His face had paled and his breathing came in gulps.

"Are you ill, sir?" Adam asked. Stealing a glance into Sid Friedman's office across the way, he was gratified to see Friedman watching wide-eyed, unable to hear what was transpiring, as Sid watched Meyers' meltdown. Adam's confidence swelled. He couldn't remember the last time a bluff had paid such rich dividends. The anticipation of solving a high profile murder in record time was a heady experience.

Bill Meyers trembled as sweat dripped onto his desk. He was white as a sheet. His voice shook as he answered Adam. "It wasn't me, it wasn't me. Please! I didn't know Harrington would be there. I had no idea. Please—you've got to believe me. I couldn't believe it when he walked in, and then he just—he just died!"

Adam continued his hard line of questioning. He saw Sid Friedman pick up the phone. *Bet he has his lawyer on speed dial. His lawyer might even be in this same building. Better hurry this up.* "How ruined was this company going to be if Harrington hadn't died, and succeeded in his takeover of your project?" Adam asked, confident he was on the right track.

Bill Meyers gulped and looked back and forth. When he started talking, his words poured out with lightning speed. "It would've shut us down. Sid, you know, he takes chances. Chances I wouldn't feel comfortable taking. The new bank building on the riverfront, the one that is supposed to be thirty stories high? Well, they couldn't make their payments and they were going under and Sid wanted it, said we could make a fortune. He committed close to all of our assets on the purchase, then Harrington stepped in and..."

Sid Friedman barged into Bill's office. "Shut up, Bill. Stop talking. We're going to wait for our lawyer. Not another word until our attorney gets here."

"He knows already, Sid! But I didn't kill that man—I swear I didn't! And I'm not going to jail for a crime you committed!" He pointed a shaky finger at his partner.

"I didn't commit any crime, Bill. Harrington's death may've been very fortunate for us, but I had nothing to do with it."

"Why were you two at the dinner theater if you didn't intend to kill Edward Harrington?" Adam asked, looking from one partner to the other.

"We were thinking about buying the place," Bill answered. His speech slowed to a normal rate, but he continued to perspire. He took a deep breath.

"We didn't know Harrington was going to be there," Sid explained, having already forgotten his lawyer's advice. "That old place was falling down and nobody has ever made a go of it. Not yet, anyway. But we had a client who wanted us to take a look-see and talk about buying Alan Cunningham out. We were stunned when Harrington walked in. He was the last person either of us expected to see."

Bill Meyers removed his glasses and mopped his face with a damp handkerchief. "We were sick when we saw him. And when he died? Yeah, we were relieved, but we both thought it was a heart attack. I swear to you, that's the truth."

Adam believed they were telling the truth. *Another road to nowhere. So much for an impending arrest.*

The door to Bill Meyers' office swung open and a man wearing a suit that cost more than Adam made in a week entered. The attorney nodded to his clients. "Sid, Bill," he began with authority. "You don't have to talk to the police." He turned to Adam and pointing a finger at him, announced, "I want to speak with my clients in private, so you'll excuse us." It was an order, not a request. The obnoxious man then pointed to the door and motioned for Adam to leave.

"No problem," Adam said. He looked the attorney in the eye. "I got everything I needed, so I'll be going." He walked out, holding his head high.

Adam drove back to the station to type his report of the morning's interviews. Kate Marlin was waiting at his desk, clutching a wad of papers.

"Hey Adam. What's with the long face?"

"Yet another dead end. Every time I think I'm onto something, it goes up in smoke. Whatcha got for me, Kate? By the way, thanks for agreeing to come on board. I appreciate the help."

"You're welcome." Kate straightened the wad of papers, setting them in some kind of order. "I've got computer printouts for all the places in the bi-state area where you can purchase cyanide. I hate to tell you, but there's nothing promising here. I've cross-checked the buyers with the names on your list. I went back 12 months, which I think is overkill, but better to overdo the research than underestimate your adversary. Nobody on the list comes up. All the purchases were legitimate businesses and I can't find any connection to our suspects. Sorry, Adam, but there's nothing suspicious here." Kate separated her pages, pulling out those that referenced the cyanide purchases and laid them out on Adam's desk for him to view.

Adam glanced at the list. Reluctantly, he admitted to Kate that she was right. "What about a home garden? Do you think someone could've made cyanide from their home-grown apricots, apple seeds, anything like that?"

"That'd be pretty ambitious," Kate chuckled. "The only person on the list who does any gardening here is Jenna. Did you question her?"

Adam crossed his arms in front of his chest. "Haha. Funny." He sat at his desk and leaned back in his chair. "And yeah, for the record, I did talk to Jenna. She wasn't able to add anything new. Amy paid no attention to anything besides the play and the brochure. Can we check out the others and see if anyone's growing anything?"

"Will do. In the meantime, I got the lowdown on the staff and the nuns. All the nuns work at Our Lady of Sorrows over on Rhodes."

"You *have* been busy. Thanks. Why don't we start with the staff?" He motioned for her to pull up a chair.

"Right." Kate sat on top of Adam's desk, making herself at home. She thumbed through her papers and pulled out a sheet. "Alan Cunningham lives on the third floor of Mansford Mansion."

Adam shuddered and recoiled. "Seriously? That guy is just plain creepy."

She laughed. "Mansford Mansion is pretty creepy. He must feel right at home."

"Okay, what about the others?"

Kate pulled out more papers. "Mike Davey lives in a small apartment in Maplewood. He's the highest paid employee, if you call his salary high. Works odd jobs as a bouncer or bartender in a variety of places around town—nothing steady. Keeps to himself. Kind of a loner, I gather. I couldn't find any indication of a girlfriend or any hobbies. No record. He's a veteran. Navy.

"Carl Mendoza and Mark Vernon are longtime friends and share an apartment in the Dogtown neighborhood. When they're not acting at the dinner theater, Carl tends bar at Helen Fitzgerald's in South County and Mark tends bar at the Cheshire Inn. No serious girlfriends, but from their credit cards, it looks like they do go out on occasion. Clean records other than minor traffic matters. No complaints from the neighbors."

"How'd you get all this information in such a short time?" Adam asked, sitting up in his chair.

"I sent the uniforms to their various homes and had them gather the dirt, or rather, lack thereof. Not *everybody's* the lone ranger around here." She put a hand on her hip and looked at Adam daring him to contradict her.

"Guilty as charged." He put his hands up in surrender. "What else?"

"Mariah Flores, the waitress who had the Harrington table. Lives alone in a small house in Affton. Belonged to her grandparents who left her everything when they died. No parents in the picture. Grandparents raised her from the time she was pretty young. Works days at a nursing home as a nurse's assistant."

"Glorified title for cleaning bed pans and all the other jobs nobody wants?"

"Right. But she has a good work record. The residents seem to like her. With no rent to pay, she makes enough between the two jobs to keep her head above water."

"Does she have a garden?" He stood to look over Kate's shoulder and read her notes for himself.

"She does, but it looks like all she grows are tomatoes and peppers. No cyanide producing culprits. Sorry."

"Right." Adam rubbed his temple.

"Anyway, she seems to have a love interest, but I haven't got any further information on that." Kate crossed her legs and sat Indian style.

"Record? Something more than speeding?" Adam walked around his small office, stretching his tired muscles.

"Yes, she does, but nothing too exciting. Juvenile shoplifting, possession of a couple of joints. Nothing came of any of it, just attributed to teenage rebellion, probably dealing with parent abandonment issues. Her grandparents paid the fines and she was released back into their custody."

Adam stopped pacing and looked at Kate with fading hope. "Nothing more recent than teenage shenanigans?"

Kate shook her head and continued. "Then there's Ava Montel," she enunciated slowly. "Head case." She re-arranged her papers.

"Oh?" Adam raised his eyebrows. "Go on." He returned to his seat.

Kate slipped off his desk and began to lay out papers where she had been sitting. "Ava Montel did three stints of six weeks each in the lockdown units of psych wards. She's a few fries short of a happy meal, I'd say." She wound her finger in circles by her temple.

Adam leaned back in his chair and whistled. "How did you get *that* information?"

"For now, it's unconfirmed. We need all kinds of paperwork to get the facts, HIPAA and all, you know, but she went to Catholic girls' schools from Kindergarten through graduation and boy, do those girls love to talk! Ava has all kinds of issues, and after her father walked out on the family, she started spending more and more time in La-la Land, as her former classmates called it. Seems to have a little trouble discerning fact from fiction. You can see why she may have been attracted to an acting career." Kate took a step backward and Adam leaned forward to look at her notes.

"Yeah, but she's a terrible actress! Any indication she might be dangerous?"

Kate sighed and shrugged her shoulders. "That's where we'd have to get her records, talk to her doctors. All I've got is rumor, but I heard the same type of stuff over and over. Where there's smoke, you know, and all that. It wouldn't hurt to be careful when you talk to her."

Adam nodded. He had dealt with his share of fruitcakes in his career. "Any connection to the Harringtons?"

Kate grinned and put a hand on her hip. "I'm not *that* good, Adam. I did just have the morning and everyone reported in just a few minutes before you returned. I'll do more follow-up. This is just the preliminary stuff."

"Sounds like you got a lot done. I appreciate it."

"Jasmine Jones is interesting. Did you know she's got her doctorate in psychology?"

"Yeah, but I promised to keep her secret. She's got an interesting project she's working on at the mansion."

"Right. She's married, but kept her maiden name. No kids. Smart cookie. Finished valedictorian. Comes from money back east. She'd have no financial motive." Kate snagged a chair with her foot and pulled it up beside Adam, sitting next to him.

"She's also a direct descendant of Hettie, the housekeeper who was murdered by Captain Mansford."

"I didn't know that!" Kate raised her eyebrows and leaned closer to Adam. She lowered her voice. "If we find out that the Harringtons are related to Josiah Mansford, then maybe Jasmine's settling a multi-generational score. Whatcha think?"

"I think you've been watching too many B-rated movies there, Kate!"

They laughed together.

"Well, that's the staff. I'm hungry. Why don't I fill you in on the nuns over lunch?"

"How exciting is that?"

"What? Lunch or nuns?" Kate joked, picking up her purse and fishing out her keys. "I'll drive. I need to stop by the house first and look in on Robo."

They left in Kate's squad car. Robo was overjoyed to see the two of them. He was graying and walked stiff-legged. Adam winced to see the change in his favorite fur-covered officer. He couldn't help but think of Blue, and how much she meant to the family. He was glad Kate had decided to keep Robo. Often, it was too much to handle an aging K-9 along with a younger dog, and the older retired dog often ended up being put up for adoption or euthanized. Adam had always found that kind of treatment immensely unfair after these magnificent dogs had served so faithfully and fearlessly. But Robo would live the rest of his days as a pampered pooch—a well-deserved fate. Kate might be hard as nails as a cop, but when it came to her dogs, she was a confirmed marshmallow.

They went to Pueblo Solis, a popular Mexican restaurant on Hampton Avenue, for lunch. Adam ordered the taco plate and Kate the chicken mole. They ate chips and salsa and talked while they waited for the food to arrive.

"Hey! I didn't see a chef on the list from Cunningham. Isn't there a chef at Mansford Mansion? Who prepares the food?"

Kate laughed. "You'll love this. It's a toss-up between the staff. Most of the cooking is divided between Alan Cunningham and Mike Davey. But some of the others pitch in here and there. It's not like there's any *real* cooking, but then, I'm sure you suspected that all along, right?"

"Okay, not much of a surprise, but it sure leaves a lot of folks with access to the food." He took a drink of water and wiped his mouth with his hand. "So, the nuns?" Adam asked.

"Right, the nuns," Kate shoved a salsa laden chip into her mouth. "All four of them work at Our Lady of Sorrows, like I said. Sister Agnes Pauline is in her early eighties and lives in a building on the church property. She's a Sacristan at Sorrows. Takes care of set-ups for service, various vessels, garments and the like. Sister Elizabeth Anne is in her late fifties. Works as a Liturgist, planning and preparing the worship programs, overseeing preparations for Lent, Easter, the holidays, that sort of thing. She lives with her aging mother in the same house she grew up in a couple of blocks from the church. She has deep roots in the community and the church. Both of them are fixtures in that parish as well as in the neighborhood."

"They don't sound too dangerous. What about the two younger nuns?" He pushed Kate's hand out of the chip basket and grabbed a handful of chips, piling them on his plate.

"Hey!" She grabbed the salt shaker and shook it into his water. "Behave. Didn't your mother teach you to share?"

"Look who's talking." Adam dumped pepper into the salsa. "It needed more spice. And leave my mother out of this. So you were saying?" He grinned and dipped his chip into the peppery salsa. As he put it on his tongue, he looked at Kate, daring her to do the same.

Kate took another chip but skipped the salsa. "Sister Mary Bernadette is in her late thirties and shares a two-family flat with Sister Cecilia Marie, the youngest of the group, at twenty-eight. Sister Mary Bernadette is the Music Director and Sister Cecilia Marie is a teacher at Our Lady of Sorrows grade school. None of them have so much as a parking ticket."

"Yeah, they sound real threatening." He took a drink of water.

"Maybe not as suspects, but they may have seen something. You never know. Ask anyone who went to Catholic school and they'll tell you—the nuns have eyes on every side of their heads. Sister Cecilia Marie has a fiery personality, but she's good with the children and they adore her. She's very passionate about the causes she believes in. She's a bit of an activist and instills those values and her spirit of commitment in her students."

Adam raised a finger to call the server and asked for another dish of salsa and a fresh glass of water. He turned to Kate. "You've been a big help, Kate. I appreciate all the legwork, and the organizing you did for this project. You've lightened my load a lot."

"Glad to help. The department has been really gracious while I sort out losing my best-ever partner." She looked down at the table and grew quiet a few moments before she looked back at Adam. She squinted her eyes and became serious. "Wish I could do something about Cranston. He's one twisted monster."

"Those are exactly the same words Jenna used to describe him."

"Great minds think alike, you know."

Their food arrived and they ate, chatting about the case and promising to get together for a barbecue when the Cranston case was over. Adam told Kate about Amy getting a black eye in a fight with the bigger boy.

Kate giggled. "I bet Jenna was thrilled about that."

"Maybe not so much. Can't wait to see them again, black eye and all." Adam shoved half a taco into his mouth and licked the spicy grease off of his fingers.

"Where are they staying? Oops, sorry. I forgot. Total secrecy. Forget I asked." She held up a hand in apology.

"They're safe, Kate. That's all that's important. Hey, do you want to go with me while I interview the nuns?"

Kate shook her head. "Thanks for the exciting invite, but I'll pass. I want to dig some more on the cyanide and see if I can get any more details on all your suspects, so *you* don't have to work so hard."

He threw a chip at her and missed.

"I hope you shoot straighter than you throw!"

"Is Adam coming home for the weekend, dear?" Emma Jo asked her daughter-in-law.

"Yes. I'm expecting him this evening. Would it be okay if we ate a little later tonight, so he can join us?"

"Of course. Don't you all have pizza or tacos on Friday nights?"

"That's right. It's always a toss-up between the two, but since we have such a limited amount of time together, I was hoping to make a nicer meal for him, until things get back to normal. Adam loves my chicken pot pie. I think a little comfort food might do us all some good. I imagine you have everything right here in the kitchen. Why don't I fix dinner by myself tonight while you stay on that sofa, sit back, put your feet up and relax? This is such a comfortable family room, and your sofa is heavenly. You need to rest and enjoy it."

"Jenna that sounds lovely. I'm feeling a bit tired today. Thank you. I can sure see why Adam loves you so much."

Jenna smiled and started for the kitchen.

Amy bounded in from the chicken pen and found Emma Jo standing by the massive stone fireplace, staring at the photographs of her children that covered the mantel. "I fed all the chickens, Gomer, and I got some eggs, just like you taught me!"

"You didn't let that dog of yours get to my chickens, now, did you, Amy?"

"No. Blue stayed outside of the pen."

Blue wagged her tail at the sound of her name, having followed right behind Amy, and begged for a treat. Amy gave her one and the dog found a corner in which to settle down and enjoy her reward for not killing any chickens.

"What are ya doin', Gomer?" Amy asked, giving her grandmother a hug.

"I'm just praying that your daddy will be safe. He's the only boy I've got left, now."

Amy stood next to Emma Jo, looking at the photos. She gazed at the photo of her father, so handsome and brave in his Marine uniform, and at her Uncle Joshua, whom she had never met, also a Marine. She knew her father had come home from the

Middle East, alive and in one piece, but his brother, her Uncle Joshua, had not. Amy did not know much more than that—did not know the extent to which her father struggled with survivor's guilt—and did not ask. She knew that sometimes, he would have nightmares about the war and wake up screaming. But her father never talked about the war. In spite of her tender age, Amy perceived an atmosphere of pain when the subject was brought up, and felt it best if she did not ask questions.

Looking over the mantel of photos, she asked her grandmother, "Is that Aunt Rachel, Gomer?"

Her grandmother pressed her lips together. "Yes," she answered and blinked away tears.

Amy remembered how her daddy's face would tense at the mention of Aunt Rachel's name and how the muscle in his cheek would twitch. "Why does Aunt Rachel make you sad, Gomer?"

Emma Jo put her arm around Amy and led her to the couch where Amy loved to cuddle with her. "I love Rachel very much, Amy," she began. "She's my daughter. My only daughter. Rachel didn't like living on a farm and dreamed of living in a big city and of being successful. She was embarrassed to be the daughter of farmers, even though she never wanted for anything. Oompah worked hard to send all three of our children to college, but once Rachel had her degree, she took a job in New York City and never came back."

"Never? Not even for Christmas or Thanksgiving or Easter or birthdays? Even before I was born?" Amy asked. No wonder her daddy didn't want to talk about Rachel. She had turned her back on her own family. Amy did not understand how anyone could do such a thing. Being away from family on special occasions was unthinkable.

"No," her grandmother shook her head. "Not for anything. She came home once, for Joshua's funeral. Her plane landed two hours before the service and took off again three hours after he was laid to rest."

Amy felt sad and hugged her grandmother. "I'll never leave you, Gomer. Never." Blue, sensing she was needed, padded into the family room and onto the sofa, a ready participant in the group hug.

Emma Jo shooed her off. "No dogs on my furniture!" Blue got down and lay at Amy's feet, looking up and down pitifully at Emma Jo while keeping her chin on the floor. "Don't give me that look, Blue. This is a farm. You're lucky you're allowed inside the house."

"Are we having salad with dinner? I make the salad now at home," Amy informed her grandmother.

"What a good helper you are! Why don't you run on into the kitchen and see if your sweet mama needs any help?"

Emma Jo lay back on the sofa, propped her feet up on the rolled arm and closed her eyes.

Adam's last stop for the day was Our Lady of Sorrows on Rhodes Avenue in an old, well-established section of south St. Louis. A priest greeted him when he walked through the church doors and showed him to a room where he could wait while the sisters were gathered together. A cup of coffee and a small plate of cookies were brought. Soon, all four sisters arrived, greeted him cordially and sat around the conference table.

"Ladies, thank you for your time. I'm Detective Adam Trent. You may remember me from the Mansford Mansion dinner theater, the night Mr. Harrington was murdered."

The nuns gasped collectively, and Adam remembered that the cause of Mr. Harrington's demise had not yet been announced as a homicide. Sister Agnes Pauline and Sister Elizabeth Anne made the sign of the cross.

Sister Cecilia Marie spoke. "We thought that man died from natural causes. How was he murdered?"

"He was poisoned. I'd like for you to think back to that evening. Did any of you notice anyone tampering with Mr. Harrington's food? Did any of you see anything that struck you as out of the ordinary?"

They all shook their heads.

Sister Elizabeth Anne sneezed loudly. "Oh, excuse me. I'm terribly sorry. I have a dreadful cold. I beg your pardon." Her voice sounded congested and her nose was red. She blew it into a tissue and moved her chair away from the others. Adam hoped she wasn't contagious.

"God bless you," Sister Mary Bernadette exclaimed. "After the detective leaves, I hope you'll allow me to make you some hot tea with lemon and honey. It'll make you feel better."

The sick nun nodded her head. "That's a very kind offer and I will take you up on it. Thank you."

"Does anybody have anything they can tell me that might be of help in this investigation?" he asked.

Again, they all shrugged and shook their heads.

Adam sighed, leaned back in his chair, and looked at each one of them. "Ladies, I was there. I saw the effect this man had on each of you when he arrived at the restaurant. You all changed in an instant from chatting and laughing to stiffening and going stone silent. Sister Cecilia Marie, you glared at Mr. Harrington until Sister Agnes Pauline said something to you. I believe an explanation is in order."

The nuns' only response was wide-eyed silence. Adam turned to Sister Agnes Pauline. "I expect to hear a little truth before I leave here, Sister Agnes Pauline. I have a family to go home to and I'd very much like to see them today. But I'm prepared to wait you out. It's your choice."

Sister Agnes Pauline straightened her posture and looked straight at Adam with wizened eyes. Her voice, though clouded by age, carried strength and weight. "Edward Harrington was an evil man. God works in mysterious ways." Having spoken, the elderly nun took a deep breath and sat back in her chair, unblinking as her gaze bore through Adam.

"Agreed. What was your connection to Mr. Harrington?"

Sister Cecilia Marie did not wait for Agnes Pauline to respond. As she answered Adam's question, her dark eyes flashed fire. "He damaged everything and everyone he touched. Just look how he treated his own children. It was shameful. I'm not sorry he's dead. I've already been to confession, but I'm still not sorry, so I guess I'll have to go back."

"I, too, have confessed that I wished him ill and was secretly pleased when he died," Sister Agnes Pauline said. She folded her hands on her lap.

"I also went to confession over my guilty feelings for being happy he died and for wishing he was dead," Sister Mary Bernadette admitted.

"I haven't been yet because of this cold, but I'll go soon," sniffed Sister Elizabeth Anne.

Adam leaned back further in his chair and surveyed the nuns. "So let me get this straight. You're all glad he's dead, and sorry that you're glad, do I have that right?"

They nodded.

"Why?"

Cecilia Marie glared at him as though he were a fire-breathing heathen. "Because it's a sin to wish someone dead. It's wrong to rejoice in the death of another human being."

Adam sighed. "I'm aware of that. I'll rephrase the question. Why did you wish him ill in the first place?" He was running out of patience and trying not to show it.

"Well, because of the children's home, of course!" Sister Cecilia Marie exclaimed passionately. "We worked for three years to raise money for a large children's home. We purchased a wonderful abandoned building. All we needed to do was finish the renovations. Fifty children could have left the foster care system to live there. We had several house parents, funding to support it and a great deal of money had been spent to purchase furnishings, decorations and the like. Not to mention the children who were excited to have a real home to live in, rather than being passed back and forth like old luggage."

Sister Elizabeth Anne blew her nose and continued the conversation. "Children are precious and society has deemed them a disposable commodity. They are aborted before they even breathe their first breath. The same butchers who prey on vulnerable women tell them it's only a blob of tissue, and then they turn around and sell the baby's body parts to make even more money. And they even claim they're doing a good thing! God have mercy! Could our society cheapen life anymore? Babies who survive an abortion are cast aside or left in trash bins to die. Children who are battered and neglected are sent into a failed foster system and turned out when they're eighteen, with no family, no future and no hope." Sister Elizabeth Anne looked into Adam's eyes. "How many calls have you answered, detective, where a baby was tossed into a dumpster?"

Adam winced at the question and looked away. *Too many. Even one call is too many. And I've answered countless calls.* The passion in Sister Elizabeth Anne's voice resonated with Adam's core beliefs. People mattered. They mattered to God and they mattered to Adam. All people.

The nun continued, ignoring the increasing hoarseness in her voice. "It was our dream to make a difference in our community— to help the hurting. And not just a dream. It was our calling. Our service to God and to His children." Her voice caught and she paused, dabbing a handkerchief to her moist eyes. She cleared her throat and sat up straight. "And Edward Harrington," she spat his name. "Edward Harrington took all of that away. He filed suit, claiming that part of the building was encroaching on land that one of his businesses owned. We doubted the authenticity of the survey, but he had more money than we did."

"Or he owned more people anyway," Sister Mary Bernadette interrupted.

Cecilia Marie jumped in. "He had our building torn down, claiming that it was on his property and it was derelict."

"Which it wasn't," Sister Mary Bernadette added.

Cecilia Marie finished. "We lost the money, but more than that, we lost the chance to give needy children a loving home where they could thrive."

Agnes Pauline cleared her throat and spoke with wisdom and authority. Adam noticed that whenever Agnes Pauline spoke, the other sisters deferred to her. They remained quiet whenever she spoke and all eyes were on her. "Edward Harrington owned dozens of buildings and plots of land. He did not need to do what he did. There were other options available to amicably settle this minor problem. He *chose* to inflict harm. It was his *choice*. He *chose* evil for the sole reason that he enjoyed flexing his malicious muscle. Inflicting pain on others was the biggest pleasure that devil had in life. Edward Harrington got exactly what he deserved."

"How many people knew about this? About the children's home?" Adam asked.

"Oh, everybody! Absolutely everybody," they all answered at once.

Adam nodded. *Terrific. At least everybody wasn't at Mansford Mansion.* The sisters were wearing him out. "I just need to ask you one more question and then you can all go. Did any of you help Edward Harrington to his eternal destiny?"

"Oh, no," they all answered in concert.

Cecilia Marie spoke again. "But we're not sorry that someone else did." She laughed half-heartedly. "Guess I'm going back to confession."

Adam rose. "Thank you for your time, ladies. Sister Elizabeth Anne, I hope you feel better soon." He left Our Lady of Sorrows and headed for the family farm.

"Daddy, Daddy, Daddy!" Amy ran to Adam as he got out of his car and walked toward the farmhouse, and jumped into his arms. He swung her around in a bear hug while she squealed in delight.

"Hey, peanut! I've missed you. Lemme take a look at that shiner of yours." He set her down and knelt in front of her, cradling her face in his hands. "Wow! That's a beaut!"

Adam stood up as Jenna hurried outside, wiping her hands on her apron. She threw her arms around him and he enveloped her in his arms, kissing her passionately while Amy made gagging noises. "I was just telling Amy not to fight anymore," he said nuzzling her neck.

"Uh huh. I heard."

"Oh."

She hugged him again. "I made chicken pot pie for your dinner tonight."

"I made the salad!" Amy chimed in.

"Well, don't just stand there like ya got all day! Get on in the house. Dinner's almost ready, and we didn't get our hugs yet!" Emma Jo was standing on the porch, her hands covered with flour, waving them in. Blue stood behind Emma Jo with her tail wagging, pawing at the screen door.

"I told her to sit back and relax and let me cook dinner. Your mother hasn't rested since we got here," Jenna mumbled under her breath as the three of them made their way to the house, with their arms linked together.

"Don't tell me. My mother didn't listen. Gee, how did I know?"

Emma Jo opened the door wide and they entered the house. She and Dwayne hugged Adam.

"Glad you're back safe with us, son." Dwayne patted Adam on his shoulder.

"So how many chickens are we down now?" Adam asked, petting Blue, who stood wagging her tail.

"We strengthened the chicken yard fencing. Blue will just have to stick to the food Amy's putting in her dish."

The family sat together at the dinner table and prayed before dinner, thanking God for another week of safety and protection, grateful for the opportunity to spend the entire weekend together.

Saturday, Adam helped his father with the farm chores. There was never a shortage of work. Sunday after church, the family played board games and relaxed when they weren't caring for the animals. Adam did not offer any information about Dr. Cranston or the Harrington case, and nobody asked.

Monday morning dawned too quickly for the Trent family. They said their goodbyes and Adam began the long drive back to the city. Ava Montel was on his radar. He did not know how she fit into the Harrington puzzle, but he was determined to find out.

He used his Bluetooth to call Kate Marlin. A hoarse, sleepy voice answered.

"Kate? Is that you?"

"Uh huh. What time is it?"

"Mornin', sunshine. Sorry to wake you. I'm on my way to Ava Montel's place. I was checking to see if you might want to wait outside as backup."

"Uh huh."

"I won't be there for a couple of hours. Meet me in front of her apartment, okay?"

"Uh huh."

Adam felt a twinge of guilt for waking Kate up so early. As he remembered, Ava Montel couldn't have weighed much over a hundred pounds. If she got violent, he could handle her with ease. But he had known several instances where head cases, as Kate called them, seemed to summon superhuman strength. Still, he thought, he shouldn't have gotten Kate up. He hoped she would go back to sleep and forget about his request for back-up.

Adam arrived on Ava's street and parked some distance from her building. City parking spots in most neighborhoods were at a premium and always difficult to find. As he walked to the entrance of Ava's apartment building, he saw Kate approaching from the other direction. He put his hand up and started to apologize.

"Hey, sorry to—"

"No problem. I went back to sleep for a bit." Kate shook her head. Her eyes were puffy and Adam thought she looked like she forgot to brush her hair. "I'll wait outside her door and listen. Here's an earpiece. What help word do you want to use so I'll know if you're in trouble?" She stifled a yawn.

"How about Robocop, in honor of our favorite German Shepherd?"

Kate grinned. "Robocop it is."

Ava Montel was still in bed when she heard knocking at her door. She ran on her tip toes to the window and looked outside, but saw nothing unusual. She scurried to the door and peered through the peephole. *That cop!* "Just a second," she called. She threw on sweatpants and a sweatshirt and answered the door barefoot. In her rush to dress and answer the door, she left her bedroom door open.

"Ms. Montel? I'd like to ask you a few questions about the murder of Edward Harrington. May I come in?" Adam showed his badge.

She opened the door and admitted him into a Lilliputian sized apartment. Adam looked around, thankful he was not claustrophobic. Her furniture—what little she had—looked like the stuff people set by the curb for pick-up after the family Rottweiler used them as chew toys. Turning his attention back to Ava, he realized she was the first person who did not express surprise that Harrington's death was murder. *So she knows.*

"What can you tell me about Mr. Harrington's murder, Ms. Montel?"

She smiled wistfully, her eyes fixed on some imaginary point over Adam's head. *Insanity defense. Nice. Start building it early, honey.*

"Ms. Montel," Adam raised his voice in an attempt to jolt her back to reality. "Why did you poison Mr. Harrington? How did you know him?"

She appeared to return to the present conversation. "Me? I didn't... Oh, um..." She appeared to be considering the accusation. She perked up. "Yes. It was me. I did it. It was for the best."

Total fruitcake. With extra nuts. This may take a while. He sat on a wood chair. "Ms. Montel?"

"Hmm?" she answered, balancing her thin frame on the arm of her sofa. Her eyes were half closed and the corners of her mouth turned upward.

"Can you tell me how you did it? I can't seem to figure out how this crime was committed."

"Oh! Um... I put arsenic in his water glass. Yes! That's what happened. But he was a bad man. He was a very bad man. It was in everyone's best interest that he die."

"I see. Do you still have the arsenic?"

"No. I threw it away."

"Mmmhmm." He rose from his seat and walked around the tiny apartment. It needed a good cleaning. All that dirt and dust had to be harboring millions of germs. He hoped he didn't have to touch anything, and wondered how long it would take before someone got sick from the place. He cast his gaze toward the open bedroom door. *Is that what I think it is? This case keeps on getting weirder.*

As he walked toward her bedroom to take a closer look, she jumped up and screamed, "You can't go in there! Stay away! I told you, I did it!"

"Ms. Montel, Edward Harrington wasn't poisoned with arsenic. Who are you protecting?" He opened the bedroom door wider, turning his back on Ava, and gasped loud enough for Kate to hear.

He heard Kate in his ear piece, "Did someone forget to say Robocop?"

"Holey Moley!"

At that moment, Ava Montel came running toward him screaming like a banshee with a butcher knife raised high above her head. Adam turned around and watched as she approached.

"Robocop," he said, and Kate was in the door with her gun drawn. Adam stepped aside and stuck his foot out, tripping Ava, who flew over his foot and landed sprawled on the floor with the knife still clutched in her hand.

"Put it down, Ava. You're outnumbered. It's over. Put the knife down," Kate said. Her voice was firm but calm. Ava looked like a wounded puppy and released the knife from her clenched fingers. Kate kicked it out of reach and stooped over Ava, handcuffs in hand.

"You can't go in there!" Ava screamed as Adam stepped toward her bedroom.

"Oh, I think I can," Adam said as Kate subdued and handcuffed Ava, leaving her on the floor, kicking and spewing invectives at them.

Kate joined Adam in the bedroom and her eyes widened. Plastered over Ava's walls were photographs and news clippings of Roland Harrington. A silver framed picture of Roland overlooked Ava's bed. They found a large photo album packed with everything that had ever been printed about the Harringtons.

"Wow," Kate muttered. "Can you spell obsessed?"

"Why did you confess to killing Harrington, Ava?" Adam asked, stepping back to the living room.

Ava began to cry. Kate helped her to a chair. "I don't want Roland to go to prison. All he wanted was a normal life. We're in love. He couldn't marry me because of his father, but now, with his horrible father out of the way, we're free to be together. Please don't send him away. He's never been free in his life. Now he has a chance at love…and a future…with me!"

Hoo boy. How did she ever get out of lockdown in the first place? "When did you first meet Roland?" Adam asked.

The corners of Ava's mouth turned up and her eyes glazed as she retreated to a faraway place. "Roland held the door open for me. I was going to Panera for lunch, and we got to the door at the same time. He held it for me and smiled at me. He said, 'After you, miss.' Roland Harrington was kind and had a beautiful smile. He stood behind me in line, admiring me and trying to figure out how to ask me out. I didn't quite have enough money to buy my lunch, and he was such a gentleman! He reached into his wallet and paid the cashier for my lunch. It was love at first sight."

"Did you see Roland Harrington after that?" Adam asked, trying to sift fact from fiction.

"Oh yes! All the time. Roland's picture was in the paper often. Not as often as his father's. I knew then that he was shy and wanted me to wait for his father to die so we could be together. He came to the play because he wanted to see me. I gave him my come hither look from the stage. He saw. He knew. And he knew what he had to do."

Is anybody connected to this case sane? Adam turned to Kate and spoke in a low voice so Ava could not hear. "Take her in and then get her some help."

"Where are you going?"

"To see Roland Harrington."

"Are you kidding? She doesn't have a single actual photo of him. Everything has been clipped from magazines and newspapers. I'll bet the rent Roland has never sent an e-mail, phone call, letter, flowers, nothing."

"He at least ought to know what went down here."

The same friendly receptionist greeted Adam and announced his arrival to Roland Harrington. Again, Adam waited less than a minute before Roland met him in the waiting area and ushered him into his office. Adam admired the view one more time. He knew Roland's practice was successful, but unlike Sid Friedman, Roland had no narcissistic need to put his success on display.

"Detective Trent. May I get you something to drink? Please, have a seat. Are there any developments in my father's case?"

Adam sat across from Roland. "Do you know a woman by the name of Ava Montel, Mr. Harrington?"

Roland furrowed his brow and pursed his lips. He shook his head. "No, sir. I don't believe that name is familiar to me. Who is she?"

"She's the young lady who portrayed Annalise Mansford in the play. Is she familiar to you now?"

"Ah, yes. Quite attractive, she was. But no, outside of that evening, I don't recall ever meeting her."

"She claims you paid for her lunch at a Panera's some time back. She didn't have money to pay for her purchases."

"Well, yes. I do remember something like that. Detective Trent, I must confess, I've done that kind of thing before. It's so easy to do, to run out of the house without checking your wallet. And it's embarrassing. It certainly may've been her. However, I have no specific recollection. Why? And what does this have to do with my father's murder?"

Adam explained the morning's events. Roland's eyes widened in surprise as he stared open-mouthed at Adam.

"Well, Detective Trent. I must say, this comes as a shock to me. Quite frankly, I was less surprised to learn that Father's death was a homicide, than to learn I have a secret admirer stalker!" Roland blinked his eyes several times. He shook his head and continued. "I assure you, Detective, I was entirely unaware of the young lady's affections. It's clear she needs help. I hope she gets it."

"She's being processed as we speak. She'll likely end up at Hyland, but at some point, she'll be released. I just thought you ought to be warned. Please call us if she bothers you. You'll be notified thirty days before Ms. Montel is released."

"Thank you, Detective Trent. I do hope she responds to treatment."

"Right. How's Fergus, by the way?" Adam asked.

"He just this morning threw up my fourth pair of slippers— thanks for asking. I can't imagine the draw."

Adam grinned. "Your slippers smell like you. It's a compliment."

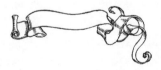

Adam returned to the City Morgue and peeked through the window of Dr. Avril Markham's door. The assistant coroner was writing on a chart. He tapped on the door and opened it.

"Hi, Avril. Got a minute?"

"Adam. Always. What brings you by? Did you get my report on Harrington? I sent it over Friday."

"I haven't been to the office yet. Any surprises?"

"Nope. Short version, he was given enough cyanide to kill a moose. He also had a heart condition, diabetes, hardening of the arteries, diverticulitis, cirrhosis of the liver and a host of other health issues. In other words, Edward Harrington was a walking time bomb. If his murderer had been patient, our vic would have departed this life unassisted within a year."

Adam nodded. "You're right. No surprises there. I've got some specific questions to ask you about the night he died."

"Shoot."

"Can I get you a cup of coffee or a soda or something?" Adam asked.

"Still can't handle the smell, huh?" Avril grinned. "Sure, there's a break room right this way." She locked her autopsy room behind them and led him down a hall and around a corner.

They sat at a table far enough away from the pungent smell of death and chemicals that Adam could think and breathe at the same time.

"I'm trying to understand exactly *how* Harrington died that night," Adam said. "I know it was cyanide, but he seemed fine, and then next thing you know, he didn't wake up. Do you just fall asleep? What's the process after ingestion? And do you have any idea when the poison might've been ingested?"

"Adam, for the amount of cyanide in his system, he should've been gasping for breath—at least for a short while, say, several seconds—before death. I don't know what the noise level was that night, but if it was quiet, I would think you would've heard him struggling to breathe. Like I said the other day, it appeared as if there may've been a number of small doses administered over the course of the meal, but at some point, a large amount was ingested. While Harrington was certainly on the road to an early death, the official cause of death was cyanide poisoning and nothing else. All the details are in my report, but I'm giving you the condensed version. There was nothing else in his autopsy that was unusual or out of the ordinary. Sorry to disappoint you."

Adam held up his hands. "No, No, Avril. I'm not disappointed. Just a little confused at how this could have happened right in front of me and I never noticed anything awry. It looked like a heart attack, like I said before. I'm just trying to sort out the details. One more question, if you don't mind."

She looked at him and raised her eyebrows.

"Is there any way the dosing could've been timed so that he died right after dessert was served?"

"Sure. If he was given small doses throughout the meal and a large dose when his dessert was being served, that would do the trick. That would mean somebody knew exactly what they were doing, or else they got very, very lucky."

Adam stood. "Well, Avril, I know you've got work to do and I have plenty waiting for me at the office. Thanks for your time— and thanks for getting on this so quickly."

They shook hands and Adam left the building while Dr. Markham retreated to her autopsy room.

Stepping outside, Adam breathed fresh air deep into his lungs, glad to be away from the morgue, the smell of death and noxious chemicals. Fall was bursting forth, painting St. Louis with rich, glorious colors and blanketing the atmosphere in cool, crisp air. It had never smelled better to Adam. He walked around the corner to the police station, took the flight of stairs to his office and sat down at his computer. Avril's report was in his inbox. He scanned it, but found nothing new, other than the technical medical jargon explaining in official terms the same thing she had told him in plain English only minutes before.

Captain Peterson approached and perched on the corner of Adam's desk. "Kate should be back soon. Ava Montel is on her way to Hyland for evaluation and admittance, no doubt. It'll be a while before she gets out. Kate told me you were going to talk to Roland Harrington. What did Mr. Harrington have to say?"

"He seemed surprised. He's quite the gentleman. Claimed he's paid for others who have run short of money. He's a gracious

man. I believe him. No reason not to. You can have someone
check his cell phone and e-mails as a follow up, but I don't think
you'll find any connection between Roland Harrington and Ava
Montel, outside of her own delusions."

Peterson rubbed his chin. "The autopsy report has been
released. It should be all over the news pretty soon. Who do
you have left to interview?" Adam pulled out his notebook and
scanned it. "Mariah Flores, Mark Vernon, Carl Mendoza and
Mike Davey—all employees of the restaurant. Mendoza and
Vernon share an apartment. I'm heading over there now. Then
Ms. Flores, and I'll try to catch Mike Davey, the bartender, at the
beginning of his shift."

"Do you want to wait and go with Kate?"

"No. She might be a while. I'd like to get the interviews over
with before we start the white board. When Kate gets back,
would you ask her to do some digging on these last few suspects
and call me if anything interesting comes up? She already did a
preliminary, so I'm not expecting any great shakes here. I just
don't want any surprises. Make that any *more* surprises." Adam
stood to leave.

Captain Peterson agreed, turned and walked into his office and
picked up his phone. "Here's his order of business today."

Adam parked his car outside the Dogtown apartment building
where Mark Vernon and Carl Mendoza lived and pulled out his
notes to review. Mark had played Josiah Mansford in the play
and Carl had played Stefan, the ill-fated lover of Annalise. Kate's

research into them revealed nothing remarkable. Mark and Carl appeared to be a couple of honest working guys trying to make a living and get discovered somewhere along the way. Adam wondered if this visit would hold any surprises as he trotted up the three flights of stairs and walked to the right to their door. He repeated to himself that somebody, somewhere, knew something and hoped this visit would be a turning point.

Adam rang the doorbell. He heard shuffling noises followed by the sound of footsteps approaching from the other side. Mark Vernon opened the door looking like he had recently stepped out of the shower. His hair was wet and uncombed and he was wearing shorts and a tee shirt that didn't match, as though he had dressed in a hurry.

"Mr. Vernon?"

"That's me. What's goin' on?" Mark opened the door so Adam could enter. He walked to the refrigerator and filled a plate with cold pizza. "Want some? I was just getting breakfast."

"No, thanks."

"Have a seat. Want a soda?" Mark plopped down on the sofa and crammed half a slice of pizza into his mouth, while Adam took a nearby chair.

Adam asked the usual questions, but, like the others, Mark had not seen anything, heard anything, or known anything. Adam saw no reason to question Mark further. There was nothing to be gained and he still had a list of others to question.

"I'll leave you to your breakfast, Mr. Vernon. Is Mr. Mendoza here?"

Mark shifted uncomfortably, avoiding Adam's gaze. He set his plate of pizza on the cushion next to him and fidgeted.

"Carl's at work. He had to cover lunch shift before the Mansion tonight. But I don't think he knows anything, either. We've all been talking about it."

Adam consulted the well-prepared notes Kate had given him. "That would be Helen Fitzgerald's? On Lindbergh?"

"Yeah," Mark replied, looking down and away. His shoulders slumped.

Curious. Mark Vernon goes from being relaxed and comfortable to defensive and defeated, as soon as I mention Carl.

"You and Carl been friends a long time?"

"Oh, yeah. Since grade school. Carl's a real good guy. Never been in any kind of trouble or nothin'. I don't think he's gonna be any help to you. Sorry, but I don't know nothin' either."

Adam thanked him and made a mental note of Mark's body language.

Adam drove to Helen Fitzgerald's, twenty minutes from Dogtown, where he found Carl pouring drinks for the early lunch crowd. As soon as he entered the restaurant he caught Carl's eye and sensed panic. Carl wiped his hands on his apron, picked up the pace of his work, and acted as though he hadn't seen Adam. He scrubbed the bar counter with more energy than necessary, busied himself making drinks and setting up glasses, napkins, whatever he could find. Adam found the act unconvincing. He stepped up to the bar, forcing Carl to acknowledge his presence.

"What'll it be?" Carl asked, but in his attempt to sound casual, his voice cracked.

Adam discreetly showed his badge and said in a low voice, "Can you take a break, Mr. Mendoza? I need to ask you a few questions."

Carl's face twitched and he looked away. He motioned for an attractive blond with her hair pulled into a pony tail stuck through a Cardinal's baseball cap to come and relieve him. Carl wiped his hands on his apron again, leaving wet streaks, and he and Adam retreated to a back table. "What's this all about?"

"I need to ask you some questions about the night Edward Harrington died at Mansford Mansion," Adam said, observing Carl's body language.

"I thought he had a heart attack. I didn't know he was murdered until I heard it on the radio this morning," Carl answered. He took a napkin from the metal holder and began to pick it apart, twisting the corners back and forth.

"What was your relationship to Edward Harrington?"

Carl slumped, defeated. He put his head in his hands. He was shaking.

"What did Mark tell you?" he asked in a flat tone.

"Mr. Vernon didn't tell me anything, but his actions indicated he was trying to protect you. So we can continue this conversation here, or we can take a ride down to the station. Your choice, but as soon as I even so much as suspect you're lying, I'll take you downtown in handcuffs. So I suggest you tell me everything."

Carl nodded, pressing his fingers on each side of his nose. "We were jam packed that night. It was so busy, we had five bartenders in that little space, trying to get everybody taken care of," he said, jerking his head sideways to the bar area.

Adam had no clue what Carl was talking about, but he nodded as though he understood.

"She came in alone, as far as I could tell, and ordered a drink," he continued.

"Uh huh," Adam said.

"Officer, I swear—I *swear* to you, I did *not* know she was underage. She looked like she was at least thirty with all that black eye make-up on. I card anyone I even remotely suspect could be under twenty-one. I had no idea. You gotta believe me. I never would've served her if I had known." Carl was sweating and trembling.

Sheesh. Adam sighed and closed his eyes for a few seconds. *So this is the big secret.* "So how old was Lucinda Harrington when you served her alcohol?"

Carl glanced around and cupped his hand next to his cheek. "She was twenty. Close, but not legal. If it came out, I'd be fired on the spot. They're very strict about that kind of thing here. I *need* this job. From that time forward, I card everyone. I swear I do."

"And how did Edward Harrington find out? Lucinda doesn't strike me as a young lady who would share that information with a man like her father."

"I don't know how he found out. He was a cruel and overbearing man. For all I know, he could've been following his daughter.

Anyway, he was waiting for me in the parking lot after my shift was over and threatened to go to the police and file charges against the bar and against me personally. I tried to reason with him, but he demanded money in exchange for his silence. You'd think a man with all his money wouldn't need to extort from working folks. I make very little at Mansford, and enough to get by here, because Mark and I split the bills."

Adam wrote in his notebook. "Okay. So did you know Edward Harrington was going to be at Mansford Mansion that night?"

"No! Absolutely not! I was mortified when I saw him in the audience. I was a couple of days late with my blackmail payment, and I thought he'd come to ruin me."

"So you hatched a plan to get rid of him that night? Did Mark help you in that endeavor?"

"No, no! I was terrified! You can bet the rent I shed no tears when that man died, but I didn't kill him. Until this morning, I thought he had a heart attack. I thanked my guardian angel for the gift. Mark told me he overheard Jasmine and Alan talking and thought there might've been foul play, but I first heard for certain on this morning's news. Mark didn't think Harrington recognized me with my hair slicked down and all the stage make-up." "Have you ever purchased cyanide?"

"Cyanide! No. I wouldn't even know where to get it. Or how to use it." Carl continued to pick at the napkin until it was a pile of confetti.

"Did you see or hear anything unusual that night? See anyone tampering with Harrington's food or drink?" Adam flipped a page in his notebook.

"No. Once my character is killed off, I put on an apron and go back to the kitchen to help. We all take turns. Alan's pretty cheap."

Adam nodded. Alan Cunningham's penny pinching seemed to be a main theme among his employees. "So while you were working in the kitchen, was anybody back there who shouldn't have been? Did you see any food dishes being prepared in a different manner than usual?"

"No. But we were busy, so I don't know that I would've noticed anything in the food prep. All we do is open cans and nuke frozen dishes. But nobody was in the kitchen that didn't belong there." Carl paused and destroyed another napkin. "Are you going to arrest me?" His voice caught.

"For what?"

"You know. Underage serving," Carl whispered, leaning forward.

"I'm a St. Louis city homicide detective, Mr. Mendoza. Helen Fitzgerald's is in St. Louis County. Not my jurisdiction." Adam had done the math in his head. Carl had served Lucinda three months before she turned twenty-one. Not exactly Adam's idea of a capital offense. "I've got much bigger fish to fry."

Carl relaxed for the first time since Adam had seen him that afternoon.

Adam stood. "I'm looking for a killer. That's all for now. Don't leave town, Carl." He left the restaurant as the lunch crowd grew. The smell of food cooking wafted from the kitchen, piquing Adam's appetite.

Adam drove toward the nursing home in St. Louis Hills where Mariah Flores worked. He would pick up a quick bite after he talked to her. His Bluetooth notified him Kate was calling.

"Hey, Kate. What's up?"

"You asked me to do a little deeper digging?"

"Yeah?"

"Mike Davey. The bartender. Got into some trouble while he was in the Navy. Served his country honorably, but had a gambling problem and got mixed up with some not-so-honest folks."

"Don't tell me. Harrington found out and was blackmailing him, too?"

Kate laughed. "Not that I know of. Davey got help and straightened out, but he can have a temper if provoked and he's plenty capable of doing some damage. He's strong and keeps himself in shape. I just wanted to warn you to be careful, that's all. So Carl was also being blackmailed?"

Adam filled her in on his interview with Carl Mendoza.

"Hey Kate. Got a question for you. Carl asked me during our interview, and I've been wondering the same thing. I've got my own theory, but I'm interested in your take."

"Sure. If you've just got *one* question on this case, you're way ahead of me."

"Harrington had more money than he knew what to do with, right? Why do you think he resorted to blackmail? And how do you think he found his victims?"

"Yeah, I've thought a lot about that, too. I suppose we'd have to talk to Dr. Gerwyn for a professional opinion, but I've got my own theories."

"I did talk to Gerwyn. He said Harrington was a classic narcissist."

"He was also just a mean old man. That's probably not the medical term. I don't need Dr. Gerwyn to see that. I think the old fart derived great pleasure from blackmail. Especially when the people couldn't pay. So if Doc Gerwyn said Harrington was a narcissist, then that means Harrington's world revolved around Harrington. I'm thinkin' it was a control issue. Sticking it to working folks fed his cruel nature. It had more to do with making people miserable and nothing to do with needing money."

"Okay, I can buy that. It fits. Harrington wanted to make others as unhappy as he was. So what's your take on how he found his victims?"

"That's a little tougher. I think in Carl's case, Harrington was probably following Lucinda. We know he didn't approve of women drinking alcohol, and she, of course was his wild child, so he decided to punish the person who served her."

"Makes sense, I guess. No point in punishing Lucinda, since nothing affects her. And the others?"

"Just speculating here, Adam. The guy's dead, so we can't ask him, but I tend to believe the others may have been coincidental. Harrington happened to be at the right place at the right time and took take advantage of another person's weakness. He was opportunistic enough to turn someone else's misfortune into another avenue to feed his narcissism. I suppose we'll never know for sure, but I think he was always looking for someone he could exploit."

"So how do you think something like that might've gone down?"

Kate was quiet for a minute, and Adam thought he might have lost the connection. Then he heard her take a breath. "For example, if you hang out at a department store long enough, sooner or later you'll see someone shoplift something. Kimber Dennison was the lucky winner when she couldn't resist that scarf. Harrington wouldn't have bothered going after teenagers. That would've been too much of a challenge and no reward. But he could get to someone like Kimber. Hey, do you remember the Coral Court No-Tell Motel?"

Adam laughed. "Who doesn't? Rooms by the hour and closed garages."

"Yeah. Prostitute heaven and a regular campground for private eyes looking for unfaithful spouses. Great history."

"I agree. How does the Coral Court Motel figure into Harrington's blackmail scheme? It's been closed for twenty years, I think."

"Say Harrington goes for a higher class of patrons than those who frequented Coral Court? Maybe he hangs out in the lobby, reading the newspaper and watching for patterns, the same guests showing up on a particular day, that sort of thing. Again, just speculating, but he notices Charlie and his side dish on Thursdays, whatever, at one of the nicer hotels, and puts the screws to Charlie. Then, he learns where Kimber likes to shop. Not like she doesn't post that stuff all over Facebook."

"Right. I see where you're going. Hmm. I wonder if there are other blackmail victims we don't know about."

"My guess is that there are lots of others we don't know about, given that human nature dictates we all screw up at one time or another. I'm betting Harrington kept a list somewhere, but you'd need a search warrant to go through that castle of his. Pretty sure Cedric and Lucinda wouldn't give permission, and if they did, it'd be because they'd already gotten rid of any list. Too hot to hold onto."

"I'm confident you're right about that. But regardless of how many other victims might be on that blackmail list, we can at least be glad they weren't all at the restaurant that night. We've got enough suspects as it is."

"Good point."

"Well, I'm pulling into the nursing home where Mariah Flores works. Thanks for your input. I think your take on Harrington makes a lot of sense. Call ya later."

Adam parked toward the back of the building, so his squad car was unobtrusive. No point in raising alarms. He observed the one-story brick facility, shaped like a wagon wheel with manicured lawns and landscaping of pink and white flowers shedding their remaining petals as summer segued into fall.

Adam walked through the large double doors unnoticed and sat in the lobby of Rosemount Skilled Nursing and Rehabilitation Center watching the staff bustling back and forth, pushing trays of medicines, snacks, clean linens and all things necessary to comfort the suffering in the winter of their lives. He noted with interest the manner in which the employees performed their duties. Several were cold as ice, doing the minimum, and spoke to the ailing residents in harsh tones. Impatient, uncaring and bored, their faces were grim as they stared straight ahead and walked briskly, putting in their time until their shift was over. Whether they were in fact, mean-spirited people or simply burned out from working long hours he did not know, but he could think of no excuse for treating another human being, particularly one who was frail and helpless, with such callous indifference. On the other end of the spectrum were the staff members who cheerfully carried out their tasks, treating their charges with kindness and compassion. Adam respected people who considered their work a calling, rather than a job, and valued the dignity of all people for no other reason than because they were worth it. Adam wondered where on this continuum Mariah Flores fell.

He had been waiting in the lobby several minutes. No receptionist was present at the front desk, no security guard was visible and no one took notice of him, which he found disconcerting. He could have been anybody. He could have been there for any reason. He could have been Dr. Cranston. The thought made him shudder.

Adam saw Mariah Flores as she walked to a linen closet and pulled out fresh sheets. He stood and approached her as she was shutting the closet door. "Ms. Flores?" he asked, cupping his hand to show his badge.

Her face showed no emotion, but she looked tired. "Yes?"

"May I have a few minutes of your time?"

She looked back and forth and answered him in a low voice. "I don't get a break for another twenty minutes. Can we talk then, maybe? I have to get back to work and get a bed changed now."

"Of course. Can you meet me outside on the bench in front of the building? It won't take long. Can I get you a soda?"

She half-smiled. "Thanks. That'd be nice. There's a snack machine just to the left of the front doors. Anything that isn't diet will be fine."

Adam exited the building as unnoticed as when he had entered it. The smell of old urine, the scent of impending death and hopelessness stung his nostrils and he was grateful for the coolness of the clean autumn air as he waited outside for Mariah. He took a deep breath, gulping down the fresh air, wondering if the staff ever got used to the stench, as Doc Sutter and Avril

Markham had grown accustomed to the chemical smell in the autopsy rooms. The morgue smelled of finality, the quietness of death and the exploration of its causes. But the nursing home smelled of the anticipation of another day of bleak futility, the last step before the end. Adam felt a wave of melancholy wash over him. He could not picture his parents in such a place, and even less so, himself or Jenna. Taking another deep breath of the cool, crisp air, he willed his thoughts from impending depression to the present. Life was a precious gift from God and every day was worth fighting for and protecting. That core value was the driving force behind Adam's decision to become a cop. It compelled him to seek justice for those robbed of life by the willful actions of those who disrespected life.

He glanced at his watch. Mariah Flores would be out any minute. Adam bought her a can of soda and a bag of pretzels from the vending machine. She appeared as promised. Strands of her long dark hair had worked loose from the clips that held it up. Mariah accepted the soda and pretzels with a nod of thanks, and sat beside Adam.

"I have fifteen minutes and then I have to get back," she said, pushing her hair back and massaging her hands as if they hurt. "What's this about?"

"I'm investigating the murder of Edward Harrington. You waited on his table the night he died. Did you know the Harrington family would be there that night?" He took out his notepad and pen.

"No. I knew we had a large party and I was assigned to their table and another table of two. Jasmine had the rest of the tables, but when she saw the type of people I'd be serving, she volunteered to take the smaller party, since she knew my hands would be full. She also promised to split her tips with me, as we both figured that was gonna be a zero night for me."

"And did she do that?"

"Oh, yeah. Jasmine's always very nice to everyone. She's a little mysterious, but she treats everybody great."

"Mmmhmm." Adam took notes as she spoke. "Did you bring all of the food and drink to the Harrington's table that night?"

"I definitely brought all the food. I brought some of the drinks, but some of the family also went to the bar, so I didn't bring all of the drinks. Why?"

"How about I ask the questions?"

"Yeah, okay, whatever." She took a drink of soda.

"Is it true that there are several people involved in the preparation of the food, depending on who is and isn't on stage?"

"Yeah. We all pretty much do something in the kitchen."

"Edward Harrington was poisoned. It was in his food and drink. Any idea how it might have gotten in there?" Adam was writing in his notebook.

Mariah's eyes widened and her mouth flew open. "No! I can't imagine! Well...well... anybody, I guess!"

"Toward the end of the drama, you started screaming offstage. Wanna tell me what that was all about?"

Mariah laughed out loud. "It was a joke we were playing on Ava."

Adam sat unmoved, remembering his first reaction to her scream. "I fail to see the humor. Why don't you let me in on the joke?"

Mariah opened the bag of pretzels and popped a handful in her mouth. "In case you hadn't noticed, Ava's a terrible actress. I mean, really, the pits. Everyone knows she only got the part because she looks like the portrait of Annalise. I've seen third grade plays with better acting than Ava's."

Adam could not disagree with Mariah's assessment. "And the joke?"

"Yeah, well, when the Captain confronts her and Stefan and points the gun, Ava, or Annalise rather, is supposed to scream. Ava's so stupid. She doesn't even have a clue how to scream. She sounds more like overly dramatic fainting, ya know? Like maybe she's got a bad headache. Well, every time we practiced, we couldn't get her to scream, like, a real scream, so me and Mike, we thought it'd be a real hoot if, like, just before she gets shot, I screamed loud and long from offstage. It was fun, just to upset her and see her jump. She's a real weird bird, in case you hadn't noticed."

Adam consulted his notes. "Mike Davey, the bartender? Is that the Mike you mean?"

"Yeah."

"And what did your boss, Mr. Cunningham, think of your little joke?"

Mariah's smile faded. "Well, of course, that night, ya know, the old guy up and died, so nothing was said until the next performance. Alan wasn't too pleased, but by that time, we had a full house with a waiting list, so he just told me he expected me to do my job, not Ava's. I'd had my fun, so I stuck to waiting tables after that."

"I see. Ms. Flores, do you have access to cyanide?"

Adam thought he saw her flinch, but he wasn't sure, so slight was the movement.

"Cyanide? Where would I get cyanide?"

"You tell me."

"I have no idea." Mariah finished her soda.

"Did you see anybody tamper with the food or drink going to the Harrington table?"

"No. We were busy. Sorry. Look. I gotta get back to work," she said, looking back toward the building. "I got a patient who gets his enema soon, so I need to like, get his bed pan. Thanks again for the snacks." She rose to leave, hurrying back inside.

Adam sat on the bench and finished writing his notes. His stomach was growling. The lunch crowd would be thinning out now, and Adam looked forward to enjoying a quiet meal during the restaurant lull of mid-afternoon. He mentally mapped his present location in St. Louis Hills to Mansford Mansion, his next stop, and decided to eat at Seamus McDaniels, home of the best burgers in the Lou. Not quite halfway if he took the most direct route, but Adam was certain he heard a medium rare pepper cheese burger with a side of toasted ravioli calling him, and it just wouldn't be right not to answer that call. He headed to Dogtown.

After a satisfying lunch at his favorite window table, Adam sat back to let his meal settle. It was too early to head over to Mansford Mansion, so he requested a cup of coffee and watched with mild interest, the people walking down Tamm Avenue. He called Captain Peterson to update him and let him know his plans were still on schedule. There was no news on Cranston. Adam wished he had Bo and Connor to work these cases with him. Twice, he thought he had glimpsed one or the other of them, but when he looked again, he had been mistaken, his mind playing tricks on him. As he lingered over his coffee, Adam removed his pocket New Testament and Psalms to read. He found great comfort in the Psalms, especially the ones David wrote when he was surrounded by enemies and feeling like everyone was against him. Twice he read Psalm 46, 62 and 69. With body and soul refreshed, Adam left for Mansford Mansion to interview Mike Davey.

Adam reached Mansford Mansion a half hour before it opened for business. The door was unlocked, so he stepped inside and walked past the dining room to the bar where Mike Davey was making final preparations for another sell-out crowd.

"We're not quite open yet, but I could get you a beer, if you like," Mike said. He sounded upbeat.

Adam declined and introduced himself. He had not been to the bar the night Harrington was murdered, and had not met Mike Davey. He found the bartender amiable, but, like the others, Mr. Davey had not seen anyone tampering with the drinks. Mike was not able to provide any information regarding the food, because he only worked the bar that night and was unaware of what transpired in the kitchen, beyond the end result of terrible food.

Adam was getting tired of hearing the same answers to his questions, and got straight to the point. "Was Edward Harrington blackmailing you?"

Mike's mouth flew open and his eyes bugged out "What?"

"Was Edward Harrington extorting money from you by threatening to expose a secret from your past?"

"Like *what*?"

"You had some gambling trouble when you were in the Navy..."

"That's hardly a secret," Mike cut him off. "Yeah I screwed up pretty bad, but I got the help I needed and I've never looked back. I haven't kept that from anyone. Look, I'm not proud of that part of my life, but the past is the past." He glanced at the clock and began setting up glasses.

Finally. Someone who wasn't paying hush money to Harrington. Getting nowhere, Adam changed his line of questioning. He was frustrated with the lack of progress.

"Which of the Harringtons came to the bar, or did Mariah serve all of their drinks?" Mike frowned and pressed his lips together. "I can't say for sure, but at least two of the Harringtons were here at the bar. Mariah was pretty busy with their drinks as well. We also have appetizers available, for an extra charge, and I know she took a few plates of those out, too. That table kept her running all night. Sorry, man, I just don't remember who got what."

"All right." Adam was not entirely convinced. The bartenders he knew had pretty good memories. "Did you notice anything unusual or out of the ordinary during the course of the evening? Anyone behaving strangely? Either before or after the murder?"

Mike's cheerful countenance fell. "There was Ava," he said with a sad note in his voice. "She was her usual flighty, ethereal self until Harrington died. Then she was—I don't know, she acted really strange, like she was relieved or something. I couldn't figure her," he sighed.

Poor guy. He's sure got a thing for Ava. Must not have realized she wasn't playing with a full deck. "I see. Was there anything else that struck you as odd?"

Mike thought a minute, taking a breath as though he was about to speak, but remained silent.

Anytime, now. Please answer before dinner. Adam was already getting hungry again. Even the awful food being prepared in the kitchen was beginning to smell good.

"One thing, but I'm not too sure about it. The more I think about it, the more I think it was just the angle messing with my eyesight."

"What was it?"

"From where I was standing, it looked like the creepy Harrington son, the one who smelled like he smoked."

"Cedric? Thin mustache?"

"Yeah, that's him. He wouldn't leave Mariah alone. She ignored him and looked pretty aggravated to me. She wasn't rude to his face, but she wasn't polite either. I asked her if she wanted me to step in and take care of things, but she said she could handle it, so I backed off. But while I was filling drinks, he was at the bar, and it looked to me, at least from my position here, like he grabbed her butt and squeezed and she lingered a second, which really struck me as odd because she'd been avoiding him all night. But like I said, I think it might've been the angle."

Mike began filling containers with maraschino cherries, slices of lemons, limes and oranges and other bar accoutrements.

Adam remembered what a slimy lecher Cedric had been and how he had seen Mariah move away each time he tried to grope her.

"Do you wear glasses, Mr. Davey? Is there a reason your eyes may have tricked you?"

"My left eye's not too good. I got in a fight back when I was havin' all my trouble, so I don't see too good outta that eye. That's why I wasn't sure I oughta say anything."

"Tell me why Mariah started the offstage screaming."

"I wish I could," Mike replied with a half laugh. "That was pretty odd."

"Did you and Mariah think up that little trick to play a joke on Ava?"

Mike gripped the edge of the counter and glared at Adam. Adam saw a flash of the anger Kate had warned him about. "Absolutely not. Where would you get an idea like that?" *He has it pretty bad for Ava. Why did Mariah lie? Who is she protecting?* "What's your relationship with Ava Montel?" Adam asked.

Mike looked away. His anger fizzled as quickly as it had sparked. "Ava wasn't interested in a relationship with me. Believe me, I tried." He looked down and wiped away a water ring from the bar. He looked at Adam with sad eyes. "I would never have done anything to hurt Ava or upset her. There's a new girl playing her part tonight. I don't even know where Ava is now."

"Thanks for your time, Mr. Davey. If you can think of anything else that might be helpful, please give me a call." Adam handed him a card and left.

He called Kate Marlin from his car as he turned onto the street.

"Hey, Kate. Need something to do, or is the new pup in action yet?"

"Nah, I got a couple more weeks. What's up?"

"See what you can dig up on Mariah Flores. She's been a little less than truthful, and I want to know why."

"On it. Later."

Chapter 12

Adam stopped at Imo's to pick up a carryout pizza for dinner. With Jenna and blabbermouth Amy, who tattled every time he ingested an extra gram of fat, at his parents' farm, he ordered pepperoni. Jenna wouldn't stand for so many chemicals, nitrates, nitrites and other poisons in her kitchen, so all pizza had to be cheese, topped with veggies of some sort, or free range chicken. *What she doesn't know won't hurt her.* Feeling the slightest twinge of guilt, Adam ordered a salad to go with his toxic pizza. *Much better*, he convinced himself. *Okay, almost much better. Queen Jenna will never know.*

He ate alone at the safe house apartment, thinking over the case, missing his team, and missing Jenna and Amy even more. He didn't blame Connor for staying with his family, presumably far away somewhere and safe. All those little ones needed their father. But Bo had no family, and he was surprised that Bo didn't stick around to hunt down Cranston and catch him in the act of taking another innocent and helpless life. Discouragement hovered over Adam. It had been a long day. He was tired and the questions he sought answers to remained unanswered. But before he could take his first step down depression road, his throwaway phone rang and his mood lifted.

"Hey, babe. I was gonna call as soon as I finished dinner. How are things going?"

"We just finished our meal too, Adam. What are you having?"

"Salad. Gotta take care of myself until you get your old job back!" he crammed the last piece of pizza into his mouth and swallowed it half-chewed.

"Uh huh. Did that salad come with a pepperoni pizza?"

How does she know this stuff? "How's home schooling going?" he asked, changing the subject.

He could hear her smile in the way she caught her breath, and in her teasing accusation. *Caught red-handed eating forbidden food, fifty miles away. Pathetic.*

"I heard you laugh, Jenna."

"I love you, too. Amy's doing better. Her school work is fine, and she's helping out on the farm. I think that's been a good experience for her. Any progress on the case?"

"Nothing on Cranston yet, but he'll screw up. Still working the Harrington murder, but nothing solid so far. Kate Marlin's helping me. She said to tell you hi. Robo's been retired and living the life of a pampered pooch, and she doesn't have her new dog yet."

"Give her my best. I'm glad she's helping you. If this is all over before the weather gets too nasty, we'll have her over for another barbecue. We'll even stick a plain burger on the grill for Robo."

They chatted a while longer and said their goodbyes. Adam promised to return Friday night. Hanging up the phone, he felt better knowing his girls were doing well. Tomorrow he would organize his notes and begin diagramming the white board. As he sat on the sofa, staring at the empty pizza box and salad carton, the events of the day flooded through his mind and overtook his tired muscles. Adam's body was exhausted, but his mind was racing. He got up and stretched, picked up the box and carton and put them in the trash bin. He yawned and his head felt heavy. *Better get to bed before I drop where I am.*

Setting his badge and gun in their usual position on the night stand, Adam checked and double-checked the doors and windows before retiring for the night. He lay in bed, trying to put his thoughts in order before drifting into restless slumber.

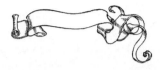

Kate Marlin picked up a cheeseburger and chili at Carl's Drive-in and drove home to eat. Robo, whose sense of smell had not dimmed at all with age, greeted her with eternal hope shining in his large expressive eyes.

"Just a little bit of burger. Chili's not a good idea for puppy," she told him, tearing off a portion. "Hey! At least chew it, ya pig!"

He looked at her with a joyful expectation of seconds, but it was not to be. "Go get your leash, Robo," she told him. A walk was every bit as good as a burger. Robo took off and returned with the leash in his mouth. Dropping it at her feet, he sat watching her with his large ears forward and tail wagging.

Kate inhaled the rest of her dinner and clipped the leash onto Robo's collar. "You're not retired yet, partner. We still have a little work to do. Don't tell anybody," she whispered. He wagged his tail in obedient agreement to whatever it was she had just whispered.

Chapter 13

Adam woke suddenly before four a.m. and bolted upright in bed. As he allowed his eyes to adjust to the dark, he felt uneasy. *Maybe Jenna's right. Too much pepperoni. Don't think I'll do that again.* He reached over to the night stand and froze. Fumbling for the switch to the lamp, he turned it on and stared at the night stand. His gun and badge were there, but not in the same place he had put them before retiring. He was certain. Adam was a man of strict habits. He knew precisely where he had laid his things. They had been moved.

Adam looked around the bedroom and listened, but the apartment was quiet. He checked his gun, removing the clip, and with his thumb, ejected the bullets. All the rounds were there. The barrel was clear. He tested the spring and the firing pin and took the entire piece apart, going through every inch of every part until he was satisfied that his weapon had not been tampered with. But it had been moved. A couple of inches. Adam reassembled the gun, testing the action. Confident the action of the gun had not been compromised, he replaced the bullets in the clip and loaded the gun. He pulled the receiver back and injected a round into the chamber. He set the safety and replaced the gun on the night stand.

Adam dressed in a hurry, skipping his shower, and checked the doors and windows again. All were locked. He looked in the closets, cabinets and under the bed. Nothing. But someone had been in his room. Watching him sleep. And letting him know of their presence by moving his gun and badge a couple of inches. *Cranston!* It couldn't be anyone else. Tossing a change of clothes and his toothbrush into a bag, Adam left the apartment and sped to the station. In the darkness of the early morning hours, he saw no one. Was Cranston watching him now? Who was the hunter and who was the prey?

He hated to wake up the captain at such an early hour, but it was unavoidable.

Captain Peterson came fully awake when told of the intruder. "What! Cranston? No way Adam. It's just not possible. Where are you?"

"On my way to the station, Cap. It's not like I'm gonna go back to sleep *now*. I'll shower in the locker room. I'm only ten minutes away."

"I'll meet you there in an hour."

"What now, Gavin?" Melanie Peterson asked her husband, her voice husky from being woken out of a sound sleep. She sat on the side of the bed and sluggishly pushed herself up in an effort to journey to the kitchen to make coffee for her husband. As newlyweds thirty years ago, she promised herself she would rise whenever her husband had an emergency call in the middle of the night. She had thought all those years back that if he could sacrifice sleep for the safety of total strangers, the least she could do was sacrifice sleep to make coffee for the man she loved. However, as they both got older, Melanie found herself questioning whether that was still such a great idea. As a twenty-five year old bride, she hadn't had arthritis. Now, her joints ached every morning. *Quit being such a baby. He's got less than two years until retirement, and then we can sleep as late as we like.*

"Go back to bed, Mel. I'll pick up coffee on the way."

"No way. It's never as good as mine." She straightened her spine, stretched and walked purposefully into the kitchen. The one small luxury they had always allowed, tight budget notwithstanding, was gourmet coffee, even when Gavin had been a young patrolman. He loved his coffee and she loved her husband. They had eaten their fair share of mac and cheese, hot dogs and ramen noodles, shopped at second-hand stores and driven their cars until the wheels fell off, but they always drank gourmet coffee. When Gavin made captain, they bought an expensive coffeemaker that ground fresh beans and immediately brewed them. It was a purchase they never regretted.

By the time Captain Peterson was showered and dressed, the aroma of fresh brewed, dark roast coffee permeated the house. He poured a cup, held it under his nose to inhale, and sat at the kitchen table to drink.

"Eggs?" she asked him, walking toward the refrigerator.

"Too early to eat. I'll grab some day-old donuts at the station."

"Liar. Donuts don't last a day at the station." She poured herself a cup of coffee and sat down across from him. Melanie could not remember Adam Trent ever calling Gavin at home. She reached across the table and touched her husband's hand. "Anything I should be worried about?"

"Of course. The world's a dangerous place. Keep the house locked up, watch where you're going, be aware of your surroundings and call me if anything seems out of place or suspicious. No sense in protecting St. Louis if I can't protect my own wife." He touched her cheek with the back of his hand.

It was a familiar mini-sermon. He rose and kissed her, then hurried out the door. The station was a fifteen minute traffic free drive at this absurd hour in the morning.

"Adam. Are you sure? Are you absolutely certain?" They were in Gavin's office.

"*Yes!* I *know* where I left my gun and badge. It had been moved two inches." Adam refused to budge on his account of the early morning discovery.

Captain Peterson sighed. If any of his men had come to him with a story of their belongings being moved two inches, he would have expressed doubt and dismissed such a claim without a second thought. But Adam was fastidious and exact. His perfectionist-driven attention to detail helped get him promoted to detective early in his law enforcement career. Gavin Peterson called the monitoring company to check the tracking device on Dr. Cranston. The monitor showed that the ankle bracelet never left Cranston's home in Clayton.

"I don't see how it could be Cranston. According to the monitor, he never left home. I spoke to the supervisor, and he confirmed it."

"Then I want the device and Cranston checked," Adam insisted. "I'm telling you, he was there."

Captain Peterson checked his watch. "I'll call the Clayton police and ask them to pay a visit to Cranston. We'll get to the bottom of this."

"Son, it's six in the morning. What's wrong?" Dwayne Trent carried the phone outside to the back porch where his conversation could not be overheard by anyone else in the house.

"Dad, keep the girls inside today. Make whatever excuse you need to. Lock up tight and keep a careful eye out. I know Blue is Amy's responsibility, but I'd feel better if you took her on short walks and kept your pistol in your pocket."

"You wanna fill me in, Adam?"

"Cranston's found a way to get out. I don't know how. But I need to know my family is safe. That includes you and Mom."

"I'll take care of it, son. You watch yourself, boy."

Dwayne hung up and returned to the kitchen. Jenna was cracking eggs for breakfast while bacon and sausage sizzled in the skillet. She heard Emma Jo walking down the hall toward the kitchen. Jenna turned to her father-in-law so her back was to the hall and her voice wouldn't carry to Emma Jo. "Was that Adam on the phone?" she asked. "What's wrong? Tell me."

"Everything's fine, honey. Don't you worry about a thing." He whistled for Blue who trotted in. "C'mon Blue, let's go for a walk."

But Jenna knew better and she did worry. Everything was not fine.

Adam arrived at Dr. Cranston's home on Ridgemoor Drive in the swank Claverach Park subdivision of Clayton. A Clayton police car pulled in front of the house at the same time Adam did. They were greeted at the front door by a smiling Lionel Cranston. Adam thought Cranston looked bloated and unwell. He and the officer from Clayton examined every millimeter of Dr. Cranston's ankle bracelet.

"Is there a problem, gentlemen?" Cranston asked, grinning at Adam.

He's enjoying this a little too much. I don't know how you managed it, but I will catch you.

"Just a routine check, that's all," Adam said. His eyes narrowed as he focused on Cranston. *I will catch you. And when I do, you will not get out again.*

"I do hope everything's okay. I'd love to invite you nice gentlemen in for a cup of tea, but I'm fresh out. It seems I don't really get out much these days." Cranston pushed his face forward, still wearing his infuriating Cheshire grin.

Adam and the other officer said nothing.

"But, you know, at *some* point, I will be needing groceries."
Cranston's chatty, sing-song voice was wearing on Adam's
last frayed nerve.

Cranston leaned toward Adam and lowered his voice. "And
other supplies."

"I wouldn't stock up too much, if I were you." Adam could no
longer hold his tongue.

Cranston straightened up and brought his hand to his cheek
in mock surprise. "Oh, officer, let's see, is it Trent? No, it's
Detective Trent, isn't it? Now, you weren't intending to threaten
me, were you? Maybe I should call Harlan. Mr. Royce is very
good at talking to your kind."

The Clayton officer spoke before Adam could react. "Yes, sir.
You're welcome to call your attorney. Would you like for us to
wait while you do that?"

Cranston appeared to consider the suggestion. He held his
left elbow in his right hand with his cheek resting in his left
hand. Then he shrugged. "No, I don't think that'll be necessary
right now. I'm on sabbatical from work for a little while and he
charges a fortune. Oh, but he's very good."

Adam clenched his teeth. He wanted nothing more than to
wipe that ridiculous grin off Cranston's face. But that would
only bring Harlan Royce rushing over with the news cameras.
Adam could find nothing wrong with the ankle bracelet. It had
not been cut or tampered with as far as he could tell.

"That'll be all." Adam said. He turned and both officers walked
together to their cars.

"Good day, gentlemen," Cranston sang out, as Adam reached
his vehicle. "Do come again."

When Adam returned to the station, Captain Peterson was on
the phone in his office with the door shut. He was talking with
his back turned to the door, but even through the closed door,
his muffled voice sounded angry. He saw Adam's reflection in
the glass and, turning around, lowered his voice. "I have to go
now." Captain Peterson slammed the phone down and rubbed
his hands over his face.

Adam was in a foul mood as well, exacerbated by a lack of sleep. He began to work on his white board in an attempt to connect the dots and make some sense of the Harrington case. Kate trotted into Homicide in time to see Adam throw the marker against the white board.

"Good morning, Susie Sunshine," she chirped.

"It's morning, all right," Adam answered. He sucked in his cheeks and sat down with a thud at his desk chair.

"All right," she backed off, putting her hands up with her fingers spread apart. "Wanna fill me in, here?"

"Sorry. I shouldn't have spoken to you like that." Adam told her all that had transpired. The more he talked, the more animated he became, flailing his arms and knocking over his pencil holder.

"Adam, you really need to work on your poker face," she told him. Kate helped him clean the mess he created on his desk. "Cranston's taunting you and you're letting him know how well he's succeeding."

Adam growled in response. "How did he, one, find me, two, get into my room, and three, manipulate the monitor to show he never left his house?"

"You can't prove those allegations, you know."

"Really, Kate? You, too? First, Captain Peterson, and now you? I. Am. Not. Crazy. I'm telling you, Cranston was in my room and he moved my things." His voice had risen in pitch and volume.

"Adam." Kate leveled her face to his and looked him in the eye. "If Cranston was in your room and had your gun, why didn't he just shoot you then? He's vowed revenge on you and your team and your families. This morning was the perfect chance."

"It's like you said." Adam stood and began to pace. "He's taunting me, toying with me—maybe he thinks it'll make me fear him. Maybe he's trying to make me look paranoid. Maybe it feeds his sick need for power. Or control. Or maybe he thinks he can discredit me by making me look crazy, who knows?" Adam was fighting to maintain self-control, but losing the battle.

Kate sat back in her chair. "You *are* sounding a little crazy there, bud. Wanna go see Dr. Gerwyn? I'll walk ya down there."

Adam sank into his chair and threw his pen across the desk. He rubbed his face with his hands and pressed his fingertips into his eyebrows. His tirade had been overheard by the rest of the department. For him to say anything further would only make the situation worse. The other detectives in the department were giving him a wide berth and avoiding eye contact. Adam knew he sounded like a raving lunatic. If Cranston wanted to discredit him by making him crazy, then Kate was right—he was succeeding. He lowered his voice and leaned toward Kate until their heads were almost touching. "Kate. He was there. I don't know how to prove it, but I know he was there."

"C'mon. Get up and come with me." She rose and motioned for him to follow.

He stood. "Where?"

Kate turned her back to the squad room, and facing Adam, responded in a low voice. "First we stop at evidence and sign out a box. Then we go to my house. Maybe *you* can't prove Cranston was in your room, but I know someone who can. Let's go."

"Robo! Of course!" Adam felt a tinge of hope. "Kate, if I wasn't married to the girl of my dreams, I'd kiss you!"

Kate laughed. "No thanks. I'll settle for barbecued pork steaks and Jenna's chocolate meringue pie."

They left together, and once they were alone in the hall, Kate turned to Adam.

"You go and wait in my car. I'll run down to evidence and sign out the box."

"That case is huge. There are lots of boxes. Do you know which one to get?"

"I'll know when I see it. No sense in both of us taking a risk. I know what Robo needs."

Adam waited in Kate's car. Minutes later, she appeared carrying a box which she placed in her trunk. They drove to her house and picked up her old partner who was overjoyed to go for another ride.

As they rode to the safe house, Kate spoke to Robo, as she often did. "Hey, partner. I know I told you last night was your last job, but we've got one more for ya, buddy. I hope your nose is up for it."

"If the wagging tail is any indication, he's rarin' to go," Adam said. "So what was last night's job?"

"First things first, Adam. I've got a little more on Mariah Flores, but let's see if our furry friend back there can restore your credibility."

They entered the apartment with the box from the evidence room. Kate removed the shirt Dr. Cranston was wearing when he had been arrested, placed it under Robo's nose, and gave a command. "Seek!" Robo leapt into action, sniffing through the living room with his head down and his tail up. Adam held his breath as he watched the dog. Robo stopped by the hall, lifted his head and stood still a moment, sniffing the air. Then he dashed into Adam's bedroom and stopped by the night stand where he sat and barked one time, looking expectantly at Kate. She met the dog's gaze for a moment, then turned a worried face to Adam.

"That's solid confirmation, Adam," Kate said in a sober voice. "Cranston was here. Let's inform Captain Peterson." She knelt by her dog. "Good boy!" She gave Robo a treat and scratched behind his ears. "You're a good boy."

"I knew I wasn't crazy."

"Whoa, there. Robo can't confirm that you're not crazy. All he did was confirm that Cranston was in your room."

Adam grinned at her. "You better hope I'm not the one that makes that chocolate meringue pie for you, Marlin." He petted the dog and the three of them left.

They dropped Robo off at Kate's house and drove to the station.

Adam and Kate knocked on Captain Peterson's office door and entered, closing the door behind them.

Gavin Peterson listened as Kate confirmed Cranston's presence in Adam's bedroom.

Captain Peterson stared at her. His teeth were clenched, causing the muscles in his jaw to flex.

After several uncomfortable seconds, he spoke to them in short, terse sentences. "I cannot *believe* the two of you went into evidence without obtaining approval through the proper channels. *Both* of you! Seasoned detectives with unblemished records. What were you *thinking?*" Adam and Kate shifted in their seats. "You could both be suspended or even fired for a stunt like this. The whole case could be thrown out of court because you tampered with evidence!"

"Cap, the Cranston case has dozens of boxes. We just took one box—the one with Cranston's shirt in it. Nothing else from his case was disturbed, removed or touched. The case has not been compromised." Adam knew his argument was weak and he regretted his answer as soon as he said it.

Captain Peterson's anger was not assuaged. He continued glaring at Kate and Adam. "A first year law student would have a field day with what you've done. What do you think an attorney like Harlan Royce is gonna do? He'll eat you alive—all the work that has gone into building a case against Cranston, and it could now be thrown out! You should've come to me. We could've gotten this authorized. There's a chain of authority that must be followed. You both know that."

Adam slumped in his chair, but Kate spoke up. "It would've taken too long to get permission. Time is not on our side, here. Sometimes getting the truth is more important than a bunch of paperwork. We had to know, Captain Peterson. And we got the truth."

"You do realize, don't you, that none of your unauthorized discovery is admissible? All because the two of you decided to play cowboy."

Admissible or not, the truth remained. Adam had exercised poor judgment by allowing circumstances to dictate his actions. In spite of that, however, he felt vindicated, and for the moment, he needed to know he was right about Cranston. Cranston had somehow gotten out of his ankle monitor and had gotten into Adam's room while Adam slept.

"Robo has no incentive to lie," Kate said. "We needed to prove that Adam was either right or wrong. Turns out he was right. And that's important."

"So how did he escape the ankle monitor?"

"That we don't know yet. But he did do it," she said.

"Yeah, yeah, I got that already. So for your next trick, figure out how Cranston fooled the monitor. In the meantime, I'll have to decide what to do about your flagrant disregard for protocol. You're both dismissed." Captain Peterson waved them out with the back of his hand as if he were shooing a fly away.

Adam closed the door behind them as they left. Other detectives in the division were watching them with curious eyes. Adam and Kate walked out of the department and into the hall. When they were out of earshot, Adam said, "Sorry I got you into this. I knew better."

"Are you kidding? We did what had to be done. Peterson sure blew a gasket. If his face got any redder, he'd have popped a blood vessel!"

"You thought that was fun?" He looked at her as if she had lost her mind.

"Okay, maybe not exactly fun, but I'm enjoying working on this case. It's keeping me sharp. Peterson'll calm down. As for you and me, we're good. I made a choice to bend the rules a little and I'd do it all over again. You hungry?"

"I'm breathing, right?"

"Let's go. You drive this time."

Adam headed to the Central West End, home of every type of food from half the countries around the world.

"So what did you learn about Mariah Flores? And how did Robo get involved in that?" Adam asked Kate over lunch at Llewellyn's an Irish pub.

She grinned as she slid a slice of Guinness steak flatbread onto her plate. "I watched Mariah for a couple of days, saw where she went, who she saw, tried to get a handle on her schedule. I think there's more to her than meets the eye."

"I don't know when she has time for a life," Adam said. "She works days at a nursing home and nights at Mansford Mansion. She's got to be on her feet constantly."

"I wish I had a couple of weeks to keep an eye on her. Two days isn't enough to glean very much with her schedule. The first night, the night the restaurant was closed, I followed her to the Adam's Mark downtown. She was dolled up and dressed to kill, if you'll pardon the pun. Nice clothes, hair up, plenty of make-up."

"Working girl?" Adam asked. He raised his eyebrows, wrinkling his forehead. He took a piece of the flatbread.

"No, I don't think so. I think she was meeting someone. Anyway, the nursing home is in St. Louis Hills, and she walks around Francis Park during her lunch hour. Probably needs to get out of there and clear her head, get some fresh air is my guess. So Robo and I decided to take a walk around the park. Mariah was talking on her cell phone while she walked. I got that her boyfriend's name is Eddie."

"Did you talk to her? Did she suspect anything?"

Kate laughed. "I told Robo to play hurt."

"Explain."

"When Robo was around three years old, he got a minor injury on duty and was limping, favoring his front right leg. I felt bad for him, so while he was recuperating, I fed him steak, burgers, anything he liked, right? Long after his injury was healed, he'd look up at me with those big sweet brown eyes and start to limp, except over time, he forgot which leg had been injured, so he would sometimes limp on the right side, and other times on the left. Anything for some beef. So I started asking him if he was hurt. He associated the word hurt with limping and being rewarded. He's such a smart boy, even beyond all the police work. He knows more words than some people I know."

Adam chuckled and nodded in agreement.

"So when Mariah was walking toward me, I asked Robo if he was hurt. He heard the magic word and yelped and began to limp. She looked up at us and I heard her tell Eddie she'd call him back. She asked me if my dog was okay. I think Robo knew what was going on and really hammed it up. I told her he must've just hurt himself, and I was a couple of blocks from home and needed someone strong to give me a hand. Since she had mentioned Eddie's name right in front of me, I asked her if Eddie could come and help. She hemmed and hawed, and I told her I'd just broken up with my boyfriend and his name was Eddie, and I hoped she hadn't picked up Eddie Smith, because that would be my ex and he was bad news."

"Eddie *Smith*? Seriously? Why didn't you pick a common last name?" he teased and took another slice of flatbread.

"She assured me that her Eddie was not my ex, and then she said she had to get back to work, but she offered to call my vet for me. I told her that I would let my dog rest and see if he improved enough to walk home. Once she was out of sight, we got in the car and left."

"Nice work."

"I'm not done. And stop eating all the flatbread pizza. The Guinness steak is my fave."

"I'll buy another one," Adam said, cramming another piece in his mouth.

"Don't talk with your mouth full. Jenna should've domesticated you by now."

"She's still trying. It's a full-time job. So what else did you learn?"

"Since Mariah would be at work for a while, I drove to her place in Affton. Most of the folks in that neighborhood are at work, so it's pretty deserted in the daytime, but there are some retirees in that neck of the woods, so it's not too smart to let your guard down. I didn't want any nosy neighbors calling the cops." Kate grinned at Adam. "So anyway, I let Robo out of the car and told him to find the kitty. For some reason, he loves cats. Go figure. So he took off and I pretended to be looking for my lost dog, in case someone asked what I was doing. Nobody did, by the way. I had a look-see around her place."

"Sheesh, Kate, please tell me you didn't break into Mariah's house. We're in enough trouble already." Adam put his head in his hand.

"No, no. Just the outside, looking in the windows and snooping around the garden. Nothing at first glance, but I took a peek in her basement windows. Know what it looked like?" She didn't give Adam a chance to answer. "It looked like an old photo lab," she announced, satisfied with herself.

"Yeah, so?" he asked.

She snatched the last piece of the flatbread pizza. "An *old* photo lab, Adam," she repeated. "That could be where the cyanide came from. Hello?"

"That's not enough to get a warrant. Cyanide purchases are registered. Remember? You're the one who checked the records and found nothing connecting any purchases in the past year to any of our suspects."

"*Now* cyanide purchases have to be registered, but years ago, photographers could buy it freely. No hassles. They used it to develop their film."

"Still not enough to get a warrant. And she's too young to go back that far. Not to mention, we have no motive. Surely, she doesn't carry a deadly poison around with her to use on every obnoxious customer she waits on."

"So we have to find the connection. That is, *if* she has the cyanide at all." Kate sat back and took a drink of water.

"Good work, Kate. Very helpful. Unless, of course there's no connection. And no cyanide. Can you keep a tail on her for a couple of weeks?"

"Until my new partner is ready. Not sure of the exact date, but it's coming up soon. I'll do what I can and let you know."

"That's all I can ask. Right now, though, I want to get back to the station and see what possible explanations can account for Cranston being in two places at one time. You in?"

"Sure. Gotta stop by my house first, and then I'll join you. Homicide's getting to be fun."

"Yeah? More fun than K-9?"

"Not on your life."

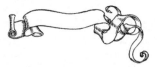

Adam's printer was hot from spewing reams of paper on the Cranston case.

"Killing a forest, detective?" Captain Peterson asked. His earlier anger had dissipated. He could never remain angry at his men. Life was too short and their work too important.

"Sorry, Cap, but I need to be able to put all this information into some kind of order and I need the hard copies for better viewing."

"Just get this guy, Adam. I've asked for some help looking into the judge that granted bail. It never should've happened. And now this."

"Yeah. Judge Dempsey's not known for being a great judge, but he's never made a decision this catastrophic. I'm glad someone's doing a little digging. Cranston never should've been released. Jenna said the judge had to be crooked, and while that may be, I just can't see who in their right mind would have allowed such a dangerous psychopath out on bail."

"I agree. I've got a team of detectives looking into Judge Dempsey. I'll be surprised if he comes up clean. But what do you hope to find by reviewing Cranston's life on paper? The case we've built against him is solid, as long as the breach of the one box in Evidence isn't discovered." Captain Peterson gave Adam a sharp look. "But even if we get a jury of lunatics, I don't see anything other than a conviction."

"From your mouth." Adam said. "You never know what a jury's gonna do, so I wouldn't bet the rent. But if we get sane, reasonable people, I think we have a great chance of putting him away for the rest of his life."

"So what do you hope to find by looking through all of this?"

"There's a clue in here somewhere. Cranston got out of that ankle bracelet somehow. If he did it once, he'll do it again, which means nobody's safe. If I can prove it, then his bail will be revoked until trial."

Kate arrived after taking Robo for a short walk. "Wow. Looks like a paper factory blew up in here. Whaddya got against trees, anyway?"

"I'm trying to organize these piles so we can go through this systematically. In spite of your snideness, I'm almost finished."

"I don't think snideness is a word. Where do you want to start?"

Adam viewed the organized mess set out on his desk, filing cabinets and chairs, and sighed. He was beginning to feel the toll the case was taking on him, physically and mentally. Friday couldn't come soon enough. He would see Jenna and Amy again. But for now, he was feeling overwhelmed, so he stared at the piles of paper, unable to answer Kate's question.

Kate studied her friend. She pulled the only available chair next to him and sat. "Adam, let me ask you this. What was your first thought when you saw Cranston today?"

"I wanted to wipe that Cheshire grin off his smug, sanctimonious face."

"So you think he was taunting you? That he knew that you knew he was out, and you couldn't figure out how to prove it?"

"That about sums it up."

"What was your impression of the ankle bracelet? We know it wasn't cut, or the alarm would notify the monitoring company. Did it look as if it had been tampered with in any way? Did his ankle look like he had greased it and it could have somehow slipped off? Was there anything unusual? Did anything about the device or Cranston strike you as odd?"

Adam leaned back in his chair. He closed his eyes and rubbed his temples. "Actually, Kate, it was just the opposite." He opened his eyes. "His skin was dry and the ankle bracelet was almost tight."

"Tight? That shouldn't be the case."

"Right. And Cranston's not a very large man anyway. He looked unwell and somewhat bloated. Now that I think about it, his ankles seemed bigger than what a man his size ought to have."

Kate looked at him, twisting her mouth and squinting her eyes, but said nothing.

"And he was quite chatty, just like a wind-up doll. Like he had a secret and I was never going to learn it."

"Arrogance was his downfall the last time."

"Yep."

"All right. Well, enough talking. Let's dig in. I'm here to work." Kate picked up a large stack of papers and retreated to a corner, while Adam, remaining at his desk, took another stack.

They pored over the piles of paperwork for hours. Kate finally laid aside the pile she was working on. She yawned and stretched. "I gotta go home. Robo needs a walk and some dinner, and I'm too tired to read one more piece of paper. Even Captain Peterson has left. Go home, Adam. We'll both think better in the morning."

Adam clipped together over a dozen separate piles of paper and stuffed them into the bag with his dirty clothes. He left the station and drove toward the safe house. As he approached the driveway that led to the garages in back of the building, he changed his mind and continued past, turning around and driving toward Highway 44. He called Captain Peterson and informed him that he was out of town until Monday, and sped toward Union. It was late. The family would be in bed by the time he got there, but his need to be with them overshadowed his sense of etiquette.

By increasing his speed, he could cut the time in half. He checked his rear view mirror every few minutes to be sure no one was following him. Adam was bone tired and rolled down the window so the cold night air could hit his face. It was bracing and kept him awake until he exited the highway. A few more miles of rolling hills and winding roads and he would be there. The car was cold, but if he turned on the heater, he feared he would fall asleep at the wheel. At last, he slowed to pull into the driveway and cut his headlights.

The farmhouse was dark, but Adam had a key. As he quietly turned the key in the lock, he heard the distinctive sound of the racking of a shell into the chamber of a 12 gauge 870 pump action Remington shotgun behind him, and he froze. Without moving, he said, "Dad, it's me."

Dwayne Trent lowered his shotgun. "What in—"

Adam turned around and interrupted, "I know, I know. I should've called. I didn't want to wake anyone."

"So it was smarter to just about get yourself killed? I could'a shot you, thinkin' it was Cranston, or some other—"

"Right, Dad, I'm sorry. Look, I'm dog tired and need to go to bed. Sorry for the heart attack. I need to be here. I need to be with my family, and I didn't want to wait until tomorrow night."

Dwayne took a deep breath and exhaled. "It's all right, son. My hair's all gray anyway."

Chapter 14

After breakfast, Jenna and Adam cleared the table and cleaned the kitchen. "Amy, help Gomer and Oompah with the farm chores, and then you get the rest of the day off from school. Mom and I need to get some work done here."

"Okay." Amy skipped off to join her grandfather. Blue trotted behind her with her tail in the air.

"I can see she's devastated to be missing school today," Adam said with a grin.

Jenna squeezed his hand. "This is more important. The sooner we can return Cranston to jail before the trial, the sooner we get our lives back. Amy will be fine when she returns to her own school," she reassured her husband. Looking at the mountain of papers spread out on the table, she asked, "So what's the plan here, chief?"

"I'm looking for any type of clue that might explain how Cranston slipped the ankle bracelet. Kate thought it was important that he appeared bloated to me when I saw him and that the ankle bracelet was tight on him. It shouldn't be so tight that it hugs the skin. I don't know for certain what we're looking for, but something in here will give us an answer. I've got to believe we'll know it when we see it. Kate already went through that group over there in the rubber bands," Adam said, pointing to a pile at the far corner of the table. "So we can do those last. She's pretty thorough, so I don't expect she'd miss anything."

Adam and Jenna each took a stack of documents to read and traded stacks as they finished, so that each pile of paperwork was read and then read again by the other. Several hours passed with no results. They continued their search.

Emma Jo brought in sandwiches and tea for lunch. Without a word, she set the plates down and retreated. Adam and Jenna ate in silence while they continued to pore over each page.

After two hours of careful reading, Jenna gasped. "Adam, I think I've got something!" He looked up at her with strained eyes, bloodshot from hours of reading and a lack of sleep.

"Do you have a list of what Cranston ate while he was in jail, before the final bail hearing?"

"It'll be in the jailhouse records," Adam answered, removing a folder from the stacks. "Why is that important?"

Jenna held up a piece of paper. "According to his medical intake sheet, Dr. Cranston is allergic to MSG."

"Huh? MS who?"

"Monosodium glutamate. It's a flavor enhancer. Most restaurants don't use it anymore because it's such a dangerous chemical and a lot of people have terrible reactions to it. I had a friend who would swell so badly, she needed an EpiPen or she could die from eating it. But monosodium glutamate is still found in some Chinese food, as well as a lot of fast food. I'd be very interested to know what he ate before he was measured for that ankle bracelet. If he consumed a meal with MSG in it, and it triggered that type of allergic reaction, it could've caused his entire body, including his ankles, to swell."

"That's quite a risk for him to take if it could be fatal, though, right?"

"Adam, the man's a doctor. And Cranston, of all people, is well acquainted with fatal dosing. I think it's safe to assume that he would know precisely how much he could consume to make himself swell without needing an ambulance. And it would be worth the risk if it meant the bracelet would be easy to remove once the swelling subsided. He would know how to time the reaction, don't you think?"

"Jenna, it sounds good on the surface, but do you think he could be exacting enough to put it into practice?"

"Maybe it doesn't have to be all that exact. It may not cause enough of a reaction to threaten his life. He just needs to swell *enough*. Maybe any Chinese dish will do it. Or maybe, a particular dish gives him the same reaction every time. We don't know how much practice he may've had, but it's at least worth looking into. We haven't come up with anything else, and there's not much left to go through."

Adam sat up straight and with a sparkle in his eyes, he smiled. *Gotcha!* "That could explain why he looked so bloated when I saw him and why the bracelet was so tight. He knew we'd be coming to check on him and he ate enough to get a reaction. Of course it would be worth the discomfort, if it meant getting away with unfettered freedom. So let's see what the good doctor had to eat before he was fitted for that ankle bracelet!"

They divided the contents of the folder and soon Adam jumped from his seat, waiving a sheet of paper in the air as though it were a flag of victory. "Jenna, honey, you're a genius! Kung Pao Beef right before he was fitted! He's been free to leave his home at will because the apparatus was too big all along. As long as he keeps something to eat on hand with MSG in it, he can show the ankle bracelet is still in place." He strode out of the room.

"Where are you going?"

"Gotta call Captain Peterson. If our suspicions are confirmed, this'll be enough to revoke bail," he called back over his shoulder. Then turning on his heel, he hurried back to his wife. "First things first," he said and scooped her up out of her chair and swung her around, stopping to kiss her passionately, just as Amy walked into the room.

"Oh gross! Get a room," she said, screwing up her face and leaving again.

Jenna giggled. A weight had been lifted from everyone's shoulders. She ran to find her in-laws to tell them the news, as Adam reached for his phone.

The Trent family was elated that evening at the dinner table. Amy was excited that she could return to her own school with her own friends, and Adam and Jenna were thankful they could return home soon. Dwayne and Emma Jo were relieved that the evil Dr. Cranston would be returned to jail to await trial, and Blue was happy that in all the excitement, the humans were dropping food on the floor.

"Captain Peterson is making sure all the i's are dotted and the t's are crossed. Then Cranston will be picked up. Kate was thrilled when I told her. She's still keeping an eye on one of our suspects in the Harrington murder. She would've never picked up on the MSG connection because she doesn't cook." Adam dumped a second helping of mashed potatoes onto his plate.

Jenna laughed. "No, she doesn't cook, but she does bring a mean bag of chips!"

"Aunt Kate's not my real aunt, is she?" Amy asked.

"No, sweetie, she's just a very good friend of Daddy's and mine. That's why you call her Aunt Kate."

"But she's still a better aunt than Aunt Rachel, who's my real aunt, right?"

The joy at the table began to deflate.

"Don't rain on the parade, Amy, okay?" Jenna shot her daughter The Look. Amy sank down in her chair. "Sorry," she mumbled.

Adam's cell phone rang, creating a much needed diversion.

"'Scuse me," Adam announced springing to his feet. "That'll be Captain Peterson calling to tell me Cranston is rotting as we speak! Be right back." He left the table to talk in the other room.

"Can we have pie for dessert, Gomer?" Amy asked turning her gaze upward to her grandmother and blinking her eyes.

"I think we can find a little something to sweeten our celebration," Emma Jo answered with a wink.

Adam returned to the table in a much darker mood. The spring in his step was gone and his jaw clenched. He took his seat, closed his eyes and covered them with his fingers. The Trents became quiet and braced themselves for bad news. Adam stretched his hands on the table in front of him.

"He's gone," Adam said flatly. He stared at his outstretched hands on the table, avoiding eye contact, and swallowed hard.

"What do you mean, gone? As in dead?" Emma Jo asked.

"As in not at home, where the ankle bracelet was found."

Stunned silence followed.

"Is he coming to get us, Daddy?" Amy's question broke the silence.

"Not if I get him first," Adam replied.

Chapter 15

The next morning as they said their goodbyes in the driveway, Jenna hugged Adam, holding on to him with her head buried in his chest. A lump swelled in her throat. She knew going into their marriage that there was always the possibility that one day her husband might not return home from work. It was a possibility every cop's wife needed to come to terms with, without going insane. But now, the threat of losing Adam loomed over Jenna like gathering storm clouds before a tornado. She pulled away and searched his eyes, fighting back tears. "I love you Adam." She stroked his face and leaned into his chest one more time, listening to his heartbeat. Jenna could not say anything else for fear her voice would crack. She would not allow herself to break. To do so would serve no purpose other than to make Adam's departure more difficult. Everything else in her heart remained unspoken, but understood.

Amy threw her arms around her father's neck as he picked her up for one last hug. "You be good for your mom, now, peanut. I love you."

"I love you, too, Daddy," she said in a quiet voice, and kissed his cheek. "Please come home."

Blue walked around in circles next to Adam. When he set Amy down, he petted her and scratched behind her ears. She stayed close to Amy with her ears cocked forward.

"I'll keep them safe, son. Don't you worry," Dwayne assured him as he hugged Adam. "And next time you get a hankerin' to come 'round here in the middle of the night, you call first, you hear? No matter what time it is. 'Cause next time, I'll shoot first and ask questions later."

Emma Jo's blue eyes brimmed with tears as she started to approach her son, but overcome, she turned and ran into the house.

"Let her go, Adam," Dwayne said as Adam started after his mother. "Your momma is scared to lose you. Don't you be worryin' 'bout nobody here. I got this covered. You go and do what you gotta do. Just be careful."

One final embrace with Jenna. Adam kissed her, holding her close, running his fingers through her hair and squeezing the back of her neck. After several minutes, he released her and drove away. Jenna stood in the driveway as Adam left. Amy stood by her mother and Blue sat by Amy. They watched in silence until Adam's car was no longer visible and the trail of dust settled.

A grim-faced Captain Peterson was waiting for Adam at the station. The all-out manhunt for Dr. Lionel Cranston cancelled weekends and vacations, commencing mandatory overtime, but nobody complained, as officers from every precinct trickled in for the morning briefing.

Assignments and admonishments were handed out like candy on Halloween. Cranston's home was under 24-hour surveillance, not that anyone credited him with being stupid enough to return home. But no chances were being taken. Security was stepped up in hospitals and nursing homes. All known and suspected people and places to which Cranston might go were being watched. Bulletins were faxed and e-mailed to pharmacies, urging them to ensure their security cameras were working and to report any sightings of Cranston immediately. His known bank accounts and other assets were frozen. Even a tail was put on Harlan Royce, Cranston's sleazy attorney, however, with instructions to stay out of sight. No sense in providing Harlan Royce with an opportunity to be the ringleader in yet another media circus.

"Cranston has screwed up before," Captain Peterson reminded the force lined up before him. "He'll screw up again. He does not react well under pressure and now he's on the run, out of his comfort zone. But he's not stupid, so do *not* underestimate him. He's been planning this for some time, so assume he's made contingencies to counteract the actions we're taking. His weapons are not guns or knives, but hypodermic needles. If he sticks you, you will not recover. It goes without saying, but I'll say it anyway. Proceed with extreme caution. Dismissed."

"Adam, the offer to take leave is still open," Captain Peterson reminded him.

"Noted and declined, Cap."

"Do you want another place to stay? Cranston found his way into your room somehow. Say the word and I'll get you into another safe house."

Adam shook his head. "No thanks. He found me once, he'll find me again. At this point, it's just a matter of who finds who first. But I appreciate the offer."

"Phone check in at least every twelve hours, Adam." Captain Peterson patted Adam on his shoulder, turned and left.

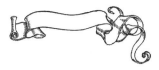

The Honorable Lucas Dempsey sat at his desk in chambers, staring at his windows, but seeing nothing. News of Cranston's disappearance was the last thing the judge expected to hear. He began to perspire underneath his heavy robe. His hands were unsteady and he struggled to keep his thoughts coherent. *If I get out now and leave Missouri, I only have enough money to last a few months.* His father's estate was still awaiting the final closing in Cook County, Illinois, but Dempsey wasn't sure how much longer he could wait. He had woven a tangled web, indeed, and saw no way out.

He was certain the probate clerk in Cook County had put his file at the bottom of the pile. He had called too many times and had been too abrasive. And now, Cranston was in the wind. Lucas Dempsey never saw that coming. He couldn't shake his feeling of impending doom.

A knock on his door jolted him. Candace, his clerk, entered. She looked at him with one eyebrow raised. "Judge Dempsey, are you unwell? You don't look well."

"No, Candace, I'm quite under the weather."

"I'm sorry to interrupt, sir, but there are some detectives out here that want to speak with you."

It had been a long day of running down leads and chasing sightings, and Adam, as well as the others, had finished empty handed. He called Jenna every two hours to check in. All was quiet on the farm, but Dwayne had every gun in the house loaded and had given Jenna a refresher course on target practice. Amy and Blue stayed in Amy's bedroom, playing together except for a few brief walks with Dwayne.

Adam needed sleep. His bones and muscles ached from exhaustion, and his head was throbbing. He longed for the comfort of even the bed in the safe house. It was long past dinner time, but he had no appetite. All he wanted was to lie down and sleep, but the locks needed to be double-checked and the room would require modifications, so if an intruder came in, it would wake him. A repeat performance of the other night by Cranston would be deadly. And Adam would sleep with his gun under his pillow.

Adam arrived at the safe house apartment and trudged up the stairs, his mind as tired and stressed as his body. He fumbled with his keys, dropping them twice before turning the key in the lock. He entered and turned to lock the door behind him. Flipping the light switch on, he turned around and froze in stunned disbelief. Sitting on a folding chair in the middle of the small living room was Dr. Lionel Cranston. Cranston grinned at Adam with the same Cheshire cat insolence he displayed when Adam checked his ankle bracelet. Adam expected that a meeting with Cranston would occur soon, but he didn't think it would be tonight. He was exhausted and his head hurt. But the immediate threat before him sent adrenaline coursing through his body.

Adam reached for his gun.

Cranston put up his hands in mock surrender and said, "I don't think you want to shoot me, Detective Trent."

"And why is that?" Adam asked, stopping with his hand on the grip of his weapon.

"I know where your precious Jenna and little Amy are staying. Nice farmhouse your folks have out in the country there. It would be a *shame* if something happened to them." Cranston opened his mouth and made his lips form a circle, and he raised his eyebrows over widened eyes.

Adam continued to finger his gun, prepared to draw it. "And if I shoot you, then they'll continue to be safe."

Cranston smiled mirthlessly again. He sat back in his chair, rotating his shoulders with the litheness of a cat eyeing its prey.

Adam felt a cold hatred envelop him. An unseen power much greater than any he had ever encountered challenged his courage, filling him with doubt, provoking his heart to fear. The room seemed to darken and he prayed for protection as he felt the presence of evil penetrate the air. His eyes never left Cranston and his body tensed as he calculated his enemy.

Cranston was not a large man. He was in his late sixties. Even without his gun, Adam could handle himself. In spite of his physical advantage, however, Adam sensed he was up against something more ominous than that over which bullets and muscle could prevail. He remained steady, while fear crept up his spine like a death adder waiting to strike.

"Give me a little credit, detective," Cranston began, his voice smooth and hypnotic. "Do you really believe I would be sitting here, in the middle of your cozy little living room, if I was not confident that you were going to do exactly as I say?" He made a sweeping gesture around the room with his arm. "By the way, the place could use a woman's touch, don't you agree?"

Adam stared at the smiling devil, refusing to blink, refusing to give him the satisfaction of seeing his fear. So focused was he on the demon before him, he could no longer see anything else in the room. Not the hallway, nor the kitchenette to the right or the windows to the left. The nefarious presence of Dr. Lionel Cranston filled Adam's entire vision, blocking out everything else. He silently asked God to give him strength to overcome evil.

"You have two choices, Detective Trent. You can do as I say and assist my escape. In doing so, you'll have enough time to warn your sweet little family so they can avoid a most painful and unpleasant death. That's your wisest choice. Or, you can shoot me now and you'll never know what's in store for them, when, or how. You'll be powerless to protect them." Cranston crossed his legs and assumed a relaxed position in his chair.

Deranged. Adam snorted, "Do you believe I'm incapable of protecting my family? Especially once you're out of the picture?" He touched his gun still nestled in its holster.

The demon grinned, showing perfect, white teeth. "I do. You have studied me. Just as I have studied you. You know, then, that I'm a meticulous planner. Every detail. And there's always a contingent plan." Cranston leaned forward in his chair. His eyes narrowed. "It took you *years* to catch me, *Adam.* Decades, if you want the truth." He spat his last sentence at Adam and Adam cringed as he understood the implication.

"You're a murderer, Cranston. Many times over."

"That's *Doctor* Cranston, Detective. Show a little respect. Please." He made a dismissive gesture with his hand, flipping his fingers in the air, minimizing Adam.

"Doctors—*real* doctors—take an oath. First, do no harm. Or did you conveniently forget that?"

"For the record, that's no longer part of the oath. And anyway, I've done no harm."

Adam's mouth flew open and his eyes popped.

"You know, you shouldn't play poker. You haven't got the face for it."

So I've been told.

Cranston continued. "If you would open your mind and admit the truth, you'd see that what I have done—what I've been doing for more than thirty years—is good. Good for everyone."

"Not good for the people you murdered. Not good for those who loved them. You have played God. You've determined who is and is not fit to live. News flash, Cranston. You are not God. You have no right to pass judgment on others. What you've done is not good. It's evil and monstrous. *You* are evil and monstrous." Adam fought for control, determined not to allow Cranston to get the upper hand.

Lionel Cranston sighed and rolled his eyes as if he was tired of dealing with a petulant child. "I've freed others from their suffering. Not just those with permanent afflictions, but their families whose energy and resources are drained from needless and ongoing caregiving. Oh, sure, they grieve—but only for a short time. They soon embrace their newfound freedom. So I have relieved suffering, not caused it."

Adam's body was getting stiff from standing in one place, yet he felt powerless to move. "You have no idea who will or will not recover from any condition. And even if you did, it's not your place to make a choice like that for someone else. For anyone else. When you love someone, not that you would know, you care for them no matter what that entails."

Cranston threw his head back and laughed. "Oh, how idealistic you are! People, the masses—the great unwashed, if you will, and that includes you—they're too stupid to make wise choices. You have to consider all the facts. The value of human life is overrated, particularly if that life contributes nothing to society. Do you even know— do you have any idea what it costs to keep a vegetable alive? The cost to society? The drain on finances and resources? The utter waste? All for nothing! You think your God is so smart and good. Why, then, would such a God allow his dear little children to suffer if he's so great and wonderful? No, Adam. We make our own decisions. We are our own gods." Cranston's eyes narrowed as he uncrossed and re-crossed his legs.

"I am not my own god. I wouldn't want to be. My God is stronger and infinitely more powerful than any mere human being can be. If you are your own god, Cranston, then you're worse than pitiable."

"You depend on your God all you want. I've already won this battle because your world view is weak. But enough of this. You have a decision to make. I know you'll make the honorable choice to die in order to save your family. I'm smarter than you are. Where is your God, Adam? Do you think he's going to save you tonight? I depend on myself. That's all I need."

"You'll never win, Cranston. I'm stronger because of my faith. I honor God when I love and protect my family, and in my work, by protecting society. You're a law breaker, a common criminal, and you're going to pay the price for that."

"So we're a civilized society, are we? We have all kinds of pills and procedures which the government has legalized. Life can be ended in an instant. We can keep people going on and on with feeding tubes, ventilators, all kinds of mechanisms. A judge can make a decision to end life. The Supreme Court does the same. All I do is save the government the legal expense. I'm the one making a better society, Adam. I'm a better servant of society than you are, for what I do shows more compassion."

"Life is God's to give and God's to take. That includes whatever blessings, as well as trials may come. He has a greater purpose in all things than we, in our finite minds, can fathom. Murder is murder. *All* life has value, from the pre-born to the eldest, from the most helpless to the strongest. Life is worth protecting. It's worth saving and it's worth fighting for. We're created in the image of God and we're created for a specific purpose. No mere man, and that includes you, has the right to take that away." Adam clenched and unclenched his jaw. He was locked in a battle of minds which he refused to lose.

Cranston rolled his eyes again and fluttered his eyelids. "All right. Have it your way. *My* specific purpose then, is to rid society of those responsible for draining it and to end the suffering of those who are too cowardly to do it themselves."

Adam took a step toward Cranston. "Who made you judge and jury? Who made you God? You can't even create so much as a worm, much less a human life, yet you destroy it with abandon. You're so short-sighted! You see nothing, no possibilities or purpose, outside the limited range of your own small-minded, demented opinion."

"I make a better God than the myth you worship. If I had created the world, I would've done a better job than this."

"You aren't arguing the existence of God, Cranston. You just disagree with His morality because your own imperfection doesn't allow you to see truth."

"Truth! Hah! Whose truth? Your truth? My truth? There is no absolute truth, only your opinion, my opinion, the opinions of everyone."

Adam laughed. "No absolute truth? Really? Are you absolutely sure about that? If you are, then that's one absolute truth. And here's another for you. We all have the knowledge of a creator inside of us. Even the devil knows. And you know it too. You can deny it, but it changes nothing."

Cranston yawned and stretched. "The *truth*, Adam, is that you are going to die tonight. If you do not agree to help me first, then your family will suffer incredible agony before they all die a terrifying death. And *that* will be on your shoulders—the last conscious thought you'll have before you meet your God. *Or not.*"

Adam tried to control his rage. He pulled his gun and pointed it at Cranston.

"You're insane. And I'm not getting into a theological debate with a crazy person. Talk about casting your pearls before swine. Stand up and put your hands behind your back, Cranston. You're under arrest. This is over." He took another step toward Cranston, retrieving his handcuffs with his other hand.

"It's far from over, Adam. You've not yet aided my escape." Cranston removed a small bag from his jacket and laid the contents on the end table beside him.

Adam stopped cold as his heart leapt to his throat. His head pounded as Cranston set out several syringes filled with an amber liquid. He felt the room drop in temperature. "You *will* help me, because it's the only way to save your family."

"You're mad."

Cranston held his index finger to his chin. "Now, let's see. You claim to be a God-fearing man, correct? So correct me if I'm wrong, but doesn't your Bible say that greater love has no man than if he lays down his life for his friends? Or some such nonsense."

Adam opened his mouth, but Dr. Cranston cut him off.

"Well, I'm sure it's in there somewhere. Maybe you're not familiar with that passage. No matter. We're going to test it to see if it's true. Give me your arm." He picked up a syringe.

"Not gonna happen." Adam bit his lower lip. He was unable to come close to Cranston without getting stuck with a syringe.

"Now this is what you're going to do. You are going to call your Captain and tell him that you killed me on the Eads Bridge and my body fell over into the river below, so the search will be called off. And in return, I will leave Missouri."

"Yeah, that's gonna happen."

Dr. Cranston clucked at him with his tongue. "Now, now. You're already forgetting about your family. Oh Adam! You disappoint me. So after you have assured your Captain that if they want to find my body, they'll have to drag the Mississippi for miles, you give me the keys to your car. Now comes the good part! I will inject you with my little syringe here, and you'll have just enough time to make one phone call before you die. You may call your sweet wife and tell her what she and Amy and your parents need to do to avoid a horrendous death."

"If you think I'm going to help you, you're out of your mind. There's no way you can predict what'll happen after I arrest you, or shoot you. Your choice."

Lionel Cranston's lips parted in a cruel, maleficent smile. "I am not alone," he sneered, narrowing his eyes at Adam.

Cranston stood, clutching a syringe with the deadly liquid in each hand. The two men glared at each other. Cranston curled his lips back, showing his teeth like a rabid dog and growled in rage as he charged toward Adam with both arms raised, ready to strike. Adam raised his gun, but before he could fire, a loud shot echoed through the tiny apartment and Dr. Cranston crumpled to the floor.

Adam looked up in surprise to see Bo and Connor, guns drawn, standing over Cranston, who was on the floor, gasping for breath.

"What—how did you guys get in here?"

"Same way Cranston got in here," Bo drawled with no further comment, pulling up the chair Cranston had been sitting in and making himself comfortable.

"That's it?" Adam asked. "Same way Cranston got in here? That's all you got?"

"Yep."

Connor was pushing buttons on his phone. "I'm calling an ambulance for Dr. Death here, but it looks to me like he ain't gonna make it anyway. I have half a mind to stick him with one of his own needles."

"I don't want him to die. Cranston needs to stand trial for what he's done," Adam said, kneeling beside the doctor. He tried to apply pressure to slow the bleeding, but Cranston was bleeding out.

"Don't think he's got that much time." Bo said, his Tennessee accent thick as molasses. He glanced toward the man on the floor and shook his head. "He don't look too good."

"I'm not alone," Cranston repeated, choking. "I have a partner. Your families will die when my partner doesn't hear from me." He reached for the syringes which had fallen from his hand and lay scattered on the floor.

Bo kicked the syringes out of Cranston's reach, scattering them. "What, Cranston? Your last ditch effort to take us down with you? Even as my buddy, Adam, here, tries to save your sorry life? I don't think so. You've murdered your last."

"I thought you guys left with your families?" Adam asked. He continued working to save Cranston, but despite his efforts, it was becoming a lost cause.

Connor ran to the bathroom and returned with some towels to aid in Adam's effort to save Cranston.

"I don't have a family," Bo said.

"Alls I did was leave that first day to get my wife and kids to safety—same as you, man," Connor said. "Man, you didn't really think we'd desert you, did you? Man, we're *partners*! We stick together!"

"I never did leave," Bo drawled. "But I thought about it. I just didn't want anything to mess up my purty face. Good lookin' guy like me. He ain't doin' so good, there." Bo pointed at Cranston, whose breathing was raspy.

"To answer your question, this building is a DEA safe house," Connor said. "They offered it to us in the spirit of cooperation. It's full of tunnels and passageways. There's a panel leading from the closet in the apartment next door to the closet in your hallway. That's how Cranston got in the night he moved your gun and badge," Connor said.

"How'd you know about that?"

"Man, we're on the phone with Cap every day and night," Bo answered. "We been stayin' here in this building, same as you. Had to have *somebody* keep an eye on you. Yeah, you, man, goin' all lone ranger on us like some kinda cowboy."

Connor handed Adam another towel. "We known you a long time and you're 'bout as easy as pie to predict. We knew you'd stay and work by yourself. So's me and Bo and Cap, we had our own plan. Cap had us divide up. Somebody to watch over Dr. Death down there, and somebody to watch over you. Neither one of yous made it very easy."

"And nobody bothered to clue me in on this ingenious little plan?" Adam asked. He tried to wrap the towels tighter around Cranston to stem the flow of blood. He could hear the wail of the ambulance siren approaching.

"One, you ain't got no poker face to pull nuthin' off," Bo began to explain. "Two, ain't nobody thought you'd go along with Cap's idea, and three—ain't nobody needed your permission anyhow."

"Cap was real mad when Cranston got into this place and we didn't know about it. That's when we found the moveable panels," Connor said. "That, and the DEA told us about them." He looked at Cranston and shook his head.

Connor continued, "We knew you wouldn't back off the case and that Cranston would go after you first if we was nowhere in sight. You was the easiest and most available target. We always had eyes on you and Cranston, until he gave us the slip. That's when things got scary."

The ambulance arrived, interrupting the team's reunion. Adam checked Cranston's pulse. He had stopped gasping for breath and was silent. "He's gone. No pulse. It was a good shoot. That's an awfully big hole in him."

His partners grinned. "Thank you," they said in unison.

Cranston was pronounced dead at the scene. The ambulance driver was instructed to take the body to the morgue, but to sit on the report because there was still an imminent threat.

When they were alone again in the apartment, Adam said, "Before we talk any further, I need to call Jenna." He retreated into the bedroom, dialing as he walked.

"Baby, it's over. It's finally over." He shut the bedroom door and sat down on the bed.

"What happened? Are you okay? Where are you? What does over mean?" Jenna was breathless as she peppered Adam with a barrage of questions.

"Cranston is dead. I'm fine. We're all fine, but it's late. I've got paperwork and some finishing up to do, but everybody's okay. You all get a good night's sleep. See if Mom and Dad will follow you back in the morning and we'll all celebrate together then. At our house. I'll fill you in tomorrow, but I'm fine. Just very, very tired. My team never left me after all. I love you. See you tomorrow."

He hung up and the three team members met back in the living room.

"While y'all was callin' your wives, I called Cap. He'll be here real soon," Bo said.

Connor arranged the seating so the four of them could face each other talking. "Whaddya think about Cranston's claim to have a partner?"

Before Adam could answer, Captain Peterson knocked at the door. Adam opened the door, and they all started talking at once. Captain Peterson raised his hand. "Sit," he ordered, lowering his hand.

"He was very sure of himself, Cap," Bo said as they took their seats. "All three of us heard him say he was not alone. So he's got some kind of a partner we don't know nothin' about."

Captain Gavin Peterson rubbed his chin. "Do you think he was bluffing?"

"Can't know for sure now with him dead. Part of me doesn't think so," Adam answered. "But on the other hand, this is the first we've heard of any partner. When Jenna and I went through his prison file, there was no indication he had contact with anyone besides his lawyer. I don't want to take any chances, but I also don't want Cranston dictating from the grave that I need to be looking over my shoulder for the rest of my life, either. He was evil enough to throw in an empty threat at the last, just for that purpose."

Captain Peterson was quiet a moment. "We *could* put the story out that he was shot and he fell off the Eads Bridge and see if that flushes anyone out. But I have a better idea, if you don't like that one."

"The problem with that, Cap, is that we don't know who the partner is, and if Cranston doesn't contact his partner and they find out I'm still alive, there's no telling what they might do."

"So what's your better idea, Cap?" Bo asked.

"There's a new and very important development that none of you are aware of yet," Captain Peterson began. The men leaned forward in their seats as he continued. "Judge Lucas Dempsey, who granted bail, did not have clean hands in this matter."

"I knew it! We all knew it!" Bo said.

"We launched a separate investigation into Judge Dempsey. It was insane to have granted bail in a case like this. Turns out, the judge's father was in his late nineties and in poor health. Estimated worth was a few mil, but Dempsey could afford to be patient and wait for his inheritance. The problem, however, was that the judge had a younger brother, Jameson. Jameson suffered a permanent injury in a drunk driving accident. He was kept alive and comfortable in a skilled nursing facility in Moline, Illinois."

"Why Illinois?" Connor asked.

"Because Jameson was on a ventilator and there's not a single facility in Missouri set up for a ventilator patient, so Illinois was the closest. Anyway, a trust was set up to cover Jameson's expenses for the rest of his life. So the longer Jameson lived, the more the cost of his care drained from the trust. Judge Dempsey could see that in a few years, it would cut into his share of the old man's estate."

"I think we can all see where this is going," Connor said. "Go on."

Adam left the room and returned with water for everyone.

"Dr. Cranston accepted a large payment from Judge Dempsey to kill Jameson. Because Jameson's health was so precarious, he was susceptible to every bug and germ on the planet. Dr. Cranston was able to inject the helpless Jameson so he would succumb to infection and no one would be any wiser. His death wouldn't be suspicious. The father's health was deteriorating, and with Jameson out of the way, Lucas Dempsey would inherit everything when his father died of natural causes." Captain Peterson paused and took a sip of water. "I believe the father suspected something was up, but was not in a position where he could prove it. His body might've been frail, but his mind was still sharp. So he moved to Chicago to live out his remaining months, knowing his estate would then have to go through probate in a state where Lucas Dempsey had no connections or pull."

Bo leaned back in his chair, tilting it on two legs. "So the old man had suspicions, but no proof."

"Not without an exhumation order and obtaining one would have been difficult. Plus, he had his own declining health to deal with. Jameson was not expected to live into old age, but as long as he was living, more and more of the father's estate would've gone to provide for his care. That would've left Dempsey with a steadily decreasing portion."

"So when Cranston's lawyer got him a change of judge, Cranston put the screws to Dempsey and got out on bail," Connor said.

"Bingo." Captain Peterson snapped his fingers and pointed to Connor.

Adam cleared his throat. "So what's your second idea, Cap?"

The Captain took a long drink of water. "My second idea is that maybe Dempsey was Cranston's partner, and maybe he had orders to do something in the event that Cranston's plan A didn't work out. There's a team going through Judge Dempsey's office and home looking for evidence in the murder for hire scheme. If my hunch is correct, that Dempsey is Cranston's partner, they'll find evidence as to that, as well. We'll know something by morning. I don't believe Cranston could've had a partner outside of Dempsey. But in all honesty, I don't believe Cranston had a partner at all. No phone calls, no visitors, no evidence that we could uncover. I smell no smoke and I see no fire. In the meantime, you're all free to go to your own homes and sleep in your own beds tonight. Of course, if you feel safer here, you're welcome to stay. The manhunt has been called off and you all have the next two days to get your families settled in again."

The men stood together. "Leave everything here as is. The crime scene techs will be here soon to collect those needles and the bloody towels. Your work on this case is done. Good job."

"Thanks for having my back. And, oh yeah, thanks for not bothering to mention it to me," Adam said.

"Like you would've listened," Bo said. "See you in two days. Then what, Cap?"

"Then you're all back together on the Harrington case. Adam has the lead on that and has made excellent progress."

"I'm not sure about the progress part, but I've sure met a lot of nutty people in the process. I'll fill you all in when we meet again in two days. I'm goin' home to sleep in my *own* bed." He left the room to pack his few belongings. "Tell the DEA thanks for their hospitality," he called over his shoulder.

Chapter 16

The Trent family arrived home the next afternoon. Blue bounded out of the car and into the house, and then promptly asked to go out into the back yard, where she rolled in the grass and brought out her toys from underneath the back porch. It was a joyful morning full of hugs, kisses, tears and thankfulness to God for protection.

Jenna loved the new doorbell chimes Adam installed. A large bouquet of red and white roses graced the dining room table next to a box of hand-picked truffles from Kakao, Jenna's favorite chocolate shop, and chocolate covered marshmallows from Chocolate Chocolate Chocolate, Amy's favorite chocolate shop. Even Blue had a new antler chew toy waiting for her.

"So where are we going to celebrate?" Emma Jo asked.

"The Fountain!" Amy and Jenna answered together.

"You're gonna love it, Gomer," Amy proclaimed with excited authority.

After unpacking, the Trents converged on The Fountain at Locust. Amy ordered the grilled cheese, Jenna ordered tomato bisque and the Mr. K salad, Adam and Dwayne got the Champion meatball sandwich with the St. Louis salad and Emma Jo got the chicken pesto with the Stutz salad.

"My, that was good," Emma Jo said, wiping her mouth on her napkin.

"You're not done yet, Gomer," Amy said. "They have the world's *best* ice cream! You *can't* come to the Fountain and not get the ice cream."

They ordered the Coconut Almond Joy sundae, the Bearcat and the Dark and Sinister and passed around the desserts for everyone to try. Amy got extra whipped cream and Jenna got extra hot fudge. As they relished the delectable combinations of ice cream and toppings, the family fell quiet for the first time that day.

As more customers piled into the restaurant, the noise level grew. Adam's cell phone rang. It was Captain Peterson. He stepped outside to take the call.

"Adam, we found boxes at Judge Dempsey's home addressed to Jenna, your parents and Connor's wife. There was also a box addressed to Bo's mother in Tennessee. The packages are on their way to the lab. Just keeping you updated. You enjoy your family and don't worry about anything. Judge Dempsey is going away for a long time. While Cranston was careful about erasing his calls and covering his tracks, Judge Dempsey was not. We found a number of calls he received from Cranston."

"Everything okay, son?" his father asked as he returned to the table.

"We're all good. Great ice cream, huh?"

Chapter 17

"I'm thinking Disney World next summer," Jenna said as she kissed Adam goodbye. He held her close, brushing her hair away from her face with his hand. "Anything you want, baby," he answered, running his finger down her nose and around her lips. "Anything at all."

"Be careful."

"Always."

Adam arrived at the station refreshed and ready to update his team on the Harrington case. But Captain Peterson preempted him with an announcement. "Excuse me, Adam, we just got the lab results in from the boxes that were addressed to all of your families. They contained a dangerous mixture of *Bacillus anthracis*, otherwise known as anthrax, and a concoction of several deadly neurotoxins, most of which I can't pronounce, but all guaranteed to cause a horrible and agonizing death. The Haz Mat crew is dealing with the toxins and the matter has been turned over to the DA."

"I knew Judge Dempsey was crooked, but I didn't figure him for something like that," Adam said. "Killing innocent women and children because their husbands put away a dangerous criminal? That seems extreme, even for a dishonest judge."

Gavin Peterson agreed. "Dempsey claimed he was following orders from Cranston who held Jameson's murder over his head in order to force him into compliance. Said he didn't know what was in the boxes, and was only going to mail them if any of you were killed. Claims he thought they were a guilt offering of some sort from Cranston. Hard to believe a judge would be that gullible, but maybe his fear of being caught or even a guilty conscience clouded his thinking. I don't think Cranston ever suffered from guilt. He was a psychopath, if one ever existed. I do believe he was overreaching when he alleged he had a partner, though. Cranston was a master manipulator and you were his most recent target. He was deluded enough to think you'd actually help him escape. That's all I've got. Unless something else turns up, I'm declaring the Cranston threat has breathed its last. I'll leave you to the Harrington case." He turned and retreated into his office.

Adam briefed his team on the Harrington murder, telling them what he knew and what he suspected. He updated them on the progress he and Kate had made, as well as her suspicions. He assigned the Harrington brothers to Connor, the Harrington sisters to Bo, and divided the staff of Mansford Mansion as evenly as possible between them. They took the case notes to review and agreed to meet after lunch to brainstorm as a team. Adam invited Kate to join them.

"I start with my new K-9 partner tomorrow," Kate announced, when the group convened. "So this is my last stint in Homicide. Not that it hasn't been a blast."

"I'm hopeful that after we've gone over the notes and brainstormed, we'll have another round of interviews, but with a smaller number of suspects. One or more of them is a murderer," Adam said.

"The way I see it here," Bo drawled, "is we got nineteen people in that building, not counting Adam and his family, right? Four's related to the victim, eight more are guests—not including the Trents, again—and seven more are employees. Right so far?" Everyone nodded.

"Okay. So then we got nineteen people—suspects—who all have a motive for murder."

"Not quite all nineteen, but most of those people had a motive for murder, and almost all of them had the opportunity. But who all had the means?" Connor asked.

"And how do we know there's just one killer? It could be two, or three, or more—even everybody," Kate said.

"You all could be right," Adam said. "Although I don't think it was everybody, because I can't find any connection between the people there. But I'd like a fresh pair of eyes on that aspect. Connor, can you go through phone records, e-mails, Facebook, any common denominator you can find, and see if you can determine if any of these folks shared a connection? Same bus route, same chiropractor, same exercise class, same grocery store, same church—*anything* that brings two or more of them together."

"Got it," Connor said, as he took notes.

"I'll take the remaining male suspects and see if anything shakes loose. Bo, you take the female suspects."

"Yeah, yeah, but why does Bo always get the ladies?"

"Cuz I'm the best lookin'. Besides, the ladies all like me and I'm good at gettin' 'em to talk." He winked at Kate.

"I wouldn't fall for you, Bo. Not if you were the last man on earth. But you can keep on deceiving yourself all you want to," Kate said. "Apparently Homicide is so used to working with head cases, the nuttiness is rubbing off."

"Ouch. I'm wounded, Kate." Bo shot back.

Kate rolled her eyes and gave her report summarizing what she had learned, then stood to leave. "Well, guys. This has been fun, but I'm going back to my old job. Anybody going to the graduation ceremony?"

They shook their heads.

"Adam, you are," Captain Peterson said, as he approached the team.

"I am? Why? I was planning on some family time."

"We've got some bright ones coming up. There's one in particular I'd like you to meet."

"Okay," he answered, trying to conceal his disappointment.

"Well, guys. Let's get to it and meet back on Friday to compare notes. Kate, thanks for the extra help. Much appreciated." She nodded and left with a wave of her hand.

The graduation ceremony was well attended. Adam sat next to Captain Peterson and his wife, Melanie.

"They look so young," Melanie said when it was over.

Her husband squeezed her hand in his. "We all did, when we graduated."

"Today's police academy graduates are well trained and well educated. Cap, you were right. It does look like a promising bunch." They stood.

"C'mon. There's someone I want you to meet." Captain Peterson ushered Adam to a female graduate with dark red hair, café au lait skin and dark eyes, standing with a couple Adam assumed were her proud parents, and another couple who appeared unrelated.

The two men shook hands. "Sir, this is Adam Trent. When Samantha makes detective, she won't do better than to be on Adam's team."

Adam shook the man's hand as Captain Peterson started a round of introductions. "Sam Hernandez, Adam Trent. Adam, Sam Hernandez and his wife, Julie. This is their daughter, Samantha Jane."

Samantha Jane introduced the other couple. "This is my Aunt Su Li and Uncle David."

"Pleased to meet you all," Adam replied. "Sam Hernandez? *The* Sam Hernandez? With the ATF?"

Sam nodded and smiled. He looked pleased that Adam recognized his name. "I'm no longer at the Bureau, Detective Trent."

"Adam."

"Adam. Mandatory retirement. I now run a private investigation agency."

"You're quite a legend in law enforcement, taking down that arms dealer and his crew."

"I had a team, and we worked as a team. Joe's retired, and Keisha works for me now."

"And now your daughter is going to join us? Didn't Samantha want to work with you?"

"She did. But I think it's important that she gets several years' experience on the police force. I started there after getting out of the military and then moved into the Bureau. Her mother did her best to start her in music, but Samantha was always more interested in what I was doing."

Julie beamed and squeezed her husband's arm. She was a beautiful redhead with fair skin and sapphire blue eyes. Adam could see both of them in their daughter. He held out his hand to Samantha. "Welcome aboard. Do you go by Sam?"

"No, sir," she answered, giving Adam a firm handshake. "Sam Hernandez is my father. I go by Samantha, or Samantha Jane, either is fine. And for the record, I *do* like music," she said, glancing toward her mother. "I just couldn't see myself practicing all those hours every day. Dad's job has always been so much more exciting."

"Julie is a cellist with the St. Louis Symphony," Sam said, placing an arm around her.

"That's why she looks familiar!" Adam snapped his fingers, having made the connection. "I kept trying to place her."

"You enjoy the symphony?" Julie asked him.

Adam hemmed and hawed before answering. "Um, er, well, my wife and daughter enjoy it. Quite a lot more than I do, to be honest. But we do go every Christmas and once or twice during the season, as well as the Summer Pops."

"I'm with you," David said to Adam. "Su Li grew up with Julie and she made sure our kids all went to the Symphony. But I do enjoy the Christmas programs."

"Adam," Captain Peterson cut in. "Since Samantha doesn't officially start work for a couple more weeks, I thought you might let her sit in and observe on the Harrington case."

Samantha's eyes widened at the suggestion, and her hand flew to her mouth. "I've been following that case in the papers. I'd love to watch your team work! I'll be real quiet and you won't even know I'm there."

Adam chuckled. "Bo will know you're there."

"Who's Bo?"

"He's the young, single, southern guy on the team. Notices anything female."

"I can handle myself," she answered, standing straight.

They all laughed. "I'm sure you can!" Adam said. "See you Friday in Homicide. That's our first official team meeting to discuss what our individual assignments turned up. You know where it is?"

"Yes, sir."

The various groups of graduates with their friends and families were breaking up to head to their private celebrations. "Nice to have met you folks. Enjoy your weekend."

Chapter 18

Connor and Bo entered Adam's office for their information sharing session. Adam had the chairs arranged in a circle. "Connor, Bo, I'd like you to say hello to Samantha Jane Hernandez."

"Why does that name sound familiar?" Connor asked.

"Her father is Sam Hernandez, the ATF agent whose team took down that big arms dealer out in Pineview several years ago. Samantha just graduated from the Academy and will be starting her undoubtedly illustrious career in District 6 in two weeks. Until then, she's going to observe on the Harrington case."

Connor shook hands with Samantha, but Bo backed away putting the back of his hand in front of his mouth. "That nun shared her cold with me." He sneezed. "Best not to make you sick as well. Welcome aboard." He sneezed again.

"Stay away from me. I don't want your germs," Adam said, backing away with his hands up.

"You never want nobody's germs," Connor said.

Adam ignored him. "So everybody's had time to study. What have we got? Bo, you first."

"Right. I'm starting with the premise that none of our suspects is in the habit of walking around with a deadly poison in their purse, or in their pocket. So somebody came prepared to kill Harrington. That means our killer or killers already knew Harrington would be there." Bo blew his nose and put the wadded up tissue in his pocket.

Adam cringed and Connor put two thumbs up.

Bo continued. "Now, I know the nuns had motive, but I see no reason to believe that they would've had the poison on their person. They didn't have foreknowledge that Harrington was gonna be there. I can't find any connection anywhere, other than their anger at Harrington over the children's home. They're so low on the suspect list I believe it's feasible to eliminate the nuns. Are we together on the nuns?"

"I'm good with that," Connor said. "I think they're about the least likely of all the suspects."

"I'm with you too. Go on," said Adam. He drew two vertical lines dividing a clean whiteboard into thirds and wrote the word nuns on the left side of the line.

"I also think that Kimber Dennison is a long shot. Now that's one gal that loves to talk. She's a nice lady, and I'm thinkin' not the brightest bulb in the socket, but based on my investigation of her and my personal interview, I don't think she's a viable suspect. And again, she had no knowledge that Harrington was gonna be there that night, and if she had, she said she never would've gone. I believe her. She was terrified her husband would find out she stole that scarf, which gave her all that much more motive to stay away from Harrington. I think it's safe to say she's off the list. Same with Jasmine Jones. Her research is well respected and she's pretty well known in the New England area, where they got a bunch more haunted houses than we do. Her family connection to the house is interesting—pretty cool history—but I don't see any motive for a crime there." He drained his coffee and wiped his mouth. "According to her cell phone records, she calls her husband every night before bed, and calls her mama three times a week. She also checks in with her colleagues and occasionally calls for room service. I can't find any red flags there, so I think we can dismiss Dr. Jones."

"As long as you're not giving her a pass 'cause she's a looker,'" Connor said. He pointed a playful finger at Bo and raised an eyebrow. "I'm okay with dismissing Jasmine Jones, but rather than dismiss Mrs. Dennison, I'd rather bump her toward the bottom of the suspect list. I'm not so sure Kimber Dennison should be ruled out just yet."

"Did you find a connection, Connor?" Adam asked. "What she told Bo is consistent with what she told me—that if she'd known Harrington was gonna be there, she never would've gone." He added Jasmine's name to the left on the board and put Kimber's name in the middle column.

"No. I just think she had a much stronger motive, what with her being blackmailed, and also believin' her husband's business was threatened. The Dennisons have a nice place there on Flora, which gives her extra motive. She was scared of losin' her home. Desperate measures and all, ya know. I agree she's a weak suspect, but I don't want her written off just yet, unless yous know somethin' I don't."

"Fair enough," Adam said. He turned to their guest. "Samantha, we're putting our least likely suspects on the left side, the most likely ones on the right and those we're divided on in this middle column."

Samantha looked up from her notebook and tucked her hair behind her ears. "Right, sir. Got it."

Bo cleared his throat and resumed his summary. "That leaves my four most viable suspects: the employees, Ava Montel, the nut case, and Mariah Flores—and the Harrington sisters, Esme and Lucinda."

"And from that list, can you narrow it anymore?" Adam asked. Bo sighed and shook his head. "I don't think so. Ava may have limited strength, but it doesn't take an Olympic athlete to drop poison into someone's food or drink. And she has, to say the least, a skewed version of reality. So there's no tellin' what in the world is goin' on in that purty little head of hers. Now you said Esme had a lot of head problems too, but she seemed like she was healing purty nice, now that daddy's out of the way. Adam, I know you said that Dr. Gerwyn wrote off Esme as a suspect. But I think there's more to her than meets the eye."

"How do yous mean?" Connor asked. "I tend to lean with Dr. Gerwyn on her. Esme oughtta go in the middle row." He wiggled his finger at the board indicating her name should be moved.

"Well, I ain't no psychiatrist, but I'll tell ya, I don't cotton to nut jobs. When I drove out to the Harrington home, Esme was dressed with her hair all combed and some lipstick on and working in the flower garden out in the sunshine. She looked to me like she's put on some weight and had a little sun on her skin. Maybe not having that tyrant around was a real good thing for Esme. She was lookin' fairly normal to me."

Adam sighed and put his head in his hands and rubbed his temples. When he lifted his head and spoke, he sounded discouraged. "If that's the case, it would point more to Roland, I'm afraid. He is altruistic enough and smart enough to go for what he would consider the greater good, which in this case, would be to benefit his little sister if he thought that Edward's death would free her to live a normal life."

"Why you soundin' so disappointed at that?" Bo asked.

"Because *if*—and I do mean if—it's Roland, I don't think we'll ever find the evidence we need to make an arrest. Roland even admitted to me that he was the only one of his siblings smart enough to pull this off, although he claimed he didn't. That's either blatant arrogance, or simple honesty. And the last thing Roland Harrington is, is arrogant."

The group fell silent as Adam's words sunk in. He added Ava's name to the right hand column and Esme to the middle column. In large letters across the bottom of the whiteboard, he printed Roland, stretching over all three of the suspect categories.

"Okay, Bo, what about Lucinda and Mariah?" Connor asked, breaking the gloom.

"Lucinda is my strongest suspect, with motive and opportunity. Plus, she's just plain psychopathic."

"Sociopathic," Adam interrupted. "That's the term Dr. Gerwyn used."

"What's the difference?" Connor asked.

"Very little. Sociopathic is the correct term, according to our esteemed psychiatrist," Adam answered.

"Whatever. But I can't find any physical evidence to link Lucinda. That bothers me a lot because I kinda like her for this."

Adam glanced at Samantha, who was listening and taking notes. *Yeah, she'll be a good one for this team when the time comes.*

"I don't see any motive for Mariah," Bo said. "Based on Kate's observation, we got a search warrant but we didn't find any cyanide at her place. That photo lab belonged to her granddaddy, but it didn't look like it had been used in years. Miz Mariah was royally ticked off when I showed up with that warrant. But when we looked over the place, we didn't find nothin'. She was dressed up real nice, like she was goin' out on a date or somethin', and we made her late. She was not happy and complained about the invasion of her privacy."

"By now, she's had plenty of opportunity to get rid of any cyanide," Adam said. "If we could've come up with a motive, it would've been better to have searched that lab weeks ago."

"I know. Woulda coulda shoulda, but I can only work with what I got here, and there wasn't no cyanide in that lab. Although, it did look as if some of that dust in there wasn't as old as the rest, but there's no way of tellin'."

"Thanks, Bo. So we put Mariah in the middle column? You got anything else to share on our female suspects?" Adam asked.

"Nope. That about does it." He winked at Samantha who appeared not to notice. "Anybody want coffee? I gotta stretch." Bo stood and began sneezing.

Adam stepped back and shuddered. "I don't want you touching anything that's goin' in my mouth, thank you very much."

Samantha stood. "I'll get everyone some fresh coffee."

Adam put his hand up. "Samantha, you're not the gopher here. Nobody expects you to wait on anybody. We can get our own coffee ourselves. Everybody pulls their own weight around here."

"Yeah, Samantha. I was just bein' a gentleman. I saw your cup was empty."

"It's no problem. I just thought that since I wasn't contributing to the case, I could keep everyone caffeinated."

Connor returned carrying a fresh pot of brew. "Well, while yous guys was all involved in such an important discussion as to who oughtta get the coffee, I just went and got it. Seemed easier." He filled everyone's cup. "Someone from Robbery just brought in a big box of bagels. All different kinds."

"I'm in," Adam said, setting the marker on the whiteboard shelf and walking toward the Robbery division. The others followed behind him.

They returned and took their seats.

"All right. Back to work. Thanks for your input, Bo. Well done. Connor, were you able to find any connection between any of our suspects?"

Connor shook his head as he swallowed a large bite of bagel. "Sorry Adam. I got nothin' to tie these folks together. Other than the obvious, I don't see where these people's paths cross at all. I got everyone's cell phone records and no calls between the suspects, outside of those who work together, of course. The only folks who use Facebook are Kimber Dennison, Sister Cecilia Marie, and the staff of Mansford Mansion. Kimber shows pictures of her latest shopping trips, recipes, her gardening, that kind of fascinating stuff. Mark Vernon and Carl Mendoza post acting related things, and sometimes jokes. Cunningham is all about promoting his business. The rest of the staff barely use it."

"If any of our suspects communicate through burn phones, we'd never know about that," Adam said.

"That's right—or if they had e-mail accounts I couldn't locate," Connor replied. "I had the folks who I considered the most likely suspects followed by some of our uniforms. Nothin' suspicious that they could tell. Only thing about that is the three Harrington siblings that live in the house. There's plenty of exits in that house. And some of those places in the Central West End have basement connections to adjoining buildings, carriage houses and the like, which could allow our suspects to come and go without being noticed."

"Thanks, Connor. Good work," Adam said and took out his notes. "I paid a visit to Bill Meyers, Sid Friedman, Roland and Cedric Harrington and Alan Cunningham. I revisited Charlie Dennison, Mike Davey, Mark Vernon and Carl Mendoza. Kate also assisted in this effort. We went over our notes together last night, so I'm combining our impressions."

Adam paused a minute while he gathered Kate's notes and reorganized his paperwork.

"Bill Meyers doesn't have enough nerve to kill a gnat, so I vote him out right from the start. He's a weak suspect in more ways than one."

The team snickered and agreed as Adam put Bill's name in the left column. He returned to his notes.

"Now, as for the rest of them. Sid Friedman's a big jerk. I think he's ruthless enough to kill and clever enough to figure out a way to make and carry out a good plan. But the problem with Friedman is what Bo said in the beginning. Nobody walks around with cyanide in their pocket on the off chance they might meet someone they hate enough to kill." Adam paused and took a long drink of coffee. "Now. That leaves us with the rest of the men—the men who worked at the restaurant. They all either knew or could have known that Harrington would be there that night. All anyone had to do was read the reservation book. Everyone's name was in there." He put Sid's name in the left column.

Connor finished his bagel and belched. "Adam, I know you like Mr. Roland pretty well, but quite frankly, anyone that perfect just gives me the creeps. What was that movie about the guy who was all normal on the outside, but turned out to be a murderer?"

"*American Psycho*," Adam said. "And I think I said I find Roland likeable. Assuming he's not our killer, that is."

"Yeah, whatever. Roland creeps me out and I think he could've done it for all kinds of reasons. He could've figured it would free

Esme, for one. Like you was sayin' for the greater good. It's not like Harrington's missed by anyone. Maybe Roland knew his old man was blackmailing good folks. That would'a rankled him good. I think *somebody* knew Harrington had a blackmail list, 'cause that cozy little crowd was no coincidence. Alls I'm sayin' is the guy gives me the willies. But while we're on the subject of creepy, here, Alan Cunningham wins the prize." Connor stood and walked back and forth in front of the group while he talked. "Cunningham had a big financial motive for killing Edward Harrington. That guy didn't have two nickels to rub together. After the murder, the restaurant was packed. They even had to open extra nights. Sales in the gift shop were way up. They sold that fake emerald and diamond pendant over fifty times, even with the price more than double the original. Folks was payin' double to sit at the Harrington table. Go figure *that* out. Cunningham is a master manipulator and he's benefitted financially in a huge way. Plus, that guy is creepier than a centipede. He *lives* in that house. Actually *lives* there!" Connor shuddered and resumed his seat.

"Connor, you and I both know there's no such thing as…"

"Hey, man," Connor interrupted him. "You grew up on a farm. I grew up right here in St. Louis. That house has earned its scary stories."

"All right. Let's stick to the case." Adam cut him off before they all went down a rabbit trail. It was close to lunch time and Adam's stomach was rumbling. He wrote Cunningham's name in the far right column. He looked at his notes. "Next up is Cedric."

"Cedric's a sniveling, sneaky womanizer with the morals of an alley cat." Bo said, stifling another sneeze.

"Hey!" Connor interjected. "That's offensive to alley cats. Take it back."

"Sorry." Bo shook his head and grinned. "Forgot we had a cat lover in the room."

Adam consulted his notes. "Cedric's got plenty of motive and opportunity, but he's lazy and not too bright. Much as I'd like to see him as our guy, I don't think he's it. But I don't like him at all, and I think that if he had a partner, he could be involved, so I don't want to leave him out of the mix." Adam added Cedric's name to the right hand column. "Now we didn't talk about Charlie Dennison when we were discussing Kimber."

"Dennison's got plenty of motive, just like his wife." Connor said. "I think he also had opportunity."

"I agree," said Adam. He held up a finger. "Problem is, there's no evidence and no reason to believe he had cyanide with him. Both Charlie and Kimber Dennison said they never would've gone to the restaurant had they known Harrington would be there. Given both of their circumstances, there's no reason not to believe that. So which column are we putting Charlie in?"

The team was split in their discussion, so Adam wrote Charlie's name in the middle column.

"What about the bartender? What did Kate think about him?" Bo asked. He sniffed and wiped his nose. Samantha opened her purse and handed him a small bottle of hand sanitizer. "Thanks." He scooted his chair closer to her. She scooted her chair away from him.

Adam rolled his eyes and turned to write Mike Davey's name in the left column. *Bo never quits.* "Neither of us thinks Davey's our guy. Can't find a motive or any evidence to support him being our killer. Objections?" The group shook their heads.

"All right," Adam said. He took a drink from his coffee mug. "That leaves Carl Mendoza and Mark Vernon. They both could've had foreknowledge that Harrington would be there that night. We can't tie them to any cyanide purchase, but that doesn't rule out the possibility that one or both of them may have had access. Mark's not as likely as Carl to have committed the crime. He had no motive other than to protect his friend. While I don't think that either of them is our perp, I'm also not convinced otherwise. I'd like to put their names in the middle column. Everyone good with that?" He wrote their names as the others nodded in agreement.

Adam paused and looked over the board making checkmarks in the air with his finger as he reviewed his notes. He turned back to the team. "Okay guys. Thanks for your hard work. We've at least narrowed down our most probable suspects." Samantha Hernandez raised her hand sheepishly. "Samantha? You have a question?" Adam asked.

All eyes turned to the rookie in the room who blushed at the attention.

"I did have one question. How was it that these particular people were at the Mansford Mansion on that particular night? If someone knew that Edward Harrington was going to be there, could they have arranged for the others to be present?"

Adam snapped his fingers and pointed upward, pleased at her initiative. "That's an excellent question, Samantha. The nuns were given tickets as a gift from the grateful family of a special needs student that Cecilia Marie worked with. Friedman and Meyers got a coupon in the mail, but they also said they had a client who was thinking about buying the place and asked them to take a look, so they had two reasons to be there. The Dennisons and the Harringtons all got coupons and responded. So the only people there that night who did not have a coupon were the nuns and my family."

"Could be that coupons went out to *all* the people on that blackmail list, but not all of them responded. Also, it'd just make sense, statistically, that people such as y'all would be there because of the advertisements." Bo said. "Isn't that what drew Amy? All the hype?"

"That's a good point, Bo." Adam said. Bo looked sideways to Samantha and she scooted her chair farther away. "Connor, will you run down where those coupons came from, and who decided where to send them?"

Connor scribbled some notes. "Will do, Adam. I'll get back to yous."

"Okay. Let me know by Wednesday. Thanks again, and you're dismissed for lunch. Hope you feel better soon, Bo. Take a couple of days off, why don't you, before you get us all sick?"

Chapter 19

"Great dinner, Jenna. Nothing like chili and cornbread on a cold fall day. And you make the best of both." Adam squeezed his wife's hand and rose to help clear the table. "Amy, you take the silverware and glasses."

"Then I gotta walk Blue and I got English homework and math sheets due tomorrow."

"I *have* to walk Blue, and I *have* English homework," Jenna gently corrected. Amy rolled her eyes as she set the dishes in the sink and called the dog.

Adam's cell phone rang. It was Connor. "Ya know those coupons? They were generated by the restaurant, but once they were printed, Cunningham says he changed his mind and didn't send them out. Thought they'd be too expensive and eat into his profits. He was real surprised and pretty angry when Friedman, Meyers, the Harringtons and the Dennisons all showed up with a discount on the same night. Not only that, but turns out no other coupons showed up for any other nights. And get this. When Cunningham showed me what those coupons looked like, they were dated for the September 15 event *only*. Whaddya think of that? Pretty fishy, huh?"

"Any idea who sent them out or why they went to those particular people?" Adam asked.

"No. Cunningham didn't even know until they showed up with the coupons. He wasn't happy but, of course, couldn't show it. It would've been bad for business."

"Good work, Connor. What do you make of this?" Adam peeked through the curtain to make sure Amy and Blue were safe.

"We know, er, I mean, we suspect that Harrington had a blackmail list, and at least some of the people on his list were sent coupons for that night. Could've been even more coupons were sent out, but just our current suspects are all that took the bait. I'm thinkin' it's looking more and more like the three siblings in the house. One or more of them found that list. Probably snooping through their father's office, is my guess."

"I agree. But we didn't have enough for a warrant before, and if the killer found that list, I'd think that by now, it's been destroyed. That'd be some pretty strong evidence."

"So, what's next?"

"Dunno. Write up your report and be sure Bo and Cap get a copy. I'm gonna have to think on this. There's a connection I'm missing somewhere. Thanks for calling. Good work."

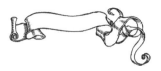

Adam lay in bed staring at the ceiling, allowing his eyes to adjust to the dark. Jenna lay beside him, sleeping peacefully. He stroked her hair and brushed his lips across her shoulder, then turned over, trying without success to quell his scrambled thoughts. Adam and his team had gathered facts, impressions, details and histories, but he was unable to use what he had learned to determine who had killed Edward Harrington. His frustration grew as sleep eluded him. He turned on his left side, then his right side. He punched his pillow and tried lying on his back.

Unable to sleep, Adam got up. Jenna never moved. He envied her. Adam walked through the house, double-checking to make sure the doors and windows were locked. He peeked into Amy's room. Blue was asleep on top of Amy, like she was every night, snoring like a drunk. How the noise didn't wake his daughter, he would never understand. The sleeping Trent household was at peace. Except for Adam.

He looked out onto the street in front of the house, the backyard and every window. All was quiet. Adam paced through the house, but was still unsettled. He spread his case notes out on the table, reading and re-reading them, thumbing his fingers on the tabletop. Still restless. He gathered the papers together and returned them to their folder. Rummaging through the kitchen, Adam found a bottle of melatonin that Jenna swore helped her sleep. He took a couple and flipped on the computer to play a game of solitaire, but before he could finish the game, his head began to feel heavy. Maybe Jenna was right about the melatonin.

He returned to bed. His last conscious thought before succumbing to exhaustion was that he had eaten too many onions on his chili, as he drifted into a restless sleep filled with nonsensical dreams and images…

Doc Sutter and Avril Markham were dancing and laughing in the morgue. "You kill 'em, we'll chill 'em! You stab 'em, we'll slab 'em!" They were chanting back and forth, while tossing beakers and test tubes into the air, their faces looming in and out of focus, larger than life.

A camera appeared in front of him, dangling in mid-air. Captain Peterson said, "Smile pretty for the camera." Then the flashbulb blinded Adam and he was immediately inside Mansford Mansion. The staff and the guests were running around the tables with their wine glasses lifted high, singing out, "Cyanide! Get your cyanide here! A little dab'll do ya!" Then the women bragged, "We have boyfriends! We all have boyfriends!" And the men answered, "We like our girlfriends! Our partners in crime!" Altogether, their voices rang out, "All for one and one for all! Money, money, money! We have coupons! Coupons for cyanide!"

Then everyone started sneezing and their germs were getting on Adam. He jumped back to get away from them and was instantly transported to Our Lady of Sorrows Catholic Church. Sister Elizabeth Anne was sick. Her nose glowed a bright red and she was sneezing, sneezing on Adam. Sick people! Germs! He ran away to the station and found Bo walking like a zombie toward him, and sneezing. Kate Marlin and Robo appeared. They were laughing and dancing. Kate whispered to him, "My boyfriend's name is Eddie. He's no good. He's a bad, bad boy." Another camera with a flashbulb clicked, blinding him and he was back at Mansford Mansion. He heard a woman screaming over and over, as Ava Montel ran at him with a knife.

Adam woke up in a cold sweat and sat up in bed. *I gotta lay off all those onions.* He blinked and looked around his bedroom. All was dark and quiet. He could hear Jenna's soft breathing as she lay sleeping beside him. He swung his legs off the side of the bed and put his head in his hands, re-winding the dream in his conscious thoughts, trying to sort out what the craziness meant. Adam knew his dream was his subconscious working to make sense of the information that eluded his conscious thoughts. The coupons were important. The boyfriend, Eddie was important. But the sneezing? Why was that significant? What did that mean, other than he didn't like germs? But why would that invade his dream? Then there was the woman's voice screaming while Ava Montel …

Adam suddenly bolted upright. And he knew in that moment who killed Edward Rupert Harrington, III, and how.

Chapter 20

Jenna Trent woke to the rich aroma of coffee wafting into the bedroom. She turned over to discover Adam's side of the bed empty. She sprang out of bed, threw on leggings and a tee shirt and hurried into the kitchen.

"You're up early, Sweetheart," she walked to her husband to kiss him, tucking her hair back behind her ears. Adam was already dressed for work. "If you needed to go to work early, I would have gotten up and started coffee."

Adam kissed her. "Do you know how beautiful you are first thing in the morning?"

"Yeah, I got a pretty good idea. Messy hair, smushed up face and no make-up. Alert the media. Hey! Whatcha got over there?" She peered over his shoulder at a pan on the counter.

"Cinnamon rolls, just going into the oven. Special treat, right out of the pop-open can."

"Coffee and breakfast? And since when do you wake up so cheerful?"

"Since I solved the Harrington case and we'll be closing it tonight," he said, hugging her so tightly, he lifted her off her feet.

"Wow! Adam, that's great! Was there a break in the case? You didn't say anything to me last night. You seemed preoccupied after you got that call from Connor. What happened?"

"You'll see tonight. Don't fix dinner. The three of us have someplace to be, so we'll grab some tacos on the way. How about this weekend we leave Amy with Kate and the new dog, and if you still have questions, we can talk about it over a kid-free date?"

Jenna laughed. "You're on! I'll give Kate a call after I drop Amy off at school. I want to hear all about this."

"Speaking of Amy—" Adam looked toward the hall.

"She's got eight more minutes before she needs to get up. Don't worry. Blue won't allow her to oversleep." She took his hands in hers and brought them to her lips to kiss them. "It's good to see you happy, Adam."

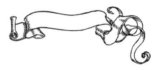

Adam and his team, together with Samantha Jane Hernandez, gathered in Adam's office at the police station on Clark Street. He reviewed his instructions with them. "Everybody clear?" he asked. The team answered in the affirmative. "Let's roll."

"Thanks for letting me tag along," Samantha said to Adam as they started up the steps to the front porch of the mansion.

"Watch and learn," he answered. He held the door open as Jenna, Amy and Samantha entered the house.

Adam, Jenna and Amy were seated at the same table at Mansford Mansion as they had been on the night of the murder. Within minutes, the nuns, the businessmen, the Dennisons and the Harrington siblings arrived and took their seats. Alan Cunningham and the staff, minus Ava Montel, were seated at the table in the back of the room. Samantha sat alone in a back corner, unnoticed by the others.

The atmosphere was thick with anticipation and nervous unease.

"Well, well, well. Isn't this cozy?" Lucinda Harrington sneered, curling her lip. "All of us together again, just like old times, minus dear old dad, may he lie tortured in hell."

"Shut up, Lucinda," Esme spoke sharply, challenging her sister. Esme's arms were crossed in front of her chest. She jutted her chin toward her sister.

A slight smile escaped Roland's lips at the new, improved and bolder Esme Harrington. Cedric squirmed in his chair, looking sideways at Lucinda.

Several of the guests shifted uncomfortably in their seats. As Adam read the group, he could see they were unsure of why they had been summoned to the scene of a crime from which they were anxious to distance themselves, yet at the same time, were secretly grateful had occurred.

Adam walked toward the front of the room, positioned himself in front of the stage and addressed the gathering. "Thank you for coming," he began.

"As if we had a choice," Lucinda snorted.

Adam continued, ignoring the rude interruption. "On September 15, Edward Rupert Harrington, III was murdered at this table. The murder was premeditated and carried out. It was no accident that this particular gathering of people was here on that evening." The Dennisons held hands and looked toward the floor. Carl Mendoza looked away, and Lucinda Harrington glared at Adam.

Adam walked the length of the room as he spoke, making eye contact with each person. Everyone avoided looking at him, except for Roland, who sat with perfect posture and an unnatural calmness, unaffected by Adam's gaze. "The one thing the killer did not plan on was that my family and I would be in attendance. Edward Harrington was the poster child for heart disease. He ate and drank anything that wasn't nailed down. He was on heart medication and had a host of health conditions. Unless the family would have asked for an autopsy, there would have been nothing

to indicate one was necessary. But I'm a homicide detective, and
when Harrington died, I became suspicious. So I requested an
autopsy, and when cyanide was ruled to be the cause of death,
an investigation was launched. Edward Harrington's death was
supposed to look like a heart attack. What I believe his killer
didn't realize, was that Harrington would have been dead within
a year anyway. It's no secret that Harrington was hated by
everyone in this room. Except for Mike Davey, the bartender,
every one of you had a motive to kill Edward Harrington."

The suspects changed positions in their seats, crossing and
uncrossing their legs, looking about the room, avoiding eye
contact.

"Everything Edward Harrington touched, he damaged. Many
of you were being blackmailed by Harrington. Many of you
lost money because of him. Others faced ruin at his hands. I'm
not here to divulge your secrets. It's nobody's business and it's
not my place to air anyone's dirty laundry. But someone else
here, among us knew. They knew your secrets and used that
knowledge to their benefit."

The group was silent.

"Someone knew who had access to the records Mr. Harrington
kept. And that person colluded with someone who had access
to the restaurant coupons and who could send those coupons to
entice you—the very people who would be present in this room,
to come on the same night. The Harrington siblings were the
only suspects who could've found their father's records. And the
restaurant employees were the only suspects who had access to
the coupons."

Everyone in the room looked to each other. Except for the
rustle of clothing as the people looked around them, the room
was quiet.

"Somewhere, somehow, there was a connection between one
of the Harrington siblings and one of the restaurant employees."

Lucinda's jaw clenched. Cedric squirmed. Esme sat clasping
her hands in her lap. Roland sat still and upright, listening with
polite attention.

Adam stopped pacing and returned to his original position. "What I couldn't figure out was how and when the cyanide was administered. Edward Harrington sat only a few yards away from me, yet I saw no sign of distress in him as he struggled for breath in the final moments before his death."

Roland studied Adam intently, but sat still as a statue.

"Sister Elizabeth Anne…"

The nun's head jerked up and her hand flew to her chest. "Me?"

Adam paused and took a breath. He looked at the nun. "Sister Elizabeth Anne, when I came to see you, you had a cold and were sneezing. You were congested and feeling under the weather. Unfortunately, when one of my team members came to conduct a follow-up interview with you and your friends, he also caught your cold. He too, has been sneezing and is congested."

Sister Elizabeth Anne looked at Adam with her head tilted to one side.

"The question I kept asking myself is why didn't I hear Mr. Harrington in his distress? While it didn't take a long time for him to die, the nature of cyanide poisoning causes its victims to suffer as they struggle for breath. But I heard nothing. And I don't think any of you did either." He swept his hand over the small crowd.

Jasmine tilted her head to one side and narrowed her eyes as she listened to Adam. Mariah looked at Cedric, then looked away. Alan began to fidget. Mark, Carl and Mike looked back and forth between the Harrington table and their own.

"The reason that neither I, nor any of you, were aware that Mr. Harrington was gasping for breath, is that at that precise moment, there was a terrible screaming from Ms. Flores, offstage. Mariah Flores screamed and screamed for an extended period of time at the top of her lungs. By the time her theatrics were finished, Edward Harrington's struggle for life was over."

Mariah began to bite her lip. She looked sideways around the room.

Adam ignored her and continued. "But Mariah Flores was offstage. She was waiting tables and tending to her other duties.

When I asked Mariah why she screamed so, she told me that she and Mike Davey, the bartender, were playing a joke on Ava Montel, because Ava didn't know how to scream and they were going to teach her."

"I never…" Mike Davey stood indignantly, his fists clenched. But Adam cut him off.

"Mike Davey would never have done that. Mariah was not aware that Mr. Davey was carrying a torch for Ava Montel, and would've sooner cut off his own arm than to have done anything to hurt or upset the woman, even though her feelings were not reciprocal."

Mike returned to his seat. His face flushed bright red as he looked at the floor.

"So the question then, is why did Mariah begin screaming like that, at the exact moment the cyanide which Mr. Harrington had been ingesting all evening, finally took effect? How would she have known? She was in the kitchen during the play, and serving the table between scenes. What was the cue that Mariah was listening for that would tell her when to start screaming and when to stop?"

"Do tell," Lucinda said. "The suspense is killing me." She yawned. But her remarks hung in the air without response.

"It was Cedric Harrington."

"*Cedric!*" Lucinda turned and faced her brother.

Adam paced the floor again, watching the faces of his suspects. The nuns sat up and leaned toward him, as did the businessmen, Sid Friedman and Bill Meyers. Cedric, Lucinda and Esme appeared uncomfortable, squirming in their seats and glancing sideways at the others. Roland remained erect and unreadable. Charlie Dennison put his arm around Kimber and pulled her close. She leaned into him. Amy sat mesmerized, open-mouthed and wide-eyed.

Adam continued. "Cedric and Mariah were secret lovers, however, each had a different agenda. Each had something the other wanted, and together, they formed an unlikely, but diabolical union. Cedric had money and upon his father's death, he'd have more money than he could spend in a lifetime. But Cedric was a little short on brains and ambition." All eyes turned toward Cedric who was beginning to look ill.

"Mariah, on the other hand, would always struggle financially. She dreamed of having money and all that it could buy her. Having money meant she would never have to wait tables again, or change another bedpan, or mop another dirty floor. She wouldn't have to work two exhausting jobs just to keep her head above water. The demands of the nursing home would be a thing of the past. And she would no longer have to wait tables or endure demeaning treatment from the likes of people such as the Harringtons. She envisioned that her days of serving would soon be over, and a new life—one where she would be served, was now within reach. Mariah had the brains and ambition that Cedric lacked."

The room was silent as a tomb. Everyone looked from Cedric, to Mariah to Adam. Adam continued. "But Mariah also had something else that Cedric didn't. Mariah had cyanide, left over from her grandfather's photography lab. Her grandfather's cyanide was obtained long before cyanide purchases were registered or traceable. She and Cedric had been dosing Edward Harrington's food and drink all night, and as we all heard, he complained that everything tasted off. No one paid much attention to him because the food wasn't very good to begin with. But when Harrington didn't succumb, a much heavier dose was administered before the dessert. A dose so strong, it was sure to work."

"Your people searched my house and never found any cyanide," Mariah spat at him.

"That's true, Ms. Flores. But as one of my team members pointed out, you had plenty of time between September 15 and the time my men came to search your house, to either move the poison or dispose of it altogether. You were the brains behind the murder for money scheme. Cedric was an easy mark for you. You referred to your boyfriend as Eddie, but Eddie was just your nickname for Cedric, taking Cedi and dropping the C, so it was similar to his father's name. It didn't take much for you to learn where Cedric hung out to drink and carouse. His reputation was hardly a secret. He had an eye for beautiful women and you know how to make yourself up to be alluring." Mariah ran her tongue over her lips and chewed her bottom lip.

Adam continued. "Plus, Cedric knew his father would not approve of you. That made you even more attractive to him. Once you had Cedric's attention, it was easy for you to hook him and reel him in. After that, it was a simple matter to plan his father's murder. Maybe Cedric would agree to marry you, and who knows? At some point, you likely would have poisoned him as well."

All eyes looked toward Mariah, then back and forth between her and Cedric. Cedric squirmed in his seat and Mariah bit her fingernails.

"The two of you cooked up a scheme in which you acted offended at Cedric's advances, so as to throw off any suspicion that you two were involved. But you couldn't resist one slip up in the bar, which, unfortunately for you, was observed. When you thought no one was looking, you allowed Cedric to run his hand along your bottom." Mariah bit her bottom lip until it turned white. "You had the most access to Harrington's food and drink, but you also gave Cedric cyanide to slip into his father's plate and glasses. However, by the time dessert was going to be served, Edward was still alive, so you gave him a large dose and listened for Cedric's cue so you would know when to begin screaming loud enough to cover the sound of his father's final desperate breaths. When Cedric saw his father in distress, he began to sneeze very loudly. The rest of us thought him rude and uncouth, but you see, *Cedric was never sick.* Sister Elizabeth Anne and one of my team members have been sneezing and miserable for days, but they were sick with a bad cold. Cedric was in perfect health."

Cedric suddenly stood, threw his chair toward Adam and bolted toward the door, shoving the nuns out of his way and knocking Sister Agnes Pauline to the floor. But Connor was waiting for him at the front door and tackled him to the ground, handcuffing him behind his back. Adam rushed to help the elderly nun back to her seat, as the other three sisters attended to her. "I'm fine, I'm fine. Stop fussing," she said, brushing herself off.

Adam glared at the handcuffed Cedric, as Connor kept watch. Then he turned toward Mariah.

Mariah's eyes darted back and forth as she dashed toward the kitchen, but Adam calmly told her, "It's no use. The house is surrounded. You have no place to go. It's over, Mariah." She stopped running and stared at him in disbelief, then slumped to the floor with her head between her knees, grabbing her hair in tightly balled fists.

Chapter 2J

Three months later

Dusk was turning to dark as Adam's squad car crept past the Mansford Mansion. A dim streetlight cast a flickering glow as Adam watched Alan Cunningham remove what looked to be the last of several boxes piled on the sidewalk to a rental van. Alan's coat flapped back and forth in the frigid wind. He wore nothing on his head and his cheeks and nose were chapped bright red. He did not notice Adam as he drove by.

After the arrests were announced in the Harrington murder, interest in the mansion waned, and despite Alan Cunningham's best efforts, he was unable to keep the dinner theater running. With no questionable aura looming over the house, reservations dropped off and then stopped altogether. He could no longer afford to pay the staff and so he let them go. While the Mansford Mansion was not responsible for claiming the life of Edward Rupert Harrington, III, Cunningham's mystery dinner theater had become the latest business to fall prey to its curse.

The people whose lives the house last touched resumed their existence, some forging new paths, and others returning to that which was familiar.

Jasmine Jones, having gleaned all she could from the event of the century, returned to Connecticut to carry on her research. Mike Davey found odd jobs and restaurant work where he could. Carl Mendoza and Mark Vernon continued bartending at Helen Fitzgerald's and the Cheshire Inn, while searching for acting jobs on their days off. Ava Montel would continue receiving treatment in the lockdown ward of the state run mental hospital for the foreseeable future.

Cedric and Mariah were denied bail and remained locked up, awaiting trial.

Charlie and Kimber Dennison renewed their vows and patched up their marriage.

Sid Friedman and Bill Meyers expanded their operations. Their business resumed as if Edward Harrington had never existed. Their client who had been interested in purchasing the mansion decided against it.

Lucinda started her own cosmetics company and Esme enrolled in culinary school. Roland donated land, cash and building supplies so the nuns could start over and build their children's home unimpeded. Roland's generosity meant the new home would house more than twice as many children as the original.

Adam circled around the block and returned for a final pass before heading home. As he approached the mansion one last time, he watched the tail lights of the rental van disappear around the corner. He parked the car in front of the place and stared at it. He wondered if the city would finally tear it down. Mansford Mansion looked empty, neglected and forlorn, yet, strangely beckoning. Adam felt himself drawn to the house, unable to break its magnetic spell and pull away. A chill ran down his spine. The St. Louis winter was bitter cold as usual. Adam felt cold throughout his body. He turned the heat up in the squad car, but could not shake the chill as he watched the house, mesmerized. He felt himself being lured in as though an unspoken invitation was being offered that could not be resisted. As he moved his hand toward the door handle, the radio chatter abruptly interrupted his silent reverie, startling him back to consciousness. He shook his head to clear it and listened to the call from the dispatcher. Another car answered. Adam looked at the clock on his radio and realized several minutes had passed. It was past time to go home. He again felt cold. With one final look, he drove away, leaving the house to whatever fate would eventually befall it.

Inside Mansford Mansion, the cold January wind blew through the leaky windows causing the dust to swirl eerily into nondescript patterns. Light frost formed a thin covering over the third floor. And the crystal chandelier swayed gently over the grand staircase.

He'll Find You

In Dumbrava, a tiny and remote mountain village in County Maramures, Romania

Ovidiu Todoran, racked with anger and grief, trudged out to the small patch of dirt he farmed to eke out another day of the poverty-entrenched existence that post-Revolution Romania called freedom. Not that life had been good under the Communist reign of Nicolae Ceausescue. But the promises of new-found freedom and prosperity remained unfulfilled in Dumbrava, as they were throughout the entire country. Although the last winter frost was gone, the cold remained, and it was time to plant potatoes. The March wind blew, cutting through the threadbare coat wrapped around Ovidiu's thin waist. He hated winter. His pants had worn so thin, they were useless, and his only pair of socks was full of holes. His sweater had been warm when his wife first knit it for him, but that was many years ago, and it hung on his slight frame, like rags on a scarecrow. The cold chilled him to the bone, and he longed for spring.

Ovidiu's heart was as acrid and barren as the countryside was beautiful and lush in the spring and summer. Life in Romania was hard. Ovidiu was born in Dumbrava, he lived all his life in Dumbrava and he would die in Dumbrava. It was the same in all the towns and mountain villages.

Winters were harsh with only a fireplace to heat his three-room shack. The frigid wind cut through the walls, coating the sparse furnishings with a layer of frost. Snow and ice would barricade Ovidiu and his daughter, Tatiana, inside for days. When Tatiana was only three years old, his young wife, Sorina, died from pneumonia. There were no doctors in Dumbrava, and the nearest place medicine might be found was Baia Mare, nearly one hundred kilometers to the northwest, close to the Ukraine border. It would take at least a week to walk over the mountains in the snow.

With a toddler to raise alone, Ovidiu could not take time to grieve the loss of Sorina, so his grief was shoved deep inside of him, where it turned to anger, and anger to bitterness.

The summers were blistering hot. There was no electricity. Even the water in the well was lukewarm. But weather, no matter how uncooperative, could not deter Ovidiu from working the small plot of land. If he did not do so, he and Tatiana would not eat. His hands, cracked and swollen with calluses, ached without relief. The dirt beneath his fingernails grew to a permanent stain, and his face was weathered so that he looked like an old man, just like the other men in Dumbrava.

Ovidiu did his best over the years to raise Tatiana. She grew into a beautiful young woman with a sweet and gentle spirit. Her long, dark hair outlined her fine-boned face in soft curls. Her large, expressive brown eyes were framed with long black lashes and full, arched eyebrows. He had worried over her and fussed, doing his best to provide for a little girl, a job he felt ill-equipped to do. Adina and Daria Oros, two sisters in the village who shared a home with their aging parents, took pity on Ovidiu. They taught Tatiana to cook, sew and clean and to be a good and virtuous woman. He had been grateful for the sisters' help, but they also had to work in the fields and care for their parents, so their time with Tatiana was short.

But now, Ovidiu discovered Tatiana was with child. He spat in anger at the cold ground beneath him. Barely eighteen years of age, and she betrayed him. He shook his fist at the sky and cried out. "How could his happen? My beautiful Tatiana! Such a good girl, and now she is ruined! No decent man will want her now. Did she really think she could hide such a thing? Was I never supposed to notice the change in her belly as it grew to shame my family?" He struck the ground with his shovel. Ovidiu continued talking to himself and shouting out loud, as he struck the unyielding ground with his shovel again and again. "She refuses to tell me who the man is!" He cried out to the heavens. "How could she do this? How could she do this to me?" He paused, leaning on his shovel and wept. The wind picked up, whistling through the chilly air. Ovidiu shivered and resumed digging and ranting. "She will have the abortion. She will have no say in the matter. There will be no illegitimate baby in the Todoran house! She will have the abortion tomorrow!"

So caught up in his diatribe was Ovidiu, that he never saw the tall figure, clad in a black coat with a black hood approach him from behind. Before he could erupt in another angry outburst, the hooded figure took a heavy rock and with great force, hit Ovidiu in the head. Ovidiu felt searing pain as he crumpled to the cold dirt beside his shovel. His attacker struck him once more. Then all went black and Ovidiu Todoran stood before God.

"He'll Find You" by Laine Boyd. Coming soon...